The SINGER *of* ISRAEL

THE SONG OF PROPHETS AND KINGS

The
SINGER
of
ISRAEL

HENRY O. ARNOLD

WhiteFire
PUBLISHING

THE SINGER OF ISRAEL

Cover design and typesetting by Roseanna White Designs
Cover images from Shutterstock

Author photo by Ben Pearson

Published in association with the literary agency, WTA Media, LLC, Franklin, TN

WhiteFire Publishing
13607 Bedford Rd NE
Cumberland, MD 21502

ISBN: 978-1-946531-29-2 (print)
          978-1-946531-30-8 (digital)

To my sons-in-law, Derek and Erik…modern-day giant-slayers

PART ONE

PART ONE

Prologue

NATHAN DROVE THE OPEN CARRIAGE INTO THE CENTER OF the compound as the sun set over the western hills. It had been a long day: up before dawn—his master, Samuel, insisting they be on the road at first light—drive over the hills between Ramah and Kiriath Jearim to the home of Abinadab where the Ark of the Covenant was in residence, sit before Yahweh, and then return to Ramah by nightfall.

His master had pressed upon Nathan the urgency of this trip as he climbed into the carriage. "Drive with haste."

"Be mindful the horse is doing all the work," the master's wife countered, tucking a thick fleece blanket around her husband's lumpy body to keep his thinning blood warm against the early morning chill of the open-air ride. "He must bring you home in the heat of the day."

"I will buy a fresh horse," his master had said, giving the front guardrail an annoyed smack with his fist. "I want to be off."

Nathan waited for the master's wife to drop the basket of food in the back of the carriage before snapping the reins. He knew the master's moods—this current disposition was one of fuming impatience. The prophet did not want to waste a moment, not even for his wife's good-bye kiss. Once Nathan snapped the leather reins upon its hide, the horse bolted out of the courtyard onto the road.

They made one stop on their journey to the village of Kiriath Jearim to rest and water the horse and for the two men to eat the dried beef strips, olives, figs, and honey cakes Shira had prepared for them. Even Samuel had to admit that taking this brief moment was a nice break from the constant jostling over a rough highway.

By late morning, Nathan pulled the carriage in front of the home of Abinadab. This humble Levite had housed the Ark since its return from Philistine captivity, and Samuel had consecrated Eleazar, the son of Abinadab, to be the guardian of the Ark. Eleazar had sent the urgent message to the prophet's home in Ramah that King Saul had requested the Ark be brought to the battlefront at the Valley of Elah, and Eleazar needed Samuel's counsel on how to proceed.

The prophet gave a cracked-lip kiss on the bearded cheeks of father and son after he climbed out of the carriage, but he said nothing to them before charging straight inside the house.

"The master's mind is on the Presence awaiting him between the winged cherubim upon the Ark," Nathan said to Abinadab and Eleazar as he climbed down from the carriage. Part of Nathan's job was to explain to others his master's baffling behavior. He had become quite the diplomat over the years. "Have the guards prepare a barrier."

Once word spread that the prophet of Yahweh was alone with the Ark in the common room of the guardian's dwelling, the yard became overcrowded with people pressing against the human barriers of armed Levites Eleazar had stationed around the perimeter of the house to protect the Ark. The crowd spoke in hushed tones, ears straining for any audible communication between the prophet and the Almighty.

Nathan spent the time swapping their exhausted horse for a fresh one and harnessing to the carriage. He wanted to be ready to depart the moment Samuel came into view. The master would be as anxious to return to Ramah as he had been to get to Kiriath Jearim that morning.

When Samuel emerged from the house by early afternoon, grim-faced and no more eager to converse than when he arrived, Nathan led his master through the people forcing them to part as they marched toward the carriage with Eleazar and Abinadab close to their heels. Nathan hopped into the driver's seat and took up the leather reins of the horse.

Before helping him into the carriage, Samuel laid his hands upon the shoulders of the guardian of the Ark and whispered into his ear. When he was finished, Samuel settled into the carriage and gave the front rail another aggravated whack. The master had not addressed the crowd gathered for a fleeting look at a rare sight of the prophet. He did not acknowledge them as they scattered like chickens when Nathan turned the carriage around and pulled out of the yard. He did not seem to care that Eleazar and Abinadab were left stunned and speechless.

Nathan glanced over his shoulder as he drove the carriage down the hill away from the house of Abinadab. Nathan had often witnessed a sullen expression on the prophet's face in times when Samuel might be quietly listening for the voice of Yahweh, a voice he had never heard, or studying the words of Moses, or copying the stories of the chosen people. This was different. This was an expression of consternation and alarm.

What had the prophet witnessed in his time before the Ark that had left him so dismayed? Nathan knew not to speak, and he knew from this pinched expression and squinted eyes the entire trip home his master would be silent.

Chapter 1

SHIRA CONCENTRATED AS SHE WROTE ON THE PARCHMENT with her slow steady hand. She was experimenting with a new dye. Bowls with different colored inks were lined across the table in the common room. But the moment she heard the carriage rumbling into the middle of the courtyard, she stopped what she was doing and rose from her chair.

When she opened the door, she was not quick enough to catch her husband before he scrambled out of the back seat, defying his age and natural hardening of bones and muscles from traveling such a long distance. He advanced toward a group of students so engrossed in stretching wet animal skins inside large wooden frames to dry in the cool air that they failed to notice the approaching human tempest. Shira recognized that her husband's mood had not improved since he and Nathan departed that morning, perhaps had darkened even, and to call out to him—as he marched into the assembly of young prophets and disrupted their production of stretching the skins—would have been wasted breath.

Shira's apron was covered with a residue of powders from dry roots and crushed flowers, pastes of egg whites, flour, goat milk, and extracts from beetles. Her hands and wrists were stained and streaked with hues of crimson and sepia dyes from a concoction of natural plants, bullock's blood, wasp larvae, and charcoal. Her husband needed just the right pigment to write his words, and her experimental alchemy had yet to produce the perfect colorant to satisfy him.

She paused beside Nathan who was unhitching the wearied horse from the carriage.

"I see we have a new horse," Shira said.

"It was either that or be stranded on the road with a dead one." Nathan ran his hand over the horse's back, causing a wave of sweat to flow down the animal's left flank.

"The trip did not go well, I take it." Shira wiped her fingers onto her apron while observing her husband's agitated gestures and the cowering response from his students.

"He spent a considerable time alone before the Ark inside the house of Abinadab and did not say a word all the way home. He seems to be making up for the silence now." Nathan nodded toward the master upbraiding his young student prophets.

Shira could hear the gruff pitch of her husband's voice but was not able to make out exactly what he was saying.

"Perhaps I should rescue the young men," Shira said, and moved toward the jittery, wild scene.

"How long has this been soaking?" Samuel shouted as he reached into the wooden trough and yanked a calfskin out of the grimy, red water. No one answered, and Samuel shouted the question again, waving the skin in the air, water dripping and soaking into the sleeve of his robe with streaks of red.

"Since morning, my lord." The voice spoke from the clump of flinching students.

"Calfskin needs a full day and night," Samuel barked. "If not soaked through, it splits when you stretch it on the frame. We need the gevil, the full skin, to write on, not just the outer layer after the hair is removed, or the inner layer of flesh, but a full skin. It is what the great prophet Moses used to write the sacred texts. Those inspired words are still with us because he wrote on the gevil. I have told you a thousand times."

Samuel slung the calfskin back into the tub then gripped the metal edge, upending the tub off the stand and knocking it to the ground. The students jumped out of the way to avoid a drenching from the spillage of bloody water. When Samuel spun around, he looked right into the face of his wife.

"How about a carriage ride to the top of the hill to watch the sunset?" Shira's cheery-pitched voice could not counter the discord in Samuel's spirit.

Samuel blinked as if he had trouble recognizing her. Her unexpected appearance had immobilized him. He held his breath. The students held their breath. All that could be heard was the sizzle and pop of the water soaking into the worn grass.

"I have been riding all day," Samuel grumbled. "A carriage ride is the last thing I want to do."

Samuel stumbled around Shira like a man suffering from vertigo and wobbled toward the house, his arms held aloft to stabilize his blundering gait.

Shira looked at the hapless student prophets and smiled. If they were to be prophets for the Almighty, they should be prepared for the unpredictable scuffles between human and divine natures. They had just witnessed a perfect demonstration.

Shira ran and caught up with her husband. She gripped his arm and helped him regain his balance. They paused before the door into the house.

"It is good to be home," Samuel said with a wearied sigh.

"I shall clear the table and we can eat our supper." Shira swept her hand over Samuel's face. His tense expression relaxed at the gentle touch of Shira's fingers.

She went inside ahead of him and began to clear the table. The common room had become a laboratory for Shira and a writing sanctum for Samuel. Samuel claimed a corner for his chair and table, surrounded by baskets and tall clay jars filled with scrolls. Shira had set up tables throughout the rest of the common area, covering the tops with bowls of natural specimens of water-soluble products: extracts of berries and plants, crushed insects and animal blood, and dishes of pasty experiments mixed together to coat the scrolls so the dyes and colors Samuel needed would adhere to the gevil skin. A pot full of gallnuts simmered in hot water next to the fire. It would produce a fine ink that would react well with the other concoctions, leaving its permanent literary impression.

The time Samuel devoted to writing the histories of Israel was precious, and Shira did all she could to minimize the distractions and interruptions from the outside world. She and Samuel were the only ones allowed into the house that doubled as an alchemy lab and library. Shira could always sense the supernatural power that had taken possession of this room, an infusion of vocabulary and products of nature confirming the deity of Yahweh—His creativity, His authority made alive by written communication. This holy word recorded by her husband with her dyes would calm the turbulent world, invoke worship, and give all people guidance and hope. The activity inside this small common room was no less than the work of the Creator scooping watery dark matter into His hands and speaking creation into existence.

Shira remained silent as she set out their plates of vegetables and mugs of wine. She chose not to inquire as to the details of her husband's day. Samuel gave himself a sponge bath and changed into a comfortable evening robe while Shira prepared their supper all without verbal exchange.

When Samuel sat down he leaned against the arm of his chair, a hand propping up his head. He ran his index finger along the rim of his clay plate and tapped the steaming vegetables, testing its heat. At last, he picked up a chunk of bread and daubed his lentils with one end, allowing the juices to soak into the dough before he brought it to his mouth.

Shira chose to take a few sips of wine from her mug before stating the obvious. "Your day has not gone well."

"The king has requested the Ark be brought to him in the Valley of Elah," Samuel said while slowly chewing. "He wants to use it against the Philistines like some artifact with magical powers to ensure him another victory."

Samuel dropped the half-eaten bread back onto his plate and began to massage the left side of his head with his fingers. He stared into the crackling flames in the fireplace.

"Eleazar is in distress. He would have to accompany the Ark to the battlefront. He wisely remembers the last time the Ark was removed from its holy place in the Tabernacle in Shiloh by Eli's incorrigible sons, whose names shall not be spoken. The guardian of the Ark does not want a similar fate for himself or the Ark of the Covenant."

Samuel snorted with disdain. A boil of disgust puffed from his mouth.

Shira heard the pain of memory in her husband's voice. He had suffered much from their abuse when he was a young priest serving in the Tabernacle in Shiloh. She rested her stained hand on top of his and began to stroke her fingers over the skin. The non-mention of the names of the wicked sons of Eli, the High Priest, who had treated their role as priests of Yahweh as a way to gain personal wealth and power, was a stark reminder to her of their own sons, whose names also were never mentioned by her or Samuel.

"I traveled today thinking I might…that I might arrange to bring the Ark home. I halfway expected to arrange its transport here. I just needed to know."

Samuel was unresponsive to her gentle touch, but Shira continued her caresses.

"I sat there. I do not know how long. I waited. I prayed. I sang a psalm. I prayed more. I spoke the Ten Sayings. I prayed again. I listened. There was nothing: no sound, no ambient light radiating from the Ark, no voice, nothing…nothing but silence."

Samuel took a sudden breath and held it as if his chest had received the blade of a knife.

"I was frightened by the silence," he said, finally releasing his breath. His voice sounded like a whispery reed in the breeze. "So close to the Presence, yet a universe between us."

Shira gave her husband's trembling hand a tender squeeze and placed the tip of her a finger beneath his wrist. She felt the rapid beat of his pulse. His candor had brought an increase in his heart rate and this frankness concerned her.

"The Ark of the Covenant needs a proper place to reside, not a family domicile. Like the Tabernacle in Shiloh had been; the Holy of Holies, a place of glory."

"Someday perhaps." Shira tried to placate her husband and calm his heart. "In time, Yahweh will make a place for Himself to dwell."

"Why not here?" Samuel sat up in his seat, his countenance brightening at this sudden inspiration. "We could build a new Tabernacle here on the property. Tear down the barns in the south pasture."

"Do you hear yourself? What are you saying?" Shira suddenly lost her wits; the shock wave of so preposterous a suggestion was too much for her.

"We could do it, Shira. It would be my life's work, my greatest accomplishment. This would be the gathering place for all of Israel."

"This is foolish," Shira blurted. Angry tears gathered in her throat. "It is too close. Too close to my hearth, to my way of life. I have shared my husband with Yahweh since the beginning, endured long absences, grieved our own sons who were no less corrupt than Eli's, watched as your mind disappeared before my eyes when the Spirit of Yahweh took possession and caused you to speak and act in ways beyond my comprehension."

Shira paused to swallow and master her resolve. She could not believe she was speaking this way, that these words were spilling from her lips, but some unknown place within her had been jolted, and her impulsive reaction was honest and true. She raised her dye-stained hands before she continued. "Whatever time I have left on this earth, I will live it as I have always done as your faithful wife, resolved to encourage and support in all ways. But I do not want the Ark of the Covenant at my doorstep or the hordes of Yahweh's chosen people who would follow."

Shira held her eyes steady, absorbing her husband's wounded expression, yet she felt no remorse for the words she had spoken. Being the wife of Yahweh's prophet had exacted a price, which had never been expressed with such vehemence until now. She could not keep from expressing the emotional toil of her feelings, but she knew there was wisdom in her words. When Samuel quietly nodded, Shira knew it was a sign of his consent.

"Perhaps Ahimelech, the High Priest, would consider building a Tabernacle in the city of Nob and house the Ark," Samuel suggested. "His Levitical school is located there. That might be possible."

"A preferable choice." Shira said.-

"I told Eleazar under no circumstances was he to transport the Ark to the king in the Valley of Elah. It is folly to risk the Philistines capturing the Ark a second time."

Shira turned her hands over and laid them on the tabletop and wiggled her fingers, signaling for Samuel to place his hands inside her open palms, which he did immediately. She was ready to change the subject.

"I finished Deborah's song while you were gone. I believe it is quite good."

Samuel entwined his fingers within Shira's stained hands.

"Finished what song?" He furrowed his brow as if in an effort to remember.

"Deborah's song of her victory over Jabin, the Canaanite king. The one you asked me to transcribe into poetry."

Shira rose from the table to retrieve the scroll stretched out near the fireplace. Its uneven four corners were held down by small stones. "I used different colored inks to test which ones might work the best."

Shira returned to the table, and Samuel pushed their plates and mugs to one side so the scroll could be laid in front of him.

"Did you know Deborah was the first woman judge in Israel?"

"Of course." Samuel huffed, pretending to be insulted by such a question.

"Did you know she was the first prophetess since Miriam, Moses's sister, herself a poet and dancer?"

"Yes," he said with a little less surety.

"You would remember it given time; I am sure. Deborah was a poet-warrior. She led an army and wrote a song about her victory."

"You want to take over teaching my students now?"

"Do you know the next prophet-judge Yahweh appointed after Deborah?"

"You are about to tell me."

"After almost two hundred years, Yahweh called my husband to be Israel's prophet, judge, and warrior."

Samuel was silent, his gaze dropping upon the parchment. He delicately rubbed the tips of his fingers over the multi-colored lettering of Deborah's poem.

"You left out poet and dancer," he said with a pensive chuckle.

"That is why Yahweh gave me to you." Shira tucked her fingers beneath her husband's chin forcing him to stop caressing the scroll and look at her. She could see the gloom of the day start to clear from his eyes.

Shira unpinned her hair. Her long, gray and brown locks flowed down her shoulders. She held her hands aloft, the color of Yahweh's emerging letters and words stained deep into the pores of her skin. Her body swayed from side to side until it flowed into an improvised dance. Shira sang as she moved around the table. In the murky light of this small room, she would rethread the soul of her husband into her heart.

> "When the princes of Israel let down their hair,
> When the people offer themselves willingly,
> Yahweh will hear praise. Bless You, O Yahweh.
> Hear this, you kings! Give ear, you princes!
> Unto the Lord will I sing.
> Unto the Lord will I sing.
> I will make music to the Lord, the God of Israel."

Chapter 2

SAUL STOOD CALF-DEEP IN THE MIDDLE OF THE COOL STREAM, stripped to his bare skin and armed with a knife. He cupped his free hand into the stream flowing out of the cave and brought the water to his lips. He did not take his eyes off the cave though he could not remember how he had gotten there. Saul was alone and did not know why. When he was alone, he was frightened, yet at this moment, he felt no fear, just the opposite. He felt strong, an earthiness that made him potent, a sense of wholeness that restored his mental state.

Laughter made Saul tilt his ear toward the mouth of the cave. Saul knew the source. His mind was clear, and he could remember the infinite number of moments he had been in the presence of such laughter.

The sunlight intensified the violet hue of the blossoms of a wild lavender bush on the bank of the stream. Saul clutched a handful of stems and sliced them at the base with his knife bringing the whorls of flowers to his face. The profuse aroma made his eyes brighten.

Saul paused at the entrance to the cave and looked deep within the cave's dark throat. He looked behind him and saw no other living soul, human or animal. The laughter came again, but with less naturalness, a forced gaiety at knifepoint. He saw a ribbon of blood in the water, a stream within a stream, and became fearful. He anchored his legs in the streambed and thrust his knife forward. The water lost its pristine clarity becoming a thick infusion of blood that bubbled with heat. He dashed into the cave. The laughter became screams bouncing off the jagged walls as he raced down the middle of the cave, his legs churning through the flow of blood splashing over his exposed body.

The appearance of a rainbow stunned him when he burst into the open cavern. It hung above him, the light filtering through variations of red he had never imagined possible. The illuminated arch suspended in the air dripped blood into the pool of water. Here was the source. But why, he thought? How?

He raised the bouquet of lavender toward the dripping rainbow as if it might stop the bleeding, but it had no power.

Saul looked on the sandbar and saw the quilt Ahinoam had brought on their last excursion into the cave. On the quilt lay a ram's horn, the bloody sleeve of a robe, and a bronzed-leaf crown. Saul recognized the items and rushed onto the loamy sandbar.

He froze the instant the prophet Samuel stepped from the shadows.

The prophet raised a sword above his head—Saul's own sword, the sword bearing the Egyptian symbols, the sword the prophet had given Saul's father and then had taken with him after the prophet executed King Agag. Blood ran down the blade, over its guard and hilt, onto the prophet's hand and bare arm extended from his robe, its sleeve torn from the body of the robe. Clutched in the grip of the prophet's other hand dangled the head of Ahinoam, her startled eyes looking toward her husband, her mouth frozen open, yet still producing the luring, pleasurable laughter Saul had heard outside the cave.

Saul lunged forward with his knife pointed at the prophet's heart, bellowing his rage. *No! No! Not this time!*

The strength of a clasp upon his shoulders brought him to a standstill. The knife slipped from his fingers. Light burst across his eyes, and the sound of a pleading voice rumbled down the tunnels of his ears.

"My lord. My lord, wake up."

Saul sat upright in bed, sweat pouring off his forehead. His ribs hummed from his deep and heavy breathing. He buried his face into the quilt.

"My lord, it is just another nightmare."

Saul began to shiver at the touch of soft hands upon his bare shoulders. He was afraid to look, afraid to remove the quilt from his perspiring face, afraid of who he might see, of who he might not see. He slowly pulled the quilt from his face.

The voice spoke correctly…another nightmare. He was returning from the deep, dream-killing sleep. The light from the lamps brought the surrounding objects within the screened-in area of the tent into focus: his writing table, the pedestal for grooming utensils and bathing basin, a stand bearing his armor, his crown suspended on a hook on the center post of the tent—all familiar, all from a present reality. He looked into the face of his companion.

"You are not who I expected." Saul's voice was husky from his distressed sleep.

"No, my lord. I am Rizpah."

The name familiar, yet not. The beauty of her face familiar, yet not. Her touch and voice familiar, yet not.

Saul let the edges of the quilt slip through his fingers. "I cannot be sure of what my dreams do to me." He sighed.

"You are back now and safe," she whispered.

"It is the same dream with the same bloody outcome." Saul felt her head rest upon his shoulder and her long red hair cascade down his chest. Her arm swept in front of his face like a wing. Her fingers began to glide delicately across his neck as though caressing the surface of still water.

"It is never safe," Saul said. At the touch of her fingers, he clasped her hand and held it in front of him. Then he kissed the back of her hand, moving his tongue smoothly over each of her fingers.

Rizpah reacted by gently kissing Saul's muscular shoulder.

The light was returning to Saul's mind, but in such moments of passion, he preferred darkness. He preferred to avert his eyes from Rizpah's flaming beauty. To look into her face was to replace the ghostly face of his one true love. And he wanted her face back, he wanted her body back, he wanted Ahinoam to return.

Saul closed his eyes and nuzzled his lips and nose into the supple crook of Rizpah's neck, allowing her lenient flesh to conceal his sight. She gave him no passion by lying on her back, guiding him over her body. Saul gave himself over to the rhythm of his need in the hope of dispelling the terror and sadness from his heart.

Abner paced in front of the king's tent. He was not accustomed to waiting, forced to stand outside and request permission to enter. If he wanted or need-ed to see his cousin, it never crossed his mind to seek an invitation before now. He always had the liberty to enter any threshold or tent flap at any time. As long as he could remember, the families of Saul and Abner enjoyed the freedom of flowing in and out of each other's presence.

But life had changed. There was restrictive protocol, a new code of behav-ior. And there was Jarib, the king's aide, standing in his way.

"Do you see the position of the sun?" Abner pointed to the sun's well-es-tablished presence in the sky. "Any time now, the giant will begin his morning tirade."

In deference to the commander, Jarib shielded his one good eye from the glare of the sun with his scribe's quill and gave a quick glance to the sun's position.

"The king did not sleep well last night." Jarib stood behind the table sta-tioned in front of the lavish tent. "I am giving him a little extra time."

"No one has slept well for weeks."

"He is the king."

"Do not remind me who he is, Jarib," Abner snapped. "I remind you we are at war, and we have been cowering in this valley for the last thirty-how-ev-er-many days. The king needs to show himself. Wake him."

Jarib looked at his scroll rolled out on the table and tapped a long row of numbers with the writing end of his quill.

"The precise number would be forty, Commander."

"Precise number of what?"

"The number of days we have been *cowering* in the Valley of Elah." Jarib lifted his face to the commander and waved the feathered end of the quill over the recorded numbers on the scroll.

"Wake him!" Abner was not interested in the exact number of days the army of Israel had been camped at the Elah Fortress on the upper western edge of this rolling valley. This tiresome siege had become oppressive, com-pounding the general dismay among the ranks. The lethargy and indecision of the king had infected his soldiers, and Abner had grown impatient beyond control.

Jarib gestured toward the entrance to the tent, granting permission for Abner to enter. He would not stand in the commander's way.

The sentries snapped to attention as Abner approached. But the moment he put his hands on the tent flaps, he balked. Instead of barging into the tent, he quietly parted the flaps and cocked his ear to listen for signs of activity. He heard nothing and looked toward Jarib seated at his table with his back to him. The king's secretary would not be a party to disturbing the king. Abner would enter without reinforcement, so he took a deep breath, tamping down his nerves. He feared what he might see.

Abner slipped inside. It took a moment for his eyes to adjust from the bright sunlight outside to the shadowy flickers of lamplight inside the spacious tent. He detected the sound of soft breathing as he tiptoed into the room and moved along a tall screen that divided the sleeping area from the rest of the space.

When he peeked around the corner of the cloth screen, he saw Rizpah on her back in bed with the king asleep next to her. She looked straight at him as if he had been expected. Rizpah did not gasp, giving away Abner's appearance. She removed a hand from the back of the king's head and held a finger to her lips then re-clasped her hand onto the back of Saul's thick mane. She continued to look at Abner, her face devoid of expression, as the king remained serenely unaware that his commander stood a few feet behind him.

Abner's frustration swiftly dissipated. These moments between the king and his concubine were the reason he had brought Rizpah to the grieving king after the death of his wife—to provide comfort and to save her life. She would have been killed by the king's order to slaughter the Gibeonites if Abner had not brought Rizpah to the rooftop of Saul's house the night of the genocide. That was understood, but he had hoped never to witness any display of affection between them. This vivid impression would haunt him perhaps forever.

He swayed, his legs nearly buckling as he backed out of the tent. He was blinded by the light outside. Abner bent over, bracing his hands upon his knees and gasped. He had been holding his breath and was almost faint from lack of air.

"Sometimes, I am thankful to be half-blind," Jarib said without looking up from his document. "It is easier to avert one eye from those things I should not see."

"Go rot in Sheol," Abner said.

"Abner. Abner," came the youthful cry from the middle of the encampment.

He stood the moment he heard his name.

Malki and Ishvi ran toward him, waving their swords in attack position just as they had been trained.

The soldiers milling about the front of their tents looked on the king's twin sons with bored amusement as they raced by. However, the men came to attention when Jonathan trailed behind his younger brothers, carrying a stuffed leather pouch.

Abner welcomed this distraction from his young cousin's feigned threat after what he had just witnessed, and he moved into the middle of the lane, drew his sword, and braced himself for the coming attack.

The twins split apart right before they reached Abner, forcing him to divide his attention, and after a few defensive blows against their sword blades, Abner yielded and dropped to his knees. His twin cousins took advantage of Abner's submission and fell upon him with a combination of kisses and chokeholds. Just the emotional reaction the commander needed.

Jonathan stopped at Jarib's table and set down the leather pouch. "Black kite feathered quills and more parchment. Just as you requested."

"Thank you, Captain." Jarib opened the pouch and carefully removed the contents. "There has not been much activity to document, but good to be prepared."

"True. True." Jonathan watched his brothers wrestle Abner to the ground. "Any improvement with my father while I was in Gibeah?"

"I regret to report the king's heart has worsened while you were gone." Jarib opened the elongated wooden box full of black kite feathers and removed a single feather. He examined the sturdiness of the quill shaft and density of the feathered barbs in the sunlight. "My prayer is he will revive at the news of your return and the arrival of the twins and his daughters."

"May Yahweh answer that prayer," Jonathan replied, and then nodded toward the entrance of the tent. "Any sign of him this morning?"

"I expect him to summon me at any moment." Jarib placed the quill back into the box and closed the lid. "Where have your sisters been encamped?"

"In the grove of terebinth trees behind the supply tents." Jonathan point-ed in the general direction of the grove. "Adriel is overseeing the task of setting up the tents. I want them to be far from the battle lines and plenty of shade for the child."

"You brought the child then?" Jarib leaned over the table to Jonathan.

"My sister insisted. Merab would never abandon Ish-bosheth, not under the present circumstances."

"That is wise, Captain, and I say this with caution, but I think it is best the king does not see his young son at this time," Jarib whispered, glancing back at the entrance to the tent. "Forgive me if I have spoken improperly, but in the king's present mental state…"

"I understand, Jarib." Jonathan raised his hand for Jarib to say no more. "I will inform my sisters to keep the child with the nurses when we are with our father."

The blare from the ram's horn reverberating from the middle of the valley brought the wrestling match between Abner and the twins to an abrupt halt. The eyes of his twin brothers widened as the shrill blast of the horn was replaced by a harsh whirring that seemed to originate from the place of the dead. The vocal resonance could not be mortal.

Once the buzzing dialect was translated into fractured Hebrew by a second more human voice, Jonathan could tell by the expressions of shock that his brothers now believed the stories he had told them about the giant. Only a giant could speak thus. Only a giant could cause such fear in the hearts of men. Only a giant could paralyze an entire army.

"The giant?" Malki slipped his arms from Abner's neck and looked at his big brother for an answer.

Jonathan barely nodded, affirming Malki's intuition.

Abner pushed Ishvi off his chest and leapt to his feet.

"Our morning berating begins," Abner growled while brushing the dust from his clothes. "I wish I could cut out his tongue."

"You would have to stand on my shoulders to do so," Jonathan said.

"Not if he were flat on his back with an arrow in his eye," Abner said.

"Is he really as big as two men?" Ishvi yanked his sword off the ground so fast he bounced against Malki, causing them both to topple into the dirt.

"Tall as two grown men plus a midget like you on top for good measure," Abner said with no hint of humor in his voice.

The twins scrambled to their feet and put their swords back into their sheaths.

"We must go see him," Malki said to his brother, and both boys scampered between the rows of tents.

Jonathan's sharp whistle through his teeth stopped his brothers in their tracks.

"Do not go into the valley," Jonathan ordered.

The twins promised to obey their brother's command, and then scurried between the tents as soldiers began meandering toward the front lines. No one but the twins was in a hurry for the giant's daily scolding.

"He must come out of his tent. He must." Abner raised his hands in a helpless gesture. "The army is losing heart, and I have lost all patience."

"Has he come out at all while I was gone?" Jonathan turned to ask Jarib.

"Late at night when he cannot sleep and most of the soldiers are in their tents, he will wander through the encampment," Jarib answered.

"Like a brooding phantom," Abner grumbled. "He does nothing to boost morale."

"The king told me last night before retiring that once Jonathan returned with the family, he wished all would join him for the evening meal in his tent." Jarib's announcement brought a measure of hope to Jonathan.

"That is encouraging, is it not, Commander?"

"A family dinner does little to rid us of our giant problem."

"Agreed, but we shall take what we can get." Jonathan began to follow his younger brothers to the battle lines but spun around. "Perhaps, such a family gathering will restore Father to his old self. Best follow the twins. Keep them from wandering into the valley."

Abner watched his nephew cross the central hub in the middle of the officer's quarters and disappear between the rows of tents.

Why had not the prophet chosen Jonathan to be king?

Abner looked back at the closed flaps of the king's elaborate shelter. The image of the tangled bodies of the king and his concubine jolted his mind. He whirled and strode after the prince, furiously shaking his head to dislodge the memory.

Chapter 3

SABA BLEW HIS BREATH ALONG THE CHISELED RIDGE OF THE large stone, scattering the fine granules into the light breeze. He took a step back to examine the skilled cut before his attention was drawn from the bas-relief on the stone slab toward the flesh and blood subject posing for him just moments ago.

"I defy the ranks of Israel. Choose a man and send him down to fight."

Each time Saba heard the absurd, vocal mixture of buzzing and thunder coming from two human voices, a chill went through his body. Regardless of their colossal size, their surging oral tones rumbling over the valley was enough to strike any mortal heart with terror. The echo of the dual intonations made the two men sound like a multitude.

Saba set his hammer and chisels on his worktable and unfolded a covering of goat hides sewn together into one large piece. He climbed halfway up the ladder beside the great flat stone set upright inside a scaffolding of sturdy iron frame designed specially to stabilize the heavy slab on which he carved. He draped the slab with the goat hide covering to protect it. The work was nearly done, and Saba wanted his patron to give it one last look before the artist pronounced it finished.

Once the slab was covered, Saba climbed to the top of the ladder. The better vantage point allowed him to see over the tents and battle lines of the Philistine encampment and watch the father and son duo in the middle of the valley hurl their insults.

Morning and evening, this verbal abuse boosted the morale of the Philistine army though the ritual had become perfunctory, indeed boring. After forty days of the same invective with no response to the giant's challenge for Israel to send down a champion so the two might fight to the death to determine a victor, even Goliath and his son, Lahmi, who bore his father's armaments and translated his curses into a derelict Hebrew, seemed to have lost heart in the routine. But it was part of the job for which this father and son were being well compensated: inspire fear in the hearts of the army of Israel to either accept this terrible offer of single, winner-take-all combat, or have the armies meet in the Valley of Elah and thousands be slaughtered.

When Saba first arrived at the encampment with his patron, Lord Namal, he was instructed to pitch his tent and workstation beside that of the Fifth Lord. Since the incident at the outpost on the Geba boundary line with Israel that had stirred a national outcry, Saba had been assigned to Lord Namal's entourage, an honor he accepted with pleasure.

On that first day while Saba was setting up his workstation, there had been an impromptu meeting of the Five Lords of the Philistines in front of Lord Namal's tents. Lord Achish made his unusual proposal and brought along his impressive visual aids.

"I will pay for Goliath's services from my own coffers," Lord Achish offered, pointing to the two descendants of the legendary Nephilim arrayed in full battle armor.

Saba trembled at the sight of the father and son standing off to the side, their heads at eye level with the top of the center post of Lord Namal's tent. Goliath's bronze helmet added another two-hand span to his height. Neither Goliath nor Lahmi would be able to stand fully erect inside the tent of a normal man.

The other lords asked for a demonstration of how the giant might intimidate the army of Israel. Lord Achish nodded to Goliath, and he took to the valley with Lahmi trundling along behind. When Goliath bellowed toward Israel's position and Lahmi translated his father's curses into Hebrew, the volume of their combined vocal power created such a pall of fear on the opposing side, the soldiers on Israel's front lines fled to their tents. Saba dropped to his knees beside his worktable, putting his hands over his ears. Who would not be terrified by these sinister, inhuman sounds?

"Remember the panic and fear we experienced in the Jordan Valley at the hands of Prince Jonathan, son of King Saul? May it now be turned back upon them," Lord Achish said as the giants lumbered out of the valley after their performance. "Day and night, we maintain this constant harangue. The army of Israel will quake in their tents like old women and lose their will to fight. When we do strike, we will avenge ourselves for the dishonor at the outpost at Geba."

Saba saw Lord Namal wince at the mention of the incident at the Philistine border garrison at Geba. Of the Five Lords, Namal had suffered the most humiliation by the disaster in the Jordan Valley. It had happened like a flash flood surging through a ravine. The well-fortified outpost in Namal's province had been overrun by the prince of Israel and his armor-bearer, his soldiers slaughtered, and his favorite artisan's sacred pillar desecrated. So, Namal's incentive for revenge was all-consuming, and he had brought Saba along in order to document his victory in a series of artistic works.

Lord Achish was the youngest of the Five Lords. He had risen in place of his father, Maoch, who had recently died. While Lords Tidal, Arioch, and Shinab were sympathetic to Namal's lust for war, the three of them were advanced in years and not enthusiastic to rush into another battle with their perennial enemies, however justified. Thinking it unwise to be overconfident, the three older lords agreed to try Lord Achish's strategy for an indefinite period to see if they could terrorize the army of Israel to their advantage.

Forty days later, the vocal cords of the father and son team were raw from a twice-daily berating of Israel's cowardice. While the Philistine army was growing sluggish from this long attrition, Achish and the older lords kept themselves amused by overindulging their appetites. It was all Lord Namal could do to restrain his impulse to charge the front lines of Saul's army by himself.

There had been little for Saba to do until, one day, Goliath approached him. He held a pouch of coins in one hand and a large flat stone, a thickness of ten fingers, tucked under his other arm. He asked if Saba would carve his likeness onto the rock face. Lord Namal gave his frosty permission with an irritated wave of his hand. Saba knew his lord would have rather kept him busy working exclusively for him, but what was the point? Namal had yet to set foot onto the battlefield.

Lord Namal stormed out of his tent as Goliath was finishing his morning rant and came to a stop in front of Saba's workstation.

Saba hastily descended the ladder and bowed to his lord the moment his feet hit the ground.

Lord Namal did not even acknowledge Saba's presence. He was focused on the approaching giant and his loyal son carrying his father's shield and spear.

Saba knew from Lord Namal's rigid profile and inflexible posture that whatever was going on in his mind was about to burst forth. "My lord, good morning," Saba began. "Is there something I could—"

"Keep silent, Artisan," Lord Namal barked, thrusting out his arm and hand and nearly striking Saba in the face.

Saba could not believe Lord Namal would confront Goliath, but he could tell this was his intention. Saba watched as Lord Namal's head began to rise higher and higher as the giant drew closer until the apple of his neck began to protrude from the middle of his gullet as though his throat were swollen.

Goliath stopped in front of Lord Namal, his shadow casting its darkened shade over the Philistine lord now standing on tiptoe, trying to gain a few more fingers of elevation to compensate for the height disparity.

"My Lord Namal." Goliath bowed in honor of the Fifth Seren.

"You do not speak for me," Lord Namal said.

"My lord, I do not understand."

"You dare offer our enemies a challenge that if their champion defeats you, then the Philistines will become servants to this Hebrew nation."

"Lord Namal, no one will—"

"I will never be a slave to a race of people whose men remove the foreskin from their manhood."

Saba had never seen Goliath laugh the entire forty days the two armies had been camped in the Valley of Elah. He had never even seen him smile, he or his son.

"Never fear, Lord Namal. Your foreskin is safe." Goliath threw back his massive head, mouth open wide, his throat a volcano of laughter.

The atmosphere seemed to crackle like fire at the flinty ricochet of the giant's laughter bouncing through the hot air.

Goliath untied the neck strap on his helmet and lifted the protective covering off his perspiring head. The sweat poured from inside the helmet onto the dry ground like a stray rainstorm. Then Goliath tossed the helmet at Lahmi's feet.

"Water, Lahmi." Goliath held out his hand after dropping his soaked helmet. The space from the tip of the giant's small finger to the tip of his thumb was equal to the wingspan of a falcon.

Lahmi thrust the spearhead into the ground then took the large leather water container from off his shoulder and handed it to his father.

Only when Goliath latched his lips around the spout and began to guzzle did his laughter finally subside.

Saba was amazed watching the leather container deflate as Goliath drained the contents.

Goliath pulled the spout from his lips and wiped the dripping excess from his beard with his forearm.

"Artisan, is it finished?" Goliath pointed to the granite slab protected by the covering of goat hide.

"My lord, it awaits your final approval before I chisel my mark." Saba's voice quivered. He was unable to move. Every hair stood on end.

"Remove the covering." Goliath motioned for Saba to climb the ladder.

Saba found his footing on the rungs of the ladder and scampered to the top of the stone slab. He carefully lifted away the goat hide from the front-piece so as not to scrape any of the relief images. After descending the ladder, he pulled the goat hide around to the opposite side of the stone. Saba did not wish to distract his patron's view of his creation.

Saba did not look at the artwork but watched the giant's eyes widen and his lips form an O-shaped expression of disbelief. When the giant reached out his hand as if he would touch the stone, Saba cringed, and then promptly put up his hand to stop Goliath. He instantly regretted his response in preventing his patron from this tactile engagement with the art. When he saw Goliath's expression of wonder change to that of a scolded child, eyes cast upon the ground, Saba felt guilt for hurting the man's feelings. He never expected laughter or awkwardness to be exhibited from such a human leviathan.

"What do you dream when you sleep at night, Artisan?" Goliath asked once he had returned his gaze to behold the chiseled beauty on the large stone slab.

"My lord?" Saba was unsure how to answer.

"The winged demons gathering up the souls of the scattered dead, the rocky landscape, my son standing to one side holding my shield, and Dagon above me. How did you have such vision?"

Lahmi and Lord Namal moved toward the piece as if spellbound by the stone-carved imagery.

"It is as if it were alive," Lord Namal whispered.

Saba reminded Goliath. "You posed for me, my lord, standing in full armor, legs apart, arm holding your spear aloft in the air. The rest I imagined."

"What do the letters say beside the crowned head of Dagon?" Goliath asked.

Saba answered. "It reads: '*In the house of Dagon, thou shalt eat the bread of honor; thou shalt drink the wine of favor.*' These words are inscribed on the walls of the temple of Dagon in Ashdod. I hope you think they are fitting."

With the slow wave of his arm and hand, Goliath began to encompass the entire work. "You see what the artist has done, Lord Namal. You see how I, Goliath of Gath, son of my noble father, Rapha, descendant of the legendary Nephilim—giants of renown before the great waters covered the earth—have laid waste my enemies across the landscape."

Goliath paused and turned to look at Lord Namal who stood transfixed before the great stone. "Do not be afraid, Lord Namal. I will avenge the disgrace brought upon us years ago when the blind, Hebrew judge, Samson, brought down Dagon's temple in Gaza and slew three thousand Philistines. One greater than Samson stands before you now. I shall fulfill what the artist has carved on my stone to the glory of our people and to the glory of Dagon, our god. Do not be afraid."

Chapter 4

A SPOTTED EAGLE FLEW HIGH ABOVE DAVID AS HE DESCENDED through the mountain pass on the road west to Socoh and Azekah, riding his horse and leading two tethered mules loaded with food and fresh clothing. David first noticed the eagle rising on the wind currents when he made the summit from the Bethlehem side of the mountain. It was difficult for him to watch the majestic creature circling overhead at the same time attempting to guide his horse down the curved, steep trail.

David glanced over his shoulder to check the mules' pace and spied a rope coming loose over a bundle of supplies that had shifted on the back of the first mule. He dismounted and secured the large sacks of dried mutton, roasted grain, cheeses, and loaves of bread. He did not immediately set off again but took time to stretch his legs and drink from his waterskin. The bird soared in ever-widening circles, and David took the eagle's piercing, raucous screech as a personal communication that required him to respond.

"Sing to Yahweh, O peoples of the earth. Sing praise to the One who rides the ancient skies." David shouted his praise, smiling as the eagle spiraled upward. "Sing to the One who thunders with a mighty voice."

He wiped his lips with the back of his hand, put the stopper into the mouth of the waterskin, and then looped the strap around the oryx horn handle attached to the front of his saddle. He reached underneath the blanket roll on his horse and pulled out the lion-skin bag containing his kinnor. The top of the kinnor protruded from the bag.

David regretted having entrusted to Joab, his nephew, the task of gutting and skinning the lion he slew when last in the high country shepherding his father's flocks. He would have carved the beast's skin in such a way that there would have been enough pelt to cover the whole instrument. In spite of his nephew's poor job of skinning, Joab had made the extra effort of excavating the claws from the four paws. David made a necklace of the lion's claws, which he wore with pride.

Since the prophet Samuel's visit to his home in Bethlehem, David had not returned to shepherding. After the secret anointing by the prophet, endorsing him as the next king of Israel, the armies of Israel and the Philistines met in the Valley of Elah. His three oldest brothers were conscripts in Saul's army, and whenever lower ranking soldiers were summoned for duty, their families were responsible for keeping them supplied. There were not enough funds in the national coffers to equip and support a large military force.

Abner, commander of the three-thousand-man professional army, saw to it that his men lacked nothing, but little was left for the conscripts other than a small wartime stipend. So, David traveled back and forth from Bethlehem to the encampment, bringing supplies to his brothers' unit. When he was at home, he still tended to those ewes about to lamb and the newborns corralled in the multiple pens on the family property, but as far as he was concerned, the lonely stretches of time spent guarding flocks of sheep were over.

He let the bag fall to the dusty road, propped a leg on a boulder, and rested the base of the kinnor on his thigh. He tightened the sheep gut strings and began to pluck them with his long, dirt-encrusted fingernails.

> "O Yahweh, where can I go from your Spirit?
> Where can I flee from your presence?
> If I ascend to heaven, you are there.
> If I make my bed in Sheol, you are there.
> If I rise on the wings of the dawn,
> If I dwell on the far side of the sea,
> Even there...even there...even..."

David looked at his kinnor as if the strings' last tremors might provide the words needed to finish his lyric, but the notes faded to silence. He looked back into the sky and watched the spotted eagle disappear over the next mountain, taking inspiration with it.

"Even there...Even there...and the words fly away with the eagle."

He sighed, slapped the strings on the kinnor, and listened to the vibrations until the sound was absorbed by the breeze. He bent and grabbed the lion-skin bag and slipped his instrument inside. After tucking the bag under the saddle blanket, he gave one last check of the ropes, securing the supplies upon the backs of the two mules, and then climbed on his horse and began the final descent. This was his third trip delivering supplies from home to his brothers on the front lines.

"Time to go." David clucked his tongue, urging his horse forward. The grade was steep this side of the mountain, but barring any unforeseen accidents, he would arrive at the encampment in time to hear the giant's afternoon harangue.

On David's first trip to the Valley of Elah, the tents of the conscripts and the layout of the encampment were orderly and well presented, sectioned out under their respective tribal banners. The professional army was located on the hill in the center section of the camp with the tents of the conscripts fanning out around it in expanding concentric half circles. The king's tent was protected with many layers of tents and soldiers between the royal shelter and the front lines.

A training ground was laid out behind the encampment. Abner had ordered intense morning and afternoon combat exercises for the conscripts to get them in shape for battle. But the longer the siege progressed there had been a steady decline in discipline.

By his second visit, David noticed the conscripts spent more time milling about their tents or around the firepits than on the training ground, voicing equal complaints of fear and boredom, generally ignoring any updates on the progress of the siege given by their tribal officers on their daily rounds.

David was not allowed on the training ground, nor could he or any civilian enter the main camp of the professional army. He was confined to the sector reserved for the conscripts from Judah. On his first two visits, he was not given the opportunity to see the giant. His brothers had taken the supplies and sent him back to Bethlehem with their insults ringing in his ears that the "favored child" needed to be home by dark, or the parents would be sounding the alarm. After witnessing the prophet Samuel anoint him with the holy oil and proclaim him the future king of Israel, his brothers continued to treat him with derision.

This time, when David entered the southern outskirts of the camp, the visible change was drastic. The training ground was empty of soldiers, professional or conscript, except for a small group of archers amusing themselves by shooting arrows into the air then racing out of the way as the arrow hurtled back to earth. No sentries were posted. The soldiers David did see when he rode through the back rows of the camp were intoxicated and chasing half-naked women into or out of the tents. Clothing and debris were scattered over the ground. Armaments and weapons lay in unorganized heaps. Animal carcasses rotted around the periphery of the firepits while dogs gnawed the discarded bones.

David gagged at the pungent smell of human waste. Many of the soldiers found it more convenient to eliminate their bowels in the pathways between the tents instead of making their way to the latrines outside camp. He guided his horse and mules to where the captain in charge of provisions and baggage for the tribe of Judah always set up his storage bins but found no captain or bins. In his place was a stubby little man garbed in a gray prophet's robe sitting behind a table, busily scribbling on papyrus.

David dismounted in front of the table and slapped the reins across his opened hand to gain the attention of the scribbler.

Gad ignored the rider's slap of the reins across his palm. He had been assigned to update the inventory of supplies brought to the camp. When he finished writing his report, he raised his head and gave the rider a mistrustful look. Gad set his quill beside his scroll, rubbed his eyes, and then removed a small wad of cloth from each ear.

"I did not hear you ride up." Gad set the plugs on his table.

"I see that." The rider pointed at the balls of cloth on the table. "Why the—"

"To block out his voice," Gad blurted. He was annoyed at what he perceived to be this young man's mild impertinence. "I can no longer endure the grating sound of his voice."

"Whose voice?" The rider turned his head to scan the designated quarter of the Judahite camp, finding it deserted.

Gad studied the young man standing in front of him, upright and confident, his arms akimbo and his balled fists dug into his slim, muscular waist.

Ignoring the rider's question, Gad continued. "Your first time, I assume."

"My third trip crossing the mountain in over a month."

"Then you are aware we have been in siege mode for exactly forty days, not counting the time it took for the army to muster and establish its position, Gad said. "I see you traveled alone. A bit risky, considering our current state of war."

"I do not call this a state of war."

Gad waited for the rider to give his appraisal of the condition of the camp and he got just what he had expected from this poised young man.

"I call this a state of deadlock in the dwelling of Sheol," he said.

"I admit to a downward spiral of discipline." Gad could not help but be impressed but concealed his admiration at this scruffy young man's self-confidence and unexpected vocabulary. "It is to be expected among the lower ranks. But you will not find these slovenly conditions in the king's professional army."

Gad pointed in the direction of the pristine accommodations of the veteran army atop the hill.

"I would hope not."

Gad felt slightly self-conscious when the rider looked above his rotund head as if questioning his pronouncement.

"My older brothers are stationed in the section of the tribe of Judah. I am David, son of Jesse, from Bethlehem."

"I, too, am from Bethlehem. I know of your family. You are livestock traders. I am Gad, son of Tekoa. My father is a spice merchant."

"I know the family name, but not you."

"I left home to study with the prophet Samuel at a young age." Gad made no attempt to mask his pride. "I am now the official court prophet for King Saul."

"I am just a shepherd, so I see why we never met." David then changed the subject. "Has the supply captain moved the storage bins? I need to unload these mules."

"The storage bins have been moved to a safer area. Too much idle time has given rise to thievery. The supply captain is currently on the front lines. Leave your mules with me. I will see that your provisions are distributed properly."

"These supplies are for my brothers and the tribe of Judah, not the whole camp."

Gad squared his back and stretched his corpulent body. Being a member of the royal court had allowed him dining privileges at the king's table with its abundant, exotic victuals. He crossed his arms over his expanded waistline.

"You are an impertinent fellow. You do not trust me?"

An eruption of war cries from the army of Israel stretched along the front lines of the camp brought an end to the two-man showdown.

David snapped his head in the direction of the bloodcurdling din, and Gad reached down for the wads of cloth to reinsert them.

"What is that?" David tightened his grip on the reins of his horse to keep it from dashing away at the terrifying screams.

"Men screaming at one another."

"Is it the giant?"

Gad inserted a plug into an ear. He could see David's whole body trembling.

"He has that effect on everyone." Gad held up the second wad. "That is why I plug my ears."

"I am not frightened, Prophet, if that is what you imply." David jutted out his chin.

"You would be the first." Gad was not impressed with David's bluster. "So go, see the giant. You rode all this way."

Gad knew David was suspicious of him, so he leaned over his table.

"If you cannot trust one from your own hometown, a prophet of Yahweh no less, who can you trust?" Gad had to shout to be heard above the rising chorus of male voices.

"I did not see the giant on my first two trips," David said.

"Then you do not want to miss the spectacle." Gad pointed toward the battle lines.

"Follow the lane through the tents until you see the banners of Judah. You will find your brothers there with our tribe."

David slung the reins of his horse at Gad and bolted toward the path.

Chapter 5

WHEN DAVID SPOTTED THE BANNER OF JUDAH, THE IMAGE OF a rearing lion with blood dripping from its front paws, he pushed his way through the screaming soldiers beating their shields with their swords until he reached the front line. The Valley of Elah spread out before him.

In the middle of the valley floor, between the two great armies, stood the giant, his arm upraised, his hand clutching the shaft of his spear.

"I curse the ranks of Israel. Choose a man and let us fight."

The voice was thunder, savage, bursting with arrogance, the single-throat volume loud enough to be heard above the constant yelling of the army of Israel. David understood why Gad plugged his ears.

David bent down on one knee and gave the giant his full concentration.

The enormous warrior stood twice the height of a normal man and wore a bronze helmet large enough for a young child to bathe inside it. His torso was covered in bronze-scaled armor with a wide leather sash tied around his waist, securing his sword and sheath. Bronze greaves covered his massive legs and slung on his back was a bronze javelin. The shaft of his spear was as thick as the main beam of a weaver's loom with the iron spearpoint reflecting the sunlight as if pulled red-hot from the blacksmith's fire.

David imagined that the earth must have opened up and disgorged this mythological creature.

"Why do you come out and line up for battle?" the giant bellowed. "Choose a champion. Send him down to fight. If he should kill me, then we shall be your servants, but if I kill him, then all Israel shall be slaves to the Philistines and our god, Dagon."

The giant's cynical laughter pealed across the valley, forcing a hushed awe upon the army of Israel. The soldiers around David suddenly lost the will to continue their defiant war cry. The giant reached for his bronze shield held by an armor-bearer of almost equal height. He lifted the shield with the embossed head of a bull on its face and turned it toward the sun. The giant rotated the intense shaft of light from the sun's reflection off the shield over the front lines of Israel.

The soldiers of Israel were cowed by the burning ray.

A different sensation burned through David as the beam of light from the giant's shield passed over him—the sensation he felt when he had killed the lion, not fear but the impulse to charge. David imagined the giant's head mounted on the top of his shepherd's crook; his mocking voice silenced forever. David ran his hand along his waist, feeling for his sling. He rose to his feet, pulling the sling from his belt and took one step into the valley when an arm wrapped around his chest. He was instantly yanked back into the group of soldiers.

"And what are you about to do, little brother?"

David recognized Eliab's voice as he was being dragged back toward the Judah enclave. His other two brothers, Abinadab and Shammah, stumbled out of the cluster of soldiers who watched these antics with amusement as each brother picked up one of David's legs, suspending him above the ground. David tried to squirm free, but all three brothers tightened their grip.

"You think you were going to fight the giant with this?" Abinadab jerked David's sling from his hand.

The trio of older brothers enjoyed a disdainful laugh at David's high and mighty aspirations. Intoxicated, they bragged to their fellow soldiers that they captured a Philistine spy and planned to torture him. Once they entered their tribe's designated space, they dropped David on the ground with a thud.

Springing to his feet, David snatched his sling from Abinadab's fingers, pushing him back against Shammah, causing both brothers to lose their balance and fall. They were not as quick as David to get back onto their wobbly legs but rolled on the ground, their useless limbs loosened by too much wine.

David spun to face Eliab who raised his arms in mocking surrender, causing him to drop the wineskin he was holding. The wine gushed from the spout the moment the wineskin hit the ground, and Eliab slumped to his knees to grab the deflating pouch before the earth absorbed any more of the contents. David's brothers crawled around his legs like disoriented sheep. It brought him shame to see the other tribal conscripts gathering and laughing at such unprofessional behavior from soldiers in the king's army.

"I unloaded your supplies." Gad pointed to the bundles stacked beside his table. "You can distribute them yourself if you would like."

David looked up to see Gad staring at him. Behind Gad were his horse and two mules, all three munching on the straw Gad had strewn on the ground in front of them. He nodded his thanks to Gad, and then spoke through gritted teeth at Eliab still on his knees clutching his wineskin. "I brought you more food and fresh clothing."

"You have done your duty. Now, go home to your sheep." Eliab tried to bow from his kneeling position, but lost his balance and fell onto his side, which caused more laughter from their audience.

The only one not amused was David.

"Do you play?" Gad asked as he held out the reins of David's horse, offering him an expression of sympathy not judgment.

"Play. What do you mean?" David asked.

"Forgive me. I noticed the kinnor underneath the saddle. Are you a musician?"

"Of sorts." David was relieved to be diverted from his drunken brothers. He stepped over to Gad but did not take the ends of the reins from the prophet's hand.

"Try not to be too hard on them." Gad and David watched as some of the soldiers helped the three brothers to their feet. "We have been here a long time without much entertainment. The siege has taken its toll."

"Why does no one fight this giant? You have been here long enough." David tucked his sling back into his belt and brushed the dust from his clothes.

"They call the giant Goliath, one of the descendants of the primeval Nephilim." Gad lowered his hand with the reins. "I have spent my time studying about this ancient race of demon-men in the writings of Enoch and the Prophet Moses."

"I remember hearing the rabbis in the synagogue tell those stories when I was a child," David said. "I thought them fables used to frighten children."

"Does this giant look and sound like a fable to you?"

David noted the mixture of weary sarcasm in Gad's voice. "What about King Saul? Has he lost heart?"

"A great fear has infected us all, like a plague, from the king down to me."

"Still this uncircumcised Goliath, with his big voice and his big truncheon, has defied the army of the living God."

"True," Gad said, a smile forming on his lips.

David could not help his coarse bravado. He may be just a shepherd, but he had more depth than his appearance revealed.

"Still, insulting Yahweh for the last forty days has not inspired sufficient umbrage for someone to step forward and meet the giant's challenge."

David looked back over his shoulder and saw his brothers stumbling toward him along with other soldiers. David leaned closer to Gad and lowered his voice. "Has the king offered any incentives to remove this disgrace from Israel?"

"Rewards, you mean, for killing the giant?" Gad asked just to clarify the question, and David nodded. "The king will shower the giant-slayer with great wealth. He will exempt the family of the champion from all taxes; and there is talk of marriage someone of noble heritage. All this will be done for the man who slays the giant."

Eliab pulled himself free of his two brothers who were propping him up. He slapped the wineskin into Shammah's chest for him to hold, then dug his feet into the earth to stabilize his legs.

Eliab glared into David's face. "Why have you come down here? To humiliate us, to reproach us? You are nothing but a keeper of sheep." Eliab's speech was slurred, his body trembling with anger. "You just chase sheep, and now you have abandoned your flock. Who is minding your sheep while you come to spy on us?"

"What have I done, Brother?" David lowered his eyes to the ground.

"What have you done? You have come over the mountain to fill your head with fantasies. Stories you can tell everyone back home that you came to the Valley of Elah and slew the giant with this."

Eliab reached for David's sling and tore it from his belt. He held it up for the soldiers to see.

David did not attempt to get it back. "I only asked a question. It is only words."

"Words that you weave into stories and songs that raise you above the rest of us." Eliab spit between David's legs. "I know you. Your heart is wicked and arrogant. You are only a shepherd, the last-born son of Jesse, no better than a servant. Do not try to rise above your rank."

43

David said nothing. He held his open hand to Eliab: a dirty and scarred hand, a hand when paired with the other was gentle enough to comfort a skittish lamb or strong enough to slay wild beasts, a hand extended to calm an angry brother, a hand of a king.

Eliab looked down at David's hand but did not take it. He balled the sling into a wad of leather and threw it into the dirt. Then he spun and pushed his way past his brothers and on through the crowd.

Abinadab and Shammah followed Eliab toward the open firepit. David retrieved his sling from off the ground and unfurled the leather straps and hollowed out the sack with his fingers before tying it back onto his belt.

"Do not lose heart because of this," David spoke, then became silent. Had he lost heart because of the sting of this brother's public humiliation? Had he lost heart because he felt the great pall of fear that had fallen over the camp? Had he lost heart because right then he began to question his earlier impulse to challenge the one who had insulted Yahweh?

These thoughts raced through his mind and then he spoke the words again but added the promise of action. "Do not lose heart because of this giant. Your servant will go and fight him."

Gad froze in place. He looked at the soldiers standing nearby. They did not move or speak. In forty days' time, no one had spoken such a thing. No one had stepped forward and uttered such words even in jest or reckless boast. These words appeared to be neither, just a simple statement of intention before the fact. No one seemed sure how to react because no one was sure how to interpret what they had just heard.

Gad was the first to break the silence. His blood flowed a little faster at the thought that this young man, at least, had courage enough to entertain the idea of challenging the giant, whether or not it proved a practical reality.

"Our hearts have been lost to us, and what you say is an encouraging word." Gad stepped beside David. "But before you do such a thing, perhaps you might sing for us."

"Why should I bother to unpack my kinnor and sing for this unruly crowd?"

"If you happened to lose your fight with the giant, and we all become slaves to the Philistines, I would hate to have missed out on hearing a fine singer," Gad offered as explanation.

"You do not know whether or not I am a fine singer."

"Nor do I know if you are a fine soldier able to go against Goliath as you claim." Gad responded with no trace of insult in his voice. "Let us put your skills as a singer to the test before we test your skills as a warrior. It would be a pleasure to hear you."

"I must admit, you have a way to soothe and persuade with soft words and a charitable demeanor. As you wish, Prophet." David gave Gad a smile and walked to the back of his horse and removed the pouch with the kinnor from beneath the saddle blanket.

Gad extended his arm toward the center of the encampment, and the soldiers made way for David to pass. Gad ordered a log be placed before the firepit for David to sit. When he removed the kinnor from its pouch and began to tighten the strings, Gad watched soldiers form a semicircle on the opposite side of the firepit.

Even David's brothers begrudgingly plopped onto a bench in the middle of the group directly opposite David and passed the wineskin among them. They sneered at their brother, but David took no notice. He just concentrated on tuning his strings.

Gad felt a strain of sympathy for David who had to be only slightly younger than himself. Here he was, despised by his older brothers, a shepherd with a high opinion of himself and imprudent enough to express it in public. Gad did not expect David to hold to his brave words and fight the giant, but he understood the need for David to fight for some kind of attention, being the youngest of so many brothers. If the lad could sing, even with modest skill, it might tamp down the tension caused by the spate of sibling rivalry, and David could save face from his boast to go against the giant—excuse it as youthful exuberance—and go home to Bethlehem sitting upright in his saddle as opposed to strapped over it.

But then David leaned his head back and began to sing, or rather he began to yowl, upward and upward, his voice soaring and circling, a lament, a cry, and shout before he ever sang a word, his vocal groan insistent that heaven and earth pay attention to the words he was to utter:

"Yahweh, you are my refuge.
In you, O Yahweh, do I take refuge.

How can anyone say to me,
'Flee like a bird to your mountain'?
How can you say to my soul,
'Flee like a frightened bird to find refuge'?
The wicked bend their bows.
The wicked loose their arrows from the string.
The wicked hide in the shadows
That they may shoot at the upright in heart.
When the foundations are being destroyed
What can the righteous do?
Yahweh is in his holy temple. Yahweh.
Yahweh, heaven is your throne."

That was all Gad needed to hear. The high register of pitch, the haunting wail of one who desperately needs refuge, the cry of fear that comes when facing insuperable odds. These words were sung with such vocal quality that Gad had to massage the expectancy rising in his chest. He understood the lyrical expressions of hurt, fear, the hope of refuge, the redirection on who might save Israel from her enemies. Gad looked at the mesmerized faces of the soldiers. It was as though they were being scolded by the singer, yet their ears were willing to listen, their hearts were willing to hear what truth the singer offered. Even the singer's three brothers had stopped snickering and refrained from passing the wineskin.

Gad turned on his heels and began a hasty retreat up the hill toward the tent of the king, the voice of the singer ringing in his ears removing all memory of the strident voice of the giant, removing all fear, removing all darkness in his heart.

Chapter 6

JONATHAN STOOD ON THE EDGE OF THE ENCAMPMENT LOOK-
ing down into the valley. At the sound of the giant's voice, his twin brothers
had fallen to their knees and scrambled behind him, each one wrapping their
arms around a powerful leg and gripping so tightly that Jonathan thought
they might cut off the blood flow. The giant's voice was terrifying, and he did
not blame them for their frightened response. It was an honest response, and
they clung to the protection of their eldest brother. But how could he protect
them? Jonathan was not allowed to fight, and in his heart of hearts, he too
was frightened by this giant.

The pervasive fear had become like the Destroyer, an invisible force floating through the army of Israel, crushing the heart of every man from king to
camp cook. And there was no Passover lamb to protect them from the demor-
alizing effect of this fear with its atoning blood on the doorpost.

The army looked to the prince, to the commander, for leadership. Jonathan looked to his father, but the fear had enfeebled his father's heart, and he
remained hidden inside his tent with his new wife that was not his wife and
certainly not Jonathan's mother. A father debilitated and taking comfort and
shelter in the arms of another woman; a giant hurling daily insults against
Yahweh and His chosen people; a forty-day siege that each passing day grew
heavier with fear and dread. Since the death of his mother, his father had not
been the same. Jonathan had watched his father attempt to clasp the reality of

life, but with hands that lacked fingers. The king could never quite grip the world around him and stabilize it.

Jonathan's place in the order of the family was clear. And when he became the first prince of Israel, the presumed king in the line of succession to the throne, he was fully aware of the importance of stability and proper order of magnitude. Yet, in the current state of his father's unstable mind, he found himself trying to think like a king, to think like a leader of men, and knew this was not right. It was too soon to assume the role of king, even in his quiet imagination.

But how to lead? How to bring confidence to the army? How to dispel the fear brought on by the harassment of the giant? Should he shake his whimpering brothers from his legs and march into the valley? And what if the giant slew him? If only his mother had not died. If only she were alive and present in the king's tent. Not this usurper. His mother would know what to say to Saul, what comforting and wise words would clear his father's mind and restore his heart.

The giant had finished his afternoon ridicule of the army of Israel, and the men were dispersing back to their tents, hearts broken and dismayed from the giant's mockery for their lack of courage, and he had done nothing.

Jeush approached Jonathan. "My lord, a word."

"Brothers, go back to the family tent and wait for me there." Jonathan tenderly grabbed the backs of the twins' heads and peeled them off his legs. He did not let go until their wobbly legs had become stable, then he positioned them in front of him. "There is nothing to be afraid of. The giant boasts and then goes back to his tent. He will be vanquished soon. Now go. I must meet with the tribal leaders."

The twins bolted away. Jonathan knew their speed was inspired more by fear of the giant than by their older brother's encouragement.

Jeush surveyed the valley, his hand covering his eyes, shielding them from the afternoon glare. Jonathan knew what was on the chieftain's mind. The other tribal leaders stood at a distance, talking among themselves. It did not take a prophet's clairvoyance to know what dominated their thoughts.

"There is no change with the king," Jonathan said. It was best to speak the truth, to give a preemptive answer to the question he expected Jeush to ask.

"Forty days, my lord." Jeush kicked the ground in disgust. "Are we all to die of old age?"

"At least the men are not deserting like they did at Gilgal," Jonathan said. "Thank Yahweh for that."

"But I do not know how much longer the tribal leaders can prevent that from happening again, my lord. Is there any encouraging sign from the king?"

Jonathan lay his hand upon Jeush's shoulder and pressed his fingers into the leather strap of his armor. "A dinner is planned for this evening. My hope is that with the family around him, the king's spirits will revive, and a decision will be made. That is all I can offer you at this time."

"I will tell the other leaders, my lord."

The forced smile on the face of this devoted chieftain was like an arrow shot into Jonathan's chest. He removed his hand as Jeush stepped away.

"Your faithfulness is a blessing to me, Jeush, and to my family."

"I love the king. I would die for the king."

Jonathan placed a hand over his heart to acknowledge Jeush's loyalty, and then trudged up the hill to the family tents.

"Catch your baby brother," Merab shouted at Jonathan as she chased Ishbosheth who had scampered out of the tent to escape the clutches of his big sister.

Jonathan scooped his brother into his hands. He held the squirming child away from his body as if it were some strange creature dropped from the sky. The memory of his father's murderous reaction to the birth of this child instantly came to mind. Jonathan had to restrain him from taking the child's life. Jonathan could understand the grief-stricken anger of his father at the death of his wife. He felt a twinge of the same reaction at the loss of his mother. Yet, surely, it was not this child's crime.

"He will not bite, my lord," Adriel said as he walked up behind Merab.

Jonathan thought his devoted armor bearer had come to rescue him, but instead he took Merab by the hand and began to lead her away. Jonathan felt a moment of panic.

"Sister, you cannot leave me with him." Jonathan's voice faltered.

"Mikal is inside overseeing the decoration of our tent." Merab waved her free hand as she and Adriel walked away. "Call her if you need anything."

"But…but I…what if…" Jonathan sputtered.

"You will be fine, Jonathan," Merab said. "Adriel and I have not seen each other since the army has been in camp."

Ish-bosheth twisted his head around at Merab's imminent departure, and his face began to scrunch into a wrinkled fig preparing to howl.

"You both are hopeless." Merab swiped Ish-bosheth from Jonathan's hands.

"Thank you, Merab. I am in your debt."

"Yes, you are." Merab bounced Ish-bosheth in her arms to keep him from shrieking. "And when do you intend to tell Father that we are here?"

"Merab, do not pressure your brother," Adriel said. "We are in the midst of a war."

"Not much of war if you ask me." Merab sniffed the swaddling cloth wrapped around Ish-bosheth's bottom.

"Sorry, my lord." Adriel held out hands of resignation.

"She is to be your wife." Jonathan gave Adriel a wink. "Are you prepared for this?"

"Jonathan." Merab slammed her heel onto her big brother's foot.

Jonathan reacted like his foot had been severed, and he hobbled around the entrance of the family tent howling in pain.

"My lord. My lord, you must come."

When Jonathan saw Gad stumbling toward him, he stopped feigning injury and stood straight.

"What is it, Gad?"

"You must come, my lord." Gad came to a stop but could not continue until he caught his breath. He braced his hands on his knees, lungs sucking in gulps of air.

"Is the giant chasing you?" Jonathan slapped Gad's thick, bent back.

With each exhale, Gad tried to speak.

The prophet's sense of urgency was obvious. It must be something important, but what? A danger to the family, the king?

Just then, Mikal came out of the tent holding different colored fabrics. "Which of these colors will work for the canopies?" Her question was directed to anyone within earshot, but she stopped when she saw Gad in such distress. "What is the matter with him?"

"I am sorry, my lady…my ladies." Gad rose just enough to bow to Merab and Mikal. "Forgive this intrusion. I think the prince needs to hear this shepherd sing. He just arrived in camp."

"A singing shepherd? Such a rarity." Mikal flavored her condescension with amusement.

"Yes, my lady. I would agree with you, but not in this case." Gad had begun to catch his breath. "I have never heard such singing. And I say this with some hesitancy, but this shepherd may be worthy of an audience with the king."

Everyone became still, including Ish-bosheth. The child stopped wiggling in his sister's arms.

When Gad finally caught his breath and stood up straight, he saw everyone looking at him. "I suggest the singer might bring comfort to the king."

"A common shepherd to sing for my father?" Mikal questioned Gad's idea.

"That is why I hope the prince will come and hear him, my lady." Gad added a meek nod toward the princess.

"Gad, take me to this shepherd." Jonathan welcomed the excuse to exit.

"Jonathan, please. You promised to speak to Father for us." Merab's protests stopped her brother in his tracks.

"I will speak to him." Jonathan dashed back to Merab and embraced her. "We want Father in the best frame of mind when I advocate for you and Adriel. If this shepherd sings as well as Gad believes, perhaps he can calm Father's soul."

"You are not serious, are you?" Mikal exclaimed. "Must we go to the pastures of Israel to find court musicians now?"

"We all want Abba the way he was before we lost Ima." Jonathan stared down his sister's scorn at a country boy's chance to sing for the king. "I will hear this shepherd and decide."

When Gad and Jonathan reached the tribal encampment of Judah the crowd had grown to listen to the singing shepherd.

"My lord, most of these men were not here when I left to come fetch you." Gad waved his hand over the thick circle of men. "Word must have spread to other tribal enclaves of the shepherd's singing."

Jonathan made no attempt to announce his presence, motioned to Gad he did not want him to disturb the men's rapt attention by announcing his arrival.

Before he laid eyes upon the singer, his heart stopped once he heard the voice.

"Yahweh is in his holy temple. O Yahweh.
O Yahweh, heaven is your throne.
His eyes behold the children of men.
His eyes will try the hearts of men.
His eyes will judge the righteous.
But the wicked, those who love violence,
Yahweh will despise.
Yahweh will rain his fire upon them.
Yahweh will send upon them a scorching wind.
The enemies of Yahweh will drink
The burning wind from their cup."

The singer paused and raised his hand as if pointing out the destination for the words to travel. His eyes were shut. His mouth was open, and yet he uttered no sound. Jonathan and the whole circle of men remained silent and inert as though the cycle of day to night had come to an abrupt halt.

When the singer found his voice, he finished his song unaccompanied on his kinnor, the lyric making a marvelous leap from his throat into the sky.

"Yahweh is righteous.
Yahweh loves the righteous.
Only the righteous will behold the face of Yahweh."

A soldier suddenly bolted from his seat, sprang over the smoldering fire-pit, and grabbed the singer's upraised arm, bending it behind his back and knocking the kinnor out of his other hand and onto the ground.

"I know what you are doing!" the soldier yelled as he yanked the singer's arm higher up his back. "You want to humiliate me. You expect me to go out there and fight the giant? Fight for the honor of the house of Jesse."

"Yes, for the honor of our house, and Israel, and Yahweh." The singer's face was a grimace of pain, yet he would not cry out. "You are hurting my arm."

"Go home, or I will break it so you will never play again."

"Release him now!"

Without releasing the singer's arm, the soldier turned to face the one who dared interfere with a sibling quarrel and almost impaled himself on Jonathan's drawn sword. The moment he recognized the prince, he released the singer's arm and fell to his knees.

The singer grabbed his kinnor off the ground and turned to see his attacker face down on the ground with the tip of the prince's sword resting on top of the man's bowed head. He looked at the circle of men surrounding him and watched them all take a knee and bow. The singer followed the example and went down on one knee.

"If you have damaged this man's arm in any way..."

"My lord, forgive," the attacker blurted.

"That depends on the condition of his arm."

"He is my brother, my lord. We were just quarreling before he returns home."

"The fact that he is your brother has spared your own arm from being cut off, but you are a disgrace to the army of Israel." Jonathan tapped the attacker's bent spine with the blade of his sword. The blade tap upon the back of the attacker was not a sign of affection or a signal to rise to his feet. He remained crouched before Jonathan.

"It is not your brother who is going home, but you." Jonathan thrust his sword into the ground beside the attacker's bowed head. It had the desired effect of surprise and fright. "And I hope you can compose a clever story for your family as to why you left the battlefield and your brother remained."

"My lord, I beg you on my brother's behalf, do not send him home." The singer held his kinnor to his chest. "He is the firstborn."

"Your composing is exceeded by your compassion." Jonathan shifted his gaze to the singer and signaled for him to rise.

"My lord, there is no harm done." The singer waved the arm his brother had attempted to damage. Then for good measure, he plucked the strings of his kinnor to demonstrate his ability to play.

Jonathan turned his head to look at Gad standing behind him. "You may be right," Jonathan whispered. "He may be the balm we need."

"Yes, my lord." Gad nodded.

Jonathan redirected his stern gaze back to the crouching attacker, his face a mere handbreadth from the dusty ground.

"Brother of this singer, go to your tent and stay out of my sight," Jonathan barked. "I do not wish to know your name. You may thank the singer for that."

The singer's brother uttered a slavish appreciation for the prince's mercy and slinked back without ever lifting his head. Two other men grabbed him, brought him to his feet, guided him through the crowd who remained on their knees, and led him out of the circle.

"I hope you did not plan to leave." Jonathan signaled for the singer to rise.

"I would have, my lord." The singer stood. "I delivered the supplies my brothers required and would have left except I heard the giant."

"Ah yes, the giant got your attention." Jonathan returned his sword into its sheath. "What is your name?"

"David, son of Jesse of Bethlehem." David bowed his head.

Jonathan looked David up and down, from bushy head to dusty sandal. "Would you be willing to play and sing for my family at the evening meal?"

David looked at Gad who quietly mouthed the words, *Yes, my lord.*

"Yes, my lord," David blurted.

"Good." Jonathan smiled at Gad's prompting of David and then turned to walk back up the hill. "Gad will bring you to the family tent when it is time."

"A bath and fresh clothes for our shepherd, my lord?" Gad asked.

Jonathan stopped and thought for a moment. Then he moved toward David and stood before him. He ran a finger along the string of lion claws hanging from David's neck as though strumming the strings of a kinnor.

"No. He comes as he is, smell and all." Jonathan enjoyed the prospect his spontaneous decision might have on the family. "I look forward to seeing my sister's face change from disgust to rapture when she hears you sing."

Gad chuckled as the prince passed by on his way back up the hill.

"And do not forget your kinnor," Jonathan said over his shoulder as he departed.

"Well, Shepherd, your fortunes have turned," Gad said. "Tonight, you shall sing for the king of Israel."

At Gad's shocking words, David dropped to his knees, his body overtaken by uncontrollable trembling. His audience was no longer the sheep he had tended all his life, or his unappreciative family, or the common soldier. He was now to sing for royalty, the most powerful people in the kingdom, and the most powerful man in the kingdom, and if the words of Samuel were true, the one he would someday replace.

Chapter 7

IN THE DIM LIGHT OF THE FAMILY TENT, SAUL TOOK THE WET cloth Rizpah handed him and pressed it over his face. He sighed and slumped back into the pile of cushions and fur blankets. Saul draped his muscular forearm over the cloth, blocking out his vision. He did not want to see or speak to anyone. Saul had not come out of his tent until after the giant had finished his afternoon reproach and the sun's intense light had waned. He made the short jaunt to the family tent without interacting with the tribal leaders, his elite guard, or common soldier. Saul wanted nothing more than to be a ghost in the shadows, to be hidden from all human sight. He ate little and did not speak during the evening meal. It was consumed without verbal communication among the family. Any personal exchange between royal family and servants was done with gestures and head motions.

The morose silence was not broken until Saul removed the cloth from his face and gave a limp wave for Ahimelech to acknowledge Yahweh for providing their sustenance. As the high priest rose, Saul looked about the tent at the solemn faces of the royal family, including Jarib, Adriel, and the servants. He lay the damp cloth over his wrist.

When Ahimelech began to pray, Saul watched his family as the words of the prayer startled everyone. The sound of a human voice after so long a period of suppressed silence was jarring.

"Blessed are you, Yahweh, our God and Master of creation, who nourishes the whole world in goodness, with grace, kindness, and compassion."

Saul moaned, which evolved into a scoff, and then his lips froze into a grimace.

Every head turned from the high priest to the king.

Saul's derisive amusement had attracted unwanted attention, so he waved for Ahimelech to resume his prayer.

After a gentle clearing of the throat, Ahimelech continued with the blessing.

Jonathan was distracted by his armor-bearer as the high priest carried on with his prayer. He watched Adriel tease the ties in the back of Merab's robe, loosening the knots with his nimble fingers until Merab playfully swatted his hand to stop him. Both Merab and Adriel were impatient with Jonathan for not bringing their suit to the attention of the king. Merab was the oldest of the king's two daughters and ripe for marriage, and everyone considered the pairing a perfect match. Even Barzillai, Adriel's father and chieftain of the tribe of Manasseh, had spoken with Jonathan, hoping to gain his blessing before he spoke to the king on his son's behalf.

Jonathan discouraged it. He knew his father's moods better than anyone. The king had been in an emotional spiral for some time and had only worsened with this inexhaustible siege in the Valley of Elah. Jonathan refused to broach the subject until he saw improvement in the king's spirits. He hoped his invitation for a common shepherd to enter the family tent to sing for his father might afford that opportunity and not be a decision he would regret.

"For He is God, who nourishes and sustains all, and does good to all, and prepares food for all His creatures which He created. Blessed are you, Oh Yahweh. Amen."

Jonathan sensed Ahimelech was anxious to exit once he had finished his prayer of thanks. When he looked to the prince for permission to leave, Jonathan nodded toward the king. In all things he would honor his father. The king granted Ahimelech's wish to depart with a grunt as he draped the cloth over his eyes again. Ahimelech's bow was not seen or acknowledged by the king, but Jonathan raised his hand in appreciation as the high priest made for the exit.

Jonathan took advantage of Ahimelech's departure to put some food in a bowl and fill a goblet with wine. When he rose to leave, Jonathan tried to make a quiet exit, but the rustling of his garments as he slipped through the tent caught the ear of the king.

"Where are you going, Son?" The king did not lift his arm or the cloth from his eyes.

"I have a surprise for you, Abba." Jonathan kept his face bright with hope.

His father lay still, his large frame motionless inside the cushions and furs.

Everyone in the tent set their eyes on Jonathan. It had been some time since anyone dared surprise the king. Everyone coddled Saul, dodged his moods, indulged his whims. The last time his father was surprised the result was disastrous. The surprise turned to horror for all who witnessed the moment at Carmel after the slaughter of the Amalekites when the prophet Samuel chopped the Amalekite king to pieces with the king's own sword, the sword the prophet claimed was his, brought out of Egypt by his ancestors at the great Exodus.

Saul had not been the same since that moment. His father had not wanted to touch the sword of execution since it had been used by Samuel for such a deadly purpose. Jonathan had instructed Abner to hide the sword in a place known only to him. So, when Jonathan offered a surprise for the king, it was not just risky for him, but for everyone inside the tent. If it did not go well, all might suffer.

Saul lifted one side of the cloth, revealing a bloodshot eye. "A surprise for me?" he inquired, as though he misunderstood.

Jonathan showed no apprehension. Indeed, he organized his features into a buoyant smile, but the saliva inside his jaw turned ice cold.

"Yes, Abba."

"Must I move from this spot?"

"Remain where you are."

His father exhaled a sigh of relief and lowered the cloth back over his eye, resting his arm firmly over his brow.

Everyone in the tent looked at Jonathan as if he had lost his mind, all their expressions congealing into a single, unnerved visage.

Mikal was the only one who tried to prevent Jonathan from leaving the tent. She dashed to the entrance and stopped her brother before he made his exit.

"Is this surprise in the form of a warbling shepherd straight out of the pasture?" Mikal kept her voice just below a whisper.

"You do not understand." Jonathan became impatient. "You would never expect to hear such singing from a sheepherder."

"Are you mad?" Mikal dug her fingers into the back of his arm.

"Yes, Sister, I am." Jonathan squeezed his fingers around the wine goblet to keep the contents from spilling after Mikal yanked his arm, then became assertive. "But I am also confident in my decision. Now, release my arm."

"Where are you going with that food?" Mikal loosened her grip.

"Feeding the singer." Jonathan used his elbow to pull back the tent flap just enough to peek outside. David strummed his kinnor and pranced around the fire in the center of the main encampment, entertaining the soldiers.

"You know Father has ordered court musicians banned from all the family meals." Mikal's disdain was evident.

"This is no ordinary musician, Sister." Jonathan nodded for Mikal to take a peek.

She pulled the tent flap back enough to get a good look at David in the firelight playing his kinnor for the crowd before she snapped the flap back in disgust.

"You must be joking. He looks common and filthy."

"And he sings like nothing you have ever heard," Jonathan responded.

"He will be as boring as the other musicians." Mikal's face displayed her disgust, but also a flash of curiosity. She pulled the flap open again. "Look at the way he is dressed. Did he come straight from the fields?"

"He arrived today from Bethlehem, bringing supplies for his brothers and smelling of sheep dung. He has not had time to make himself presentable. But he will make your heart melt into little puddles."

"I doubt that."

The intensity of his sister's protests was beginning to wane, so Jonathan could not pass up the chance to tease her. "You will bleat helplessly like one of his little lambs."

"Even more doubtful."

"Baaaaaa. Baaaaaa."

"Will you stop?" Mikal hissed.

"Let me go. I want him to eat something before he plays."

She stepped aside for her brother to pass. "I hope he enjoys it. It may be his last meal."

Jonathan chuckled and slipped out of the tent.

Gad was the only one gathered around the blazing fire to see the prince approach. The rest of the crowd was enjoying David's melodious parody of Goliath as he stomped around the fire with exaggerated steps, imitating the giant.

Gad cleared his throat, attempting to gain the attention of the soldiers and alert them to the approaching prince, but they were too amused by David's clowning. Gad saw Jonathan pause outside the circle to observe the comic spectacle and was relieved to see a smile appear on the prince's face.

"My lord."

When Gad spoke and bowed, everyone turned toward the prince and did the same, and then stepped aside so Jonathan could enter the circle.

David hugged his kinnor and bent over to catch his breath.

"I hate to stop this entertainment, but there is a request for your services." Jonathan stretched out his offering of food and drink to David. "But eat something first before we go inside."

"Thank you, my lord. I am not hungry." David declined the plate but reached for the goblet of wine. "However, I will take a swallow of this."

David took a large gulp. There was no savoring the wine, just a hard gulp, and then he tipped the goblet to his lips again and emptied the contents with another mouthful. He swished the wine inside his mouth, dropped back his head and gargled, and then spat the liquid at Gad's feet, causing him to hop backward.

"My apologies." David appeared indifferent to Gad's mortified expression.

Where was the modest shepherd from this afternoon, Gad wondered? The young man who had fallen to his knees trembling at the prospect of singing for the king and the royal family? Were these actions before the soldiers and the prince just bluster to hide his nerves, or was he a showman at heart who enjoyed the focused attention of others?

"Are you ready then?" Jonathan asked.

"Lead on, my lord," David said.

The prince thrust the plate of food and empty goblet into Gad's hands as he led the shepherd back toward the family tent. Gad lurched forward, plate and goblet in hand, but stopped just outside the tent. He waited for the tent flaps to close behind David and Jonathan, and then he eased forward, stopping at the entrance. He cocked his ear and prudently separated the tent flaps just enough to catch sight of the backs of the prince and the shepherd. In the torchlight, they moved to the center of the tent.

Gad made a silent plea to Yahweh that the prince would not suffer any repercussion if the shepherd did not please the king. The idea for David to sing for the king was initially his, and if this did not succeed, the prince would take the brunt of the king's displeasure. Jonathan would never allow the king's ire to fall on him.

Gad set the plate and goblet on the ground and quietly reopened the tent flaps and moved through the entrance. The reduced light inside covered his movement as he slipped behind one of the screens that concealed the tables of food. When the servants gave him a harsh look for being where he was not allowed, Gad put a finger to his lips for them to remain silent. If the shepherd did not please the king, then irritating the servants for entering their terrain would be the least of his worries.

Chapter 8

ALL EYES STARED AT DAVID. MOST OF THE FACES OF HIS AUDI-
ence expressed suspicion and alarm. Except for King Saul. His eyes remained
covered by a cloth weighted down by his arm.

Jonathan pointed to David for him to take a seat in the middle of the tent.
Before ushering through the entrance of the tent, the prince told David he
had done nothing to prepare the audience. "It will be a complete surprise,"
he had said. At this news, David felt a knot tightening inside his stomach.

David's assessment of this crowd was one of indifference though a few of
them seemed ready to do more than just protest the intrusion: a one-eyed
courtier, all the women, and especially the commander of the army appeared
ready to toss him out.

David exhaled a sigh of relief when he witnessed Jonathan restraining
Abner from his forceful advance. When Jonathan whispered into the ear of
the commander he retreated to a position behind a thick tent pole. Jonathan's
gesture might have kept the commander from tossing him out of the tent,
but it did nothing to remove the scowl of disapproval on Abner's stern face.

It was not until Jonathan grabbed a large cushion, chucked it into the
center, and then motioned for him to take a seat, that David was able to
unlock his legs and take his place. He had never seen the king or his family
or any of those in service to the royal family until this moment. He knew all
the accounts of the military exploits of the king, his son, and the commander.
He was keenly aware of the rivalry between prophet and king evidenced by

Samuel's secret visit to his home, and he had heard tales regarding the strange torments experienced by the king. Now, the main character of these stories and his family were assembled before him waiting for him to sing.

Everyone was in royal dress. Even the servants wore finer attire than he, and David felt self-conscious, an emotion new to him. He caught a whiff of the stale odor emanating from the lion-skin bag hanging off his back mixed with the smell of his own lack of hygiene. He glanced down at the stains of dirt and horse sweat on his leggings after riding all day and being thrown to the ground by his brothers. Why had the prince not heeded the suggestion of the prophet Gad and allowed him to bathe and find fresh clothing?

He had always aspired to perform for more appreciative audiences and wished to be more presentable. Now, he had made the leap from pasture to the inner circle of the royal household. He took a deep breath to calm his nerves. He would sing for Yahweh and sing for himself. He would pretend the audience was nothing but the sheep he cared for, though well-dressed, royal sheep.

David took his seat on the cushion. His audience did not stir but remained silent as he reached inside his bag and removed a small bow he had fashioned from willow wood and strung with horsehair. David nestled the kinnor in his lap and ran the tips of his fingers the length of the strings, warming them before he began to pluck. He did not sing immediately. Instead, he began by playing a soothing rhythm, a rhythm that permeated its consoling sound throughout the tent.

The music calmed his jumbled emotions and formed them into one melodic flow. The melody had a strange power: it had a knowing, an understanding as it collected all fears and desires and secrets and dark troubles of the soul, shepherding them into the heart of the kinnor. The rhythm of this tune took the shared knowledge of the audience and the words of their hearts that none could utter and turned them into a solacing, invisible cover spreading itself over the heads of everyone. It was then that David sang:

> "Give ear, O Yahweh.
> Give ear to me and answer,
> For I am poor and needy.
> Keep my soul, O Yahweh.
> Guard my life, for I am devoted to you.
> O Yahweh, save your servant.

Save your servant for I trust in you.
Have mercy on me, O Yahweh,
For unto you do I cry all day long."

Saul's arm rose off his forehead without any effort on his part. He thought Rizpah had lifted it for him, but when he sat up and the damp cloth fell from his eyes, she sat to his side, motionless, too far away to have removed his arm, her attention directed at the singer in the middle of the tent. Saul examined his forearm, flexed his fingers, felt the warmth of blood beginning to flow. Then he looked around the room and saw shadows and forms.

"More light," Saul spoke, his voice a whispery rasp, but no one responded to his request. He lifted a goblet of wine to his lips and felt the quickening dazzle in his mouth as he swallowed. He leaned forward, straining his eyes as he tried to bring clarity to these obscure images that did not move. His ears were opening to the music emanating from the center of the tent, his heart was reviving from its effects, but it was as though he had awakened inside the chamber of the dead after a long sleep. He kneaded his fingers into his chest.

"More light. I need more light," he said, this time with more force.

The music stopped abruptly. In the shadows, forms moved about the tent in response to his request.

The singer seated on the cushion appeared confused by the swift movement and his reflex action was to spring to his feet.

"Do not move." Saul's command carried no threat. "Stay seated and play. Just play."

The singer settled back, studied the strings of his kinnor, and found his melody again, this time using the bow, shifting the mood of the song from ecstatic melancholy to a rising exaltation.

"Rejoice the heart of your servant,
For unto you, O Yahweh, do I lift up my soul.
For you, O Yahweh, are good,
Ready to pardon,
Abounding in love,
Full of mercy unto all who call upon you."

The light brightened as more oil pots were set aflame, and the phantoms in the tent took human shape. An imperceptible force had possessed Saul, a transcendence rising within his heart. He could not detach himself from it. Even more, he did not want the sensation to depart, ever. Each note played, each word sung, echoed inside his heart and seemed to reverberate to the far rims of creation. The power that had lifted Saul's arm from his forehead a few moments before, did so again, and directed his open left hand toward the singer as though, were he within reach, he would caress his cheek.

The singer paused again, unsure if the king's gesture meant for him to stop.

"No, no," Saul said, beckoning with his fingers. "Play on, play on."

Saul's mouth twisted slightly. He felt his eyes emerging above the sunken cheekbones, blinking away the former invisible entrapment. His slumped posture began reshaping itself into upright determination.

"I have no court musician who can compare. Please..." Saul beckoned again for the singer to play.

The singer forced his fingers to respond to the command.

> "Give ear, O Yahweh.
> Give ear unto my prayer.
> Attend to my cry for mercy.
> Listen to the words of my supplication.
> For in the day of trouble
> I cry out to you, O Yahweh.
> For you will answer me, O Yahweh.
> I know you will hear me and answer."

Saul leaned toward the singer, a smile streaking across his face, though this time, the muscles of his upraised expression were not helpless, lost in vexation, but molded into serene joy, so much so, that he began to chuckle. It was a quiet laughter, one of amazement at the tune and lyrics he was hearing and wonder at how this glorious song had lured his soul out of hiding, brought him out of the long, dark sweep of these days.

Saul saw a tray of vegetables and meats at his feet. He took a thin, wooden prong placed to the side and stabbed morsels of food and stuffed them into his mouth. He could taste again; the flavors exploding onto the buds of his tongue intensified his appetite.

All eyes turned from the singer to the king, all eyes except Mikal's. His daughter crouched on her hands and knees; her eyes locked on the singer like a creature poised to spring on its prey. Her mouth was open, her breathing low and steady. Was this conjuring on the part of the musician, Saul wondered? Was he a sorcerer in the guise of a shepherd, transferring his madness onto the princess?

The music flowed from the flesh of man, from the wood, from the gut and hair of beasts into the soul of the king, and by all appearances, the princess, unlocking chambers inside his heart and the heart of his daughter that neither ever knew existed. Mikal was unaware of the drool spilling over the side of her mouth, and Saul motioned for Merab to wipe the moisture from her sister's chin.

Merab took the edge of her robe and subtly wiped the moisture away. Mikal never noticed what care was given to her. Saul was not the only person who had been altered. The singer's song had also transformed the bearing of a princess into a panther.

"Do not forget to blink, Mikal." Saul was delighted to see his daughter so taken with this singer. He washed down the crumbling food with another gulp of wine.

There was now enough light filling the tent for Saul to see Mikal emerge with a jolt. Ishvi and Malki could not contain their laughter at their sister's expense and were not silenced until Jonathan stepped forward and cracked their heads together. The commotion caused David to stop singing. This time, Saul did not insist the young singer keep playing. He continued to pierce the tasty food with his long, wooden prong and pop the morsels into his mouth.

"There is a change. I feel a change." Saul kept repeating as if he was the only one who could believe this wrought miracle. "There is a change in my bones."

"This is good, Abba," Jonathan said.

"This is good." Saul continued to gorge on the rapidly disappearing chunks of food. "This is very good."

Saul was not sure if he meant the food or if he referred to his brightening disposition. He was just thrilled to be taking pleasure in something. When he drained his goblet of wine, Rizpah quickly had a servant refill it.

"This was quite a surprise, Jonathan." Saul took his goblet from Rizpah and leaned back into the cushions. He gave David a curious scrutiny, and then once again turned his attention to Jonathan. "And where did this surprise come from?"

"Over the mountains from Bethlehem."

"Bethlehem of Judah." Saul took another mouthful of fresh wine, savoring it before swallowing. "And why has this surprise just now come to my attention?"

"Gad brought him to my attention just today." Jonathan looked around the tent for the court prophet.

"Is not Gad from Bethlehem?"

"Yes, Abba."

"Singer, do you know the prophet Gad?" Saul turned his gaze upon the singer.

David had not anticipated being spoken to or being asked to speak. His mind was still inside the composition of his song. He had more to sing. He was not finished, but for the royal family, his solo was over. The interruption surprised him. Sheep never interrupted him when he was composing, and he was a little perturbed at being cut off in the middle of a verse. But then he never wanted to play for sheep, and he had to accommodate a human audience, especially a royal one. David looked at Jonathan, who signaled for him to stand and speak, so he set down his kinnor and rose but bent to bow before the king.

"We knew Gad's family, my lord, but I did not set eyes on the prophet until today." David maintained his bent posture, keeping his eyes focused upon the tent floor until he heard giggling from all sides. The lion-claw necklace swung back and forth as he spoke, so he clasped it with both hands to stop it from swinging. He angled his head toward Jonathan and saw the prince's exasperated expression. The prince hissed at his siblings for their rudeness at the sight of David's primitive choker and gave them stern looks of reproof, which caused the snickering to stop instantly.

"Bethlehem is a small town." The king spoke, ignoring what was going on with his children. "Why would you not know him? You look roughly the same age."

"Yes, my lord, we discussed that this morning." David's eyes returned to their downward gaze. "Gad left home at an early age to study at the school of the great prophet Samuel, while I spent most of my time in the hills with sheep."

"The great prophet Samuel."

David glanced up to see King Saul gazing into his cup of wine. He sensed everyone in the tent had stopped breathing at the mention of Samuel's name. Could he, in all innocence, at one moment so deftly lift the king out of his black humor only to send him spiraling back into the depths of the debilitating mood that had held him captive?

"You have lifted my spirits tonight, Singer," King Saul said emphatically, then raised his face, displaying a cheery expression and took another sip of wine. "Please, stand up straight. You are making my back hurt just looking at you bent over like that."

When David stood upright everyone breathed a sigh of relief.

"Would that you could make my giant problem disappear as magically as you have vanquished the darker spirits in my head." The king lifted his goblet to David as a gesture of thankfulness, but instead of taking a drink, King Saul set his goblet aside and leaned forward. "And does this excellent singer have a name?"

"I am David, my lord, son of Jesse and my mother is Nitzevet," David answered.

"If you have always been a shepherd, where did you acquire your skills as a singer and composer?"

David's sensitive ears detected a clear tone of mockery in the king's voice.

"My lord, my family has always raised and traded in livestock since our forefathers settled in the land of Judah. What skills I have as a composer and singer is a gift from Yahweh."

"Then Yahweh is generous." King Saul nestled his large frame inside the cushions.

"I have only composed or sung for my sheep in the high country above Bethlehem."

"I would send my pitiful court musicians to the hills of Bethlehem for a time under your tutelage if I thought they would return with your talent and skill."

"My lord is kind." David was beginning to relish the king's praise.

"You may not know this, but I too came from humble beginnings." The king stretched out his long legs. "I was once a farmer. I had livestock. I plowed the earth, before all of this." Saul gave a tired wave of his arm to include the entire tent.

"I know the great history of your rise to power, my lord." David nodded in deference but remained looking at the king.

"Then you know I keep multitudes of people in my service." He paused and looked about the tent. "So, what is one more addition?"

"He would make a great addition to the court, Abba."

Everyone turned to look at the princess standing on her toes to extend her height, her eyes blinking rapidly, making up for the deficit of moisture her eyeballs had lost while staring wide-eyed as David sang.

David observed her flushed face and determined its rose color was not from embarrassment for interrupting the conversation, which had so far excluded her. Rather, her wine-tinted complexion belied an excitement at the prospect of having David at the king's beck and call, a decision David was not necessarily keen on since it could mean an obligation that might prove restrictive. David was not used to being confined.

"My, my, how Princess Mikal so quickly repents from her first impressions."

David did not understand the prince's playful dig at his sister, nor her attempt at kicking her brother for his comment, which the prince stepped back in time to avoid.

"You are an inspiring singer." King Saul smiled at his impulsive daughter. He looked like he might be about to snap at his daughter for her impulsive behavior, but David had sung away his melancholy and his improved state of mind made him more composed. "Certainly, the princess seems to think so."

"My lord is kind." David's heart welled with pride as he looked at Mikal, sure to share his thankfulness. "As is the princess."

Mikal did not return David's admiring gaze. Instead, she lowered her head, allowing her golden hair to fall forward to cover her profile, but David could still see the smile that fit tightly across her lips.

"Abner, perhaps we can affect a surrender from the Philistines if this shepherd will just sing to them," King Saul said with a burst of energy as if this was a splendid idea.

"I will take it up with the Five Lords first thing in the morning." The commander chuckled to reinforce his stab at humor, but King Saul did not seem amused.

"My lord, I fear my talent is not that persuasive," David said, quick to sense the unease caused by the commander's remark. "But the king is most kind to say so."

David glanced at Jonathan, and the prince's only response was an expression of concern and a shrug as if at a momentary loss for words. David observed this complex family with its complex emotions that seemed capable of shattering at the slightest unguarded word. He was not accustomed to such an intricate family dynamic. Being the youngest of eight sons, including several older sisters, he had to fight for the scraps of attention and affection from his parents.

"I want to reward this young man," King Saul blurted. "Jarib, send word to the family of Jesse and Nitzevet in Bethlehem and tell them—no, no. Ask them to allow young David to remain in my service, that we are pleased with him." The king raised both arms to encompass everyone inside the tent.

To David's amazement, everyone, even Abner, gave a positive if not hearty response.

"Would you like that, Shepherd? Get away from your sheep for a while? Sleep on soft bedding under warm fur blankets instead of the hard, cold ground?"

David's family would never believe this. He had sung his way into the hearts of the royal family. He could hear his brothers' jealous objections for his good fortune. Their scoffing would be never-ending, but then he would not have to listen. His talents had gained him this promotion to a more refined audience.

"Speak up," King Saul barked. "Your talents are wasted in Bethlehem."

The king had spoken the truth. David was done with his sheep and his family.

"My lord is too kind." David bowed to affirm his acceptance.

"Kind? Most kind? Too kind? What is that?" King Saul roared. "You may be able to sing but you are slow in manners of the court."

"I will teach him." Mikal spoke too quickly and too forcefully. She took a step back, retreating from the sudden attention and right into the arms of her older brother.

"Baaaaaa." Jonathan drew her shoulders into his chest.

"I am going to kill you." Mikal tried to squirm out of his grasp.

While David did not understand this sibling dynamic, he could not deny that he sensed the princess's infatuation with him or the pleasure he gained from it.

"My children are acting foolish." King Saul shook his head. "Do you accept the king's offer, or must I conscript you as a court musician?"

"Yes, my lord. Yes, I accept your kind—no, your generous offer," David blurted. He was almost undone by what was happening to him and embarrassed by his fumbling responses.

King Saul turned to his aide as a minor uproar of cheering took place inside the tent.

"Send word to Bethlehem straight away, Jarib."

"First light, my lord." Jarib acted thrilled to see the king restored to normal.

The woman next to the king reached over and placed her hand upon his arm. "My lord, your head...you seem restored."

"Yes, my dear. Restored." King Saul pointed at David who still had not moved from his position in the center of the tent. "This young shepherd..."

"Court musician, Abba," Jonathan corrected.

Saul rose to his feet. He was glad his legs were strong, balanced, and his feet were not numb and tingly, but planted firmly. "Yes, our new court musician has driven away the pounding in my head and quickened my mind. I am inspired to take drastic action." Saul turned to his commander who was partially hidden behind a tent pole. "Abner, this giant, this Goliath has been a thorn in our side for how long?"

"Forty days, my lord." Abner stepped into view.

"Forty days," Saul mumbled as he thought to himself. "Forty is a familiar number, is it not?" Saul looked at the faces before him who responded with puzzled expressions at his pondering of the numeral. "The number forty; I remember reading something of this in the Scrolls. There is something significant about this number. It means something to our nation."

"Forty days the great prophet Moses sat in the cloud atop Mount Sinai, conversing with Yahweh." A voice spoke from behind the screens.

Everyone cast their eyes to the screens that concealed the tables of food and those who prepared and served it. The servants scurried around the edge as if they wanted nothing to do with the one who just spoke, and to a person, pointed behind the screens to the owner of the voice.

"Gad, is that you?" Saul grinned.

"Yes, my lord," replied a timorous voice.

"Come out from behind the screen." Saul kept his tone mirthful. He was enjoying himself. When Gad stuck his head from around the side of the screens, the king smiled and beckoned him forward while everyone else tried to conceal their amusement.

"Good to see you, court prophet. Come closer. I need your knowledge."

Gad moved to the center of the tent next to David and bowed low.

Saul appreciated the court prophet's show of devotion. King and prophet had not laid eyes on one another for some time. Saul had been in no frame of mind for studying with his court prophet. Since the death of the queen and the slaughter of the Amalekites, Saul had kept his distance.

"What significance is the number forty with the prophet Moses?" Saul asked.

"During Moses's life he lived forty years in Egypt and forty years in the desert before Yahweh chose him to lead our people out of slavery. Once out of Egypt, our people wandered in the wilderness for forty years. Before crossing the Jordan River, Moses sent twelve men, one from each tribe, to spy out the land Yahweh had promised to our people as an inheritance. They were gone forty days."

"That is quite the historical address," Saul said. "Thorough, to be sure."

"And finally, as my lord has remembered from our studies, the prophet Moses sat atop Mount Sinai forty days and nights, communing with Yahweh, shrouded inside his holy cloud, and receiving the Sacred Sayings. Not once, but on two occasions."

A divine silence followed the instruction as though the cloud of Yahweh had settled over the tent, penetrating the hearts, controlling the minds of all inside—for a brief moment placing everyone under the draw of holiness.

"I have missed our lessons, Gad," Saul whispered, breaking the shared spell.

"As have I, my lord." Gad bowed in deference.

"So, the prophet Moses sits on Sinai forty days with Yahweh, not once but on two separate occasions, and after the second encounter, he descends the mountain with the two stone tablets bearing Yahweh's Ten Sayings for our people. Am I correct?"

"Yes, my lord. Forty days alone with Yahweh...in a cloud."

"In a cloud, like the inside of my head. What a daunting prospect to be alone forty days with…" Saul paused, but then shook his head, ruffling the thought out of his newly cleared mind as if expelling a tremor. "Forty days. Yahweh and Moses seem fond of that number. So, it shall be with the king. Forty days is long enough for the army of Israel to be disheartened by a single man. Not one day more. I shall face the giant tomorrow."

Saul enjoyed seeing the disbelief rising on everyone's faces; his pronouncement clearly shocked them. He had not even worn his armor in recent memory let alone been in actual combat.

"Behind your eyes, I can see the calamitous results you are all imagining." Saul relished the thought of catching the members of his inner circle off guard, but he was ready with a defense. His chest swelled, and he stretched out his arms.

"The giant may have a cubit or so of height advantage." Saul patted his raised forearm, indicating the length of measurement. "But I do not see that as…"

"Abba, you are talking about facing the giant yourself…alone?" Jonathan interrupted.

"Is this not what the giant is requesting? Single combat?" Saul scanned the faces inside the hushed tent. "Gad says the prophet Moses sat with Yahweh alone for forty days. Surely, I can face a giant alone."

"My lord, the king shows great courage." Abner stepped between Adriel and Merab, passed Jonathan and Jarib, and approached the king. "In these forty days, no one has come forward to encounter the giant even with the generous incentives offered by the king for any champion who would accept the challenge."

"All the more reason then." Saul pointed to David. "Our new court musician has inspired me."

"My lord, the king is too…" Abner paused as if searching for the right words.

Saul knew this was the part of court behavior his cousin hated. Abner wanted to tell him he was a fool for thinking this way, something he would have said to Saul before he wore the crown. But now, his cousin and his commander had to choose his words, and he was not a man of words. Saul appreciated his cousin's restraint.

"The king is too what? Too old? Too weak?" Saul's voice rose in intensity, but not with anger. Saul was gaining strength, and he could imagine himself a giant-slayer. "This young shepherd says I am too kind. Too old. Too kind. Perhaps they go together."

"On the contrary, my lord." Jarib stepped forward to stand with Abner in solidarity. "You are too important to the army and to all of Israel."

The family immediately began to echo the words of the commander and the secretary. As thrilled as they were to see the improvement in the king's state of mind, it was unthinkable for Saul to contemplate such action.

"Just the point." Saul held out both hands, cutting off the family's expressions of concern and appeals for reason. "If the king were to face this giant, would it not inspire the army of Israel? Jarib, how could you forget Jabesh Gilead?"

"I can never forget, my lord." Jarib affirmed his memory by placing his hand over the patch covering the empty socket of his right eye. "The king of Israel liberated my city from the Ammonites."

"Following that victory, we routed the Philistines with only axes and mattocks and plowshares for weapons in the Valley of Zeboim after Jonathan and Adriel knocked over their sacred pillar. You remember this, Jonathan?"

"It was a great victory for my father." Jonathan spoke as if he felt the rush of his father's exuberance flowing into his heart.

"We have not lost a war to these pagans. Why should I allow a giant to stop me?"

"My lord, as your commander, we should not risk—" Abner stopped again.

"Risk what? Me losing my head?" Saul snapped. "You will not offend me, nor will you set me back down the path of dark brooding. We have always spoken plainly. Finish what you were about to say."

"Let Israel remember to the thousandth generation the glories of the king's past victories." Gad interjected his near-worshipful praise, giving Abner no time to respond. "Yet, let him not risk anything that could mar the memory."

Saul did have past victories of which he was proud. Some were more like slaughters, but not all. The people of Israel had demanded a king for the purpose of fighting her enemies, and he had been fighting almost since the day the crown was placed upon his head. The country had enemies on every side, and indeed Gad was correct; Saul had fought valiantly and had delivered Israel from the hands of those who had plundered the nation. Saul had reached near-mythic status with his bravery and the number of victories over Israel's enemies yet going hand to hand in single combat with another warrior taller, stronger, and more battle-hardened than he would not be a wise decision. He was clearheaded at the moment and thought the court prophet's line of reasoning should be contemplated. Saul looked at his cousin and saw the relief on his face after Gad had spoken. He decided not to insist that Abner speak his mind.

"Jarib, remind me of the incentives offered to the one who slays the giant." Saul turned to his secretary.

"The king's generous proposal offers great wealth to the warrior who slays the one who has cast reproach upon the nation of Israel and Yahweh. And for the family of the man who kills the giant: they will be free of further service to the king; they will never again pay taxes; and they will be raised to a rank of nobility in the kingdom."

"In forty days, wealth is not reward enough, nor is rank and privilege. There must be something extra, an additional boost to the fortunes of the man who steps forward." Saul's mind raced with alternatives. He was thrilled to be thinking so clearly, to have risen out of the murky slough in his heart. This unforgiving siege had gone on long enough and something more precious than gold would have to be offered.

"Has there been talk of a bride for the giant-slayer by offering a daughter of a tribal leader?" Saul asked.

"Yes, my lord," Jarib replied. "It has been discussed among the tribal leaders. They are all amenable."

"That is good. Any daughter from the tribal leaders would be a prize," Saul said, but then he furrowed his brow, inspired by a new thought. "Why not enhance the quality of the incentive. Would it not prove a greater enticement to our prospective champion if the offer would be that of a son-in-law in the royal house of the king?" Saul turned to Merab, pleased he had thought of the perfect solution. "My oldest daughter. Merab shall be given in marriage to the man who slays the giant."

The whole tent gasped. Merab howled as if she had heard her death sentence. Her strength went out from her, and she collapsed. If Adriel had not been standing behind her, she would have fallen onto the tent floor. Adriel knelt with Merab in his arms as she sobbed.

Mikal dropped to her knees beside her sister and wrapped her arms around her waist. She too began to weep.

Saul was confused by this unanimous reaction to his brilliant idea. Why had no one seized this as a potential solution for getting a soldier to accept the challenge?

He looked in disbelief at his two daughters, their bodies wracked by uncontrolled grief. They were both of marrying age, and Merab was the eldest. This was the proper order for marrying. Why would either of them not want the opportunity to marry a hero of the nation? If only his wife were still alive. She would have helped them to understand.

"Abba, you must not do this." Jonathan's face betrayed a sense of panic.

"Gad, is there no precedent for this in the history of Israel?" Saul asked. "I may be the first king of our nation, but surely I am not the first ruler to make such an offer."

All attention shifted to Gad. He delayed an answer by slowly raising his hand.

"My lord, while it may appear to be unfair of the king to offer his daughter as a prize to a potential champion, my duty to you, O King, is to speak with honesty. Much is at stake in this moment. The siege needs to end for the good of all, and if the king included his eldest daughter as a part of the total reparation to entice a warrior to slay the giant, then so be it."

"This is not a test of your loyalty, Gad. I am asking for clarification. You are saying there is precedent? This has happened in the history of our people?"

"Yes, my lord, there is an instance of such a gift. When our forefathers came out of Egypt and the land was being conquered, Caleb, son of Jephunneh and a great military leader, offered his daughter, Acsah, to the man who led the attack and captured the city Kiriath Sepher."

"There. Gad has made a case for me." Saul nodded. "And what was the outcome, O prophet of Yahweh?"

Saul was enjoying this bit of useful information. Having a prophet around was not always an uncomfortable provision.

"Othniel, son of Caleb's younger brother, captured the city and took the hand of Acsah in marriage."

Saul beamed as he glanced around the tent, but none were smiling at the history lesson. He returned focus to his court prophet, in need of one more substantive tidbit to sway the royal family to his way of thinking.

"My lord, I would add that Caleb's offer included a stretch of land in the Negev Valley. Then when his daughter and son-in-law asked for the territory to include some natural water sources, Caleb gave them the upper and lower springs on either end of the property."

"I should have stopped you before that, Gad." Saul guffawed. "Why not improve the offer with some land as well. Yes, why not? Jarib, write down the new proposal and circulate it throughout the camp."

"No, Abba, you must not," Jonathan said, this time with a calmer voice. "I will fight the giant."

At Jonathan's announcement, Ishvi and Malki leapt to their feet, shouting in excitement, thrilled at the thought of their big brother vanquishing the giant, but both Abner and Saul shouted them down.

"You are my firstborn." Saul lifted a hand toward the twins, halting their mimic slaying of the giant by Jonathan. "If I cannot fight the giant, neither can you."

"You are heir to the throne, Jonathan," Abner said. "This is not wise."

"But it is not wise for this siege to continue." Jonathan did not bother to cover his look of worry. "The damage to the reputation of our country and king and to Yahweh is beyond measure. We must do something."

David believed this giant should and could be faced regardless of the odds, but he kept silent. He did not see any reason to jeopardize his newfound position inside the court. Impressive as his singing had been, it would be presumptuous to declare himself a warrior as well as a court musician. So, he had slipped into the background. He might start playing again and see if that would have the same effect as before and calm the intensity of the debate, but he caught sight of Mikal looking directly at him.

She sat on the tent floor; her arms wrapped around Merab's waist. Mikal's beautiful, moist face blazed in the torchlight. It bore a fierce and uncompromising expression as though she would battle to the death anyone who might harm her sister.

The statement blurted from his mouth as spontaneously as any lyric of praise from one of his songs. "Let no one lose heart on account of this giant." David spoke, looking right at Mikal, and the general noise level began to fall. "Let no one lose heart because of this Philistine." David repeated, this time with more vigor, inspired by Mikal's passionate and unappeasable gaze. It was as if the singer and the princess were of one mind, one heart, one goal: kill a giant and save a family, save an army, save the nation, take the risk. "Your servant will go and fight the giant."

With that declaration the tent fell completely silent. Merab sobbed twice more, and then her voice was hushed as well.

David watched the princess slowly release her clasp around the waist of her sister, her ardent features transforming into one of desire.

"What nonsense is this?" Abner's eyes narrowed on David standing to the side with his kinnor raised in the air as a show of defiance. "Are you going to kill the giant with your harp? Sing him to death?"

"You are brave, but we are soldiers trained for this job," Jonathan said.

"I have faced many dangers as a shepherd, my lord." David lowered his arm, resting the kinnor at his side. "Yahweh has been faithful to deliver me each time."

"I have just found the best musician I have ever heard." Saul nodded in gratitude to David. "I do not want to lose him now."

"Nor do I," Jonathan said. "You have brought comfort to my father, to my whole family."

"Nor do I." Mikal spoke just loud enough to catch David's ear and eye.

He glanced back at the princess. She had turned her kneeling posture away from her sister and faced David, her hands pushing gently along her thighs. If he had not quickly returned his eyes to the king and commander, he would have lost his train of thought.

"You will not lose me, my lord." David was confident, but not boastful. "The battle is Yahweh's. The Almighty will give the giant and your enemies into your hands."

"Why did I not think of that?" Saul said in an outburst of exuberance.

"And what dangers have you faced as a shepherd?" Abner gave his question a raspy chuckle of derision. "From what battles has Yahweh delivered you?"

David set his kinnor on the tent floor, removed the lion skin from off his back, and held it before his audience. He clutched the necklace of lion claws in his other hand and took it from around his head.

"Two seasons ago, I faced a bear, my lord, when it attacked my flocks, and killed it. Then not long ago, a lion attacked my sheep, and I went after it. I hit it with a rock from my sling. When the lion turned to attack me, I seized it by the hair and slit its throat. I present you with the skin and claws of the dead lion. I will present to you the head of the uncircumcised Philistine because he has defied the army of Yahweh."

"What an imagination." Abner's ridicule burst into laughter. "Gad, be sure and take note of the tales from this shepherd. It will make for good reading."

Gad nodded out of respect, but he was not laughing. No one was laughing but the commander, and even he stopped when the king placed a firm hand upon his shoulder.

"Why risk your life for sheep?" Saul's eyes narrowed their focus upon his new court musician. "They are just sheep. Why not sacrifice a few lambs to a hungry lion or bear? Is it not the cost of doing business as a shepherd?"

"They are my father's sheep, my lord. He put me in charge of their care and protection." David paused, but then thought better of continuing.

"And?" Saul asked, grinning with intrigue.

"It is nothing, my lord." David lowered his eyes. "Forgive me."

"You were going to add something? Please, what were you going to say?"

David glanced to Mikal to see if she was still paying attention.

Her gaze had not wavered. She leaned toward him on her haunches.

"It angered me, my lord." David returned his eyes to the king. "It angered me that those wild beasts should try to steal what my father had entrusted to me."

Mikal placed a hand on her neck and felt the rapid beating of her pulse. She closed her eyes and inhaled slow and deep. She would not embarrass herself by swooning. She would not humiliate herself by sobbing like her sister. But, if he, a shepherd now court musician could defeat the giant, she would give herself to him as a reward. She would offer herself to him in a burst of unimaginable pleasure, and perhaps save her sister in the bargain. She began to imagine her body cradled inside David's arms, her lips kissing his, her strength ravished by their mutual passion. A sudden movement of someone striding through the tent brought her back from this imagined reverie, and her father stopped in front of the object of her fantasy.

"It angered you and you acted." Her father scrutinized David's calm visage for any hint of deceit in character or embellishment of story. "Simple as that."

"Yes, my lord," the singer answered softly. "Simple as that."

"A wild beast is only acting on natural instincts." The king patted David's right arm, the arm that plucked the strings of his kinnor, the arm Mikal imagined pulling her into his side. Then her father clenched the curvature of the taut muscle in the singer's upper arm. She could die inside the grip of that arm, and with no regret.

"So was I, my lord," was the singer's answer.

David resisted the king's test of his strength by flexing his sculpted muscle. Mikal too would gladly test the strength of his arm.

"Well, you surprised us with your singing. You may surprise us with your bravery." Saul clapped David's shoulders with his hands. "Come to my tent. We must try on some armor."

The world went still. Even the flames of the torches were startled static, providing light but no sound or flickering shadow.

Saul made for the exit, barking the inertia from everyone's legs with a loud, "Follow me."

Bolts of energy flew through the tent and into everyone's limbs.

Mikal watched Jonathan pass in front of David and grab his arm as he went by, forcing him to follow. David barely had time enough to snatch his kinnor from the tent floor before being hustled away. He took one last glance at Mikal as he exited through the tent flaps, and she sprang to her feet as if shocked by a spark beneath her.

"This is madness!" Abner shouted.

Mikal did not share her cousin's sentiment.

Her only intent was to follow. There was more to see and hear—more to this shepherd turned court musician, this lion-killer, this potential giant-slayer—and she must bear witness to every moment of this rapid transformation. She had entered a mad dream, and she felt more alive than she ever had in her life.

Chapter 9

ABNER COULD NOT GET HIS LEGS TO MOVE. HE STOOD IN THE family tent near where the king had been standing, listening to the king's voice inside his head repeating what he thought he had heard: *Come to my tent. We must try on some armor.* Abner trusted his ears had not deceived him, but surely the king spoke in jest. Surely, he was not intending for this shepherd, this musician, this scruffy whatever-he-was that the prince dragged in, to go against the giant, and surely not wearing the king's armor.

Abner did not care that David had sung away the blackness in the king's heart. The singer had engaged the king with a different kind of madness. What had happened to the king? What had happened to his cousin?

Yahweh could have left the family in peace on their farm in Gibeah. They were happy, living quiet lives. Then Saul was plucked out of obscurity and anointed king, the family became royalty overnight, and the madness soon followed. Now, a new folly beyond a general malaise had captivated his cousin. Would he, the mad king's commander, ever be able to gain control over this recklessness?

Not until the pointed fingernails of Rizpah scraped his forearm as she passed did Abner come to his senses. Jonathan, Gad, and Jarib had all followed the king and the singer out of the tent. Then his niece, Mikal, as if shot from a bow, rushed after them, her golden hair and silken robe billowing from her haste.

Abner looked down and saw three tracks of white, upturned flesh; they had been dug deep, swift, and long, from mid-forearm to wrist. He studied the marks and saw traces of blood. Rizpah meant business.

"Abner, my father would turn me into a bribe for some brute soldier." Merab's sobs were uncontrollable. "He cannot do such a thing."

"He can and he would." Abner lifted his hand and gently stroked Merab's moist cheek. Her sorrow brought him grief, but he knew the truth, and the truth was a blunt instrument. He caught sight of Rizpah dashing out of the tent. "But you need not worry. You will not be a spoil of this fight. The giant will skewer this singer with one spear-thrust, and we will have a much larger problem. I must go."

"Commander, should I accompany you?" Adriel released his hold of Merab's shoulder, causing her to wobble as he took a rigid stance beside her.

"No, the king's tent will be crowded enough." Abner gently took Merab's elbow, stabilizing her balance. "And no one but family is allowed inside—until now."

"May we go with you?" Ishvi and Malki bounced with excitement.

"Stay with your sister, boys, and calm down." Abner made his way to the exit, rubbing his scratched forearm. "We all just need to calm down."

When Abner emerged from the entrance of the tent, the guards already stood at attention. He could only imagine what they were thinking. These elite soldiers knew to be discrete, but Abner hated that they had witnessed such a rapid exodus from the tent as if the royal family were fleeing some menacing force. Abner prided himself for having control, but he had no control, the mere appearance of control was false.

"Say nothing of this." Abner nodded toward the entrance of the family tent, his order clear.

The guards stiffen their straight backs and gave a sharp nod of their helmeted heads.

Then Abner marched swiftly over the hard ground through the dark night toward the king's tent set a good distance from the rest of the encampment and far from the battle line.

"My love."

The moment he heard the whispered voice break through the darkness, Abner stopped as if struck by a stone. An awakening of life flamed up inside of him, burning away the frustration and confusion of the last hour. He raised his hand for the voice to remain silent. Abner looked down the path toward the entrance of the king's tent.

In the torchlight glow around the entrance, the prince, Gad, and Jarib rushed inside past the sentries. The guards might wonder why he was not with the trio that hastily followed the king and the singer into the tent, and while they might strain their eyes to look for him, Abner knew they would be unable to see into the darkness beyond the shadowy perimeter of light cast by the torches. The guards could wonder a little longer. He had a brief moment, and he would take it.

Abner stared into the black, empty space between the two tents and waited for his eyes to adjust. When the ghostlike form of Rizpah came into focus, he bolted off the path.

The moment the two embraced they dug into each other: arms and cheeks and breath and lips. Abner lifted Rizpah off the ground, carrying her deeper into the shadows between the tents. Time was still their enemy, not the king or royal family or the giant or the arrival of the singer. In fact, the singer had afforded them this stolen moment. The king's spirits were lifted, creating a new turmoil, but here Abner held Rizpah in his arms and he in hers, their hands stroking the curves of their bodies, fingers clawing at their clothing, wishing their robes were not a hindrance to further pleasures, and for this time he was grateful.

"I have but a few moments." Abner spoke through his lips barely removed from Rizpah's mouth.

Their future was unimaginable to him. The present was all they had, and this flickering moment of passion hidden between the tents of two worlds, the taste of each other's lips and the warmth of their bodies was enough to ease the heaviness of their shared plight.

Rizpah pulled away first. He could tell that she must share an urgent word with him. It could not be delayed. She removed his arms from around her waist, kissed his hands and placed them on her belly.

"I am with child," she whispered. "The lump inside me is growing. Soon, the plumpness will appear beneath my robes."

"With child?" Abner gasped. He removed his hands and stepped back. "The king's child? My cousin's child?"

"Or yours, my love. It is impossible for me to know."

The ground beneath opened to swallow him. The earth began to activate its hungry pull. Abner felt in his feet and legs the earth preparing to gulp him down, and this would be desirable. What could be worse? What other shocks could he bear tonight?

"Say something?" Rizpah pleaded, retaking his limp hands into hers.

"Does he know?" Abner fixed his eyes on the open chasm beneath their feet.

"No, I wanted you to be the first."

Abner could not squeeze her hands with any life-affirming pressure. The strength was flowing out of his legs.

"What must I do?"

Her question brought him back to life. Abner felt a surge of strength and clasped Rizpah's hands, bringing them to his lips. He kissed them. It did not matter. In this illogical and unfathomable instant, it did not matter who fathered this child. The king may claim it and boast of his virility, but Abner knew that the mother of this child belonged to him, that on the long road before them, their secret love was a living truth that someday would stand before the world. No, the earth could wait, its appetite would not be satisfied tonight, and the great chasm closed its mouth.

"You will bring this child into the world." Abner enveloped her in his arms. "If he chooses to accept the child, we will celebrate with the king. Regardless, I will treat it as my own."

Rizpah nuzzled her cheek against the side of his bristly face.

In his chest, Abner could feel her heart dancing. He placed his hand on her belly and thought he felt it bounce in response.

"Once the king is asleep, I will come to your tent," Rizpah said placing her hands on top of Abner's.

"The king may never sleep tonight. Not after what the singer has done to him. In his present state of mind, he will be up all night. I should go. He will expect me."

"Should I come with you to the king's tent?" Rizpah asked.

"No. Go back to the family tent. Comfort Merab. Let him send for you."

They embraced once more, kissed as lovers in a long farewell, and felt the chill of the night on their bodies as they parted at the path, each to their separate destinations, carrying their own diminished warmth and longing.

Mikal stretched upon the ground and lifted the bottom seam of the tent, inching her body forward just enough to see inside. She had not thought of who might catch her lying on her belly with her head under the king's tent. She had only one clear thought: to see more of this singing shepherd. It never crossed her mind that she might appear foolish. When she had taken the mantle of princess, she took pride in embracing the duty with a higher standard of manners. She wanted Israel to see her as worthy of her role. All of that changed with one song.

Nothing like this had ever happened to her. She felt wobbly and ill, the pores of her body flowing with icy sweat, and her eyesight a mixture of clarity and haziness as if experiencing a vision shrouded by a mist. This vision was the singing shepherd playing only for her, singing only for her, loving only her. She watched the others whirling inside her father's tent begin to settle around the singing shepherd who stood before the wooden frame supporting the king's armor.

"More light," her father barked. "Fill this tent with light."

The servants scurried to ignite every torch, flooding it with light.

Mikal lowered the hem of the tent until she was sure no one detected her presence by the sudden illumination. When she raised it once again, all eyes were on the shepherd.

"Strip down." The king pointed to the singer's filthy clothes. "You cannot fight in those shepherd's rags."

Mikal had not expected this good fortune, to watch the singer remove his garments. David unfurled his head wrap. Mikal could see the others self-consciously trying not to watch this stranger disrobe, but she sensed from this young man that he did not mind everyone looking. In fact, he appeared to enjoy it. He did not seem uncomfortable from the king's command or reluctant to obey, instead looked at ease and proud of what he was about to reveal of his appearance. The singer dropped the head wrap onto the tent floor, and then untied the leather shoulder strap, loosening the upper garment. He yanked it over his head.

Had she not already been lying prone on the ground, she might have swooned. His muscular physique revealed well-earned scars of his encounters with the fierce beasts. These were not just fanciful stories to win the hearts of his listeners, to win her heart. If the singer only knew the simple victory he had achieved over the heart of the princess. He wadded up the woolly shirt and dropped it at his feet, and then ran his hand over the claw scarring across the left side of his abdomen as though pointing out the example of his bravery in case a viewer might have missed seeing it.

The others in the tent might be looking away and not notice the singer highlighting his earned scars. Not the princess. Mikal's fingers clenched the furry edges of the tent when she sensed David was looking for her, that somehow he had expected her to follow. She wished to make some motion to let him know she was watching, even more she longed to rush into his arms. It was all she could do to restrain herself.

When an unexpected strike of a firm hand struck her backside, it startled her out of her reverie. Mikal bit down on her lower lip to keep from squealing. Two hands gripped her by the ankles and pulled her from beneath the tent. She whirled around.

Abner stood above her holding her twisted legs in the air.

Mikal wriggled free of her cousin's grip and bounced to her feet. She did not bother to brush the dirt from her gown but raised an arm ready to strike.

"You are a wildcat," Abner whispered and put a finger to his smiling lips, cautioning her to remain quiet. "I saw you watching him while he played for us tonight."

"Was I that obvious?" Mikal began to lower her fist.

"Everyone was too entranced by this singer to notice you drooling," Abner snickered. "I should let you indulge your daydream of this boy, because if your father goes through with his harebrained plan, the giant will make a splash of piddle and blood out of him tomorrow."

"I do not think so. I believe David—this singer-shepherd—may just defeat the giant." Mikal straightened into her full princess posture. "Yahweh is with him."

"May your confidence in Yahweh and this singer prove true." Abner turned to make his way to the front of the tent. "But I am not so sure."

"Cousin." Mikal forced Abner to stop, but he did not turn to face her. She was grateful. Even in the darkness she could make out his strong features. It was easier to make the request to his back and not his face. "You will not mention any of this."

"Your secret is safe, my dear," Abner said. "We all have secrets that need protecting. Just be kind to me. Your momentary lapse of propriety might play to my advantage."

"Ah, the commander's sword is now poised above my head."

"Not my sword, the giant's sword that is poised above all our heads. But if your shepherd defeats the giant tomorrow, try not to embarrass the family by throwing yourself upon him."

"I would never." Mikal's tone was one of mock protest. "A princess would never give over to such unruly behavior. And yet…"

"And yet, should the shepherd be the victor, the princess may not be able to control her impulses and just might throw herself upon him," Abner said with a chuckle.

"What a spectacle that would be, and yet, perhaps, worth whatever shame may follow."

"Of course, Princess, I would never judge you. Just beware of your impulsiveness. Lustful heat can distort one's mind. Passion is difficult to control and can cause harm."

"You speak as though you have experience with such matters."

Mikal heard her cousin's swift intake of air, and she waited for him to respond, to deny or play ignorant.

"Just be sure to brush the dirt off your gown before you return to the family tent."

"Yes, Commander." Mikal watched Abner disappear around to the front entrance. He was hiding something. She was sure of it but was not about to concern herself with what secrets her cousin might be harboring. There were more important visions to behold and ponder. Mikal threw herself to the ground and thrust her face back under the tent.

Chapter 10

WHEN ABNER BROKE THROUGH THE ENTRANCE INTO THE king's tent, he squinted at the brightness of the light. He had not been inside the tent since early morning when he came upon the king and his concubine in mid-intimacy. The mental picture came crashing back, more poignant now after his encounter with Rizpah. He hissed in disgust at the reminder and hissed again in an effort to dispel the vision.

"Why are you hissing, Commander?" Saul said. "Come, look at our champion."

Abner wiped the moisture from his burning eyes and stepped closer. His jaw dropped at the freakish shape lumbering around the tent.

David, swallowed up in the king's protective clothing, walked in a stiff-legged circle. He wore a full-length coat of scaled bronze and leather armor that should have buckled securely beneath his chin, but instead fell off his shoulders, exposing the top of his chest and neck. The hem of the coat dropped to mid-calf while the shin guards rode above his knees. The king's gold wrist guards came to David's elbows, and Abner could see how they were chafing the skin. The bronze helmet enveloped David's head like a dome. He had to keep lifting it and raising his chin just to be able to see where he was going.

Saul looked proudly upon his creation, but then moved to tie a loose knot in the tunic around David's waist.

"You must keep this wrapped securely around your middle at all times.

It must support the sheath." Saul pulled on the knot until satisfied with its tautness. Then he grabbed his sword and sheath lying at the base of the armor stand.

"This sword has drawn buckets of Philistine blood," he boasted as he unsheathed the sword and let the torchlight glisten off the polished iron. "Now, soak it with the giant's blood." He slammed the sword back into its sheath.

Saul motioned for David to continue his fashion walk, so David obediently made his way around the bare armor stand. The tip of the sheath dragged over the animal skins spread along the tent floor and kept snagging in the bunched clumps of hair. Saul waited for Jarib and Gad and Jonathan to give their approval, but their stone faces were undecipherable.

Saul nodded to the commander. Abner was expected to support this decision. After all, it was Abner who had designed the king's armor.

"Well, Abner? What do you think?"

How could Saul think this was the answer for the giant unless he expected Goliath to laugh himself to death?

"He waddles like an armored duck." Abner blurted what he believed everyone was thinking, and then he laughed to keep from more critical comments. He thought it better judgment to just laugh. That was enough of an insult. No need to add words.

Jonathan seized the moment to offer a less blunt observation.

"Abba, you see how he has trouble walking. How might he maneuver the field?"

"Well, of course. He's a shepherd. He chases sheep all day in those rags," Saul pointed to the pile of garments lying to the side of the armor stand along with David's kinnor and lion-skin bag. "Take him through some training exercises tonight. By dawn, the lad should know how to defend himself and slay the giant."

"Training in one night to kill a giant. The word 'impossible' comes to my mind," Abner exclaimed, his laughter turning into thinly veiled scorn.

"I will fight Goliath," Jonathan interjected.

Abner knew Jonathan was trying to distract Saul from his sarcasm.

"And who shall wear the crown of Israel when I die if this Philistine cuts off your head? No, my brave son. Your fighting days are numbered. We need to get you a wife, and then a grandson and an heir to the throne."

"But Abba…"

Saul stepped up to his son, cupped his face between his powerful hands, and stopped the protest of the prince.

"My son. My firstborn. Your place in the hall of Israel's heroes is secure for all time." Saul's smiling face was full of pride. Then the king looked at David. "Shepherd, do you know how many Philistines my son killed at the military garrison at the 'Tooth of the Rock?'" Saul did not wait for David to answer but returned his gaze to his son and stiffened his hold on Jonathan's downcast face. "How many was it, Son? Fifteen, twenty?"

"I do not keep count of the foreskins of our dead enemies, Abba."

"Did you hear that?" Saul shouted to the whole room. "What modesty. Another mark of a true hero."

"My lord, the stories we tell in Bethlehem is that the prince slaughtered twenty Philistines that day," David exclaimed.

Abner could tell the shepherd knew the stories of the prince and was proud to be standing in the very presence of the idol of those stories.

"That the Philistine army fled in panic when they saw the prince."

"That is correct. You see?" Saul sharpened his focus on Jonathan. "Even a shepherd from a backwater village knows of the heroic deeds of my dear son."

"I just waved my sword a little," Jonathan said almost dismissively. "It was Yahweh that caused the panic."

"Hush, now." Saul placed his forefinger on top of Jonathan's lips. "This shepherd boy here needs material to compose new songs of the legends you have inspired among the people. You will do that, will you not?"

"It would be an honor, my lord." David straightened his back in acknowledgment of the king's request. "Just as soon as I slay your giant."

"And how would you slay this giant if not in the king's armor?" Saul asked, releasing Jonathan's face and turning to David who panted and sweat from the enclosed heat of the weight of the king's armor.

"My lord, you cannot be serious," Abner insisted, attempting to stop the growing momentum of this scheme.

Saul raised his hand and silenced him.

"If I may, my lord," David said, signaling permission to remove the helmet, which the king granted. David removed it, carefully placing it atop of the armor stand. Then he pulled his right hand inside the loose-fitting leather coat, searched inside the folds of his undergarment, and pulled out a sling and held it up for everyone to see. "With this, my lord."

Everyone looked in amazement at the leather sling dangling from David's upraised hand. Abner had to strike the axe to the root of this folly before he lost all control.

"My lord, it is utter foolishness to send this boy—"

"I agree, Commander, and why have you not faced the giant in these last forty days?" Saul asked, a question which brought Abner up short with its blunt force.

"If the king commands," Abner replied, the air in his voice beginning to deflate.

"If the king commands," Saul repeated quietly, glancing at his cousin with a smile.

"My lord, this is just madness," Abner said in a humiliated murmur.

"Madness?" Saul asked, a cool brusqueness in his voice.

"It is a mockery to the army of Israel and her tribal chieftains." Abner instantly regretted his description of the king's brainstorm yet chose to speak the truth with the hope of not causing more damage to the king's heart and mind. "These men are trained and seasoned veterans, and now you slap them in the face by sending a musical shepherd with a sling to fight the champion of our enemies."

"Mockery and madness; concise descriptions of our current state," Saul said.

Abner was about to defend himself, but Saul raised his hand.

"Commander. Abner. Cousin." Saul uttered each word as a term of endearment not chastisement. "Our seasoned veterans, our tribal chieftains, have all spent these last forty days quaking in their tents."

Saul laid his hands upon Abner's shoulders, then lifted Abner's chin.

"I do not blame them, Cousin. How can I blame them? They were only following the example of the king. I have been terrified these many days until tonight. When this shepherd played and sang, Yahweh lifted my heart. I am back. I am of sound mind. I believe this young man will do as he says."

Saul gently patted Abner on the cheek and then kissed his forehead. "I know your heart, Commander. I know you love me, but we shall let this singer lead us to victory over our enemies."

"Yes, my lord," Abner replied, all the fight taken out of him.

"Take off the armor," Saul said, turning to face David.

Jonathan and Jarib immediately went to work unfastening the straps, untying the tunic, and stripping David to his undergarments.

Once all the king's armor had been removed, David put on the leather girdle over his loincloth and secured the strap over his left shoulder. The head wrap, the cotton tunic, the leggings, and the camel hair outer garment remained in a heap on the tent floor.

"My lord, it is an honor for the king to offer me his armor, but I will wear only this leather girdle."

David poised before the group, his strapping, perspiring body glowing in the torchlight.

"You play your harp and sling your stones with your right hand." Saul pointed to the sling David held.

"Yes, my lord."

"We Benjamites are famous for our left-handed prowess." Saul glanced at Jonathan. "I am sure my son could teach you."

"I would benefit from anything the prince could teach me," David said.

"Just carry enough stones in case you miss," Jonathan said.

"I will not miss, my lord," David said.

Abner heard no boasting in this statement, no cockiness in the shepherd's voice. He did not stand with the posture of a braggart. There was no attempt to shame the king or the prince or him as the commander. This young lad spoke with quiet assurance as if he could not conceive of any other outcome.

Abner did not take offense. No one in the tent took offense. No one reprimanded him for impertinence. They all looked at him in wonder—the near-nakedness of his strapping physique, the torchlight providing a shimmering glow to his tanned, moist skin. Abner accepted the flow of peace through his heart. He accepted the dissolving of all fear and disquiet and self-reproach for the unified inaction of the king and his army to stand against the enemy of Israel.

Saul stepped in front of David, dropping his hands upon David's bare shoulders.

"My son, you have slain a lion and a bear; impressive, to be sure, but it is nothing like that of taking the life of another human being, especially when he is your enemy with the same objective as your own. There are thousands of men in this valley, two armies poised to kill each other. Do not be deceived.

"When the order is given and the trumpets are blown, we will kill or be killed. There are no laws or morality on the field of blood, and with each murder, each soldier, each man, must appease his conscience with any justification he may muster. But know this also, when you have slain your enemy, an ecstasy will follow. A transcendence that captures your soul. It is your death or the death of your foe, but death is the victor, and you will never experience anything like it in this world."

"My lord, I can only imagine what the king has spoken. Should I die, I must consider my vanity motivated me to accept the challenge. If I am the victor as I believe I am to be, then Yahweh will have played a role, and the king's words will become a fast truth burnished into my heart forever."

Saul kissed David on each cheek, then turned to speak to the others.

"This day shall be remembered for as long as Israel remains a nation. At first light, this singer-shepherd shall walk into the valley—alone, armed only with his sling—and stand before the giant. If Yahweh rules the day, David shall bring me the head of our enemy, silencing his mocking voice forever."

Chapter 11

SABA AWOKE AT THE SOUND OF HEAVY BREATHING OUTSIDE his tent. He opened his eyes in the darkness. He listened for what he first thought might be the commotion of soldiers rising in the camp, but no one was stirring. He rolled over on his cot. The torchlight outside his tent cast the undulating shadow of an oversized head of a man in profile. He reached his bare arm from beneath the fur coverlet and felt along the ground for the mallet he kept by his cot. Once he gripped the mallet, he slipped from under the coverlet. Saba carefully pulled back the woolly entrance flap and stretched his head above the top of the tent.

Goliath, holding a torch in each hand and sitting cross-legged on the ground, stared at the great stone the artist had carved. Saba was puzzled by several burnt-out torches lying on the ground around Goliath.

The morning light peeked out of the eastern horizon. The camp would be rising soon, so Saba tossed the mallet back inside the tent and made his way toward the stone. He had not expected this commission and was thankful for something to do during the interminable nature of this campaign, but he had grown attached to the mythology of the piece and was taking more than the usual pride in what had been created. Each day Saba would stand before the massive stone and contemplate. If he found a flaw he would take his chisel and smooth it out. If he envisioned a new image, he would carve it into the whole. He had never worked on such a large piece, nor had the time to devote to one creation. He was always discovering something new with each viewing. Saba could not start on another project until he returned to his shop in Aphek, so why not perfect this commission?

He hoped the opposing armies would tire of the monotony and depart without incident, but if not, he hoped Lord Namal would just send him home. Saba would be on the road before the sun grew hot were that to happen.

Saba found that during the time it took to create Goliath's commission, his respect of the giant had grown into a fondness. When Goliath was not insulting the enemy, he was exercising or training. His diet was strict though ample: dried fruit, nuts, vegetables, no beef, only lamb or goat meat, and no wine or beer. He refrained from the solicitations of the camp prostitutes while most of the soldiers were not so disciplined. Even the Five Lords had their own traveling harems to keep them occupied.

Some days, after hurling his morning insults at the enemy, Goliath would come by Saba's tent and work area to see the artist's progress. He was not a brute mercenary looking only for glory and to enrich his purse. He was a warrior, one of renown, known for his ruthlessness, boastful, even, of his prowess, but he also displayed an innocent admiration when presented with the mystical wonders of creativity.

Saba was happy his work was so appreciated by someone he had not thought capable of such respect. He had never had a patron sit for any length of time in front of his work just to admire it. In one way, Saba would be sorry for the siege to end and for Goliath to depart with his creation. When that time came, Saba would be sure the stone slab was properly crated for transport to withstand the rough roads.

"The images on the stone come to life in the torchlight," Goliath said, as Saba approached. "I enjoy watching their movement."

"So, they move?" Saba slipped beside Goliath. He now understood the reason for the burnt-out torches on the ground.

"With enough torchlight, yes," Goliath said.

"I had not noticed." Saba leaned forward, focusing his eyes on the winged angels gathering the souls of the dead.

"Observe." Goliath wave the torches in the air in a slow circular motion. "Do not the angels look as though they are flying?"

"Yes, my lord," Saba replied, moved by the stunning sight. "They do."

"Take note of my spear," Goliath continued. He waved the torch in his right hand toward the center of the stone. "In the light it appears as if I am throwing my spear."

This amused Goliath, and his childlike reaction to the artifice of imagination pleased Saba. He had never considered any of his works as having an intrinsic life of its own and how that might deepen the experience of a careful observer.

"I still should not touch it," the giant said as if needing to remind himself to obey the instructions of the artist. He returned the torch to his side and drove the end into the ground.

"I would suggest not," Saba said. "It is best not to rub the relief images. The granules will wear away in time, but it will last longer if you refrain from…"

"I know where I will place this work," Goliath interrupted as he thrust the other torch pole into the ground. "Inside my dwelling where I sleep, near my head so it may inspire dreams."

Goliath uncrossed his legs and massaged his thigh and calf muscles to restore the circulation.

When Saba stepped away to give the giant room to stretch, he lifted his eyes to the enemy encampment on the opposite side of the Valley of Elah. He was normally not awake at this early hour, but it seemed unusual even to him for so much activity at the break of sunrise.

"My lord, you must look across the valley," Saba said.

Goliath was bent over with his massive hands curled over his sandaled feet. He exhaled a blast of air and turned his head toward the opposite side of the valley. In the early morning light, the distinguishable forms of the enemy were arrayed for battle and taking their positions. He tucked one leg under the other, twisted his body, and thrust himself forward, got to one knee, and let the momentum and the strength of his legs bring him to his feet.

Saba was amazed that the giant's hands never touched the ground to aide his ascent.

Goliath turned toward the tent he shared with his son and cupped his hands around his mouth. "Lahmi," he bellowed with one huge breath. "My armor."

Chapter 12

SAUL EMERGED FROM HIS TENT DRESSED FOR BATTLE. ABNER pointed for Jeush, the chieftain of the tribe of Benjamin, to step forward and hand Saul a tribal banner with its wolf-head emblem. Saul smiled as he accepted the banner, and then tucked the banner into his left wrist guard. Jeush bowed to the king and took his place with the chieftains from the other tribes standing in formation at the entrance of the tent holding poles bearing the banners of their tribal insignia.

Abner had ordered that everyone be assembled before the king's tent when he appeared. Gad, Jarib, and Ahimelech, the High Priest, stood before the chieftains. In front of them were Abner and Jonathan with Malki and Ishvi on either side of their older brother. Behind the king's tribal leadership stood members of Saul's elite honor guard, soldiers selected from each tribe, holding torches above their heads to illuminate the grounds in front of the royal tent. All bent the knee before the king.

Abner was the first to rise. He drew near to the king and, in the bright torchlight, gave Saul a hard, judicious look.

"You will see no sign of madness in my eyes, Commander," Saul said, his face composed with self-assurance. Saul gripped the neck of his coat of armor, raising it from his chest enough to tuck his nose inside it. He inhaled deeply, closing his eyes.

"My armor smells of the shepherd. It smells of victory."

"My lord, if this goes badly—"

Saul raised his hand to Abner, cutting him off before he could finish his statement.

"Is everyone assembled, Commander?"

"Yes, my lord." Abner's back stiffened from the king's gesture of rebuke, but it did not deter him from one last attempt to urge the king to reconsider his decision. He stepped closer, dropping his voice. "My lord, I fear the king risks humiliation."

"I have been humiliated long enough by my dread and idleness." Saul placed his left hand upon his cousin's shoulder. "What could be more humiliating than hiding in my tent these last forty days?"

Abner gave no answer. He too had endured the humiliation since the army had arrived in the Valley of Elah. He had done all he could to keep the morale of his army from deteriorating along with the spirits of the king. He was exhausted from shouldering such a responsibility. It would be a relief for this burden to be lifted. He hated the debilitation that came with inaction, and now it was about to end.

No matter the outcome between David and the giant, he would lead the army of Israel into battle. They would never submit to the giant's bargain that the victor of a single combat would determine what nation would be subservient to the other. Today, he would kill or be killed defending the honor of his king and his nation.

"Where is my singing shepherd?" Saul scanned the crowd for the hoped-for hero.

"Jonathan had Adriel escort him to the battle line," Abner replied. "He stands with his brothers and the tribe of Judah where he awaits you."

"This is good. This shows tribal unity. Commander, have you told the chieftains someone will face the giant?"

"No, my lord." Abner lowered his eyes. "That duty belongs to the king."

"Duty and responsibility, should it turn out to go against us this day," Saul said with a chuckle. "Do not fear, Commander. Do not fear."

Saul patted Abner's shoulder before moving toward his sons who ran into his arms. Saul embraced Malki and Ishvi with his warm strength. He had seen that the twins were given a level of military training appropriate to their young age, even fitting them with armor, but they were still too young to step onto a battlefield. If Saul had his way, his sons would never see battle, yet he knew he could not keep them off the field forever.

"You will see something great today." Saul patted the twins' helmeted heads. "A wondrous event that will remain in your memories forever."

"Abba, let us fight," implored Malki, his hand tightening the grip of his sword.

"I know the shepherd will kill the giant, and we will be victorious," Ishvi added.

"Maybe it is time you shed a little Philistine blood," Saul said, his face somber and thoughtful. "Let us see if Yahweh favors us today with our shepherd."

"Abba, I am not sure." Jonathan motioned for his brothers to return to him.

Saul noticed the apprehension across the faces of his young sons before raising his eyes to Jonathan. "If I remember, you were not much older than your brothers when you decided it was time to slay a few Philistines."

Jonathan nodded.

"Your brothers cannot always be kept within the relative safety of the camp. They will have to face the enemies of Israel someday, or they would grow resentful."

"Yes, but not today." Jonathan clinched the twins to his side, erasing any hint of misgiving in their hearts that their father just might grant their wish to fight.

Saul moved to Carmi, chieftain of Judah, and gripped the long pole he held with its banner of a roaring lion. Carmi bowed to his king and allowed him to take the pole from his hand. Saul then paced in front of the chieftains, holding the banner high as the early morning light began to fill in the cloudless sky.

"Brave and noble chieftains, my brothers, I have brought shame upon us," Saul began, his voice a woven strand of authority and conviction, his eyes clear as he passed before the grave faces of each chieftain. "For the last forty days, I have been a man standing in darkness, one leg drifting toward the light, but unable to find solid ground. I have neglected my responsibilities. I have hidden from you. I have not faced you as I should, but remained in my tent, fearful and drained of any courage expected of a king.

"As leaders of our twelve tribes, you could have revolted and taken matters into your own hands, but you did not. You remained faithful. You may have grumbled against your king and wondered about his sanity, but you remained loyal, and I am grateful to you and to my family and, most important, to Abner the commander of the army of Yahweh."

At Saul's confession and expression of gratitude, the chieftains pounded the blunt ends of their banner poles into the hard ground and stomped their feet in respect for Saul's honesty. The honor guard waved their torches above their heads.

Saul felt a flame of encouragement rise in his chest at this reception. "For forty days, the army of Yahweh has been insulted by the uncircumcised," Saul continued. "I have cowered in my tent. Not you, noble chieftains, but I, your king. But out of this dark time of waiting has come a champion. Last night, a brave young man from the tribe of Judah came forward. He will fight this giant. He will defeat him and remove the shame of cowardice and bring honor to our nation and to Yahweh."

Ahimelech stepped forward, unprompted by human command, opened his mouth, looked to the heavens, and cried. "Hear O Israel: The Lord our God, the Lord is one."

The tribal leaders, the soldiers, the commander, the prophet and priest, the royal family repeated the phrase again and again in a spontaneous eruption of praise: praise to dispel the collective fear; praise to dispel the shame and guilt; praise to thaw the blood; praise to strengthen the body and bones; praise to implore the one true God to favor them this day. A mystic trance descended upon the men as individual voices fell into the unison of a chanted rhythm of this central prayer of Israel.

Saul looked to the sky as it brightened with the rising sun. It began to fill with flocks of clamorous birds sensing the pure smell of blood and flesh and death they would feast upon that day.

"My brothers, the sun is bright!" Saul shouted above the chorus of manly voices. "The sky is clear. The vultures are gathering in anticipation of battle. May Yahweh give us victory today over our enemies."

"For the love of Israel!" Jonathan shouted.

Every man fashioned his voice around the words of the prince. "For the love of Israel," came the chorus with one voice. "For the glory of Yahweh. For the honor of the king."

The echoes of their chant flew into the air, elevating the flight of the carrion birds circling above. Then the group became silent, allowing the words just spoken to be absorbed into their souls to strengthen their limbs and calm their hearts in the face of death, for surely today death was the true victor.

Saul gripped the banner pole of the lion of Judah and approached Carmi.

"Today the lion of Judah will roar, and Yahweh will scatter our enemies." Saul handed the banner pole back to Carmi who accepted it with bowed head. "Carmi, bring your soldiers to the center of the camp alongside the tribe of Benjamin. When the giant is slain, the tribe of Judah will lead the charge against the Philistines."

"It will be our privilege, my sovereign," Carmi said. "For the glory of Yahweh."

"To the front," Abner barked. "Disperse to your tribe and be prepared to advance at my command."

At Abner's order, the chieftains disbanded and hastily proceeded to their respective tribal positions stationed across the battlefront.

Jeush went before Abner and Saul, escorting them through the middle of the encampment toward the front, proudly hoisting the banner of the wolf. Jonathan held each twin by the neck to keep them from running ahead. Gad and Ahimelech fell in with the king. The tribe of Benjamin was stationed in the center of the army stretched along the perimeter of the landscape before it descended into the valley.

As Saul passed the family tent, he noticed Mikal squeezing moisture from clothes draped over a makeshift drying rack. A pot of steaming water was placed beside the rack. Saul broke stride, leaving the others to wait as he approached his daughter.

"When did the princess start washing clothes?" Saul asked with a curious smile. "I thought such domestic duties were beneath you."

"Not just any clothes, Abba." Mikal stretched out the tunic. "They are the shepherd's clothes."

"Ah." Saul shook his head with amusement. He was not sure if the redness in his daughter's face was caused by her labor or by the blush of admitting for whom she labored. He wondered how she might have obtained the shepherd's garments but chose to allow that fact to remain a mystery. "You are smitten, my child."

"As are you, Abba," Mikal replied, and then added hastily. "As are we all."

"Indeed," Saul responded. "As are we all. Except for Abner. He remains skeptical and uncommitted."

"Abner is always skeptical and the last to commit, but even he will come around after the shepherd slays the giant." Mikal held up a damp leg of David's leggings. "And the shepherd will need clean clothes to wear."

"My dear, once David kills the giant, he will never wear shepherd's rags again."

"My lord, we must move to the front." Abner drew Saul's attention back to the task at hand.

"Yes, Commander," Saul said, but looked at Mikal. "Where is your sister?"

"In the tent with Ish-bosheth. She does not wish to see her fate unfold before her eyes on a battlefield."

"She is my firstborn daughter. She is a princess. Her fate was determined the moment the prophet Samuel placed the crown upon my head as was mine, like it or not."

Saul lowered his head, an overcast of memories rising behind his eyes: he and Ahinoam lying on the blanket inside Rainbow Cave; his wife beckoning him out of the baggage to accept the crown; his wife shrouded in clothes of the dead, cold on a slab of stone inside the family burial cave; her untimely departure caused by the birth of their last child he could not bear to see or stomach the mention of his name. He began to tremble and fought to hold on to the exuberance he had enjoyed since hearing the shepherd sing.

"Leave the wash, get your sister, and bring her to the battle lines." Saul restrained his voice to keep from sounding cross. He must not allow his tongue to be bitter. He must not allow his dispiriting thoughts to send their tendrils into his heart and mind. He must not return to the inexplicable sickness.

When Saul bolted toward the battle lines, his mind chastened by the near miss of being drawn into the darkness, Abner and the others had to jog to catch up with the king.

Chapter 13

DAVID TROTTED ALONGSIDE HIS BROTHERS AND THE REST OF the soldiers of Judah as they hastened to the center of the camp to join the Benjamites. Carmi, the tribal chieftain of Judah, had rushed to inform the Judah company that their tribe would now be stationed next to the king. Three other tribes shifted their positions to make room for the Judah contingent as advanced up the hill to join the king and the company of Benjamin.

Once the company of Judah moved into position, David did not try to maneuver closer to the king. Instead, he remained in the middle of his bustling tribe. He knelt on one knee. The Philistines across the valley were assembling before their camp. David held his breath as two giants rose above the gray sea of countless soldiers like two mythical monsters.

He was amazed how laborious it was for one giant to dress the other with armaments that must weigh more than three times his own weight. He was underdressed by comparison, but to be agile was to his advantage. He needed to be swift and daring, fast on his feet, accurate with his aim, and dependent on Yahweh.

David scratched his fingers over the hard earth, collecting stones and discarding all of them. He needed stones to be smooth and round; stones designed for kill shots, not for wounding.

An announcement had circulated throughout the army of Israel that someone had consented to face the giant in single combat. No one in the army knew the name of this potential champion. David's brothers and their fellow soldiers in their company were shocked when Carmi had announced that a champion had come forth from their tribe. Men speculated and interrogated each other as to who might be the secret volunteer.

David ignored the comments from his tribesmen boasting that the lion of Judah would devour the uncircumcised giant of the Philistines. David quit searching for the stones and rose. He spotted a small stream running through the heart of the valley and determined the stones he needed would be along the banks of the flowing water.

When Jonathan and Adriel approached, Carmi called out the advancing prince and his armor-bearer, and all knelt.

Jonathan stopped in front of David. "Have a change of heart?"

David raised his head and smiled at the prince, and then turned his head and looked at his three brothers kneeling behind him. He enjoyed watching the shocked expressions on his brothers' face as it dawned on them that the prince was summoning their little brother to join him.

"Make our parents proud today," David said to his brothers before he rose and followed Jonathan and Adriel into the valley.

A tremble of uncertainty poured through the camp like a flood as the three men walked into the valley. They recognized the prince and his armor-bearer, but who was this ruddy, half-naked shepherd boy walking behind them?

David paused to look back to the king standing in the center of his tribe, the banner of the wolf raised high above him. The royal audience he entertained the night before flanked the king. Abner stood at the king's right hand while the twins peered from either side of Abner's armored body. Merab at her father's left, her face red and beleaguered. Mikal stood beside her, one arm secured over her sister's shoulder, while in her other hand she held David's clothes.

He had forgotten his outer clothing when he left the king's tent last night. He wore only the leather and goat-hair garments for freedom of movement. David spent a sleepless night wandering the camp, praying to Yahweh, singing his songs, practicing with his sling, and imagining the giant's tactics. The giant would be surprised once he saw a shepherd had come to face him.

David knelt in honor of the king and rose to his feet once the king nodded to him. When David continued into the valley with Jonathan and Adriel, the uproar began. The choral sounds of shocked and angered male voices rippled along the battle line as the twelve tribes began to realize that their hope of victory lay upon the shoulders of an unarmed, unarmored, and unidentifiable newcomer.

Saba had the advantage of being the first to see Goliath spring into action in response to the army of Israel assembling along the eastern rim of the valley. He placed his ladder upon the scaffolding next to the great stone and climbed to the top to watch as Lahmi helped his father into his cumbersome armor.

The camp had quickly come to life the moment the trumpeters awakened the soldiers. Saba assumed the opposing army had become complacent during the interminable standoff between the two nations, each side suffering from indifference to discipline. Saba watched the Five Lords rush from their individual tents, a couple of them still being dressed in armor before being lifted into their chariots. The Philistine army, half-dressed and half-awake, scrambled into a hasty and haphazard formation.

Lahmi finished fastening the straps around his father's waist and chest, securing the sword on his side and a javelin on his back. When Goliath finished adjusting the armor to ensure a snug fit over his great bulk, Lahmi grabbed the massive shield, and the two of them marched toward Saba. Father and son appeared like a pair of metal monsters thawed from an ancient ice mountain.

Goliath paused before Saba and raised his spear into the air, holding it just like the bas-relief image the artist had carved. "My stone. My story."

Goliath released a final roar before marching to the valley.

With Goliath's departing footsteps, the added weight of his armor made the ground tremble so that the vibrations ran up the wooden ladder, into Saba's spine, forcing him to tighten his grip on the top rung. The tremors continued long after Goliath had entered the valley with Lahmi marching beside his father. Saba realized the tremors he continued to feel were originating within his body.

Three men approached from the other side of the valley, pausing before the shallow stream that ran through the heart of the landscape. He recognized the prince and his armor-bearer: the pair who toppled his monument at the military outpost at Geba; the duo who slaughtered twenty Philistine soldiers before his eyes; the one who had wounded him, the other who had healed him. Saba flexed the fingers of his left hand. The prince had broken his wrist that day with a well-aimed stone hurled from his sling. His armor-bearer had reset the break and wrapped a splint around the wound. The break had healed after a few months, and other than the occasional numbness caused by hours of work or cold weather, he was able to sculpt.

Saba did not recognize the third man kneeling at the stream and collecting rocks, but a premonition of dread rose from his belly and ascended into his head. Saba dropped from the ladder and raced into his tent. He had firsthand experience of the combat skills between the approaching warriors. While the Philistines had the imposing Goliath, the nation of Israel had the prince and his armor-bearer. If this third, unknown warrior was anything like his two companions, Saba could not be sure of the outcome.

He was not taking any chances. He threw open his trunk and pulled the contents out until he found the leather-bound parchments. He loosened the strap, opened the volume, and filed through the parchments: contracts for commissions, rough drawings, unpaid bills, lists of art supplies he would need once he returned to Aphek. He searched until he found what he desperately sought.

He carefully unfolded and reread the Canaanite translation he had paid a Philistine temple scribe to write beside the Hebrew script: "This man shall have safe passage. He is an artist." Beneath the script was the mark of Jonathan, Prince of Israel.

Saba had never destroyed the letter of safe passage Jonathan had written for him after Geba. Now, his heart was telling him he might have need of this very document once again.*

Chapter 14

DAVID GRABBED A ROCK BENEATH THE CLEAR, ANKLE-DEEP stream and bounced it in his hand. He wiped the moisture from the stone on his soft leather girdle and then rubbed his thumb over its round smoothness before dropping it into his pouch with the others.

"How many stones is that now?" Jonathan asked as he knelt beside David.

"Four." David cupped his hand and brought some water from the stream to his mouth.

Jonathan picked through the stones at their feet until he found one.

"Here." Jonathan smiled as he handed David a fifth stone. "This should work even for a right-handed slinger."

"If I miss, I know who to blame." David took the stone from the prince.

David was happy to hear Jonathan chuckle at his good-natured gibe. This exchange of humor proved there was a growing camaraderie of equals that defied the bounds of rank and station. A shepherd and a prince could be friends. This type of bond was not something David had with his older brothers. He had never experienced such good will and harmony with another man. This was new and unique for him, a stirring of kinship, a recognition in the heart and soul of each man that a respect, a trust, an admiration had begun to take shape. David did not want to disappoint the prince. He did not want to compete with either. His regard for him was too high.

David would always appreciate that Jonathan had led the way in this friendship by risking his introduction of David to the royal family and encouraging him to play for the troubled king. The joyful impetus brought on by the king's bright response to the concert, had inspired David to accept the challenge of meeting the giant in mortal combat. The rapid succession of events was overwhelming. David knew he had the impulse for action, something he shared with the prince who had led an attack against a military outpost when the odds of victory were against him. Now he would face a giant in single combat, again with unfavorable odds for victory.

This boldness for action was not a whim or caprice, but a righteous compulsion for honor and to share this honor with others. In the Valley of Elah, the two spirits of David and Jonathan were becoming one spirit in the quest for honor, an honor that would rise all the way to heaven. It was the power of a warrior's bond, and its power could not be explained, for its source was Yahweh.

"The giant approaches, my lord," Adriel said, his hand on the stock of his bow.

David and Jonathan rose to their feet.

The ground trembled as the giant and his shield bearer moved toward them.

David stretched his body to full elevation, but the effort to compensate was futile.

From shod feet to the tip of their bronze helmets, the two giants were almost three times his height.

"Do not miss," Jonathan said as he faced David. "We are close behind you."

"My lord." David bowed his head in thanks. He bounced the stone Jonathan had given him with one hand while he removed his sling from its pouch with the other.

"Should the giant kill you, I will attempt to slay him myself," Jonathan said, and he bent to the ground to retie a leather sandal that had come loose.

"I do not believe that will be necessary, my lord," David said keeping his eyes on the giant.

"Adriel, do you see a spot on the giant you can hit with your bow from this distance?" Jonathan asked as he stood back on both feet.

Adriel scrutinized the giant's potential vulnerable body parts. "Between the forearm and shoulder, my lord. An ankle. Perhaps the slot in his helmet between the eyes."

"Just be prepared to unloose your whole quiver of arrows," Jonathan said, and then he patted David on his shoulder before he and Adriel took positions far enough up the valley for the giant to know he was not fighting all three, but close enough for Jonathan and Adriel to be in range should it come to that.

Goliath paused to study the boy standing across the stream bouncing a rock in his hand. Had he just wandered into the valley unaware of the danger? He certainly could not have been sent down to fight him, yet he had come with an official escort from the army of Israel.

Goliath was confused, so he shouted his usual invective. "I defy the ranks of Israel!" he roared. "Send me a man and let us fight."

"I am here to fight you." The boy stopped bouncing the stone in his hand and swiped his forefinger around the base of the cup of his sling, cleaning out particles of dirt.

Goliath heard Lahmi's translation and could not help himself. He pounded the shaft of his spear into the ground and burst out laughing. After forty days of berating his enemies—twice a day—had it come to this? A ruddy shepherd boy with a toy sling had come to face him?

"Go back to your mother's breasts," Goliath bellowed. "You still have her milk on your upper lip."

Lahmi's face reddened when he translated his father's words into Hebrew as if embarrassed at such a thought expressed for all to hear.

The adversary stepped away from the flowing stream.

Goliath surmised that this runt of an opponent did not want to get his feet and sandals wet. He needed traction. Perhaps Goliath underestimated this lad. So, he stepped closer but kept the stream between them.

The lad spread his legs and dug his feet into the earth, then tossed his sling across his left shoulder, allowing the pouch to hang off his back while he held on to the two leather straps, an imperious gesture in response to Goliath's enjoyment of self-humor.

Goliath quickly replaced amusement with annoyance and cupped a hand over his mouth, funneling his disdain. "Saul, send down Abner, or is the commander still in his tent?" Goliath shouted but could not avoid following the taunt with laughter.

"You come against me with sword and spear and javelin," cried the callow boy. "But I come against you in the name of Yahweh the Almighty, God of the army of Israel, whom you have defied."

Goliath's amused expression distorted into a sinister scowl. "The little flea invokes his god, his one god." Goliath reared back his head and spat in his opponent's direction. "The Philistine gods are countless in number, and in all their names, I curse you. In the name of Baal, in the name of Astarte, in the name of the great god Dagon, I flout the one god of Israel."

The fledgling pulled the sling off his shoulder and allowed it to swing back and forth just inches above the ground.

Goliath felt the eyes of the flea focusing not on his eyes but on the nose slot in his helmet that extended its opening to the midpoint of his forehead. Not only was this half-naked worm an insult to his prowess, but he was also cocky enough to think he might hit him with a stone flung at his head.

"This day Yahweh will hand you over to me, and I will strike you down and cut off your head."

While Lahmi translated, Goliath maintained the frozen scowl on his face. He would not dignify such a boast with his own venomous curse.

"This day I will give the dead bodies of the Philistine army to the birds of the air and the beasts of the earth, and the whole world will know that there is a God in Israel."

Goliath grunted, his only retort in the face of such bold predictions. He considered the words less insulting than the fact that, out of the entire army of Israel, this upstart had dared come into the valley to face him. After forty days, this was the best Saul could muster. Goliath lifted his spear and bounced it in his hand like his contender had done moments ago with the little stone. A little stone, a foolish choice of weapon.

He would skewer this mite. The energy he exerted would bolster his appetite for breakfast.

"It is your carcass, the kites and vultures will feast upon, your blood the jackals will lap, and your soul that the winged demons shall carry off to the Underworld," Goliath bragged, as he took backward steps up the slight incline. "And it will be your bones the gods will grind up and scatter far and wide."

David followed his opponent's example and stepped backward up the slope of the valley, but it was not within him to allow the giant to have the last word. "This day all who are gathered here will know that it is not by sword or spear that Yahweh saves; for the battle is Yahweh's, and he will give all of you into our hands."

The giant continued to bounce the spear, searching for the feel of the perfect grip while his other arm stretched and waved to give him balance against the throw.

David used the grade of the valley to build his speed as he advanced toward the giant. On the run, he placed the stone into the cup of the sling. The sling began to purr above his head.

The giant too began to charge.

The whistle of David's sling became a sharp treble.

The giant's fingers were wrapped around the center of the shaft, pumping the spear against the air.

David's sling was a whirling scream.

The giant's legs pummeled the earth, his beard and hair, a flying mane.

When David reached the stream, he leapt into the air. At the same time, he released the stone, the giant hurled his spear. David used the momentum of his release to twist his body as he leapt over the stream just in time to avoid being impaled. The iron point of the spear was so large and heavy it would have split him in two had it struck home.

David landed hard, and with his forward motion, flipped onto his back.

The spear was thrown with such force that it sank to the midpoint of the shaft beneath the surface of the earth.

David scrambled to his feet and reloaded his sling with another stone from his pouch. He raised the sling above his head and began his windup, but realized the giant was not advancing. Instead, he stood still, his breathing labored. All the boasting, and stamping, and dreaming of men was forced into a hushed awe.

The giant appeared surprised that his spear had missed its mark and impaled only the hard earth, not human flesh. His face was concentrated as if in study of a puzzling question.

David stood still on his side of the stream. It was better not to advance, just to watch. Let this beast make the next move.

The giant's hands began to rotate. Voluntary or not, David could not tell, but the giant did not reach for his sword or javelin. Instead, he pulled on the chinstraps of his helmet until he ripped them out of their sockets and yanked off his helmet. He held it before his face and examined the damage, straining his eyes to see the dent and scratch marks along the open edges of the noseguard. He slammed the helmet onto the ground in vexation and dug his fingers along the crown of his head, moving forward until he felt the notch in the front of his skull.

The skin around the indentation was soggy and flayed. David could see the darkened imprint above the giant's eyes as he frantically dug his fingers into the wound. It surprised David that the giant's efforts did not seem to induce any sensation of physical pain.

The giant only grunted, only whined in curiosity, the skin of his face losing its elastic strength, his mind descending into a last unknowable thought. The giant dropped his arms to his sides and faltered on his legs as if attempting to dislodge his feet mired in the ground.

When the giant began to fall forward like a great tree chopped at its base, David dropped to his chest in a reflex of empathy with his felled victim. A human life had been taken by his hand, an enemy of the chosen, but still a human life. Once the giant collapsed facedown not a dozen paces in front of him, David felt the vibrations like shock waves rushing from the ground into his arms and legs.

"Yahweh," whispered David, unable to utter any other word; no other word was splendid enough to encompass the enormity of the moment.

David did not rise to his feet. He looked at the giant's armor-bearer to see if he would attack or at least come to the aid of the giant. Instead, he dropped to the ground and howled in an expression of grief.

David felt it was safe to move toward the sprawled giant. Like a lion stealthily approaching its prey just before it pounces, David crawled forward with caution. He moved in close to the giant's head and heard him babble like a child. He looked down the length of the reclining body. It seemed to extend far into the horizon. Waves of heat pungent with sweat and excrement billowed from the openings of the giant's armor as though his body was baking in an oven.

David rose, gripped the hilt of the giant's sword, and tugged on it. He lurched back in case his action might revive the giant to counter and resist, but when David got no response, he inched closer. The giant's hair and beard were so thick that David could not see his face, so he cautiously pulled the thick strands away from the giant's swelling head and protruding eyes. In the center of his forehead, blood oozed through the damaged flesh, flowed around the creases of the giant's smashed nose and dripped onto the ground.

A bolt of energy rushed through David; an ecstasy similar to the one he felt as the oil flowed from the flask of the prophet onto his head when Samuel anointed him to be the next king of Israel. This sacred flow now ran through his veins, and he clenched the hilt of the giant's sword in both hands, yanked the imposing weapon from its sheath, raised it above his head, and brought it down upon the giant's neck. One slash was not sufficient. A second was required, then a third, a fourth, and a fifth, each hack spraying blood over the future king—this blood-shower, a second, mortal-to-mortal anointing— before the giant's head was hewed from his neck and rolled a full stride from the carcass before coming to a stop against a rock protruding from the soil.

In the unbearable light of the sun, the giant's trunk seemed to deflate right before his eyes.

David dashed to the head and entangled his fingers into a thick swatch of hair matted with blood and gore and lifted it off the ground. With the head of the giant in one hand and his sword in the other, David turned to the army of King Saul, of Commander Abner, of Prince Jonathan, of the royal family, of all Israel, of Yahweh, the God of the chosen, the God of Israel, and raised both trophies high into the air.

He inhaled the heated air of the valley down to his bowels and bellowed an unnatural sound—a mixture of human and animal; a sound never been uttered by any known creature; a sound never heard by human ear; a primordial sound from ancient men and beasts long buried in the earth and rising so high as to rend the sky. There would be no other kill like this one. There would be no other victory like this one. This warrior's sound, this aberrant, vocal cry resounding from David's open mouth, was the ecstatic issue of killing his first human.

The king's words were fulfilled: this was an ecstasy he had never expected.

David was unable to move from his spot in the valley as he held the giant's head in one hand and his sword in the other. His feet were planted into the ground and his legs were locked. He stopped screaming only because his vocal cords had been stripped of sound. He panted for breath, and with each intake, the dusty air burned his raw throat. He twisted his body around, looked at Jonathan, and nodded.

The prince sprang into action, spinning and raising his sword to the army. Upon Jonathan's signal, Carmi waved the banner of the lion and led the charge toward their stunned enemies.

David turned back to the Philistine army.

The Five Lords with its officer corps were aligned across the battlefront. Realization dawned on the faces of the Five Lords that the head of their high-priced champion dangled from the hand of this Israelite champion, and his lifeless body lay prone in the middle of the valley.

The fight immediately drained out of them, and to a man, the instinct to flee took over. The chariot drivers for the Five Lords turned their horses and raced away, trampling any poor soldier in the path of the charging horses. The generals made no attempt to amass the troops and stand against the oncoming warriors of Israel, but instead ordered an immediate retreat.

David's slaying of the Philistine giant lifted the dark covering of fear and shame from the army of Israel. They were set free to massacre and plunder, which was much easier to accomplish with an enemy showing their back. Few paused to consider the magnitude of David's kill as they rushed past their champion in the frenzy of easy slaughter and abundant looting.

Jonathan was the first to reach David.

"I cannot move, my lord." David's voice could barely produce a sound. So much blood flowed from the head and carcass of the giant that David stood mired in the blood-soaked soil.

The prince grabbed David's arm that held the giant's head and helped pull his feet out of the wet ground.

Adriel ran up beside Jonathan just as David was regaining his balance. "My lord, the panic of Yahweh has seized our enemies." The prince's armor-bearer let fly an arrow from his bow that found its mark in the back of a fleeing Philistine soldier.

"I must lead this charge," Jonathan shouted into David's ear.

David watched as the Philistine armor-bearer crawled to the slain giant and collapsed upon the body, howling in grief. David was not sure he understood the blurred frenzy around him as the valley filled with thousands of Israelite warriors charging their enemies.

"We are victorious, my lord?" David needed confirmation.

"Because of you...and Yahweh," Jonathan shouted again.

Just then David's three brothers surrounded him.

"Take him to the king," Jonathan ordered. "Let no harm come to him."

"Yes, my lord." Eliab answered for the trio. Then he, Abinadab, and Shammah bowed their heads to the prince before forming a protective shield around their brother as the army of Israel roared by.

Ishvi and Malki ran up to Jonathan wild-eyed and breathless.

"Abba said we could join the fight," Ishvi shouted.

"He wants us to learn to be brave like the shepherd," Malki added.

"Stay at my side," Jonathan said and broke into a run, joining the surge.

Chapter 15

SABA HAD RETURNED TO HIS LADDER LEANING AGAINST THE scaffolding to watch the contest from above the heads of the soldiers. The moment Goliath fell, he reached inside his garment and clutched the letter. When the young man raised Goliath's severed head, Saba removed the letter and read it once again. It was his only hope. He looked up and across the valley when the army of Israel surged forward with a roar.

He returned the letter inside his garment and calmly descended the ladder. He felt no sense of urgency though all around him was sudden chaos. It was foolish to join the stampeding hordes and be trampled to death.

He would never leave behind his stone monument. The safest place for him was in front of his latest and possibly his last creation. If he was to die, he would die in front of his greatest artistic achievement.

Saba ran his fingers over the bas-relief images of the large stone—the very thing he had asked his patron not to do. The tips of his fingers caressed the winged demons gathering the souls of the scattered dead; the rocky landscape; the image of Lahmi beside his father bearing his shield; Goliath in the center, a defiant arm holding his spear in the air with Dagon floating above him. These stony images were alive, alive to his touch, to his eyes, and in spite of the day's events, this engraving would live on unlike its main subject.

He read the lettering next to Dagon's crowned head: *"In the house of Dagon, thou shalt eat the bread of honor; thou shalt drink the wine of favor."*

"I never saw this as prophetic." Saba spoke as if in confession for any role he might have played in the death of his patron. "These descendants of the legendary Nephilim—giants of renown before the great waters covered the earth—are now laid waste by their enemies. The winged demons reap the harvest of their souls. 'Do not be afraid,' Goliath had said. 'Do not be afraid.' And so, I shall not be afraid."

The blade of a sword glided over Saba's left shoulder and from the corner of his eye he saw it was covered in blood. Was it his own? He had not felt the metal pierce his skin, but he could not be sure.

The blade tapped his shoulder, and Saba turned. The tip of the sword held steady in front of his eyes until it gradually descended so he could view the man who held it. It was the man he had encountered at the outpost in Geba, the man who had written the letter folded inside his garment. Though spattered in blood, the man was dressed in finery of a prince.

On either side of this man stood younger, smaller versions of himself, a matched pair, both with drawn swords, but lacking any red-colored stains. The metal of their swords remained pristine.

Saba gestured that he had something inside his garment for his captor, so the man motioned for him to retrieve it. When Saba produced the letter and unfolded it for him to read, the man did not take it—his hands also were covered in blood—but leaned forward to read it. Once read, the man motioned for Saba to step aside, and when he did, the man and the twins stepped forward to view the stone.

For one moment, Saba broke his gaze away from inside this protected space around his stone sculpture to behold the massacre of the fleeing soldiers at the hands of their enemies, and then observed the man and the matching pair of younger versions, their eyes roving over his creation. He could tell by their expressions of wonder that they had seen nothing like it.

The man looked at Saba in amazement. He then gave an order to the two young men before disappearing around the stone, entering the flow of slaughter.

The two young men took their eyes off the stone and moved into position on either side of Saba. They held the swords aloft, a position of gallantry and protection.

Saba refolded his letter and slipped it back inside his garment. Though the carnage was great all around him, though he felt a terrible sense of sorrow witnessing the death of his fellow citizens, hearing their last cries, Saba was at ease. He knelt before his stone and placed his hands upon the grand images he had chiseled. He prayed for his slain countrymen whose souls were even now being transported by winged demons to the Underworld for their final feast in the house of Dagon.

Once Jonathan, the twins, and Adriel were absorbed into the torrent of Israelites flooding the enemy camp in pursuit of the Philistines, Eliab bowed toward David in mock compliance. "'Be brave like the shepherd,' the young prince said. We shall never hear the end of it."

But David did not pay attention to his siblings. They barely existed in this pandemonium he had created by slaying the giant.

"Perhaps you did kill that bear and the lion, after all." Shammah spoke as he cut his thumb across his neck and stuck out his tongue, causing the three brothers to laugh.

"Let me see this giant's head." Abinadab reached for the head, but David jerked back his arm, splashing fleshy tissue and blood onto his brother. Abinadab groaned and stepped back, wiping away the pulp splattered onto the front of his armored skirt.

"No one is trying to take your trophy, little brother." Eliab raised his hands before David then slammed his fist into Abinadab's shoulder. "We are proud of you, are we not?"

Eliab scowled at the brothers, and each shook their heads in shamed admiration.

David felt as if he were thawing into life at a slow speed while all around him there was swift chaos and confusion.

"What have I done? What has Yahweh done?" David began to tremble, his teeth chattering, his skin, coated in blood, shivered for lack of warmth. He turned to the morning sun, closed his eyes, and raised his trophy toward the shining ball of light.

> "Shout with joy to Yahweh, all the earth!
> Sing the glory of his name;
> Make his praise glorious! Say to Yahweh,
> 'How awesome are your deeds!
> So great is your power,
> That your enemies cringe before you.'"

David paused to see if more spontaneous words would pour from his lips. For a brief time, he had existed inside a small universe completely unaware of the thousands on either side watching this brief contest. Now, the perimeters for this duel were opening out to the valley's broad spaces to include the multitudes. It almost came as a surprise to David that he had done exactly what he said he would do. He said he would slay a giant—he gripped the evidence in his hands—and give Israel a great victory. Today, the whole world would know there was a God who saves, Yahweh the God of Israel, his God.

Abinadab reached out to take David by the arm and lead him up the valley, but Eliab slapped his hand away. They must have sensed David was not yet finished. He had more to say, and they must wait.

> "All the earth bows down to you,
> And will sing praises to you,
> They will sing praises to your name.
> Come and see the works of Yahweh."

David's blood-encrusted face held its direction toward the sky. His eyes remained shut. His lips moved but no longer made any sound. They continued to move until there were no more words of adulation to utter, and his arms came to rest at his sides. He tilted his head forward, and his eyes opened═ and focused upon the barren ground.

"They would try and harm me?" David's question was directed toward the ground, hard packed by the stampeding army of Israel.

Eliab stepped in front of David and gently cupped his head between his hands. "Who would dare try to harm the giant-slayer?"

David felt Eliab might be sincere and did not resist his efforts to bring him back into an existence where he was present with his three siblings.

"Are you with me, little brother?" Eliab asked.

David smiled and blinked in recognition of his kin.

"Forgive me for all the harm I may have caused you, for all the anger and annoyance I expressed with you."

To David's ears, Eliab sounded earnest, sounded as though his brother was contrite, and David forced his chapped lips into a smile. These men would come together, a healing bond bringing together brother to brother, flesh and blood to flesh and blood.

"What may I do for you?" Eliab asked.

"Like the prince said, take me to the king," David responded.

The quartet looked up the valley toward the camp and saw the king and the commander along with the king's daughters and the royal retinue looking down upon the Philistines in flight and the ensuing carnage.

The commander signaled for the four brothers to advance toward the royal party.

"The king is waiting." Eliab stepped forward and directed David to follow.

Abner waved for him to return to the camp. The king also raised his hand of welcome. It was a call for him to return from the world of dreams where a young man had killed a giant and rejoin humanity. Had all this been a dream?

David looked down at the head hanging from the tight grip of his left hand: the weight was real; the wound in the forehead, real; the prince, his brothers, the army of Israel, and now a beckoning king and commander, real. If this were a dream, everyone was acting as if they too agreed with the witness of the same reality. David felt the ache in his arms from holding the weight of a severed head and sword. He set them on the ground and shook his arms and wiggled his fingers to restore the feeling and give the muscles a moment to relax.

"I must carry the head and sword and present them to the king," David said.

"Yes, little brother, you must," Eliab affirmed then he waved to Abner that they were coming. "You are a true champion."

"I am glad you three were here to witness this," David said. "You never would have believed me otherwise."

His brothers could never again treat him with indifference. In one panting breath, in one instant, David's unimaginable feat had changed all their lives forever.

"I believe your days as a shepherd are over," Eliab said.

"Thank Yahweh," David shouted with no regrets at the prospect of never chasing after sheep again. Then he started laughing, surprising his brothers, for he saw the absurdity of their new world brought about by him, the giant-slayer.

"Come." David's laughter trailed off. He bent over and yanked the severed head off the ground, then took the hilt of the sword in the other hand. "The king awaits."

David marched up the hill as his brothers quickly formed ranks around him. There was no need for a protective detail. The Philistine army had fled, and the army of Israel was too preoccupied with plundering the enemy camp to follow the giant-slayer up the valley to witness his audience with the king. They had witnessed the death of the giant. That was enough.

Chapter 16

BEFORE DAVID AND HIS BROTHERS REACHED THE CREST OF THE valley where the royal family and the commander awaited, David heard someone call his name. He turned to see Jonathan riding a horse, holding the bridle of a second horse that pulled a wagon with Malki and Ishvi seated in the front and a third passenger riding in the back. Adriel rode his own horse on the other side of the horse-drawn wagon. David waited for them to catch up, and the two parties entered the camp together.

"What of the battle?" Abner demanded of Jonathan as he dismounted.

"There is no battle," Jonathan answered. "The bodies of the Philistines are strewn along the roads to Gath and Ekron. The battle is Yahweh's, and the day is ours. The tribal chieftains are finishing with the last of the Philistine army and gathering the plunder."

Malki and Ishvi did not wait for the wagon to come to a stop before they leapt to the ground and raced to join the rest of the family. They could hardly contain themselves as they embraced their father.

"And what have you brought home?" Abner asked, looking at the bound and blindfolded prisoner abandoned in the back of the wagon.

"An artisan," Jonathan replied.

Adriel dismounted and stepped into the wagon bed to help the man out. Adriel guided him around the wagon and tied his hands to the wheel. He then glanced at Merab who had brightened at the sight of him unharmed, but whose light faded when he did not return her smile. Adriel was all business as he took his place beside the prince.

"That is strange. You captured an artisan?" Abner smirked.

"We have artisans in Israel," Saul said.

"None quite like this one," Jonathan countered. "I did not appreciate his skill the first time I saw it. He might make a good addition to the court."

"First a singing shepherd and now a Philistine artist," Saul said. "You are quite a gatherer of oddities."

"We can discuss the Philistine artist later. Now, we must celebrate," Jonathan said, walking toward David.

David's familial guard detail bowed and stepped aside as Jonathan approached David and wrapped his arms around him with an intense embrace. When Jonathan released his hold of David, he ushered him toward the king.

"When the history of Israel is written, this day shall rank among its greatest moments," Jonathan said and bowed his head before the giant-slayer.

Mikal stood beside her father, clutching David's damp clothes. She wanted this rustic apparel and refused to leave them behind when her father told her to fetch Merab and join him at the battle line. She wanted the man who wore these garments. She wished for her arms to be wrapped around the giant-slayer, for her body to be pressed against the giant-slayer as her brother's had been, for her words of praise to be spoken of him, to him.

She was not frightened by the sight of David's blood-grimed appearance, though her heart pounded hard enough to flutter her blouse. The giant's head dangling from David's hand did not horrify her, though she did have to clench her sister's elbow to keep her from fainting. She did not scream or hold her breath when David bent his knee and presented her father with his prize, though the smell of blood and fresh rot had attracted a swarm of buzzing insects. Mikal was not squeamish, but remained poised and upright, a princess any man could take pride in. Gone were the days of contented life on a farm. Gone was the youngster with the girlish fantasies of marrying a prince. In in this present moment, Mikal became a woman of inner force, able to withstand any barbarity that confronted her, and capable of being stirred with passion for a man whose skin was covered in dirt and gore and who held the foul head of his first human kill.

Saul stared down at the kneeling David, shaking his head in amazement. He had believed. He had believed the moment David had accepted the challenge. He had believed when his commander had not. He had believed when the tribal chieftains wondered if the king had slipped even further into madness when they watched as David, dressed only in sandals and a shepherd's girdle, walked into the valley. Saul had believed.

"In the name of Yahweh, the God of Israel, I give you the head of your enemies." David's voice was broken and hoarse, but he spoke with pride for the gift he had promised Saul. "May the king live forever."

All were silent. Even the insects stopped buzzing and feasting. All waited. All waited for the king to respond.

"Who are you, my son?" Saul whispered, his question one of wonder at this living, breathing creature kneeling before him holding the head of a human monster. A young man who had played and sung for him just the night before. The same young man who had brought him out of his dark mettles and propelled him into the high spirits of hope.

"As surely as you live, O king, I do not know," Abner spoke softly into his cousin's ear.

Saul smiled at Abner in amusement. His cousin had taken his question as a literal inquisition and supposed Abner had mistaken his perplexed look as a return to delusion. Saul appreciated this moment of sensitivity not to expose him were it true. Saul then turned back to address David.

"And whose son are you, young man?"

"I am David, the son of Jesse of Bethlehem. I am a shepherd."

Saul dropped his head back and roared with laughter, and everything poured out of him: his joy, his madness, his fear of living up to the unattainable standard set by an unreasonable prophet who seemed to care so little about him. He was in the presence of a savior that freed him with his song and with his sling, changing the course of a nation. Saul looked beyond David and Jonathan and saw hundreds of his soldiers, spoils of battle overflowing in wagons, returning to the encampment led by their tribal chieftains under their banners.

Saul raised his arms in welcome. "Army of Israel, army of Yahweh, the God of Israel: today you have witnessed the greatest act of courage since our forefathers entered the land of Promise!" Saul shouted to the approaching soldiers who were wild with the blood-scent of their enemies still fresh in their nostrils. "A shepherd from the tribe of Judah is now your champion. From the hills of Bethlehem, he left his sheep and came and slew the giant. He will never again tend sheep. Welcome David, son of Jesse of Bethlehem, to the army of the king."

When the soldiers began moving toward their hero, Eliab signaled to Shammah and Abinadab to lift David to his feet and have him face the soldiers gathered around. Their pent-up excitement broke into delirium. The soldiers had a champion they could touch and call their own. Chants of David's name echoed in the air, and many threw offerings of Philistine spoils at his feet. When Shammah and Abinadab lifted their brother onto their shoulders to parade him through the mass of soldiers, Jonathan took the sword of the giant, and Eliab grabbed the severed head, wrenching it from David's hand.

"I will protect it!" Eliab shouted above the fray.

Eliab held aloft the giant's head as his little brother was tossed and jostled in the air by adoring soldiers. Then he knelt behind the growing pile of armor and treasure offered to David and cradled the head in his hands. He looked into the bearded, leathery face and brushed away the knotted hair covering the forehead. He took his knife and dug the blade point into the wound to remove the stone from the massive, thick skull. Once Eliab freed the stone, he dropped the head on the ground and kicked it onto the rest of the plunder. He held something of more value. The giant's head would rot and disintegrate, but the stone would become an object of adoration, a talisman full of conjuring potency, a stone that could match the power hidden in the high priest's breastplate, those magic stones of Yahweh. Eliab wiped the dried blood and bone fragments off the stone, wrapped a linen cloth around it, and dropped it into his leather pouch.

This object of death contained the brutal precision of Yahweh. Eliab would never allow it to fall into the wrong hands.

Mikal took Merab by the arm. This was a warriors' celebration.

"I cannot marry him, Mikal." Merab's sobs welled up in her throat. "I do not care what our father says or what a grand singer he may be or that he killed a giant."

"I know." Mikal squeezed Merab's shoulder as she led her away.

Mikal looked back at the shouting mass, a multi-armed beast tossing their champion in the air, a human feather rising and descending, floating above the fray.

"Do not fear," Mikal said as they passed out of sight behind the large family tent. "I shall convince Abba that giving you to the singer would be a mistake."

Mikal led Merab to the entrance and encouraged her to lie down. There would be feasting and celebrating throughout the day and into the night. She would need to be present for much of it, so now would be a good time for her to rest. She kissed Merab on the cheek and sent her inside.

Mikal held out David's clothes then she pressed them into her face and inhaled deeply. The scent of David had not been completely washed away. It gave her a slight intoxicated feeling, and if she had her way, she would smell him again and again, in the flesh, their bodies locked in a coitus knot creating a new scent.

The fire Mikal used to heat the water to wash David's cloths still smoldered. She stepped over to it and removed the pot of warm water from the coals. Then one by one, she dropped the head covering, the shirt, and finally the leggings onto the embers. The damp clothes hissed as the heat of the fire dried out the moisture before igniting the cloth.

As her father had said, once David killed the giant, he would never again wear such rags.

She had taken it upon herself to retrieve and wash his clothes. She had taken it upon herself to destroy them. She would take it upon herself to see him dressed in royal attire, fit for a giant-slayer, fit for a husband to a princess.

Chapter 17

AFTER BATHING AND DRESSING IN CLEAN GARMENTS THAT Jonathan selected from his own wardrobe, David returned to the king's tent with Jonathan. The king had requested that Jonathan, David, and Abner join him. Jonathan wanted to give David a proper introduction to the chieftains in each of the tribal camps. They went throughout the encampment, stopped before the banners of each tribe, and allowed the chieftains to greet their champion and bestow him with honor. Most of the chieftains were generous with their praise and offerings, but several did not extend the good fellowship toward David that should have come after such a feat.

Jonathan hid his annoyance with those chieftains who, while they all applauded David's bravery, were suspect of his motives. Some even expressed the idea that the fortunate shot with his sling, while indeed skillful, was not that of a trained warrior and more providential in nature. Jonathan knew it would take more time for David to win over these chieftains. Until a day ago, David was only a shepherd—a brave and inspiring one, yes, but he would have to do much more to prove his kill shot was not happenstance before he would be considered a professional soldier. Jonathan would see that David was given all the training required.

For Jonathan, it took no convincing that this shepherd from Bethlehem was in all respects a good man and worthy of devoted friendship.

When they returned from meeting the last tribe, David's own tribe of Judah, it was well into the night, and the king and Abner retired to their tents. But Jonathan pulled David aside. He had in mind a special bond of friendship that required a covenant celebration before Yahweh.

"We should cut a covenant together." Jonathan slung his arm over David's shoulder as they walked away from the king's tent.

"What covenant is that my lord?" David asked.

"A covenant bond of brotherhood. It is a mutual covenant between two equals who willingly accept the terms."

"But we are not equals, my lord," David said.

"This bond will change that." Jonathan paused and removed his arm from David's shoulder. He stepped in front of David and placed his left hand over his heart and his other hand upon David's chest. "It will make us brothers, which means you will no longer refer to me as 'my lord.' You were ready to die for the army of the king, for the nation of Israel, for Yahweh, our God. You are more than equal to this covenant."

Jonathan looked into the face of David. No guile, no conceit, just a pure center, the rare man who would never deceive or assert his ambition at the expense of someone else, a man of action, impulsive perhaps, but one who would not falter in conflict when other, lesser men would yield. This was a man who would face any foe, a man to unite the hearts of men, a man worthy of a warrior's covenant bond.

"Do this with me." Jonathan removed his hand from David's chest.

"I am willing, my lord. This is a great honor."

"Then we shall awaken the high priest and have him make the preparations for a blood covenant between the prince and the giant-slayer."

In the predawn hour, Jonathan and David sat quietly on a boulder in the hills above the encampment watching as the Levites took their positions. Each Levite led a sacrificial beast into a natural contour of the earth that sloped below the ridgeline and formed a gradual funnel shaped by the eroding rains. Gad and Ahimelech, the High Priest, stood at a high point along a ridge above the priests with the animals. Other Levites encircled Gad and Ahimelech along the ridge, holding torches. When Ahimelech nodded toward the five priests standing in the ravine, each drew a dagger and positioned their blade at the throat of their respective animal. Each creature remained quiet and docile, unaware their life would soon be extinguished.

Gad held an open scroll in his hands and raised it for Ahimelech to read.

"And Abram believed Yahweh the Almighty, and Yahweh credited it to him as righteousness. And Yahweh made a covenant with Abram saying, 'Bring me a three-year-old heifer, a three-year-old female goat, a three-year-old ram, and a dove and a pigeon.' Then Abram brought all these things to Yahweh and Abram cut them in two, down the middle, and placed each piece opposite the other, but he did not cut the birds in two. And on that day Yahweh made a covenant with Abram."

Gad lowered the scroll, rolled it up, and placed it inside a leather pouch strapped over his shoulder.

At Ahimelech's signal, each Levite performed their duty.

The creatures made no sound as the blades opened the veins in their necks. Levite and prophet, high priest and warrior stood in reverential silence as they waited for the last breath of each creature to be exhaled and absorbed into the cool temperature of the breeze.

Once the life had passed from all five animals, the Levites with the heifer, goat, and ram cut their beast in half, placing the two parts on either side of the ravine from smallest to largest. The dove and pigeon were not cut asunder but placed on the ground opposite each other. Like a sudden rain shower, animal blood filled the ravine.

Ahimelech signaled for Jonathan and David to join him at the top of the ridge, and the two of them climbed down from the rock and joined the high priest and prophet.

Jonathan slipped off his princely robe of purple hemmed in gold and draped it over David's shoulders. "This is the robe of a prince given to you from the first prince of Israel," Jonathan began, his voice quivering but solemn. "The robe is the symbol of my authority. It is a token of friendship and love. You will no longer appear in court in the garments of a shepherd, a soldier, or a common man, but that of a prince, a brother."

While David slipped his arms through the sleeves and tied the sash of the robe around his middle, Jonathan untied his leather belt, securing the sword around his waist and laid them at David's feet. He then had a Levite hand him his bow and quiver, and Jonathan laid these weapons beside the sword.

"At your feet lay the weapons of my strength," Jonathan continued. "You will be a prince and a soldier. With these weapons you will be trained as a warrior."

David trembled before the prince as he looked up from the weapons and gazed upon the holy witnesses who stood around them. "My lord, I have nothing to give you in exchange for this friendship."

Jonathan raised his hand. "These are only gifts to bear you up to a place of respect and honor, which you deserve, and to aid in your training as a warrior. What we exchange with equal measure is our loyalty."

Gad put forward the scroll in his hand to speak what the covenant makers must now do and what they must swear. He did not read these words from a scroll. His learning gave him the confidence to speak.

"To complete the covenant, you must walk the way of the blood. The covenant makers must walk to-and-fro between the cut pieces of sacrifice, two interweaving circles ending with both covenant makers standing face-to-face in the middle of the blood and swear by Yahweh, the Eternal One who perfects and completes this covenant. The covenant makers will remain loyal to one another, do no harm to the other, defend one another, protect the name of the other, bear authority for all actions in the name of the other. The covenant makers will keep faith with the descendants of the seed of the other, that you shall surely stand on all the covenant promises. And should either of the covenant makers breach the covenant, the covenant breaker may die for this violation."

Jonathan took the initial step and he and David did as they were instructed, walking a circular pattern around and between the carcass halves in two rotations, and then faced each other, standing in the stream of blood that flowed over their feet and down the slope. Face-to-face, as they stood in the current of blood, the two men swore by Yahweh to keep all parts of the covenant and finished their recitation with: "I will hold you forever in my heart, as if I were standing here in the blood of the covenant."

"Love the Lord your God with all that you are," Ahimelech spoke, and Jonathan and David repeated the words.

"Love your neighbor as yourself," Ahimelech said, and again the two covenant makers repeated his words.

Then Gad took a scroll from his pouch and raised it before Ahimelech so he could read the ancient words.

"And it came to pass, when the sun went down and it was dark, that behold, there appeared a smoking firepot with a blazing torch that passed between the pieces. On that day Yahweh made a covenant with Abram."

Ahimelech took a torch and waded into the blood flow as David and Jonathan stepped back out of the ravine. Ahimelech walked along the trench of blood, between the covenant makers, holding the torch of Yahweh to represent the supernatural passing of fire through the carcasses when Yahweh made His covenant with Abram centuries ago.

"Hear O Israel. The Lord our God. The Lord is One."

Once Ahimelech had passed through the stream of blood, he circled back around and positioned himself between the two men. He withdrew his sacred knife and held it in the air before the covenant makers.

"Do not enter into a covenant lightly, for Yahweh will require it of you," Ahimelech admonished. "This is a last opportunity to break from this commitment, the last opportunity to avoid entering into a sacred relationship. To enter into a covenant is to bring Yahweh and His glory as a witness and judge. He will protect His name, and you must do the same of each other and of Yahweh, the Lord Almighty."

The covenant makers held out their favored hand in agreement to enter this holy state of friendship, this bond of brotherhood—Jonathan his left hand and David his right.

"It is written, 'Do not swear falsely by my name and so profane the name of your God. I am Yahweh, the Lord Almighty.'"

Ahimelech made a quick cut across the palm of each covenant maker. Ahimelech held up the knife with its tip of mingled blood, and David and Jonathan pressed their palms together with the knife blade in between, smearing the blood of each man into the stream of the other. Their feet were submerged in the blood of beasts. Their palms were wet with human blood. Their souls were eternally entwined in this blood-washed bond.

Yahweh was in the cut. Yahweh was in the words. Yahweh was in the fire. Yahweh was in the light. Yahweh was in the blood, the pure sacrificial blood of beast and man, the pulse of Yahweh made manifest in all blood—celestial blood from the heart of Yahweh, for Yahweh inhabited it all.

Chapter 18

THE DAWN BROKE CLEAR AND BRIGHT OVER THE PUTREFIED landscape. Once Gad had finished packing the last of his professional materials and personal items and made sure the caravan master had stowed them carefully onto the military wagons, he walked out to the edge of the encampment and looked out over the valley floor.

For the last three days, the Philistine dead had lain where they fell. For three days, the bodies and battlements and camp had been scavenged. For three days, the sun's heat had been relentless, yet it did not burn off the ocher-colored miasma that floated above the Valley of Elah. The ground was saturated in the fetid entrails of soldier and beast, leaving a pungent haze that resisted the sun's evaporating rays. The only signs of movement across the valley were the thousands of winged and four-legged creatures feasting on carrion.

Citizens of Israel from the nearby villages and cities converged on the camp, bringing with them wagons of bounty to celebrate with the king and his conquering army. The revels were full of excess: too much eating, too much drinking, too much whoring, too many inner-tribal skirmishes—since the Philistines had not put up a fight, many of the soldiers, denied the heart-rush of combat, chose to release their bloodlust upon each other with inner-tribal rivalries causing multiple injuries among the ranks.

By the third day, Abner ordered the tribal chieftains and the captains of the king's elite force of warriors to break camp and for everyone to depart.

The army had plundered the battlefield for two days, taking anything of military value and killing all wounded who had survived the initial onslaught before turning the area over to the local citizens to rummage for any over-looked items of value. The conscripts were the first to disperse after collect-ing their stipends, returning to their homes across the country. The standing army had to mobilize as a unit and required time to organize before its return with the king and royal family to Gibeah.

Gad raised a strip of cloth to his nose to filter the stench. "What a reeking broth."

"Take some dried mint and place a few flakes inside your nostrils." Jarib walked up beside Gad and removed a pouch from his belt and handed it to him.

Gad opened the pouch and inhaled its aroma. Then he took a pinch of flakes, crumbled them between his fingers, and inserted the herb into his nose to counteract the disgusting odor.

"How will we record this event?" Gad asked, returning the pouch.

"Not since we annihilated the Amalekites have I seen such carnage." Jarib tucked the pouch behind his belt. "You are the royal historian. You write for Israel, for Yahweh. Your role as prophet should be to record the truth. The truth is the best course."

"What a terrible truth. What a terrible sight." Gad sighed and formed a visor with his hands above his eyes.

"Generations from now, what might remain? What might be uncovered from this moment?" Jarib waved his arm over the valley. "Will there be some discovered artifact that would tell the story of this event? Everything must be recorded, every detail."

"I would be selective, but Yahweh must guide my words. I might exclude some things from the text, leave details of memory buried and forgotten, allowed to pass into Sheol along with the dead, but Yahweh may have a dif-ferent notion. Yahweh must guide my hand. I am unreliable."

"The bones and flesh of the Philistines will rot and fertilize the soil, leav-ing no trace of the story."

"The Philistine artist's carved stone will mark their resting place." Gad pointed to the stone slab lying flat on the opposite side of the valley.

"The commander wanted nothing to do with it. The prince argued for it to be brought home to Gibeah as a spoil of war, but the commander refused to waste a wagon and team of oxen to transport a pagan artifact."

"Let the marker be a warning to Israel's enemies that Yahweh is not to be trifled with," Gad said, his words enhanced with an immodest tone of pride.

"Perhaps, in the future, Yahweh might prove His superiority with less carnage," Jarib replied. "I am but the king's secretary. You are a prophet of Yahweh. What do I know of such things?"

Both men turned to see David approach, leading his horse by the reins. Gad recognized the robes and weaponry of the prince that David wore from the night of the covenant. For this reason alone, Gad bowed in honor, but he was not ready to swoon at his presence, nor offer praise for his heroics. The king and the prince might be enamored by the giant-slayer, but Gad chose to reserve his affections. The story of the shepherd-singer-turned-giant-slayer would spread across the nation faster than a desert sandstorm. But who was he really? And who might he become? He was a bright star that fell from heaven. But how long would his starlight burn?

David stopped when he reached the two men and beheld the sight of the valley. He had never seen such a thing. He had never wanted to see such a thing, let alone ever consider being a participant in such carnage.

"You packed and ready to depart for Gibeah?" Jarib asked.

"I have nothing to pack." David pointed to his horse. "Except for my kinnor and bedroll. My brothers have returned home with the supplies I brought them. I do not even have the clothes I wore to the camp. I never intended to stay. I never intended…" In that moment, his lips failed him.

He had never anticipated such fortune. He could not have formulated a scheme to achieve it. He had no aspiration to be in such a place of honor. He had only wished to be something other than a shepherd, to sing and compose, do anything that would get him out of the sheep pens and away from provincial Bethlehem.

Then the prophet Samuel upended his whole life and future. The prophet said Yahweh had chosen him out of all his brothers. He had come to the encampment at Elah not on a mission to slay a giant but to deliver food to his brothers, and now he wore Prince Jonathan's purple robe, the royal sword strapped to his waist, his right hand bandaged to conceal the covenant cut he had made with the king's oldest son.

No, David never intended any of this.

"Words fail you," Jarib said. "They are inadequate to explain the mysteries of circumstance. I have my own strange circumstance that brought me to the king's service." Jarib pointed to the patch over his eye.

"I would love to hear it," David said. "Maybe compose a song for your story."

Jarib smiled at such a thought. "My story told with music."

"How do you explain it?" Gad asked.

"Explain what?" David asked.

"How a shepherd who must have a gentle, kind spirit to care for creatures with brains the size of a shriveled date, who has a beautiful singing voice, who composes music sweet enough to please the ears of Yahweh and dispel the madness in kings, how this same man with a single stone can cause this." Gad swept his arm over the valley below them.

All three shared the vision: a pestilent landscape overflowing with countless dead.

"It is a terrible wonder, and I have no answer," replied David.

"With one stone," Gad said, marveling at the sight of slaughter. "One well-aimed stone shot into the air, and men, without number, lie dead upon the ground. It is a wonder, a terrible wonder."

"I told the royal family the story of killing the lion. It is true, but I lost count of the stones I hurled at him before one found its mark. Perhaps this stone was guided by Yahweh." David pointed to the corpse of the giant prone on the ground at the bottom of the valley. "I am qualified to husband sheep. My skills as a musician are raw and untrained. As a marksman, I fall short of the prince and many other warriors. But I walked into the valley when no one else would, and here we are."

"Here we are indeed," Gad said. "You were the only one to come forward in forty days and accepted a challenge that seemed certain death to the one who volunteered. Were you not afraid?"

David's answer was given in a solemn tone. "Very much afraid, but the fear blocked out all other distraction."

"What did you do with the giant's sword?" Jarib asked.

"Given to the high priest, a gift to honor the bond with Yahweh," David replied. "And I would rather carry the prince's sword." He gripped the hilt and smiled with pride.

Jarib pulled the pouch from his belt, offering it to David. "Some mint flakes for the smell."

David raised his hand to decline the offer. "I must take in all that has happened in the last few days, including the smell." David began to lead his horse into the valley.

"We will depart as soon as the commander gives the order," Jarib said.

"I will be ready." David turned to Gad before continuing his descent. "Prophet, I need your knowledge of writing. I will bargain with you to teach me lettering. I want to write down what I compose. I have it up here." David tapped his forehead with his finger. "But I want to scribe it."

Gad could not help but chuckle at David's presumption. He had not paused to hear Gad's response to his request before marching into the Valley of Elah. David had presumed the prophet would teach him the lettering skills he needed to write down his songs and poems. Was life always so affirming for this young man? It would be difficult to deny his appeal, and Gad rolled his eyes as he turned to walk toward the assembling column.

"You are going to teach him, are you not?" Jarib said with a laugh.

"I am ignoring you," Gad replied, but a smile appeared on his lips. He could not deny it. He was being taken in by this singing shepherd.

David paused at the stream where he had collected the stones for combat with the giant. He still had four in the leather pouch attached with the sling on his belt. He squeezed the leather pouch, feeling the stones. He would keep these stones, the emergency stones, reserved in case he had missed his first throw. These stones might become a small altar, an altar of "stones of remembrance." But how could he ever forget that day, the day Yahweh made true his aim?

He looked into the water. His horse threw his head back and snorted, forcing David to tighten his grip on the reins. The day he faced the giant, the stream flowed clear. He had been able to drink from it. This day, the water ran a murky crimson, carrying the waste of human compost. He tried to persuade his horse to wade to the other side, but it dug in its forelegs.

David dropped the reins and locked his arms around its neck, whispering in its ear until it calmed and became still. Then David took a skin container from the saddle, cupped his good hand, and poured water into it for the horse to lap up the liquid. Next, he cut some straw from a wrapped bundle and dropped it on the ground. This would occupy the horse long enough for David to take one last look at his conquest.

David made a running start and jumped over the stream. He landed hard and propelled forward with his hands outstretched to break his fall. He smashed his bandaged right palm against a dead root stub protruding from the dry ground, reopening the cut given him during the covenant ceremony with Jonathan. Once he regained his balance, he moved toward the body of the giant, unwinding the soaked bandage to reveal the slice inside his palm. He would not wash it in the polluted stream but would wait until he could use the fresh water from the skin container.

David drew his sword and waved it as he approached the giant's carcass, scattering the vultures and ravens filling their gullets with decaying flesh. The headless giant lay on his back stripped of armor and undergarments, completely exposed to the sun. Humans stripped the body of its garb, and then vermin and beasts stripped the bones of sinew, muscle, and hide.

Blood flowed from his palm, and he extended his arm over the giant's bare chest pecked and slashed by a hundred fowl beaks satisfying their hunger. He examined the bright red flow dripping from his hand and splashing onto the giant's body, his third kill. A bear, a lion, and now a human being. Two beasts and a man, all raging beings with blood and bone like his and a surge to kill. Yet here he stood splashing his blood over the body of the vanquished. There was life in his blood yet not enough that a few spilled drops might resurrect the giant. In this harsh moment what did the life-blood reveal?

David knew that somewhere in the ancient Levitical commands recorded by the great prophet Moses the blood of any beast was never to be drunk. All life had breath and blood and all life came from Yahweh, and in this escalation of his blood, exposed to the light, this life of Yahweh began to ascend from his heart to his lips and into air.

> "May Yahweh arise, may his enemies be scattered;
> May his foes flee before him.
> As smoke is blown away by the wind,
> May you carry them away;

As wax melts before the fire,
May the wicked perish before Yahweh.
Sing to Yahweh, sing praise to his name,
Extol him who rides the clouds—
His name is the Lord and rejoice before him.
Kings and armies flee in haste;
In the camps men divide the plunder.
The Almighty scatters kings in the land.
Yahweh is a God who saves."

David raised his bloody right hand to the heavens and closed his eyes against the brightness of the sun. His skin shivered from a chill despite the heat. His body emptied his spirit and it floated like a ghost above the battlefield. In the desolate space, he saw the field of death, the host of bodies disintegrating into the earth's floor, softening its top crust.

This is how we seep into Sheol, he thought. One day, this is how my body will disappear from sight. His spirit reentered his body, and he lowered his arm. He reexamined the blood on his hand. This was what the blood revealed. This was what he saw in the thin, persistent drip of his blood from the wound of his covenant cut.

"If I am to be king, O Yahweh, let me never forget this day. You are the Creator of life. May I remember that my life is only a drop of spilt blood. May I take refuge inside your heart. May I forever remain in the shelter and shadow of your Presence."

He could not keep from weeping. He could not stop the flow of tears nor shut his mouth against the howling. Of the thousands of warriors who could have responded to the call to face the giant, it was his heart that was roused, his heart that was awakened to the challenge. He alone had entered the valley. He alone had invoked the God of Israel to empower his heart, to steady his aim, to direct the flight of the stone. And he alone stood in the field of death mourning the dead, those enemy warriors who were condemned to die the moment he walked into the valley.

Chapter 19

SABA STOOD INSIDE THE CAGE AS THE WAGON DRIVER GUIDED the team of oxen into the back of the long military convoy. Had there been an abundance of captives to display, the prisoners would have been stuffed onto the wagons and placed near the front of the column behind the king so the people could see the evidence of the king's victory as the army returned home. Most of the Philistines were slain except for those few who had escaped. There was a single cage with a single occupant. Saba was not even an enemy combatant. His captors thought him an unworthy spoil for exhibition.

Saba looked over the valley. From that distance it was impossible to tell what had happened to his carved stone if it had been destroyed or defaced. It appeared to have been toppled, but he could not be sure.

In the days that followed his capture, Saba had little interaction with anyone other than as an object of humor and derisive insults from passing soldiers. The morning of the departure, the king's secretary had come with the prince and communicated to Saba that the prince desired for Saba to be treated well and that no harm come to him. He would return with the royal family, and there his fate would be determined.

When the secretary asked if he wanted or needed anything, Saba requested to collect his carving equipment from his campsite and workstation. He had used these tools since he began his artist's life, Saba explained. When the secretary conveyed this to the prince, the prince nodded, but Saba was told it was unlikely such items would be found after days of scavenging. The prince sent soldiers, and they returned with one small chisel.

Saba held the chisel in one hand and gripped a wooden bar of the cage with the other to steady himself as the wagon bounced over the rough terrain. This was all that remained of his life, a chisel used to cut the finer points in a stone: the eyes of a god, the fingers of a man, the lettering of a quote.

When Lord Namal had summoned him to the Valley of Elah, Saba had taken most of his tools before closing his shop in Aphek. This chisel was all he would carry into his uncertain future, the one item of his artistic life. Lord Namal would presume him dead, and if word came that Saba was held captive in Israel, he was not the type of man to send an envoy requesting the return of a court artisan.

Aphek was filled with artists eager to replace Saba. His shop in the heart of Aphek would be taken over by another artist; the work he had left unfinished would be tossed aside or broken into pieces, the reclaimed materials used for another artist's work. His creations in private collections, temples, public squares, burial sites, and remote outposts were all that was left of his existence in the world. His survivors nothing more than inanimate objects, dumb and blind. The only reminders to those who might care to remember him at all.

Saba placed the chisel inside his leather pouch next to the document Jonathan had written giving him safe passage a few wars ago. The document with the prince's seal and signature had saved him twice now, and with his chisel, these two items might prove yet another salvation.

Mikal pretended to sleep in the back of the wagon. Her face was covered with a cloth that allowed her to keep her eyes half-open. Through a slit, Mikal watched her sister struggle to keep the wriggling and screaming Ish-bosheth from falling off the bench as the family wagon bounced along the uneven road. The child had soiled his swaddling clothes, and the odor permeated the enclosed space. The royal transport might have a luxurious interior, but it did not ensure a smooth and comfortable ride.

"Mikal, help me." Merab kicked her back leg like a donkey, striking Mikal stretched out on soft bedding. "How can you sleep anyway?"

"Leave me alone," Mikal griped as she drew in her legs to protect herself from Merab's repeated blows. "He should have stayed in the wagon with the nurses."

"Baby brother needs time with us. He gets no affection from father," Merab said. "He has rejected him, but for mother's sake, we cannot. Now, come help me."

"If he is old enough to walk, he should be old enough to change himself."

When Merab kicked her again, Mikal yanked the cloth from her head and released a frustrated growl as she rolled onto her knees and crawled to the back of the wagon to aid her sister. Crawling was safer than walking given the rough road through the countryside. When she reached the bench, she tapped her fingers on Ish-bosheth's exposed belly, and then glided her fingertips over his skin.

She placed her lips next to his ear and whispered. "Hush now. I have a tale to tell you, Ishie, a tale of a giant-slayer."

"A giant-slayer who turned your sister into a fool," Merab blurted as she pulled the soiled garments around the child's legs and feet. "Do not leave that out of your tale."

"Yes, but your other sister may be the one to end up in his bed," Mikal cooed.

At first, Merab pretended she had not heard, but then she dropped the stinking undergarment, fell back onto the cushions, and burst into tears.

Ish-bosheth had begun to calm down when Mikal had rubbed his belly and whispered in his ear, but the moment Merab burst into tears, the child resumed his crying, creating a double-act of wailing.

"Quiet, both of you," Mikal snapped, and she grabbed the foul cloth from the table, raised the curtained flap hanging from the rear of the wagon, and flung it onto the road. She would not endure the foul smell inside the family wagon any longer and ignored the complaints from the soldiers marching behind them. Mikal took a clean cloth from a basket, moistened it with wine and perfume, and wiped her hands.

"Merab, take your hands away from your face," Mikal chided. "You just changed Ishie's undergarment. It is disgusting."

Merab dropped her hands, and Mikal began to rub them with the cloth.

"What am I to do?" Merab cried as her sister wiped down her limp hands, even cleaning the webbing between her fingers. "What am I to do?"

"Stop crying to start with. Both of you," Mikal scolded, and then she turned her attention to her brother. She wiped down his baby parts, then grabbed his ankles and raised his legs to swab away the last residue of baby stink. Mikal's firm voice and action brought an end to the duet of sibling weeping. "Jonathan will talk with Father. You saw how his disposition has changed by defeating the Philistines. He is his old self again. The moment is fortuitous. I will help persuade him as well. Father will understand that you and Adriel are better suited, and he and the shepherd will just have to accept that."

Mikal raised the back flap to toss out the second cloth when she saw David and Jonathan riding past the carriage on their horses, trying to catch up to the front of the procession. During the day, the column had slowed periodically so people from the towns and villages could honor the king, bestow their offerings and gifts, and sing praises to Yahweh for the king's continued victories over the Philistines.

David smiled and nodded at Mikal as he rode by, an expression she received as an invitation, though to what she did not know. She let the curtain fall, concealing them from the world, yet her heart was caught unaware by a vibration as if it were a plucked string on the shepherd's kinnor.

Once David and her brother had passed by, Mikal heard a sustained cheering rise from hundreds of voices. Then the wagon driver gave a sharp whistle for the mule team to stop, and she felt the driver pull the lever of the emergency brake, forcing them to a halt. Mikal had to grip a corner of the bench with one hand and drop her forearm over the naked Ish-bosheth to keep them both from tumbling forward as a result of the abrupt slowdown.

Merab had nothing to brace herself and rolled forward to the midsection of the wagon, landing safely upon a pile of cushions.

Once the wagon stopped, Mikal yanked another clean cloth from the basket.

"All will be well." Mikal tossed the cloth to Merab who lay in a heap amidst the cushions. "Now, dry your tears and swaddle Ishie."

A chorus of loud voices transformed from chanting into a musical call and response. Mikal recognized the melody of an old, national folk tune. Her skin tingled. The ends of her hair began to dance to the pounding rhythm of the drums and tambourines. A leaping impulse possessed her, and she left Ish-bosheth on the bench, arms and legs waving at the ceiling, his disposition pacified, as she crawled across the floor of the wagon toward the front.

"Where are you going?" Merab dabbed her moist eyes and sniffed.

"To see what there is to see," Mikal answered as she reached the steps of the wagon's front curtains.

The shepherd had to be the cause of this commotion. His appearance inspired this human outburst. Could this be the reason behind the shepherd's nodding, smiling invitation for her to see, to witness this adulation, to join in, to become one with this morass of praise? Was it his invitation to open the door and enter his world?

Mikal reached for the curtains and pulled them back, and the drums of her ears were met with an aural wall of human voices.

The atmosphere crackled above and around Saul and his cohort. Were it not for its celebratory nature, the fervor would have bode an air of danger. It was a sudden ambush, and Saul slammed his forearm over Jonathan's chest, the protective response of a father, and forced him back onto the road, horse and all, out of the human maelstrom that had encircled him and David the moment they had rode up beside the king.

The spectacle caused the whole column to a complete stop. It forced the eyes and ears of all to fixate on the shepherd. Human rings encircled the giant-slayer.

David yanked hard on the reins to keep his horse from bucking until someone grabbed the bridle and held his mount in place. David tossed Jonathan his pouch and kinnor before being separated from the military caravan. Stringed instruments and drums were playing, shofars were blowing, and hundreds were dancing and singing in alternating choruses:

> The king has done his mighty deeds;
> His enemies fled in terror.
> Shout for joy O people of Israel;
> For the king has brought low his enemies.
> The kings of the earth belong to Yahweh.
> The kings of the earth assemble to praise Him.
> For Saul has slain his thousands,
> And David his ten thousands.
> Saul has slain his thousands,
> And David his ten thousands.

The anger within Saul's soul began to smolder at these words praising this new star of the people. The people pressed all around David, their shepherd, their singer, their slayer of giants, attributing one kill the equivalent of ten thousand, for indeed this giant was the martial force equal to ten thousand, and was not David a champion worth ten thousand mortals?

A group nearest to David broke from the ecstatic throng and rotated around horse and rider, the pressure of nameless fingers gripping, pulling, tearing, pinching flesh and garment. Some were satisfied with just a touch of their champion, others needed a token stolen from horse or rider: a piece of cloth, a waterskin, the sling—oh what a prize that would be—the instrument of death, anything of which the possessor could boast.

Women threw themselves into his saddle, devouring his face with kisses. Men pulled his legs in high-pitched pleading for his blessing. Children—too small to glimpse the giant-slayer from their natural height—were bounced in the air.

Saul had never seen such adulation. Saul had never been the object of such adulation.

David wrenched free from his adoring captors and stood on the back of the horse. Everyone went into a frenzy, repeating again and again the refrain, "Saul has slain his thousands and David his ten thousands." He could not remain standing for long and threw himself off the horse into the fray of worship.

They were worshiping the giant-slayer, Saul realized, like some being fallen from the sky, like some graven image come to life, stealing the esteem, the adoration from him.

David scrambled to his feet and joined the whirling circle, becoming one with the dancing throng in rapture.

Saul, his sons Jonathan and the twin brothers, Abner the commander, the twelve tribal leaders and the high priest, prophet and aide, Gad and Jarib—all who rode with the king at the head of the procession—observed in awe and wonder at this focused boil of human emotion. Saul began to feel humiliated in front of this group of men. Saul had never received such affection, not even for his coronation.

The effect David had produced in these people who swarmed out of their towns and villages to greet the king and his giant-slayer was complete abandon of all composure. Neither Saul nor those closest to him were invited into the human turbulence on the side of the road.

From his seat on the back of his faithful Adara, Saul looked toward the family wagon and saw Mikal standing between the drivers in their front seat. She was clapping her hands, waving them in the air, and vocalizing with the others the chorus of the king's diminished stature in triumph over his enemies compared to that of the slayer of giants. She had been ensnared, caught up in the adulation.

Saul turned to Jonathan, clutching the lion bag containing the kinnor, protecting it as though a loved one. He could see by his son's hypnotized expression that he too was enthralled by this frenzied scene and its main character. Saul immediately tasted the bile of an old wound reopened within his soul and the pitiless worm once again began to gnaw.

"You are to be married immediately. A daughter of one of the tribal leaders!" Saul shouted to Jonathan, shaking his arm, but the prince was too engrossed with the dancing to give his father full attention, so Saul shook his son's arm more forcefully. "Are you listening? You are to be married and produce an heir. I want a grandson. I want a second-generation prince. Right away as soon as it can be done."

"Yes, Abba. Right away," Jonathan replied.

Saul could tell his son did not fully understand to what he had agreed.

Adara began to pound his right hoof upon the ground and blow out an angry whicker at the euphoric crowd. Adara sensed his agitation. Through the saddle and blanket, his steed absorbed his master's distress and anger into his hide, into his blood and bone.

Saul released Jonathan's arm. With the heavy pounding of Adara's hoof upon the ground, Saul felt the black mood drift through his body like the pulse beat of blood flow. Each stomp escalated the intensity in Saul's ears, deafening the wild human cacophony before him. A new and darker hatred in his heart was bolstered. It surprised him to find such clarity in that moment provided by the repetitive pounding of Adara's hoof. Saul knew what he must do.

He must crush the threat to his kingship, the threat to his future progeny. He must crush this shepherd before all was lost.

PART TWO

PART TWO

Chapter 20

SHIRA SAT IN HER CHAIR WITH A CARVING KNIFE, PEELING THE rind from the pomegranate into a bowl in her lap and separating the seeds into another bowl on the table beside her. The acid contained in the peeling would be useful in making ink colors for the students to use in their writing. When she finished carving, Shira cleaned her hands and knife on her apron, set the knife and the bowl of rind on the table, and leaned back in her chair to enjoy the morning sun. The sunrise was too beautiful to remain indoors. Shira had to cajole her husband to join her on the rooftop.

He preferred the writing sanctuary of the main room in their house, closed off from the outside world. He claimed the writing was more focused in the darkness by oil light—better to hear the voices of the stories, the voices of the characters, the voice of Yahweh. But Shira had threatened to open the windows in the house, and she lured her husband into the light, claiming she needed him to proof the latest version of her transcription of his early childhood stories.

Samuel plodded around the perimeter of the roof, reading from the scroll. Shira had not given it to him until he made his way to the rooftop. Otherwise, he never would have walked out the front door. Samuel paused beside her and rested a hand upon her shoulder, giving her a gentle squeeze. She kissed the top of his hand, and then he reached for the fruit bowl on the table. He ran his fingers over the figs and dates, rejecting them all. But when he came to the tray of honey cakes beside the bowl, he scooped one into his fingers and put the entire cake into his mouth. He gazed out over the landscape and moaned in delight at the sweet savory taste.

Shira had to be careful with her husband's diet. So many foods upset his stomach lately. She had reduced his intake of food to vegetables, dates, figs, and, of course, her honey cakes. Samuel could not get enough of her honey cakes.

"I know nothing of the afterlife, but I hope for your honey cakes." Then Samuel bent over and kissed the top of her head before continuing his rotation around the rooftop.

Shira smiled at his affection. What she had presented him would be difficult to read, and his kiss was a sign that he might approve. She shielded her eyes from the bright sunlight as she looked beyond the courtyard, beyond where the barns once stood, beyond the private quarters where she had lived with her family as a child. The barns and her living quarters had long since been torn down and replaced with a single hospice for the first novices who had come to sit at the feet of the prophet Samuel.

In time, a single house of study with additional space for lodging was not enough. The ranks of the young men grew as they arrived from all over the country to receive prophetic training as well as learn the divine origins of creation, the lineage of their ancestry, the wanderings, the truth behind the Ten Words of Yahweh, propositional laws of Moses, the whole history of Israel, and the final great sermon of Moses on the plains of Moab before climbing Mount Nebo to die. Several buildings had to be erected to accommodate the increasing number of students: structures to house the young men, a hall for meals, two buildings just for classrooms, and a library to store all the scrolls and manuscripts as well as the space required to manufacture materials to record the stories of Yahweh and His chosen.

The success of this school for prophets helped Samuel and Shira achieve a level of peace with the painful reminder of the failure with their sons. Samuel had banished Joel and Abijah to the precinct of southern Israel where they could practice their compromised version of the law. What judicial damage resulted from their perversions of justice and what dishonor they brought to the profession of judge, would be upon their own heads. Shira and Samuel had little contact with their sons, which was preferable to both, but Shira knew her husband took the parental failure much harder than she did. Shira had hoped for grandchildren. And her husband had hoped to pass the mantle of prophet and judge on through the generations of their family. But regardless of the deep disappointment they shared, neither Shira nor her husband would want the abasement their sons brought upon themselves to come home.

Three men emerged from the library and started up the worn lane toward the house. She recognized Nathan and Jashar, a younger student in his second year at school. Then she smiled in recognition when Gad's shape came into sharper focus.

"Samuel, Nathan and Jashar are coming up the road, and I believe Gad is with them." Shira turned to see Samuel standing motionless as if he were a sculpture, his head buried in the crook of his arm, the scroll he had been reading lying at his feet.

Shira rose from her seat and raised her hand to the approaching men, signaling for them to wait and not climb the stairs to the rooftop. Then she slipped over to her husband and placed both hands on the arm covering his face.

Samuel resisted at first, not giving in to Shira's effort to pull his arm away. He exhaled a swollen breath of grief. "Do not look upon me. I am ashamed to reveal my face."

"My love, what pains you?" Shira dug her fingers into his thick arm.

"My mother's voice." His anguish expressed a long sleeping torment that had now awakened. "I hear her voice as clear as I hear yours: her words, her prayer in my ear, my howls of terror on that day. I thought I would feel no more pain from that memory at the Tabernacle, that the grief had been expelled. I was mistaken."

Shira looked down at the scroll fluttering from a slight breeze and bent to retrieve it. She spread it open and saw the marks of her husband's tears and the smudged lettering. A new copy could be rewritten, and she quickly rolled it up.

"My dear, shall I tell Nathan this is not the time to be disturbed?"

Samuel lowered his arm and shook his head. "No. No. I was just taken by surprise. I did not realize the memory would have such a sharp pierce."

Shira tucked the scroll underneath her arm, lifted the corner of her apron, and dabbed the slivers of moisture from beneath Samuel's red eyes. "This is painful, I know. As you say, the ways of Yahweh are past knowing."

"And the older I become, the less I seem to know the purposes of Yahweh."

The apron slipped from her hand as she caressed Samuel's face with her fingers.

"This I understand." Samuel took Shira's hand into his own and pressed his lips upon her palm. "This I feel. This I know. Your touch is all I need to know."

Shira leaned her body into Samuel. She wrapped her arms around him as he did the same. Inside the comfort of their embrace was the solace of heaven.

After a long silence Samuel asked, "You say Gad is here?"

"With Nathan and Jashar. I can tell them to return later."

"This is unexpected. I should see them at once."

Shira began to pull away, but Samuel gently guided her back into his arms and kissed her lips before fully releasing her. She smiled from the pleasure of his kiss. Then she raised the scroll before him. "The prayer and prophesy belong in the book."

"We shall see." Samuel nodded. "We shall see."

"I will fetch them." Shira went to the front of the roof's ledge and waved for the three men to come up the staircase outside of the house.

Long ago, Gad had chosen the king over the prophet. When Samuel had sent word through Nathan for him to return to Ramah after the death of Queen Ahinoam, Gad determined that he should remain in Gibeah and serve the royal family. He had witnessed certain traits within the prophet's character that had given him pause, traits he believed revealed an unnecessary and unfair bias toward the king. Since Samuel had severed his ties with the king and refused more dealings with him after the murder of Agag, king of the Amalekites, by the prophet's hand, Gad believed he had a responsibility to be a prophetic presence in the court even if his spiritual connection with Yahweh was underused or even ignored.

While remaining faithful in his role as prophet, he served the king and the royal family in whatever capacity they required. He had provided little spiritual service or religious instructions since the early days of the king's reign. Much had happened since the victory in the Valley of Elah when the shepherd had slain the giant. Gad witnessed a steady erosion of stability inside the court, and it had all begun with the arrival of the shepherd. He believed the king might not be suffering such mental turmoil and the royal family might not be on a present course of potential ruin if the shepherd had never entered the camp and opened his mouth to sing.

Gad was not sure how he would be received. He and Samuel had not laid eyes on one another since the slaughter of the Amalekites. While Gad respected and honored Samuel, he had had enough time and separation from his master to shape and determine his view of his own role as a prophet of Yahweh and how he might serve the Almighty. Gad was often bewildered as to what he might do as a prophet of Yahweh. While he did believe his presence was vital inside the royal court, he did not want to cut himself off from Samuel or the community of prophets. He needed them and their support, and most of all, he needed to know that Samuel would not treat him as he had treated King Saul.

"Are you faithful, my son?" Samuel spoke into Gad's ear as he embraced him.

Shira led Nathan and Jashar toward her worktable, leaving Gad alone with Samuel at the top of the stairs.

"I hope I am faithful in my heart to Yahweh, my lord," Gad replied, a slight quiver in his voice, unsure his answer would satisfy the prophet. "And faithful to the Almighty by my service to the king and the royal family."

"So, this is a visit and not a return to the fold," Samuel stated flatly.

Gad looked into the prophet's inscrutable face and chose not to waver. "I come with reports and documents. I come for council and prayer, but I intend to return to the court."

"Good. Good. It is enough, then." Samuel placed his arm on Gad's shoulders. "The king knows you are here?"

Gad took this fatherly gesture as an encouraging sign of his master's favor.

"Prince Jonathan knows. He said he would inform the king of my journey."

After a firm squeeze of Gad's shoulders, Samuel allowed his hands and arms to fall to his side. "You trust the prince?"

"I traveled yesterday and arrived after dark, so I was not in attendance for the evening meal with the royal family. If the king notices, he may inquire after my absence. I trust the integrity of the prince. He will speak for me, defend me if necessary."

"Defend you."

"If the prince tells the king that I am paying you visit, it may not go well for him or for me upon my return. The mood of the king has dramatically shifted. He has become much more unpredictable since the new arrival to the court."

"I understand the king's concubine has given him a son."

"Yes, Lady Rizpah has given birth to a son. They named him Armoni. That and Prince Jonathan's recent marriage has brightened the king's mood. But the arrival I refer to is the singing shepherd from Bethlehem, of the tribe of Judah."

"The one who slew the giant in the Valley of Elah," Samuel said.

"The same." Gad patted the leather satchel hooked over his shoulder. "I wrote the story of the siege, of how the shepherd came into our midst and defeated the champion of the Philistines."

"Based on the reports I have heard, it was a miracle to be sure," Samuel said.

"My lord, a miracle is the only explanation." Gad's voice quivered at the wonder of his memory. "The shepherd and I are from the same village, and though I did not know him, I knew of the family. He comes out of the hills and slays a giant. And by this one act, all of Israel is smitten with him. I cannot account for it."

"The young man did an amazing feat. I look forward to your report, my son."

Gad could not discern any nuance of ill or favorable emotion toward the young man from Samuel's stern expression.

"My lord, it is so much more," Gad continued. "He is a shepherd with no military skill, and yet he kills a giant with a sling and a stone. Then, after the battle, if one can even call it a battle, more of a mass carnage, Prince Jonathan and the shepherd are bound in a blood covenant. I assisted in the ceremony. Then the king makes him a captain over a thousand men. Abner puts him through intense military training, and the king sends him on campaigns against the Philistines. My lord, he is victorious in every campaign. He never returns empty-handed, but with carts full of spoils. He comes home with no wound, no physical sign of the slightest scratch. Even his armor does not appear to be damaged."

The words poured from Gad, driven by the sheer force of his incomprehension at what the shepherd had achieved in so short a time and his effect upon the royal family, indeed, the whole nation. Indeed, upon Gad's heart.

"The king had offered his eldest daughter in marriage to the man who slew the giant, and this is so outrageous I cannot take hold of it in my mind, but the shepherd refuses the king. Says he is unworthy, that his family is of low esteem. The king, however, goes through the charade of a betrothal, but at the last minute, the king changes his mind and betrothed Princess Merab to another, the prince's armor-bearer, to keep from shaming her. Yet, no one speaks against the shepherd. His behavior is shocking, and no one holds him in contempt."

"He dances in the hand of Yahweh, my son," Samuel said quietly.

"His dancing is agile enough to escape the king's attempt to impale him with his spear," Gad said.

This information came as a shock to Samuel. When he had anointed David to be the next king, Samuel had no idea how or when a transfer of power would take place. To have a new king arise from another family and different tribe was not the natural order. The stability of the nation could be thrown into jeopardy if the king's firstborn did not assume the throne after Saul.

Samuel knew his credibility would be in question for having anointed two kings from differing clans and tribes. It could be construed as the prophet trying to play one king off another for his own advantage. Samuel had hoped Saul would live out his days without ever learning of his secret visit to Bethlehem to anoint a new king, and that David would remain in obscurity, a shepherd in the hills, far from the life of the court and the king.

But the unexpected had happened without regard for Samuel's council or desires. The shepherd had vaulted into heroic status: a giant-slayer, a captain in the army, a member of the royal court, in covenant relationship with the prince, living the secret life of a future king, and according to Gad, whose life had almost been snuffed out.

What was Yahweh doing, or what was Yahweh allowing to take place?

"The king attempted to kill the shepherd?" Samuel's mind reeled. He had simply obeyed the will of Yahweh to anoint another to be the king, and now the two kings were in constant contact, one attempting to kill the other. He had warned the tribal leaders of this. If they wanted to be like other nations and have a king, then such unpredictable misbehavior should be expected.

He had no pleasure in this news. He had had to face the truth in his heart that he had little affection for Saul and had struggled with his resentment in

Saul's rise to prominence, yet to hear of such turmoil in the kingdom, made his heart feel as though it had been run through. He looked at Gad who clutched his chest.

His breathing accelerated and the sweat beaded across his forehead. "I witnessed it myself," Gad gasped.

"Why would the king be threatened by the shepherd?" Samuel posed the question to see if David had gone against his wishes to proclaim himself king and how the prophet had anointed him as proof of the title. Samuel's body was not agile enough to dodge a spear that would most certainly be hurled at him for such a treasonous act.

"The king is fearful and jealous. But it is much more than that, my lord. There is an evil malady that possesses the king's soul." Tremors shook Gad's body.

Samuel took Gad by the arm and guided him to the ledge where he sat. Samuel called, "Bring me a cup of wine, Nathan."

Shira took her husband's empty cup and filled it with wine, and then handed it to Nathan who brought it immediately.

"Here, my lord," Nathan said, handing the cup to Samuel.

"It is for Gad," Samuel instructed, and Nathan gave the cup to his friend. When Nathan started to leave them, Samuel spoke, "You need to hear what Gad has to say."

"What of Jashar?" Nathan asked.

"He should remain with Shira," Samuel replied.

Nathan waved for Jashar to remain with Shira.

"The fewer the ears, the better," Samuel said.

Gad took several sips, but Samuel removed the cup from the young prophet's trembling hand and set it upon the ledge next to him.

"Pace yourself, my son. You need a clear head to relay this story to us." Samuel lowered his voice to address Nathan. "Do not overreact to this news, Nathan. Do not let your face or voice belie your heart, but Gad was witness to the king's attempt to take the life of the shepherd."

"He attempted to kill the shepherd?" Nathan turned his back to Shira and Jashar. He kept his voice neutral, though Samuel could see in his eyes that Nathan was startled by the news.

"The king hurled his spear in the middle of a prophetic frenzy," Gad interjected. "I wrote of the incident in my report."

"Did the shepherd say or do anything to provoke the king?" Nathan asked.

"Nothing. The shepherd has kept his distance from the king since our victory in the Valley of Elah. He presents himself only when summoned, and the summons are rare and usually for one purpose."

"Which is?" asked Samuel.

"To sing for the king."

"Sing for the king," Nathan repeated, stated as such for clarity.

"Until recently, the shepherd's playing was the only balm the king received for his unpredictable moods," Gad explained. "I was the one who first heard the lad sing for the soldiers when we were camped at Elah. I was the one who insisted the prince hear him play. I was the one who suggested the shepherd's music might comfort the king who had been forlorn since the beginning of the siege. Yahweh has gifted him with a voice like no other. No court musician can compare. And his music worked its spell. That night in the king's tent, the shepherd's playing lifted the king's heart. He lifted all our hearts. I have written the story down. It is in the report."

"I understand," Samuel said. "But when did the king try to kill the shepherd?"

"The king and I would study the Sacred Scrolls together in those early days of his reign. You remember, Nathan, how he would come to our tent before dawn, and we would pour over the writings of Prophet Moses?"

Nathan gave a cursory nod to the truth of Gad's memory, but Samuel sensed that Nathan did not want him to perceive any sympathy for the king. "Continue, Gad. Where did this attack take place?"

"In the king's sleeping chamber of the new royal dwelling. I was thrilled when Jarib, the king's secretary, came and said that I had been requested to bring the scrolls to the king's rooms. The shepherd had recently returned from another successful raid on a Philistine village, and he had been summoned by the king to bring his kinnor."

"Was there anyone else with you in the chamber?" Nathan asked.

"When I arrived with the scrolls, Jarib greeted me at the door. I could hear the shepherd playing and singing from inside the chamber. Before Jarib ushered me into the rooms, he expressed his pleasure that I and the shepherd were there, that the king had summoned us, and that the king desired to be engaged in worshipful experience.

"After Jarib closed the doors, only a curtain separated me from the open space on the other side. I expected to see Rizpah and the king's newborn son when I parted the curtains, but they were not present. Out of nowhere, the king rushed by me like a phantom as I prepared to step into the large room. His lofty, dark presence startled me. The shepherd sat in a far corner, and he caught my eye and motioned for me to enter. By his expression, I could tell the circumstances were abnormal.

"The king was pacing the room, moaning, growling, uttering the occasional intelligible word, sounding more like a prowling beast in heat than a human being in enthusiastic praise of Yahweh. His armor was on its display pedestal in the opposite corner from where the shepherd was playing, and as he passed by it, King Saul gripped his spear and brandished it in a threatening manner as he continued to pace."

"Could you understand anything of what he was saying?" Samuel asked.

"I could not call it prophesying. I could not call it worship or prayer. Nor was he singing along with the shepherd. It was a jumble of words, more like tormented denunciations laced with the name of Yahweh, who the king evoked to do his bidding, to make his aim straight, for his spear to hit its mark. 'Yahweh, pin him to the wall,' I heard him cry before hurling the spear."

Gad's face was etched in what Samuel assumed must have been the expression he wore when looking upon the king in his state of mental disturbance. Gad was now deep inside the reminiscence of his story, locked inside the focused rhythm of music and motion and madness. The skin on Gad's face quivered like the flesh of an antelope before it flees from danger.

Both Samuel and Nathan placed their hands upon Gad's shoulders to steady their student and friend.

Samuel took the cup of wine from the ledge and lifted it for Gad to sip, but he refused.

"I dropped my satchel at my feet the moment it happened." Gad placed his hands over his mouth. He removed them at intervals, so he could finish the dreadful story. "The sound, I remember the sound of the spear as it flew through the air. Its flight was too fast for my eye, and then the smashing of the iron point into the wall was like the blow of a smithy's hammer. The king stood immobile beside his armor, glaring, a deep, bestial breathing emitting from his lungs.

"The shepherd lay on his back, clutching his kinnor to his chest, his eyes bursting from their sockets. Had he not flattened himself upon the floor, he would have been impaled. In the next instant, the shepherd was at my side, gripping my arm and dragging me back through the curtain and out the door. The king's baleful stare remained fixed on the point where the spear was lodged in the wall, and as we burst through the doors, the king exploded with a howling I could only describe as gruesome. Jarib raced into the chambers and closed the doors after him. I have not seen the king in private or in public since that day."

Gad remained motionless. Samuel sensed it was to keep his soul intact.

"By retelling this story, I feel the depth of my failure. My failure to you, my lord, to the king, and to the Almighty. It is as if the king's spear has pierced the breast of heaven and the blood of Yahweh is raining upon the nation."

Samuel raised the cup of wine to Gad's lips once again and held it for him as the young prophet drained the warm liquid.

Then Samuel bent and kissed the top of Gad's head. "I never expected this. I never wished for this."

"The king's mind appears diseased by many shadows," Nathan said.

"David casts numerous shadows," Gad offered. "Shepherd, singer, soldier..."

And king. Samuel did not utter the word.

"All shadows point to the shepherd, though everyone now refers to him as 'Captain,'" Gad said. "The king's melancholy was manageable until the captain arrived. At first, we thought he would prove a healing agent, and now... now, I fear the worst."

"You need not return, my son." Samuel set down the empty cup and laid a hand upon Gad's shoulder. "You can remain here and be safe."

"What of our people, my lord?" Gad asked. "What of our kingdom, our king? Surely, Yahweh has not abandoned us or the king. Surely, Yahweh means to forge and shape His people into a strong, unified nation. Must I not bear witness to this process?"

Samuel could not deny his admiration of this young man. He had taken it as an insult when Nathan first told him that Gad would not be returning to Ramah and his school of the prophets, that he had chosen to remain with the king and serve in his court. Time had allowed Samuel to view what he first perceived as a personal affront could be the hand of Yahweh. Why should not a prophet of Yahweh, that he had trained, be present in the court of the king?

"Yes, my son. A prophet of Yahweh must bear witness. I believe your shoulders are capable of bearing the heavy weight of such a task."

Samuel helped Gad to his feet. Then he cupped his hands around Gad's plump face and kissed him on each cheek. "Yahweh is with you, my son."

The prophet's kiss and blessing flooded Gad with acceptance and peace, and he nodded his thanks. To be safe, to be back among his own kind, to just write and study and debate the decrees of Yahweh and precepts of Moses, that would bring him such joy. But he was compelled otherwise.

Gad embraced Samuel. Then he reached into his leather satchel and took out the scrolls, handing them to Nathan.

"I made a copy for Ahimelech," Gad said. "After the victory at the Valley of Elah, Ahimelech did not wish to return to Gibeah, but went to the city of Nob and his Levitical school. He wants to be near his son, Abiathar, train him to take his place someday. I believe these young priests and Levites must know the stories of Yahweh and his people."

"I agree with you Gad." Nathan took the scrolls. "Will you stay the night?"

"I must return by nightfall. I wish not to put the prince under any additional stress to defend me to the king."

"Jashar and I will get your mule from the stables." Nathan waved to the young prophet to follow him down the steps.

Gad and Samuel watched as the two prophets headed toward the outside stairway.

Samuel turned Gad toward him before he spoke. "You are a brave man, my son. It is why I must tell you that it is no accident David of Bethlehem resides at the king's court. And that it is the will of Yahweh you must return to look after the present king as well as the future one."

"Yes, my lord. I think the prince will make an excellent king when it is his time."

Samuel checked that Nathan and Jashar had descended the stairs before he continued.

"Prince Jonathan will never be king." Samuel returned his eyes to Gad. "I did not know how Yahweh would work his will with the shepherd. After the defeat of the Amalekites and the death of their ruler by my hand, I was instructed of Yahweh to anoint a new king: the shepherd from Bethlehem. He is now a captain of a thousand men. And in due time, by the divine will of Yahweh, David will become king of Israel."

Gad sat on the ledge to keep his spinning head from causing him to fall to his knees. He had just eased the burden of his mind and begun to feel some relief by telling his story. In truth, he could not fathom that he had witnessed an effort by a reigning king to kill a future one. He could not imagine what he had seen or believe what he had just heard. He could not absorb that it was he who had introduced the shepherd to the prince. It was all too astounding.

"My son, listen." Samuel bent to look Gad in the eye. "This is the will of Yahweh. We only bear witness and do not stand in the way or attempt to thwart. The plan is unalterable, and a prophet of Yahweh must wait and watch no matter how painful the circumstances or our desire for a different course. Do you understand?"

Gad nodded stiffly, still in mid-comprehension of this news.

"Besides David and his family, only Nathan and I, and now you, have this knowledge. For the survival of the kingdom, this secret must be kept until Yahweh further reveals the purpose behind the destiny."

"Should I speak with the captain, tell him of my knowledge?"

"I will leave that to your judgment. Given the circumstances, do not let this knowledge increase the danger to you or the captain. Just remember, Yahweh is at work."

Gad rose. He lifted his eyes and looked into the face of the prophet. Its severe expression had softened. "I return with your blessing, my lord?"

"With my blessing and my prayers, my son." A smile broke through the curtain of Samuel's white beard. "One last thing. Did you write down the incident of the king's attempt on the life of the captain?"

"I did not, my lord. Should I?"

"Such knowledge is dangerous to all concerned. If others in the kingdom became aware, it could create such upheaval that would cause irreparable harm. But it cannot be ignored either. If this is a new pattern of behavior with the king, then it must be documented. So, yes, you must create a written account of the event, but no one is to read it, and you are not to send it by courier. You will bring the scroll next time you come to Ramah. Now do not be afraid, my son. Yahweh is with you."

"Yahweh is with you, my lord," Gad replied, his heart filling with courage as he turned and made his way down the steps.

Nathan and Jashar met Gad in front of the house with the mule and a skin of fresh water and food for the journey back to Gibeah.

"I was angry with you for not returning with me to Ramah and remaining with the king." Nathan handed Gad the reins. "I see now I was wrong to be so."

"I am finding that I am wrong in so many things."

The two friends embraced before Gad climbed onto the mule.

"And what of our young student prophets?" Gad settled into the saddle. "Do you see potential?"

"Here stands one of our brightest." Nathan pointed to Jashar, and the young man instantly blushed and took a few steps in retreat. "An inquiring mind with a depth of understanding that excels. Skilled at lettering as well."

"That is good to know. I may have a job for you at court should the day arrive. There is a certain captain who sings and plays music like no other. He needs someone to transcribe the words to his songs and to teach him lettering."

"You mean the giant-slayer?" Jashar said.

Gad gave Nathan a knowing look. "One and the same. When Nathan says you are ready, I may call upon you."

Jashar was unable to conceal his elated grin though he covered his lips with his hands.

"Yahweh is with you, my brother." Gad snapped the reins.

"And with you," Nathan said, slapping the mule's rump as it plodded away.

Glancing to the roof as he rode out of the courtyard, Gad caught sight of Samuel leaning over the ledge waving.

Gad turned his face toward Gibeah and dug his heels into the sides of the mule. With the blessing and approval of the prophet, he could face any adversity.

Shira wrapped her arm around her husband's waist and together they watched Gad ride out of the courtyard.

"I am sending him back into the unknown fraught with danger." Samuel nodded toward Gad as he disappeared over the crest of the hill.

"Much like your parents did with you so long ago," Shira said.

"So long ago, yes," Samuel said. "My life feels like a long series of departures."

Shira pressed against Samuel, and he drew her closer into his side.

"Your parents' stories are too important to leave out of your book," Shira said.

"I am concerned how my parents will be remembered. I do not want to leave the impression they abandoned me. I thought it better to begin the book with me in the Tabernacle hearing the voice of Yahweh for the first time."

"How many of us ever hear the voice of Yahweh?" Shira asked. "It is too rare an occurrence. What most know to be true comes from a slow revelation of faith, of a life filled with struggle and only enough joy to make it tolerable. Your parents' stories show the truth in perseverance, a faith lived daily, not the sudden wonder of divine visitations."

"I wrote those early stories for me in the room above the stable when I returned home to stay: my mother's prayer, my father's prophesy, both spoken in the Tabernacle. I did not intend them to be included in the story of Yahweh and the history of His people."

"Such expressions of truth in the hearts of your parents reveal the truth in the heart of Yahweh."

Samuel looked into the shadowed and creased face of his beloved wife. She had never left their property except for the occasional journey in those early years of his traveling judgeship when the boys were young. She had experienced and seen so little of the outside world, yet her soul contained so much of its wisdom.

His fingertips traced over her features, sparking tiny lightning bolts connecting flesh to flesh and restoring color to her ashen cheeks. There was no turning from her. There was no sad destiny with her at his side. There was no tale of wounded souls and weary bodies left to the judgment of history. There was only the holiness of her smile and the deep-bone strength of her arms around his frame.

Chapter 21

KISH HAD DIED DURING THE NIGHT. IN THE DAYS LEADING UP to his death, Saul never left his father's side. The time with Kish, caring for his every need, provided a calming effect on Saul's mind. Bathing his father, changing the soiled bedding, serving him the little food and drink Kish could tolerate, brought Saul into sharp focus.

Jonathan handled the duties of governance, and Jarib organized the burial preparations, including summoning Ahimelech the High Priest from Nob. When Kish finally breathed his last, all procedures for the burial were in place.

The Levites, charged with the preparations of burial, washed and anointed the body with oils and spices before wrapping it in strips of linen soaked for days in a vat of aromatic resins. A heavy cloud of perfume mixed with smoke from burning oil lamps and candles, and the decay of death, enveloped the room.

When Saul took a roll of linen from the hand of a Levite and began to wrap Kish's right leg, the Levite solemnly told the king he would be defiled by touching a dead body. Saul ignored the admonishment and encased the leg from thigh to toe. He knew the feeling of defilement, yet this simple rite had the opposite effect on Saul's heart. It cleansed his soul and brought him peace.

When the Levites finished, they collected their funereal supplies and left Saul alone with his father.

Saul knelt beside the bed. "My father: son of Abiel, son of Zeror, son of

Bechorah, son of Aphiah, the clan of Matri from the tribe of Benjamin, the last-born son of our great father Jacob. You leave your bones and body to the dust, but your soul has passed into the shadows of Sheol."

Saul tucked some loose wrapping underneath Kish's shoulder.

"You lived long enough to bounce the last of your grandsons on your knee. I confess I have not spoken to the child or held him since Ahinoam died. Perhaps I should crack the door open to the boy. I was a good king with her at my side. You believed in me as well. Now, you both have departed. And I? What may become of me?" Saul rose and gently laid a hand upon his father's head. "May the abode of the dead have thick walls to prevent you from seeing my follies."

Saul returned to his chambers and dismissed his servants. He chose solitude. After bathing, he wrapped his loins and buttocks in a grain sack. He laced his sandals around his ankles and slipped a loose, russet-colored garment of sackcloth over his head, the hem of which dropped to just below his knees.

When soft knocking came from his chamber doors, Saul opened them and stepped into the hall. The king looked at his secretary for an opinion of his appearance, and Jarib nodded in approval.

When Saul exited the private residence, escorted by Jarib, the Levites who had prepared Kish for burial were gathered around a wooden altar where the body rested waiting transport. Jarib slipped from behind the king and signaled to the Levites who snapped into position, three on each side, and gripped the wooden poles with the canvas frame that bore the body.

Saul smiled at his cousin.

Abner bowed his head in response. The commander had stationed the king's elite soldiers along the path that led up the hill, a column on each side. Those citizens who had come to pay respects to the king and his family crowded in behind the soldiers.

Jeush approached Saul, carrying the long pole bearing the insignia of the wolf and the crown, the tribe of Benjamin and the king's clan, and knelt before the king. "My lord, I request permission to lead the procession to the burial cave."

"My faithful friend," Saul said. "You do my family a great honor."

Jeush took his place in front of the Levites and awaited the signal.

Saul shifted his eyes to his children assembled to the side of the altar bearing the body of their grandfather. He reached out for them to gather around, but it was Ish-bosheth who broke and ran toward his father, nearly tripping on the hem of his robe as his little legs carried him over the uneven ground. Ish-bosheth's older siblings gasped at the child's bold action. Saul could see the freezing dread on the faces of his children at their youngest brother's un-restrained action. He had never spoken the boy's name or acknowledged his existence. Now, in front of this gathering, an innocent child was forcing Saul to pay attention.

"Where Abba-Kishie go?" cried the boy. He wept as he clutched Saul's robe.

When Merab and Mikal were about to rescue their father from this un-settling moment, Saul raised his hand for them to remain where they stood. He placed his hand on the boy's head and pressed him against his leg to stop his desperate tugging.

"Your grandfather has departed this life." Saul spoke calmly and patted the top of Ish-bosheth's curly blond hair.

This small child stared up at him in wonder. Saul had spoken to him. He had placed his hand upon his son to comfort him. At Saul's great height, his child must think of him as some giant able to reach up his hand and touch the sky.

Saul noticed the Levites carrying the shrouded body of his father were barefoot.

"We are going to take your grandfather to that cave." Saul pointed up the hill to the entrance. "There he will sleep next to your...next to the others."

"Will Abba-Kishie awake?" the boy asked, tugging again on Saul's robe.

"He will sleep until you come to understand such things." Saul felt this immediate urge to wrap his arms around his son. He knelt in front of the boy so he might be eye level with Ish-bosheth. "I wish your Abba-Kishie had not gone to sleep. I wish he could stay here to watch you grow into your man-hood. But I will watch you, my child."

Saul began to unlace his sandals. "Now, I need you to do something for me. I must take off my sandals and walk behind those men carrying your grandfather."

In imitation of his father, Ish-bosheth plopped onto the ground and be-gan loosening his own sandals.

"You do not need to remove your footwear." Saul placed his hand on the boy's arms. "But would you carry my sandals for safekeeping?"

The child nodded and rose. Once Saul removed both sandals, he offered them to Ish-bosheth. The boy curled his small fingers around the leather thongs and drew them to his tiny chest.

Saul rose and eyed Ish-bosheth clutching the sandals as if holding a great prize. A deep weariness of being a king, of being a father, of being a man settled over Saul.

If only he was a child again with a child's perplexed and curious mind at the world around him, ready to accept a strong and compassionate figure to give comfort and guidance. If only.

Mikal ignored Ish-bosheth and went straight to her father. She let Merab scoop up the child and hand him to his twin older brothers who would look after him during the procession and burial. Mikal clutched Saul's arm as she waited for Merab to slip around to the other side.

"I feel your strength, Abba." Mikal dug her fingers into her father's upper arm.

"You are my strength this day." Saul patted Mikal's hand.

Once Merab stood beside the king, Mikal looked behind her to assure that the family members were in place and ready to begin the funeral march. She gave an encouraging smile to Levana, Jonathan's young bride, who stood beside her brother looking pale and unstable. Because the king had been preoccupied with caring for Grandfather Kish, Jonathan had been unable to tell him the good news, so he confided in Mikal the reason for Levana's recent bouts of nausea. Mikal knew the good news of this addition to the royal lineage would help ease her father's grief at the loss of his father.

When Merab took Saul's other arm, Mikal whispered. "It is time, Abba." And she led him toward the wooden altar.

Once Mikal had positioned her father behind the Levites, Abner ordered the procession to commence. Jeush began his solo march up the hill, carrying the banner of the king and the tribe of Benjamin. The Levites hoisted the pallet with Grandfather Kish's body off the wooden altar and marched behind Jeush.

Mikal watched carefully for any sign her father's sadness could bode a darker turn in his ever-shifting moods. Her father appeared calm and stable as they proceeded up the incline.

She glanced behind her to see Jonathan put his arm around Levana, giving her the support she needed. Adriel walked behind his future wife, Merab. The twins, Ishvi and Malki, followed with Ish-bosheth between them clutching his father's sandals to his chest. Abner fell in beside Rizpah behind the others and holding her newborn son, Armoni. Mikal caught sight of Rizpah's furtive smile at Abner whose face remained impassive and unreadable as he stared down at Rizpah and her child. Mikal could not help but wonder if the child Rizpah carried was truly her father's progeny.

The two columns of soldiers provided a protective funnel from the base of the hill to the cave, keeping the lamenting crowds from getting too close to the grieving family. Mikal appreciated that each soldier bowed his head in reverence as the Levites passed with her grandfather's body and remained bowed as she and her father and sister passed.

When the procession approached the mouth of the cave, a select group of court musicians led by Paltiel, the court composer, began to sing a somber lamentation accompanied by their musical instruments. Mikal cringed as she listened to what passed for music, glaring at the musicians. She and her family were spoiled by David's exquisite musicianship. She checked her father's face for signs of disappointment in the lament or fatigue from the strain of the last days tending to his father.

Saul looked healthy. His eyes were clear and fixed on the cave entrance, his arms strong, his footing sure, even though he wore no sandals. His arms seemed to be carrying her and not relying on any assistance.

She turned her attention back to the crowd and caught sight of David briskly approaching from the stables. He still wore his armor, exactly what he was wearing when she had surprised him outside the stables just days ago as he and his men were preparing to leave on their latest raid by order of the king.

Mikal was never one to shy away from what she wanted. As David was adjusting the saddle on his horse outside the stables, Mikal needed to know if by rejecting Saul's offer to marry her sister that the captain's heart might be inclined toward her.

"You stood your ground against my father," Mikal said. "Why did the giant-slayer decline my father's generous offer to marry my sister? You won her."

"I had rather have faced another giant than tell your father that I could not accept his bountiful offer," David replied. "But who am I, and what is my family that I should be given such a place in the king's household?"

A faint smile hovered over Mikal's lips as she listened intently to David's words and observed his eyes and the expression on his face.

"Regardless of your reason for declining, my sister's suffering was brought to an end," Mikal said. "And I am grateful and pleased that you remain free."

Mikal knew her beauty could inspire. The folds of her garments, the fall of her hair upon her shoulders, the smell of rosewater from her body, the jeweled adornments glittering around her neck and forehead had a powerful effect.

"You slay giants. You battle the Philistines. You have the courage to face down my father. Is there anything you fear?" Mikal asked.

"Yahweh," David said without hesitation, and then added, "And you, my lady."

Mikal's gasp came as a surprise. She felt the heat of a flush to her face and a lightness in her head. Her tingling skin was brightening in color, but it brought her great pleasure to see a shade of pink rising in the captain's cheeks. It seemed that such impulsive honesty had brought mutual pleasure to their blushing faces.

"I cannot speak for Yahweh," Mikal said, her breath coming in short bursts. "Only for myself, and you have nothing to fear."

In every waking moment since their encounter outside the stables, Mikal had indulged in this memory savoring each detail. And seeing him now, her attention was drawn away from her father and the burial of her grandfather. She raised herself on tiptoe while they walked and watched David maneuver through the crowd and stop at the entrance of the cave behind Ahimelech, the High Priest, and Gad, the prophet.

David was looking for her, no one else, and she remained on tiptoe when the procession halted. In David's presence she was always on tiptoe. The captain was armored, dusty, and bedraggled after raiding Philistine villages, but the sight of him even in this slovenly condition made her skin quiver with a burning chill.

Saul watched as Jeush stepped to the side of the path once he reached the cave entrance, allowing the Levites to follow Jarib inside with the body. Jarib unlocked the gate into the burial crypt, and the Levites entered to deposit

Kish's body onto the stone slab. They would then exit, so the family might view the body one last time.

While Saul and the royal family waited for this process to be complete, Ahimelech and Gad stepped forward in front of the king and bowed low in reverence.

Ahimelech gave Saul a reassuring smile before he began his priestly blessing. Ahimelech placed his left hand inside the Breastplate of Judgment with its twelve precious stones and clutched the bag containing the Urim and Thummim. He placed his right hand just above Saul's heart.

"The Lord bless you and keep you," Ahimelech said, and then retrieved his hand from Saul's chest and reached into the bowl of ashes that Gad held. He grasped a handful of ash and held it before the king for him to lower his head. "The Lord make His face to shine upon you," Ahimelech continued, and he sprinkled the ashes over Saul's head. "And be gracious unto you."

With the residue of ash on his fingers, Ahimelech rubbed the powdery substance over the king's damp forehead and into his beard.

"The Lord lift up His countenance upon you." Ahimelech finished his blessing by directing his hand above the king's heart. "And give you peace."

"Let it be so," Saul whispered.

"Let it be so," Ahimelech said, and removed his left hand from beneath the Breastplate of Judgment. The high priest then unsheathed the knife attached to his waist and raised it to just below Saul's neck.

Saul did not even flinch. A part of him wished Ahimelech would take this opportunity to redirect the blade from the neckline of the sackcloth and plunge it into the penetrable skin below his chin. But the high priest remained true to the ceremony and only slit the garment. He replaced the knife into its sheath, then placed both hands onto the neckline of Saul's robe and rent the sackcloth.

"To honor the passing of Kish into Sheol, the land of the shadows, the king's garment is rent, exposing the king's torn heart at the loss of his father."

But Saul gently removed Ahimelech's hands from the torn material, and by his own strength, ripped the garment down to the middle of his chest.

"Like this garment, my father has been torn from me!" Saul cried, lifting his head. "Like this garment, my heart has been sundered. Like this garment, a son can no longer fulfill the command to honor his father in this life. May my father, Kish, the son of Abiel, pass into the land of the shadows and know the peace of the Almighty."

Ahimelech and Gad stepped back from the king and his daughters just as Jarib and the Levites exited the mouth of the cave.

"You may enter, my lord." Jarib pointed the way inside the cave.

"Will the high priest accompany us?" Saul looked at Ahimelech.

"Please forgive me, my lord, but Yahweh's anointed cannot enter the place of the dead." Ahimelech bowed his head to affirm his request for the king's remission. "As for my students who helped prepare the body of my lord's father, they too will be unclean until sundown. I cannot approach them until they have been made clean with the ceremonial waters and put on fresh robes. The sacredness of my holy office forbids me. I pray you understand."

"Sacredness. Holy. Anointed." Saul mulled the words he spoke. He wondered if the divine terms had any flavor on the tongue, any favorable effect on the heart and mind of a man. Would any truth arise? Would the words bring clarity to his soul? He muttered the words again, chewing them to detect a nuance of taste, but all he could savor was brackish spittle. He hoped the words might provide nourishment, but instead, he felt only harsh thirst. "I too was anointed once. Some time ago now."

Sweat coated in ash trickled down Saul's face. He could not step forward.

"Come, Abba. We should go inside."

Which daughter spoke he could not tell, but both were tugging on his arms. Still, he could not respond, he could not step forward.

"Abba," Jonathan said softly. "It is time we bid our grandfather farewell."

The gentle voice of his son, the first prince, the one in line to be king had come forward to lend his support to his sisters, his dutiful and loyal son.

Saul took a deep breath and said, "Yes, we do not want to be here any longer than we must." Then he pulled free from his two daughters' shared grasp, lunged between Ahimelech and Gad, and headed straight into the cave.

David observed Ahimelech and Gad as they stepped aside to allow the royal family to follow the king inside the ancestral burial cave, except for Mikal. She paused long enough to look in his direction. He had not moved. His eyes were focused upon her. For a reckless instant, it appeared that she was about to step toward him, that she did not wish to be standing in front of this cave any more than he did, that if it were at all possible by some magical

THE SINGER OF ISRAEL

feat they could both be transported from this distressing spot of earth. But David motioned to the princess, indicating he would wait, so Mikal entered the cave.

David came to attention as Abner passed by. The commander paused before Jeush standing at the mouth of the cave holding the pole with the tribal banner firmly in place.

"Jeush, once we are all well inside the cave, thank the people for showing their respect for the family, and then dismiss the crowd and the soldiers. The king has had his public display of grief. He will not want any more attention."

David waited for Jeush to carry out the commander's instruction, then he hurried toward Gad and Ahimelech as the two of them walked away from the cave.

"Have you just returned from battle?" Ahimelech turned toward David and held up his hand as he approached.

"I have, my lord."

"This is a foolish question, but did anyone die by your hand?" Ahimelech took a step backward.

"A few." David was baffled by the high priest's awkward retreat.

"And by your appearance, you have not bathed or changed your garments?"

"You are observant, my lord." David rapped his knuckles upon his armored breastplate. He was amused by Ahimelech's odd behavior and line of questioning. "I was on a mission for the king and came straight here."

"You must remain at a distance." Ahimelech raised both hands to be sure he was understood. "I cannot be contaminated by the presence of so much death."

Ahimelech began his brisk departure down the hill.

"My lord, Ahimelech, a moment please," Gad said, trying to stop Ahimelech.

When Ahimelech turned, David could tell that Gad's request did not sit well with the high priest.

"Gad, I have carried out my duty for the king. The other Levites will see to any final details required of the burial. Before the funeral, I performed my priestly blessing over a large vat of water from which the Levites will ceremonially cleanse themselves, as well as provided each man a clean and purified garment to wear after they burn and scatter the ash of their funereal garb.

Now, I would like to get to my carriage. The sooner I return to my home in Nob, the better."

"My lord, Ahimelech, for all your duties as high priest, I know I speak for the house of Saul in expressing gratitude, but it is another matter I wish to discuss."

"What is it, Prophet? And please be brief."

Gad glanced at David who thought the prophet wanted him to depart, so he began to walk back up the hill.

"Please stay, Captain." Then Gad turned back to the high priest. "Did you receive my report from the prophet Samuel? I left a copy for you when I was last in Ramah."

"What report is that?"

"Of the siege in the Valley of Elah and our victory over the Philistines."

"I have not seen it." Ahimelech started to move away again.

"This is puzzling, my lord. There has been ample time since my visit to Ramah for a copy of my report to have been delivered to you. You should have received your copy long before now. Perhaps, the prophet has forgotten."

"There is very little the great prophet forgets. I am the twelfth high priest in the line of our father Aaron, and I will die a young man because the father of the prophet Samuel pronounced a curse upon my lineage at the Tabernacle in Shiloh when my great-grandfather Eli presided as high priest."

"Was it not the word of the Almighty that was spoken that day?" Gad asked.

"And the sins of my fathers have been handed down to me." Ahimelech opened his arms and lowered his hands in a sign of submission to the truth of his future. "I am well aware of what was spoken and the bad blood between us. I will have a short life while the prophet lives to his ripe old age. It is hard justice from the Almighty and no mercy from Yahweh's prophet. I will never read that report, Gad, not if you delegated your master to deliver it. However, I am sure what you recorded is accurate and to be trusted. Now, I must be off. Yahweh is with you."

Ahimelech turned and hastened to make his exit.

"I did not know there was this ill feeling between the prophet and the high priest." David sidled up beside Gad stunned by this disclosure.

"The unalterable word of Yahweh is fulfilled through the generations of his people," Gad said, his shoulders drooping under the weight of this truth.

"It is why such stories must be written. If I do nothing else with my life, I will write and preserve the stories of Israel."

They silently watched Ahimelech rush down the hill, finally disappearing around the corner of the new royal dwelling.

"What of our story, the fearsome night in the king's chambers where I was nearly impaled against the wall?" David asked. "Have you written it down as well?"

"Not yet. The prophet did instruct me to write of the incident but said that it must not be shown to anyone."

"Who would believe such a terrible moment?" David said. "I hardly believe it."

"The great prophet Moses wrote that two witnesses are enough to establish a truth," Gad said as if to reassure both of them the veracity of their shared experience.

"Then we witnessed an alarming truth at the hand of Yahweh's anointed king," David said.

"And I fear it may only get worse before..." Gad stopped speaking.

"Before what?" David's eyes widened; his unease apparent at the prospect of what Gad might say. Did this prophet know he was looking right into the face of the king's successor? The tongue of the prophet caught in his throat seemed to indicate this was so. "Before what? Do not be hesitant with me."

"Before the will of Yahweh is fully known."

When he had spoken, Gad and the captain were immediately distracted by the royal family making their way out of the cave.

Mikal was the first to appear, skipping ahead of her father, her face lighting up when she spied David and Gad standing a little way down the slope. Gad easily discerned that the countenance of the princess did not brighten at the prospect of seeing him, and he could not help noticing how David responded in kind at the sight of Mikal.

"By all appearances the princess seems not to have suffered excessively at the death of her grandfather," Gad commented under his breath.

"Is she not beautiful?" The level of David's voice matched the prophet's.

The captain's ears must not have detected Gad's irony, the prophet concluded. He was surprised by this question, not of its earnestness, but that it was addressed to him, or so he thought. It was not asked in a commoner's elbow-to-the ribs crudity, but in the wonder of beholding something rarely seen. Gad had been included in David's appraisal of what he gazed upon, and his question to Gad made him his confidante. The invitation to friendship pleased Gad.

"I am no great judge of beauty. All I know is that her face does not enliven so when she looks at me."

Just as David was about to walk toward the princess who waited for him at the top of the slope, Gad reached out and took his arm. "Be careful, Captain. You move rapidly up the echelons and into the hearts of the royal family. Yahweh may be with you, but your destiny may be fraught with dangers."

David's expression took a sudden turn as if pricked by something sharp. "Are you using your powers as prophet to warn me of dangers ahead?"

"I do not have the prophetic ability of my master. You are a bold young man. I only encourage you to be careful which paths you choose to tread."

David gave Gad a look of admiration and replied, "Well said. Well taken." Then he pulled his arm free and moved toward Mikal, but then abruptly spun. "Gad, have you found a scribe to write my music?"

"The search has begun, Captain."

"I have melodies in my head that pour out of me." He held out imploring arms as if these songs would evaporate if Gad did not find that scribe.

A premonition grew in his spirit as Gad watched David move up the slope toward Mikal and the royal family gathering at the mouth of the cave. This bold young man, resplendent in his armor, embodying the charms of his newfound heroism, would someday destroy the house of Saul.

Gad did not know how or when. He did not know if this was an oracle forming in his mind or just a notion. He did not know if he should share any of this with anyone. What Gad knew, as he departed for his quarters, was that a terrible weight lay upon his heart.

Chapter 22

SAUL GLANCED BACK AND FOUND ISH-BOSHETH TROTTING
out of the cave, still clutching Saul's large sandals to his tiny chest. Saul motioned for him come and stand beside him. Ish-bosheth's puffy face spoke of
the child's hungry expression for a father's attention. *Just to be noticed.* Just to
be noticed and appreciated. This young lad, his flesh and blood son, reminded him of the disposition of his heart when he once had coveted the attention
of the prophet Samuel.

"You did well in there, my son." Saul pointed inside the cave, and then
he haltingly patted his son's head. "It must have seemed frightening. But you
did well."

Ish-bosheth's face beamed with pleasure.

"May I have my sandals please?"

When the sandals became entangled by the material and laces of his gown,
Saul knelt to help take them from his son's tiny hands.

Saul looked up to see Jonathan holding on to Levana as they exited the
cave. His wife was bent over, her hand covering her mouth. As soon as they
came into the open, Levana swerved past Saul, who remained kneeling beside
Ish-bosheth, and stumbled to where the musicians were about to play a final
lament in honor of Kish, composed by Paltiel. She emptied the contents of
her stomach with a beastly grunt.

The musicians scattered, but Paltiel stood directly in front of the expulsion, and his robe took the full brunt of Levana's spew. Paltiel's droopy-eyed

174

expression, wrapped in a well-groomed black beard, exploded in shock waves as he beheld his saturated garment.

Were it not for Jonathan, Levana would have collapsed onto the ground. Merab came to the rescue as did Rizpah. She handed her baby to Malki who immediately handed the child to Ishvi. Rizpah gripped Levana's elbow, and then she and Merab escorted the weeping young woman down the hill. Rizpah waved for the twins to follow with Armoni, which they did after their older brother sternly pointed for them to comply.

"The pungent smell of the cave must be overpowering," Saul said, flashing Jonathan a look of worry for the well-being of his daughter-in-law. "We stayed too long."

"It is not the smell, Abba. This has been the pattern for several days."

"What?" Saul finished tying his sandals and rose. "Is she in need of a healer?"

"No. But a few months from now, she will need a midwife."

Saul's face shifted from concern to elation, and he threw his arms around his son. The mood of sorrow had been overtaken by joy. The remaining members of the funeral party surrounded Jonathan, slapping his back and rubbing the top of his head.

Someone gripped Saul's arm and pulled it from Jonathan's neck.

"Abba, Captain David approaches," Mikal said.

Saul could see the flush of excitement on his daughter's face and her sudden attempt to appear poised. But the moment Saul heard Mikal speak the name of David, his body trembled as though stabbed with icy needles. His daughter's fingers dug into the ridged muscles of his arm as David approached and knelt before them.

"My lord, King of Israel." David bowed his head. "On the day my sovereign lord buried his father, I take the king's sorrow as if it were my own."

Saul tried to remember how long it had been since he last saw the man kneeling before him. The details of their last encounter were shadowy and tumultuous in his mind. The agitation in his body seemed a more accurate reaction to the lack of clarity in his memory. The darkness lurked at the edges of his vision, and he clasped his hand on top of Mikal's fingers curled over his forearm.

"You are dressed in battle armor," Saul growled. "This is a funeral, the day I lay my father to rest. Is this what you wear on such an occasion?"

Mikal removed her hand from beneath her father's clammy palm and rubbed his tense shoulder. She leaned her head forward and looked to Jonathan to say something.

"The captain was sent on a mission against our enemies," Jonathan said.

"Our enemies, yes," Saul stammered. "Our enemies, yes. Yahweh's enemies."

"We must be diligent to protect the kingdom," Abner said, stepping next to Jonathan. "Maintain a proper defense against your throne, my lord."

"You signed the order, my lord," Jarib said, adding his voice to the explanations.

Saul did not want to be calmed or treated like a child. "Yes, yes. I remember," Saul blurted with an edginess he hoped might disguise his confusion. "The wars of the Almighty. Rid the land of Yahweh's enemies. I know."

Had he not hurled his spear at this man? Had not the captain vanished after that? How could the giant-slayer be kneeling before him now?

"I just expected, well at least hoped, that my favorite musician might be home to sing for my father's burial." Saul began to regain a semblance of control.

David rose, but kept his head bowed.

Saul wanted to look into his face, but his captain kept his gaze lowered. David seemed hesitant, even fearful of making eye contact. What might David have seen in Saul's expression the last time the captain had come into his presence? Eyes like two coals burning with murderous intent? Saul felt a crackling of such a memory in his mind, yet he tried to keep the agitation from inflaming his heart.

"My sovereign king, if it is not too late and you desire it, I would be honored to sing for you now," David said.

"Yes, let David sing for you now." Mikal cut her eyes from David and smiled optimistically at her father.

Saul sensed that his daughter was too quick to approve of the captain's suggestion to sing a spontaneous lament for his father.

"You have no harp, no instrument," Saul said, his voice soft with disappointment.

"He refuses to rehearse or perform with any of the court musicians. He did not compose anything for this occasion, like some of us, and he never practices."

All heads turned in shock at Paltiel's outburst. Paltiel was the only one who thought this high-spirited commotion at the entrance of the burial cave inappropriate.

This was a funeral, and Paltiel had gone to great lengths to create and rehearse these laments in honor of the royal family. He had hoped the king would praise his creativity. Instead, a member of the royal family retched all over him. Paltiel was dumbfounded by the turn of events. His musicians had abandoned him, scurrying away with their instruments, and he stood alone in the musician's corner completely mortified, holding the front of his garment away from his chest with his pinched fingers flapping the front of his robe to circulate the air around him to dry his soiled garment.

Paltiel could have offered David the use of his kinnor and perhaps kept his dignity as court composer, but in his dejected state he lost all self-control and expelled his pent-up frustration with the royal family's favoritism toward this undisciplined musician.

Mikal positioned herself between her father and David. Her face expressed no humor at the sight of Paltiel's dismal countenance, nor did she show any sympathy for his unfortunate circumstance or his current disagreeable mood.

"The captain might not practice a day in his life and still play brilliantly," she said. "You, however, could practice daily and never match his skill."

Paltiel froze, stunned by the public critique of his musical mediocrity. The front of his damp garment slipped from his pinched fingers and sealed itself upon his chest. No one came to his defense. No one scolded the princess for her remark, nor did he detect a moment's regret on her face for having spoken her insult. He was thoroughly humiliated and the foul odor emanating from the sullied garment caused his eyes to water.

When Jarib slipped over and stood between him and the others, Paltiel knew by the secretary's grim countenance that the words he spoke out of frustration would be ones he regretted the rest of his life.

Still, Jarib tried to salvage some of Paltiel's dignity. "The king told me how he appreciated your efforts in honoring his father and instructed me to pay you double."

Whether the secretary spoke the truth or a benign falsehood, Paltiel could not tell. What registered in the court musician's eyes was the retrieval of his kinnor from where he had dropped it and the secretary pressing it into his damp chest.

"I will have payment sent to you before the day is out." Jarib indicated to Paltiel to make his departure.

If Paltiel could have evaporated into thin air it would have been preferable, but instead he allowed Jarib to guide him a few steps before launching him to continue under his own power. Paltiel clutched the kinnor to his breast as he stumbled down the slope, sure that his life as court musician had abruptly ended.

Paltiel was quickly dismissed and as quickly forgotten. The puerile scolding of a court musician did not dampen Saul's joy at the news that he would soon become a grandfather. By the time Jarib rejoined them, the subject of David creating an impromptu lamentation in honor of the king's father had turned to the captain congratulating the prince that a child would be arriving soon.

"Yes, the heir to the throne has secured our dynasty." Saul clapped a hand on his son's shoulder. "Save your music for the birth of my grandson, Captain."

"Do not be hasty, Abba. We do not know yet what we are having." Jonathan tried to tamp down his father's expectations.

"Correct. You might bring another Mikal into the world." Saul took perverse pleasure in angering his daughter with his icy sarcasm.

Mikal raised her hand to defend her honor but was interrupted by the captain.

"The world would be richer for it." David's whispered comment did not go undetected by her or the king.

Mikal looked at David to see if her ears deceived her. She clung to her father's arm not because she felt faint, but because she had this powerful urge to fling herself into the captain's arms. She had told him days before he had nothing to fear from her. Could this be the first sign of his growing boldness and affection?

"I was impertinent. Forgive me." David bowed his head.

Mikal suspected that David had never given such a compliment to anyone, and that he had said such sweet words to a princess—in front of her father, the king, and on the day of the death of the king's father, no less, while standing in front of the family burial cave—came as a complete surprise. Yet the words had not been held back, nor taken back.

"Yes, that was impertinent," Saul said. "You shall make it up to me at the evening meal. We are in mourning and must not eat till sunset, but you shall play for me then."

"As you wish, my lord," David replied.

"Until tonight then." Saul removed Mikal's hand from his forearm and stretched her open palm out to David. "Play well, and you may have a second chance to become a member of the royal family."

"Abba." Mikal yanked her hand out of Saul's grasp, hiding it behind her back. She might be in love with David, but she did not want to be treated as if she were a docile child used as strategy or reward.

Saul was amused by his daughter's indignity while savoring his captain's discomfort at the contingent opportunity before he marched down the hill. Everyone was surprised by the king's sudden leave-taking and hastily began to follow. Except Mikal, she remained where she was, as did David, though once the king passed him, he straightened his stooped posture.

Saul had not gone far when he turned around. Mikal looked as if she expected him to command her to follow, but his eyes were on Ish-bosheth standing at the mouth of the cave looking bewildered by the adult world.

"Come along, Ishie." Saul motioned the child forward.

Ish-bosheth raced toward Saul, his uncoordinated body causing him to slam into his father's side. He clung to his father's leg and pulled his face out of the sackcloth robe, looking into Saul's grave features. Saul gazed upon the boy as though he were some curious object he could not quite comprehend. The boy's eyes, the sparkle, the blueness, the luster and curl of his locks, the cheekbones, all converged to bring the image of Ahinoam to mind. The tiny existence of this boy brought him an unexpected pleasure he had not anticipated. He placed his hand upon the boy's head and ran his fingers through his golden curls.

"Remember, you are no ordinary child," Saul said. "Keep pace with me."

Saul gave a quick glance at David and Mikal, and then moved toward the family residence at a slower speed, enabling Ish-bosheth to keep stride, which he did with a child's, short-legged gallop.

When Saul moved out of earshot from Mikal and David, he spoke to Jarib. "Look back and see what they are doing."

Jarib did so and said, "Conversing, my lord."

"And their faces? What do they express?" Saul asked.

"As best as I can tell, they seem pleased with each other's company." Jarib looked back and forth between the couple and the king.

"What is going on in the king's mind, my lord?" Abner expressed his question with misgiving.

"Plots and schemes, Abner." Saul playfully slapped the commander on his shoulder to cover a boding evil. "My daughter is in love with the captain, is she not?"

"From the night in our tent at the Valley of Elah," Jonathan said. "She soared from flinty disregard to melting ice when he began to sing. Killing a giant has made it worse."

Worse for us all. But the notion that Mikal was in love with David pleased him. His daughter's infatuation with the captain offered an advantage. Yet he must keep his counsel. He could not openly plot David's demise and expect support from others. In the heat of mental fury, he had hurled a spear at the unsuspecting captain and missed. Perhaps another spear could be employed to rid Saul of this threat to his kingdom. He must tread through this sinister design alone but were he to emerge the victor with no blood on his hands, he would have beaten the prophet at his game and secured the throne for Jonathan. The kingdom may be torn from his hands as Samuel had spoken, but it would remain in his bloodline. The monarchy would be given to the son of his loins, the rightful heir and not an obscure shepherd with a beautiful voice who killed a giant with a slingshot.

"What do you think of a double wedding, then: Merab and Adriel, Mikal and the captain?" Saul turning to Adriel. "Would that be unsettling in your mind, Adriel?"

"My lord, I am humbled you would even consider me in your deliberations," Adriel replied, clearly taken aback by the king's thought process. "Sharing the wedding day with Princess Mikal and Captain David would be an honor."

"Good. Good. I know you almost lost Merab once to the captain when I offered her as his prize for slaying the giant." Saul's volatility had caused his son's armor-bearer much grief, and he would not want to risk the chance of losing her again.

"If a double ceremony secures my future with Merab, I gladly accept."

"Good. Good. I promised a wife to the one who slew the giant, and a king should be true to his word. Fortunately, I have two daughters, one of whom is available and eager. Surely, the captain will not rebuff a second offer to be my son-in-law."

"Abba, while that prospect might please my sister, I believe David's answer will be the same as with Merab."

"What was that argument again, my son? Why did he turn down my offer?"

"He is a poor man from a humble family. To become the king's son-in-law requires wealth, a fortune he does not possess to offer as the price for a princess."

"It is true, my lord. He has no position in the kingdom other than being a captain," Abner concurred. "Adriel is worthy of marrying into the family. His father, Barzillai, is chief of the tribe of Manasseh, and a great contributor to the royal coffers."

"Yet I did not kill a giant," Adriel asserted. "This is no small matter. The kingdom has its share of mighty men, but none chose to face a giant after a forty-day standoff."

"And you did give your word, my lord," Jarib added.

"And a king should honor his word," Saul mused, and then he observed Ish-bosheth beside him. "Should I not, Ish-bosheth? What say you?"

Saul had spoken his son's name for the first time since his circumcision and name day. The sound of pronouncing the name tingled in his mouth, providing a sweet, gratifying sensation. He smiled down at the lad.

"Yes, Abba." Ish-bosheth's reply had no understanding of what was asked. He had been addressed by his father, given a smile, and rewarded with a pat on the head. That was enough.

Saul now had everyone poised to hear and perhaps agree with what he would say without any of them knowing the nature of his plan. What unfolded in his mind came with amazing ease. He half expected everyone to laugh at the absurdity of the plot when he spoke it, but there was also a beauty to it, should each man accept its implausibility.

"We are all in agreement, down to the least of us." Saul continued to stroke his son's head and hair as he spoke. "The king must keep his word. So, this is my offer to David: assure him that he need not feel inferior in any way, in wealth, in family name, or in notoriety. Tell him I have only one bride-price for my daughter: a deed of service. If he should accomplish this before the day set for Merab and Adriel's wedding, then it shall be a double wedding. The price for his bride requires his skills as a soldier, which has, thus far, proven satisfactory. He shall bring me one hundred Philistine foreskins."

Saul smiled at Ish-bosheth and waited to hear the reaction from the others, but there was none. He raised his eyes to a group of frozen, incredulous faces.

"This is madness," Abner blurted, his eyes glaring at the audacity of his cousin.

Saul stopped stroking Ish-bosheth's hair and pressed his fingers into the boy's head to keep from exposing his trembling hand. Had his cousin seen the nefarious nature of his scheme and was calling him on it?

"I know what you are doing, and this is madness, a brilliant madness." Abner could not conceal his enthusiasm. "Take Yahweh's war with the pagans and strike the very essence of their manhood. A brilliant madness, my lord."

"You approve then," Saul said, his shaky hand restored to calm.

"I will draw some strategies as to how this might be executed." Abner's voice rose with excitement. "Such resourceful barbarity will generate terror in the hearts of the Philistines."

Saul looked to the others for their approval or dissent. Jarib and Adriel quickly agreed with the commander. Saul then locked eyes with Jonathan. "What say you, my son?"

"Why one hundred foreskins?" Jonathan shook his head in disbelief at such an extreme plan. "Why not one hundred heads?"

"Whose heads might they be?" Saul asked. "Some unsuspecting travelers, some defenseless villagers, his own men fallen in battle?"

"If David should accept the king's challenge, you expect him to cheat and prey on the innocent to fulfill his obligation for a dowry?" Jonathan asked.

"I do not believe the captain would be deceptive," Saul answered, his tone a hint defensive at his son's accusation. He looked into Jonathan's eyes, his well-repressed desire to rid his house of this potential challenger to the throne concealed by a mask of love for his son. Saul did not want to awaken any suspicion within his son that his father might be harboring a malignant intent. "Our covenant with the Almighty is the mark of circumcision, an easily identifiable sign. As the commander has stated, we must be zealous in Yahweh's war with the Philistines. If the captain is successful, we strike an extra measure of terror in the hearts of our enemies when after we slay them, we mutilate their manhood."

"One hundred foreskins? Is the number not excessive, Abba?"

"For the giant-slayer? For the price of your sister?" Saul retorted.

Jonathan had no response.

Saul removed his hand from Ish-bosheth's head and placed it upon Jonathan's shoulder. "Tell David the king is pleased with him. Remind him how he is beloved by all. And tell him the king would consider it the highest honor to embrace him as a son-in-law. We agree then?"

Saul did not need Jonathan's approval to implement his plan, but to have it would strengthen the bond with his son, something he desperately wanted to maintain. Jonathan was deceived by this giant-slayer, and Saul must protect him. The captain could have his daughter's heart and the hearts of the people, but not the heart of his firstborn, the prince and heir to the throne of Saul's dynasty.

"Yes, Abba, I agree."

Saul responded quickly to avoid any second thoughts his son might have—Jonathan answered out of deference not conviction. "Jarib, write the terms of the dowry, and Commander, devise some plans of attack. This task must be accomplished before Merab's wedding day. Present these conditions to the captain, and if he agrees and succeeds in this challenge, we shall celebrate a double wedding."

Saul cupped his hand over the back of Ish-bosheth's head. Saul could get used to speaking his name. "You approve, my son?"

Ish-bosheth nodded, his beaming face basking in his father's attention.

Saul had unanimous agreement. His commander had called his proposal "A brilliant madness." If he was going to be mad, why not be brilliant at the same time.

Chapter 23

DAVID DID NOT NEED A BODYGUARD TO WALK THE STREETS OF Gibeah. He could move about the city free from assault, though his status as the giant-slayer made him a more recognized figure among the citizens. Only the royal family would be distinguished with a higher status. Even the king himself could move among the citizens with minimal escort and receive deference and honor. The city had been transformed from a crossroads of inhabitants to that of a single nationality: a military, mercantile, religious, and political population of Hebrew tribal ambassadors, professional soldiers, merchants, and Levites all there for one purpose, to serve the king and the nation.

The original citizens of Gibeah, who had lived there for generations and existed peacefully with the nation of Israel after their treaty with Joshua when the Hebrews began to conquer the land of Promise, had been purged from the city. Those Gibeonites not slaughtered in Saul's zeal to annihilate them where resettled in remote villages spread along the Salt Sea in Judah and Benjamin's tribal coastal lands. There the Gibeonites could be contained or just die out. They would retain their treaty rights as a people, but if the Gibeonites could not fend for themselves, they could be consumed by the natural eliminations of time. To those in power in Israel, it mattered not.

While David could move through the streets of Gibeah without a security detail, he did have to contend with being numbered among the renowned of Israel. If a group of children spotted him, they usually swarmed. And while no woman would ever throw herself upon David, often as he approached them, a scarf or piece of jewelry might be dropped in his path, forcing him to stop and retrieve it from the ground.

He enjoyed the public attention. He loved the hero worship. He thrived when in front of a crowd. Men, women, children, everyone wanted to be with him. He was, after all, the shepherd with the honeyed voice, the captain of a thousand men, the one who defeated a giant. All of Israel was smitten with the "slayer of ten thousand." Who would not want his company?

Passing through the streets of the thriving city, he kept a brisk pace: past street hawkers selling fabrics, jewelry, and fresh produce; merchants of clothing, farming equipment, and smitheries; what dwellings that were not used for housing were converted into bakeries, fruit shops, eateries, inns for travelers, lending establishments, Levitical and military schools, offices for local municipalities. The city was large enough to have several synagogues to accommodate the population growth.

Whenever David was out in public, he could rarely pass a food vendor and not be offered an ample portion of beef or lamb, or mounds of fruit, or sacks of grain. No seller accepted David's coin. He would never go hungry or become destitute in Gibeah.

His cohorts at the Wolf Den were waiting for him, but he paused in front of the city livestock pens to tighten the strap on the lion-skin pouch containing his kinnor. The sheep inside the pen were racing around the circumference in a mad stampede as though in flight from a hungry beast. At the far end of the pen, a man lashed another man lying prone on the ground and trying to crawl away from the repeated blows of the whip.

With his kinnor tucked under his arm, he climbed over the fence. He did not break his stride as he scooped up a handful of fresh sheep excrement. When he was close enough to the man with the whip, David shouted then hurled the dung.

The man with the whip spun, angered at this intrusion and angrier still when undigested sheep bile splattered across his front. He drew back his whip to strike David, but David dropped to one knee and laid his kinnor on the ground. He raised an arm to receive the blow of the frayed tail end of the whip and clasped the leather strap as soon as it hit, coiled it around his forearm, and then jerked so hard that the wooden handle flew out of the man's grip. David rushed toward the man who had started to back away, but David clasped a fistful of the man's tunic.

"Who are you?" David thrust the butt end of the whip into the man's throat.

"No concern of yours." The man growled and choked as David pressed the wooded handle into his neck.

"It is now my concern." David dug the whip handle deeper.

"This worthless shepherd is one of the king's herders," the man confessed, and David released some pressure on his neck. "I caught him sleeping in the stalls."

David looked down at the whimpering young man lying on the ground, his leggings shredded and stained with blood.

"Whipping for falling asleep?" The punishment did not fit the crime.

"These are the royal sheep for the king and his court," the man said. "This fool should be punished for his neglect."

"Must you be so brutal?" David's cheeks burned; his eyes inflamed. "Who are you to mete out such penalty?"

"I am Doeg, the king's chief herdsman." Doeg slipped one hand behind his back.

"I hope you are just scratching an itch on your back and not reaching for a dagger. I would hate to use that against you as well as this whip."

Doeg let both hands drop to his side.

David glared into the man's dark, recessed eyes quivering from side to side. His turban had fallen to the ground, revealing his hair slick from sweat. His teeth were jagged and filed as if he supped on a diet of hardened grains like his livestock, and his gray, cracked lips were framed by a black beard.

"You dishonor the king by such cruelty to his herders." David released his hold on Doeg, who immediately stumbled backward.

Doeg unscrambled his legs and planted his feet firmly on the ground, trying not to appear humiliated by this affront.

"In the future, find less cruel ways to discipline your herders." David tossed the whip at Doeg's feet. "Such roughshod actions may return onto your head with equal recompense."

David moved toward his kinnor lying on the ground. He scooped it up and bound over the fence, clearing it by the span of a man's outstretched hand, pinky to thumb, between him and the top railing. David turned to Doeg.

The herdsman scrunched his face and spat on the ground in David's direction.

"You need to build a taller fence. If I can clear it, so can a hungry lion or wolf."

Benaiah stood at the entrance of the Wolf Den hostelry, drinking vessel of wine in hand, his third, looking up and down the street. His large frame blocked the entry of the crammed eating house. Complaints were shouted from inside by the owner to move his strapping girth, but Benaiah ignored the protests.

A hand reached from behind and patted Benaiah's bald head, imploring him to come back inside.

Benaiah swatted at the hand as if it were an annoying insect and grumbled. "He should have been here long before now."

"You are like a mother hen," the voice replied in a mocking falsetto, pecking the bare skin of Benaiah's head with jagged fingernails.

Benaiah grabbed the arm connected to the hand and jerked the rest of the body from behind him. His strength tossed Jozabad into the street where he crashed into the side of an ox cart.

Were he not in such good humor from his wine consumption, Jozabad might have responded with hostile intent. "Men have died for less," Jozabad announced, after bouncing off the wooden rails of the cart.

The pile of hair on the top of Jozabad's head that wrapped around a concealed weapon fell like a waterfall about his face and head, covering his eyes. Jozabad squatted to pick up the dagger that lay on the ground.

"So have those who poked at my bald head," Benaiah growled.

"You are just jealous." Jozabad braided his long black locks on the top of his head, inserting his thin dagger inside the tight knot of hair.

"Someday, I will slice off that horse twine you call hair." Benaiah patted the hilt of his sword.

Benaiah's attention was distracted as David dashed around the corner of a municipal building, his kinnor bouncing on top of his back. "Late as usual."

"You state the obvious," David said, running up to Benaiah and embracing him.

"You smell like a sheep pen." Benaiah scrunched his nose in disgust.

"There is a good reason for it." David started to go around his mountainous friend, but Benaiah stuck out his arm.

"The Wolf Den is full, and you smell like you just came from mucking out the king's stalls." Benaiah stiffened his arm against David's effort to pass him.

"Are you going to stand here complaining, or are you going to let me pass?" David asked, his irritation beginning to show. "You are worse than my ima."

"He is your mother," Jozabad said, approaching the two. "Now, I am thirsty and in need of a drink. Enter or stand aside, both of you."

Benaiah exhaled a contemptible snort and allowed David to enter the eatery.

Jozabad stepped beside Benaiah. "He does smell, I grant you."

"He could try bathing." Benaiah shook his head in unhappy defeat.

"He lived too long with his sheep." Jozabad gave Benaiah's shoulder a pat of understanding. "The stink has settled into his skin."

"Next time, he must bathe with sand."

The crowd began to chant the giant-slayer's name, and Benaiah turned his head and looked inside the tavern.

"But they care not how he looks or smells." Benaiah looked back at Jozabad.

Jozabad took Benaiah's wine cup and drained it before handing it back empty. "Now, come inside, and let me fill your cup."

The moment David entered the Wolf Den, the crowd cheered. Several patrons rushed toward him only to be blocked by a wild man who leapt between David and the oncoming enthusiasts. The wild man did not hold up his bare muscular arms or expand his burly chest to halt the advance of the excited admirers. He howled, distorting his face, bulging his eyes, and shaking his woolly beard and hair as if he were a lunatic. The people recoiled and the noise level dropped to a fraction of what it had been.

David placed a hand on the shoulder of the wild man and spoke to the awestruck crowd. "Uriah is why the Philistines drop their swords and run when we approach."

David's declamation brought a fervent response, and Uriah grinned at the adulation, but did not budge from his protective position in front of David.

A second man slipped beside David, which brought a smile to his face. "I knew you would be hiding somewhere, Eleazar."

Eleazar winked at David through the slit in the cloth mask wrapped around his head. The only exposed part of his face.

David had only seen Eleazar's youthful but scarred features in private settings: a campfire at night or shared barracks. A Philistine raiding party had attacked his village, setting fire to many of the homes. He was struck in the face with a flaming torch by a Philistine soldier while trying to defend his village. David was impressed with Eleazar's stealth and control in combat; most of the slain men never knew who struck them. Unlike most warriors who basked in the idolization of the masses, Eleazar preferred anonymity.

"Captain, the stage is ready." Eleazar escorted David through the crowd as Uriah led the way toward the raised platform in a back corner of the room.

Benaiah, Jozabad, Uriah, and Eleazar made up David's elite warrior team, and in addition to his kinship with the prince, these four had become his closest companions since joining the military. They were all of the same age, all bearing a warrior's heart, all fiercely loyal to David, yet hailed from different corners of the kingdom. They had chosen to fight for the king when the call came for the tribes to battle against the enemies of Israel. And when Abner had asked for volunteers to be a part of the king's standing army, these four went through the training, proving their natural fighting skills were beyond normal human scope. Their first encounter with David had been in the Valley of Elah. Witnessing such courage drew them to the shepherd, and when the king appointed David to the rank of captain and Abner gave him a command, these four requested to be assigned to David's contingent.

David sat upon the chair on the stage. He removed his kinnor from the lion-pelt bag and opened a pouch full of fingerpicks. His fingernails were too brittle to pluck the strings, and he had to rely on the fresh cut animal bone and bird quill plectra to play the instrument. Before heading to the Wolf Den, he had been in his barracks voicing the different plectra with his knife to create the proper slant and smoothness to produce the best tone quality from each string and chord strum.

Benaiah set a mug of water beside David's chair before taking his place with the other three who leaned against the wall behind the wooden platform facing the audience. Most of the patrons stood shoulder to shoulder.

The larger tables were moved outside behind the tavern to accommodate the numbers. All drink and food service had ceased. Outside, the people jostled around the open windows and the entryway for any advantage. Every available foot of space in and around the Wolf Den was occupied.

David cocked his ear close to the strings for final tuning. This performance was not like any other time: not for family who never appreciated his talent, not dim-witted sheep, not the soldiers in the camps or the barracks, or the royal family or for the king. This was what he had longed for all his life, an audience whose hearts were turned toward him, who had chosen to leave hearth and home for an evening and come to the Wolf Den to listen to his music. Having been secretly anointed king, having killed a giant, having a daughter of the king in love with him, all these facts did not compare to the pure pleasure of this moment before this audience, and he would not disappoint them.

Satisfied with the tuned strings, he faced the rapt crowd. He craned his neck over the people's heads bobbing in the diffused light and found Gad seated at an elevated table, a blank scroll and bowls of dye spread before him, and two oil lamps for illumination. When Gad lifted his hand, a black feathered quill clenched inside his plump fingers, David closed his eyes and started to play.

The tune began with a series of harmonic chords, a gust of sound from the kinnor, forcefully played and seizing control of the room. The hearts of the listeners fell under the spell of divine sound. Then David shifted to a slower cadence, the notes set free to reverberate and float above the heads of the crowd. The tempo increased gradually, the notes building, until finally ushering in the human voice. Overcome by the musical vibrations surging through him, David tilted back his head and burst forth in exaltation.

"O Yahweh, our Yahweh
How majestic is your name in all the earth.
You have set your glory above the heavens."

No listener could have predicted such an outburst of voice and rhythm. To take the name of Yahweh and blast it from human lips came near sacrilege, but for David it was a cry of wonder, of familiarity with the Creator of the universe, of greeting the supremacy of the Almighty with a personal joy. David decided this lyrical declaration was worthy of repeating.

"O Yahweh, our Yahweh

> How majestic is your name in all the earth.
> You have set your glory above the heavens."

David felt his soul possessed by Yahweh, and by extension, so did the audience, for they did not merely hear his words, they absorbed its praise-inspired language the moment he began to sing, separating them all from the material world.

> "When I consider your heavens,
> The work of your fingers, the moon, the stars,
> Which you have set in place,
> What is man that you are mindful of him;
> The son of man that you care for him?"

No one was prepared for such divine impact, for the heart of every listener to yield to such a force of imagery that Yahweh, Creator of heaven and earth, would ever set his eternal mind upon them. Who would speak such a word? Who would imagine such a thought? Who would dare conjure such a vision and set it roaring through every heart in the room?

Only the singer of Israel could make one imagine Yahweh's hands and fingers powerful enough to shape the universe yet gentle enough to clasp the human soul.

> "You made him a little lower than the angels.
> You have crowned him with glory and honor.
> You made him ruler over your creation.
> Every created thing is in his care.
> Flocks and herds, beasts and birds,
> And all that swim in the paths of the sea.
> O Yahweh. O Yahweh. Our Yahweh.
> How majestic is your name in all the earth."

The music flowed with fervency. No prophet or priest had ever set their minds on such a path. From human voice, from the strings of sheep gut, from harden, shaped wood, from the plectra of animal bone, came the resonance of Yahweh enfolding all inhabitants of the earth, all creatures that drew breath, all beings owing their existence to the Creator. These musical notes, these lyrical phrases did not evaporate into echoes and dissolve into the atmosphere once sung but were absorbed into the hearts of every listener, expelling fear and despair.

The Wolf Den was transformed into a house of worship, each patron transformed into a lover of the One they worshiped, if the power of the song and the singer brought all the glory of heaven and earth inside the cramped tavern. And when David played his last note, the natural world was silent, all the universe, all created life was stilled, awed by the breadth of creation and the infinity of the Creator.

Gad scratched the last words onto the scroll. He held the quill inside both trembling hands. As soon as he finished the last of the letters, he blew his breath over the words to hasten the drying. He looked up at the crowd.

No one moved. Everyone seemed depleted of life. Was he the only one alive?

He heard the splash of moisture on the scroll and looked down to see a tiny pool beading on the calfskin below the last line he had just written. The words were blurred, not from an unsteady hand or smeared dye, but from his tears. He had been so stirred by the music he was unaware of weeping. He had never considered Yahweh could be so personal as to be "our" Yahweh. He did not know Yahweh could be accessible beyond the rituals of sacrifice, of incense and altars, of prophet-masters and priests. He did not know his soul had been so empty until the majesty of Yahweh had curled his fingers around his heart.

How could a singer and his song perform such a feat? How could Yahweh funnel his Presence into the soul of a man?

Was this a similar encounter Samuel had experienced and instructed his students to expect in their role of prophet?

Perhaps the unexpected flow of tears answered these questions. He wiped his face and then daubed the moist sleeve across the calfskin. This salty liquid from his damp eyes would be his personal mark on these inspired words.

Chapter 24

THE SILENCE INSIDE THE WOLF DEN TAVERN WAS SHATTERED with an explosion of human scuffling and barked orders: make way, clear a path, step aside. The commotion brought David's short concert to an abrupt end.

There was no room for such an order to be obeyed, so the soldiers who had imposed the command began removing the patrons from around the door. When the space around the door had been cleared, Abner, followed by Jarib, entered the Wolf Den. Every soldier in the room rose and stood at attention, including David, who jumped from his seat clutching the kinnor to his chest.

"Quite a crowd." Abner scanned the room, impressed by the number of people crammed into one space. "They come to hear you, Captain?"

"Yes, Commander," David answered, his throat not yet fully stable after giving voice to his song of unbridled praise.

"Impressive." Abner was not sure what to make of so many eyes staring at him, so he pointed to Jarib for him to speak.

"We seek an audience with you, Captain."

David's four-man team approached from behind the stage and took positions near him, so Abner added, "And your men."

Abner caught the eye of the proprietor of the Wolf Den as he stepped from around the corner of the serving table. "We will meet behind the tavern at the roasting pits." Abner waved for David and his men to follow. Then Abner looked back at the proprietor. "With refreshment."

Abner posted sentries around the eating area. Behind the tavern, large roasting pits had been dug and meats were arranged on grills or onto spits and set over the hot coals. Cooks cut portions of meat, laying out the slabs on trays for the servers to carry inside the Wolf Den for patrons to consume. Near the roasting pits was an eating area with oak tables and benches. With Abner's men set around the perimeter, no one was allowed to enter the area. A fire blazed in a circular stone pit in the center, providing warmth against the cold wind.

Abner waited for the proprietor to set out the trays of fruit, cheese, and bread along with cups of wine on the table. The distraction of food and wine would help in relaying this unusual order. Once the proprietor had gone back inside the Wolf Den, Abner nodded to Jarib. He did not have the gift of language, so he had Jarib state the king's offer.

"This is not a secret mission, but nonetheless, a delicate one." Jarib addressed David who sat across from him. "The marriage of Princess Merab to Adriel is soon, and the king would like his youngest daughter wed at the same time."

David held a cluster of grapes in his hand. He pinched a single grape from its stem and popped it into his mouth. Then he offered the cluster to Jarib, but the secretary refused. However, Abner plucked a single grape from the cluster and raised it to David in thanks before placing it into his mouth.

"I am listening," David replied, then squished the grape between his teeth.

Abner glanced at the faces of David's men, expressionless and shining in the glare of the flames rising from the firepit. He would have preferred this conversation be for fewer ears, but he was not in control of the circumstances, only to see the message delivered. And the commander knew that were David to accept the offer, he would need the assistance of these men to fulfill the obligation.

"The king is pleased with you." Jarib looked to Abner to affirm this statement and he obliged with a nod of his head. "He is pleased with you; with all you have done for him and for the kingdom since our great victory in the Valley of Elah. He is pleased to offer you a second opportunity to become his son-in-law by marrying Princess Mikal."

"Jarib, I am the same poor man, from the same insignificant family and clan as when the king made his first offer. Who am I to—"

"Yes, who are you?" Abner blurted. "Who are you to embarrass the king by refusing to accept his generosity?"

Abner was not a diplomat like his counterpart. He did not believe in the soft approach but preferred getting straight to the point. He stepped closer to the fire and stretched out his hands toward the flames. "Jarib, explain the bargain and conditions. It is cold out here."

The commander stood on the side of Jarib's patched eye, and Jarib did not turn his head to give Abner the look of scorn that lurked just below the surface of his blank exterior. The secretary was a loyal servant of the king and that meant respect for all members of the royal family even when they asserted themselves in an unbecoming manner.

Jarib wanted to carry out the king's unusual request in such a way as to ensure a positive outcome. He wished to tell the king of a successful negotiation and not of a second refusal from the captain or of his acquiescence to loutish coercion from the commander. Jarib was a diplomat and had come to meet with David to have a discussion not issue an order. Given the unusual terms, Jarib wanted to use the art of statecraft.

He cleared his throat, highlighted his expression with a smile, and started over. "Captain, to become a member of the royal family by marrying Princess Mikal is something I happen to know would be pleasing to her as well as the king. She considers you worthy and equal to her affection. It would be an honorable match between a princess, the king's daughter, and a brave hero among the ranks of Israel. So, here are the conditions: you are not required to provide coin, livestock, or material goods of any kind to secure the price of the bride. Only a deed of service."

"Deed of service," David repeated. He tossed the uneaten grapes onto the lion-skin pouch containing his kinnor on the table.

"Yes, a deed of service." Jarib reached across the table and brought a mug of wine to his lips. He took a sip to provide some moisture to his dry mouth. "The deed is, no doubt, something unusual, the requirement a bit delicate, not a standard military operation, yet we are confident of your skills and those of your men."

"By the name of Yahweh, you take forever," Abner blurted and spun away from the fire to face David. "One hundred Philistine foreskins. You collect one hundred Philistine men, cut off their tiny shafts, and bring them to the king."

David was silent as were his companions. He waited for Abner to clarify. The conditions for the bargain were clear, but David waited for the commander's stern face to crack, his mouth to drop open and guffaw at his jest. When Abner's face remained stern, David could not believe what he had heard.

"Do you understand, Captain?" Abner asked.

"Should we kill them first?" It was all he could think to say. It was not his first thought. His first thought was how absurd was this offer.

"I am sure they would appreciate it if you did," Abner snarled.

David continued to scrutinize Abner's face. His impatience, his blunt speech, his disagreeable expression said to David that he no more wanted to be the bearer of this news than David wanted to hear it. Abner had never warmed to him. He had advised the king against David fighting Goliath, and while Abner promoted him to rank of captain as reward for slaying the giant, since then, he had barely tolerated David's presence in the army and among the royal family. Yet, the commander was a loyal servant of the king and kingdom and would fulfill the desire of the king no matter how preposterous.

"We understand this is out of the ordinary, Captain," Jarib added hastily.

"Is the prince aware of this offer?" David asked.

"Yes, and he approved." Jarib stretched his body over the top of the table and dropped his voice. "But Princess Mikal is not aware of this proposal, and we think it best she remain uninformed. She might not feel flattered by such a mission."

"I dare say," David said. Abner was not a man known for his humor, but still David could not believe he was being given such an offer. "I do not quite understand."

"What do not you understand?" Abner interjected. "You bring the king one hundred Philistine pikes, and you get the princess for a bride."

"Commander, you want me to cut off their..."

"I care not who does it, but yes, cut them off, bring them to the king as proof, and you get to marry my second cousin. Simple. Now, is this a task for the giant-slayer or not?"

David knew this was not just a reckless mission; it was foolhardy, one that would most likely get him killed. And the mission itself was not just dangerous but vile.

"Captain, do not look at this request with contempt." Jarib tapped his finger upon his leather eye patch with the face of the wolf embossed upon it. "I know what it is like to be set upon. I know the cruelty of the heathen. These are the wars of Yahweh, and we are taking the fight straight to the Philistines. As the giant struck fear in our hearts at the siege of Elah, so too will your courageous act strike fear in the hearts of Yahweh's enemies."

Jarib's assertion rang true to David. The face of the secretary offered no appearance of guile or subterfuge in his speech. Jarib had incorporated Yahweh into the argument. The Philistines were Yahweh's enemies, and by extension, Israel's enemies.

Yet, David still struggled. He looked into the faces of his four friends. He could not accomplish this without them. They would have to agree to risk their lives for him, for his reward, for his advancement, not their own. This would stretch the bonds of friendship should they agree to help. Slaying one hundred Philistines for their uncircumcised foreskins just so he could marry a princess would be an ignoble way to die should it come to that.

"We will help you with the killing, but do not ask us to do the cutting."

David smiled in appreciation of Benaiah's offer, but he spoke only for himself, not for all four of them. David knew these men loved him and were loyal, but did the others feel likewise? David lay his hand upon the shoulder of Benaiah, then studied the faces of Eleazar, Jozabad, and Uriah. They appeared resolved and not inclined to contradict Benaiah.

"Any dissent?" David insisted on surety. "I will understand."

"Should I die on this mission, I do not wish to be killed with a limp Philistine rod in my hand," Uriah asserted, his somber face conveying a depth of unease.

Everyone had been able to restrain their level of amusement up to this point, but Uriah's honesty broke the floodgate with laughter.

"Do not worry, Uriah," Jozabad slung his arm over his friend's neck. "I would kill you myself before I would let that happen."

In the firelight, David detected a smirk on the commander's face at the raw humor found in Uriah's comment. And while Jarib did not join in with the laughter, David could see a hopeful smile appear on the secretary's lips that the giant-slayer was about to accept the abnormal mission.

David stood, and he and his friends raised their cups and drank to one another. Then David faced Jarib and Abner, set his empty cup upon the table, and placed his hands on the oak top.

"I accept the king's offer." David leaned forward; his face illuminated in the firelight. He wanted the king's emissaries to clearly see his resolve. "Should I survive such a 'deed of service' as you say, I will gladly take Princess Mikal to be my bride. As Yahweh gives me strength, I will serve the king in any capacity he requires."

David scooped the grapes off the lion pouch with one hand, grabbed his kinnor and slung it over his shoulder just as the proprietor of the Wolf Den arrived carrying a large tray piled with meat still sizzling from the grill. He set it in the middle of the table, but David was not interested in lingering to eat with his friends much less with Jarib and the commander. He allowed the distraction of the heaping pile of roasted meats in the center of the table to divert everyone's attention as he disappeared into the night.

This was a peculiar day indeed, and he needed time to think. He had felt a divine flash of Yahweh expressed in his lyric, his vocals, his instrument, and the crowd's reaction that filled him with joy, but this was followed by a cold pulse of bitterness with the king's proposal. He wanted to do all he could for the king if for no other reason than out of loyalty to Jonathan and in honor of their covenant. And to be married to Mikal would be pleasant, even desirable, but what did it mean to love a woman?

He had never been instructed in such matters, what it might require, or how it might feel. He did enjoy seeing himself reflected in her adoration, but he was as ill-prepared to be a husband as he was to be a king. Friendship with Jonathan was trouble-free, its requirements a pleasure, a mutual and spontaneous reaction of the warrior's bond.

But to become a son-in-law of the king, to be married into the royal family, this was altogether different. This prospect felt more like coercion, not a welcomed invitation, more like a potential death sentence than a chance for advancement or preparation for the eventuality of becoming king.

Even the means by which he was to become a son-in-law was life threatening. He might not make it to the marriage bed if he died in the process of fulfilling the king's requirement for a bride-price.

As he made his way through the darkened, empty streets of Gibeah back to the barracks, an arrow of foreboding lodged in his heart, a vague yet lurking sense of danger. For the first time since leaving the solitude of the mountains of Bethlehem, a yearning for the campfires—for the loneliness of those starry nights listening to the bleating sheep, even a longing for his family— came upon him. There he felt safe, but tonight he felt pursued, pursued by a hungry wolf, a wolf that remained hidden in every black shadow cast before his path.

Chapter 25

MIKAL NESTLED IN A HEAP OF CUSHIONS IN THE CORNER OF the spacious bed chamber she shared with her sister, embroidering a banner of a lion with a warrior riding on its back. She had balls of gold and brown threads piled in a bowl set on a table and a selection of bird bone needles to weave the thread in and out of the banner. Oil lamps burned brightly to give enough light for the intricate stitchery.

Mikal kept her back to the room. She did not want to watch the servants supervising yet another bath for her sister and observe yet another rub down of oils and perfumes into her bare skin or massaging her scalp with hair treatments all in preparation for Merab's wedding to Adriel. How many baths did her sister need? How many oils and perfumes could the skin absorb?

She was already a fragrant cloud of spice and myrrh, pungent enough to deaden the nerves of the nose. And if Merab had another scalp treatment, her hair would fall out.

Mikal did not want to listen to the girlish palaver between servant and princess or have Merab solicit her opinion on the wedding day gown or wedding night garment.

Mikal and Merab had shared a bed from infancy. The moment Mikal was weaned, her parents put her in the room with her older sister and, since then, they never spent a night apart. Their entire lives together forged a bond impossible to break. Two distinct personalities, both opinionated and headstrong, they did not allow their differences to drive a wedge between their love for each other. The most intimate personal detail, the most elaborate fantasy, the darkest of secrets, was known by the other.

Their father's unpredictable temperament and loose grasp of reality following the death of their mother was the severest hardship they suffered, but they stood together, became mother and sister to Jonathan and the twins, Ishvi and Malki. They had even bonded in caring for Ish-bosheth when their father nearly killed him the day he was born and rejected him thereafter. Only of late had Saul taken an interest in the lad, including him in all gatherings.

But now, they faced the greatest test to their bond: marriage for one and not the other.

When the marriage advisor arrived to give expert knowledge on the mysterious pleasures to be had between husband and wife, Mikal stuffed a scrap of cloth into each ear. Merab invited her to join the group. Her time to be a bride was sure to come and she needed to be prepared.

She did not want to listen to the squeals and giggles of Merab and her female servants as they listened to instruction on the multiple ways to pleasure her husband or study the anatomies of life-size male and female teraphim brought in by the advisor and used for demonstrations and to provide oracular, fertility blessing.

How are such pleasures taught, Mikal wondered? How can every mystery between man and woman be explained? Was there not mutual discovery between husband and wife to be found? Where was the adventure for two lovers coming together in the marriage bed unencumbered by instruction and free to explore, free to imagine, free to delight?

Mikal had her flights of imagination, but there had been no face to these fantasies until David. Now, he was the only one she could imagine and accept as a husband. She had set a standard for herself early in life. She would not be the wife of some farmer or field hand. She would not marry a merchant or Levite. And when her father became king, she would not be given away to just any son of a tribal lord and certainly to no common soldier.

Then David appeared. She had to repent of her first impression: disdain for a common shepherd, his clothing and revolting smell on the day he arrived in the camp. But then, he sang, and then he slew a giant, and then her father made him a captain, and now he was on a quest that, should he succeed, would allow her fantasies to become reality.

Abner had informed her that the king had offered David a second opportunity to become his son-in-law on condition he carry out a deed of service, and that the captain had accepted the challenge. Her uncle refused to offer any details of the mission other than this was the reason for David's sudden departure.

Mikal chose not to mention the conversation with Abner to her sister. She did not discuss the subject with Jonathan whom she assumed also knew of David's commission. She contained her anticipation and hope in her heart. Mikal wanted—no, she prayed—David be successful in his quest to win her, whatever it might be, wherever it took him, however long it took him, though she preferred he be swift in completing the task and return to Gibeah in time for a double wedding.

She tried to imagine what her father might have demanded of David as a price for her hand. He had already slain a giant. She could not envision a greater task. He was already a captain over one thousand men with successful missions to his credit. What more could he do to prove himself?

Needle and thread, needle and thread. That was her distraction. Complete the artistic design on the banner, that was her task. She and David had separate missions, but once completed, their mutual reward would be the living flesh of the marriage bed where their only quest would be to satiate each other's passion.

Tapping on her shoulder startled Mikal from her reverie, and she pierced her finger with the needle, breaking off a fragment inside her flesh. She stuffed the banner into a pocket of her gown so as not to smear it with blood and rolled onto her stomach ready to pounce on whoever had intruded upon her solitude. Mikal was stunned to see Merab standing above her, propping up the life-size, terracotta, female teraphim that was as tall as her sister. Merab and teraphim, side-by-side, a bizarre juxtaposition of figurine and flesh. Mikal removed the wads of cloth from her ears.

"My marriage tutor encouraged me to sleep with her until my wedding night to ensure fertility." Merab patted the wide hips on the anatomically correct clay figure with one hand while her other hand stabilized the upright idol. "What do you think?"

Mikal looked about the bed chambers. They were alone. She had not heard the servants or the marriage expert depart. This was when she really missed her mother. Were Ahinoam alive, she would have prepared her daughters for this day. There would have been no need for a marriage tutor giving lessons on intimacy using household gods as models. Their mother had helped them through the trauma of youthful flowering of their bodies, so Mikal was confident, had she been here, Ahinoam would have eased the anxieties of her daughters about conjugal matters. Until her death and the loss of their father's mental stability, their parents were a wonderful example of matrimonial stability.

"Where is everyone?" Mikal scrambled to her feet.

"I sent them away. What do you think? Sleep with the teraphim or not?"

Mikal waved in exasperation at such a foolish question, but she did not want to insult Merab's gullibility. "I do not know. You want to have children in the first year?"

"What happened to your finger?" Merab pointed to Mikal's hand.

Mikal saw that the blood streaked over her hand where the bone splinter was lodged in her fingertip. "You startled me when you tapped my shoulder, and I broke the tip of the needle in my finger." Mikal began sucking the wound.

"Sorry, I did not mean…I just need your advice."

Mikal removed her finger from her mouth and picked at the splinter. "Go ahead and sleep with it." Mikal responded with irritation. "Am I the expert? What do I know about what you do with your husband? But I do believe sleeping with a dumb idol never got anyone pregnant, certainly not a female one."

It pained Mikal to be so blunt. Merab's question was an honest one. Merab wanted her sister's valued opinion, and Mikal just bit her head off. She did not deserve Mikal's harsh reaction, and when Merab's lower lip began to quiver, Mikal stepped around the pillows and embraced her sister, knocking the teraphim from Merab's hand.

Mikal's quick reaction saved the clay figure from crashing onto the floor and breaking into pieces. She caught it and held it awkwardly.

"I am sorry, Merab. We have slept together as sisters since we were children. Giving up that place beside you for a husband is one thing; for an idol, it is another."

There came a knock on the door and a female servant entered to tell them Captain David and his men had returned and were now meeting with their father and brother in the Hall of the Wolf King. This was all the incentive Mikal needed to push the teraphim back into Merab's hands before dashing out of their bed chambers.

Mikal paused at the door and turned to speak.

Merab had placed the teraphim upon the pillows where Mikal had been sewing and was now wiping away a streak of blood on the brown surface of the left shoulder of the clay figure, Mikal's blood.

"Sister, I can bleed for you, something an idol could never do. I can speak to you, listen to you, embrace you. This idol will never do that for you. So how could this speechless object ensure your fertility?"

Merab did not or could not respond to Mikal's question fast enough, and Mikal sprinted away vanished like a startled deer.

Construction of the Hall of the Wolf King had been completed shortly after Saul's victory over the Philistines in the Valley of Elah. The family living quarters had also been transformed into a palace with multiple rooms and chambers and attached to the massive building.

At the dedication of the Hall, Ahimelech conducted priestly blessings. Saul had requested a burnt offering during the ceremony, feeling a religious impulse to gratify Yahweh. When Ahimelech pointed out in the sacred text that sacrifices could not be performed just anywhere one pleases, but only where Yahweh pleases, Saul became petulant.

"Yahweh has too many stipulations to keep the Presence happy," he fumed.

On the day of the ceremony, the Hall was filled with the citizens from Gibeah as well as tribal leaders and chieftains from all over the country. Saul sat proudly upon his throne while Gad stood in the middle of the Hall and faced the king. He was to read from the Laws and Blessings scribed by the prophet Moses. A Levite unfurled a scroll of calfskin and held it before Gad. He read the Ten Sayings given by Yahweh to Moses at Sinai after the people of Israel had departed Egypt.

Saul listened with intent as Gad read. The words fell upon his ears but melted like snowflakes upon his mind—even as sacred liquid, the words evaporated before dripping into his heart.

When Gad finished, the Levite placed the scroll inside a leather cylinder, and he and Gad stepped to one side. Ahimelech and another Levite came forward with a second scroll and took their places in the center of the Hall. When the Levite opened the scroll and held it before the high priest, Ahimelech looked at the king.

Saul sat perfectly still; his massive head wreathed with a wide band of gold.

On the front of the crown was the image of a wolf, its own head crowned. The only embedded precious stones were upon the face of the wolf: two polished eyes of red jasper. Two pairs of eyes—one human flesh, one sparkling stone—stared back at the high priest before he began to read from the second scroll.

"And it shall be, when the king takes the throne of his kingdom, that he shall write him a copy of this law in a book, out of that which is before the priests and the Levites. And it shall be with him, and he shall read therein all the days of his life; that he may learn to fear the Lord his God, to keep all the words of this law and these statutes, to do them; that his heart be not lifted up above his brothers, and that he turn not aside from the commandment to the right hand, or to the left; to the end that he may prolong his days in his kingdom, he and his children, in the midst of Israel. Amen."

The Hall remained silent as the Levite carefully rolled up the scroll and placed it inside another leather cylinder and handed it to Ahimelech. The high priest took it and then retrieved the other cylinder containing the Ten Sayings of Yahweh and approached the throne, kneeling before the king. He lifted the two cylinders before Saul.

"The words of Yahweh, Creator of heaven and earth, the Almighty, the one and only God of Israel as recorded by the great prophet Moses; may the Lord be exalted forever by the king and by the people of Yahweh." Ahimelech waited for the king's response.

The bitter taste of gall rose in Saul's throat, and a surge of fear gripped his bowels. His long fingers curled over the face of each wolf carved into the end of each armrest of his throne. If he released his grip, he might crumple in his chair or spring to his feet and run. His gaze darted back and forth, searching for assistance. He could not take the leather cylinders. He dared not touch its sacred contents.

Saul cleared his throat, and Jonathan stepped from behind the throne, leaned in and accepted the leather cylinders on the king's behalf. Even Jonathan's reassuring smile did not bring any comfort. Saul looked away to keep his son from seeing the terror that lurked behind his eyes.

After the ceremony, Gad was given the two cylinders. Saul ordered Gad to store them in his quarters with his other writings. He would call for the prophet when he felt inclined to study them. But Saul had not requested to have Gad read or to study the scrolls since that day.

The southern entrance to the Hall of the Wolf King had a set of wide and high double doors large enough to welcome the public. At the north end of the Hall, an oversized door was built into the wall which led directly into the king's chambers. In the middle portion of the great Hall was a restricted entrance leading to the palace rooms and private quarters of the royal family.

When Mikal arrived, the sentries came to attention, allowing her to pass through the family entrance. She heard the restrained male voices the moment she entered and hid herself immediately behind the nearest column. Three large windows on the east and west sides of the Hall, allowed in the natural light and, when the weather was pleasant, breezes to cool and clear the air inside the spacious room. But as it was cold, thick curtains of animal hide and hair hung from the interior of the windows to block the chilly temperature. Mikal shivered as she leaned against the thick column. She wished she had grabbed a wrap before rushing out of her bed chambers.

Mikal carefully extended her head around one of twelve massive columns, rows of six on each side, supporting the heavy timbered roof. Each wooden pillar was dedicated to one of the twelve tribes of Israel. Her father had insisted on this design when consulting with the master builders before construction began. On the top of each column an artisan had carved the crest of a respective tribe. A fire blazed from hammered iron pots resting inside a tripod of brass legs and placed in front of every column, providing heat and illumination. Mikal felt some warmth, which gave her comfort.

The floor of the Hall was one level except for the king's throne, a raised platform, its height the length of a man's forearm from fingertip to elbow. Guards stood at the four corners of the platform with two more guards positioned at the door behind the throne leading into her father's private chambers. The throne itself with its high back and wide seat to accommodate the king's tall stature was not ornate. The wooden legs were covered with the embossed design of sword and spear and at the end of each armrest was the carved head of a wolf. Coverlets of fine goat hair cushioned the seat.

Mikal caught a whiff of an unusual smell mixed into the smoke from the chamber fires which made her face scrunch. It brought to mind the aroma of bloody membranes of afterbirth from a heifer or mare, but she had not smelled that scent since the days of her family's agrarian life so long ago, and certainly not one she expected to inhale in the Hall of the Wolf King.

She eased around the column just as two soldiers removed the covering from an object she had never before seen positioned in front of the throne. The moment her father saw the golden object, he sprang from his throne and paced excitedly. This odd-shaped carriage that had spellbound her father appeared capable of transporting one or two passengers. It was covered in gold with fierce images of gods and warriors engraved all around the half-circular shape. Each of the two wooden wheels was wrapped with an iron band and a scythe was mounted on the inside of the double spokes. A long rod extended from the center attached to a crossbeam yoke to harness two beasts.

When Mikal saw David standing at the crossbeam with two buckets at his feet, she pulled back. She did not dare risk being seen.

David did not speak. He stood at attention. He kept his eyes latched onto the king as Benaiah gave the report.

"Benaiah, how was it that you accomplished this task so swiftly?" asked Abner. The commander stood with Jarib and Jonathan on either side of the king's throne.

"The intelligence provided by my lord, the commander, was accurate," Benaiah answered. "The Philistines are building defenses along our southern borders. There was a military encampment and training area in the Valley of Sorek."

"What would you estimate to be the number of troops?" Jonathan asked.

"Two hundred less than there were before." Benaiah pointed to the two buckets on either side of David. "Forgive me, my lord, you did not send us on a scouting mission, but one of a different nature. We arrived at nightfall and were gone before daybreak."

Saul ran his fingers along the top edge of the protective side-screens on the vehicle. He appeared indifferent to the report, and his attention to the chariot shifted everyone's focus upon him. This sleek vehicle was a marvel of military invention.

"We have captured the iron chariots of the Philistines in previous battles, and we know the Philistines are masters in designing war machinery, but this scythe coming from the wheel, we have not seen that before."

"Yes, my lord, nor have we seen a golden chariot before," Benaiah replied. "This was the chariot of a general who led his troops into battle."

"How do you know this?" Abner asked.

"The pouches on the inside panel carried his weaponry." Benaiah pointed to the receptacles on the interior. "And the leather straps on the floor anchored the feet so as not to spill from the chariot when riding over rough terrain."

"And he arrived at the military barrack driving it himself," David added, and immediately regretted speaking.

"You confronted him?" Abner asked. "Why did you not make him a captive? We could have interrogated him, ransomed him, at the very least."

David felt weak in the knees. He dropped his gaze and shifted his body weight. His stomach tightened. His throat constricted.

"Captain, why did you not return with the general?" Abner demanded.

Even Saul stopped admiring the golden chariot and looked at David for his response. David had never before been either silent or downcast before the king.

"Captain, a captured Philistine general would have been beneficial to us." Saul folded his arms over his chest. "Explain yourself."

"My lord, I thought the chariot would be enough: a windfall for the king, in addition to fulfilling your requirements for the bride-price." David raised his eyes to Saul. "Besides, the general was in no condition to be of any use, even as ransom."

"What was his condition?" Saul asked.

"His mind was rendered unbalanced, my lord," David answered, and again he regretted his choice of words.

"Unbalanced," Saul responded, piqued at the suggestion of the general's precarious mental state. "How so?"

Benaiah stepped toward David to intervene on his behalf and complete the report, but David raised his hand to stop his loyal friend then looked into the faces of his other companions standing behind Benaiah, those who had carried out the plans, each one slaughtering dozens of disorientated and terrified men apiece. These men knew his heart and how he had struggled with the ignominy of this obligation. This mission was not something David would boast of in the barracks or at the Wolf Den. It was not a moment of glory on the battlefield. He would not turn this story into song for the people to sing as had been done when he slew the giant. This had been a brutal task none of them wished to discuss or remember, but an account had to be told, and it had to be told by the one who had accepted the challenge of his "deed of service" required for the hand of the king's daughter.

Jozabad, Eleazar, and Uriah gave their captain a bold look, a look of unquestionable support, that though his deed of service commissioned by the king might be distasteful to them all, they would not flinch in risking their lives for him. It gave David the poise he needed to proceed.

"My lord, as Benaiah reported, we arrived at the Philistine encampment after dark." David spoke dispassionately. He would give his report as though it were an odious fable, not a story of heroics. "A large barrack housed the soldiers on the far end of the training grounds away from the rest of the compound. When all were asleep, we killed the sentries then barricaded all entries but one. Once the fire was set, it was only a matter of slaying the men as they made their escape."

"What of the general?" Abner asked. "When did you capture him?"

"He arrived in his chariot with a contingent of unarmed men in wagons from the other side of the encampment. They had arrived believing they were to battle the fire, not their armed enemy. When all were killed, we had the general and a few boy soldiers remove the requested body part from each dead soldier. The work was swift for the soldiers wore no armor. They were either naked or wearing flimsy bed clothing. We were surprised by the number of dead. The general begged to be slain with his men, but there had been enough killing."

"There is never enough killing of Yahweh's sworn enemies," Abner interjected.

"Forgive me, Commander," David said. "The required number was one hundred Philistine foreskins. We collected twice that number. We were exhausted."

"Two hundred Philistine foreskins," Saul spoke, awed by David's answer.

"Double the price you asked for the honor of wedding Princess Mikal." David pointed to the two buckets on either side.

All eyes fell upon the buckets. The barbarity was beyond mental grasp, beyond the realm of dreams. The most intimate male part of the body had been sliced from two hundred dead men and tossed into buckets.

"What did you do with the general?" Abner broke the uneasy silence that had fallen on everyone. "You should have returned with such a prize."

"We left him on his knees, howling in madness, his body covered in the blood of his men," David said.

"Good." Abner snapped his jaw as if taking a bite out of the atmosphere. "He can go back to the Five Lords and tell the tale of Yahweh's vengeance."

***

"It is a ruthless vengeance," Saul mumbled, an acrid taste moistening his tongue.

This was not the vengeance to which Abner referred; dead Philistine soldiers were to be the favored option. Why was David still alive?

It was Yahweh's vengeance that was disagreeable toward him. How was it that two hundred men could not kill one man? Was one man so precious in the eyes of Yahweh that he could escape death?

Saul must plot a new scheme to dispatch this favorite of Yahweh.

"My lord, my deed of service is complete." David knelt between the two buckets.

To Saul it looked as though his captain's countenance was one of sorrowfulness for his actions than in honor of the man who had dictated the terms.

"For the love of Israel. For the glory of Yahweh," Saul said.

"For the honor of the king." David placed a hand on the rim of each bucket containing the loins of bitter corpses and lifted them before the king.

"Captain, the king will keep his word," Saul exclaimed.

"You did this for me? This was your deed of service to win me as your bride?"

All heads turned.

Mikal stood in the middle of the Hall, the light from the fires radiating the look of wonder on her face.

Neither Saul nor the others had noticed Mikal quietly slip around the column and position herself before them. Saul felt as if his daughter might have powers of a spirit who appeared and vanished at will. Could she also read the hearts of men, of her father?

David set the buckets back onto the floor and rose, but kept his head bowed, eyes fixed upon the floor.

"I thought my daughter worthy of a great feat and to exact punishment upon our enemies all at once." Saul responded hastily. It was all he could think to say given Mikal's surprise entrance and her question.

"A convenient scheme," Mikal said.

The glint in his daughter's eyes told Saul that Mikal suspected more than her father was revealing.

"With one stone he kills a giant, with another, two hundred of our enemies. Captain, is there no limit to your powers?"

"Yahweh provides the victories, my lady, but my companions are to be praised," David asserted as he raised his head. "You would be hard pressed to find braver men."

"I am sure that is true, Captain." Mikal gave an admiring nod to the four men across the room standing at attention.

"Mikal, your sister is to be wed in three days' time." Saul wrested control of the moment. He moved forward, extending his hand to her. "Could you be ready as well?"

"Ready for what exactly, Abba?" Mikal replied, taking his hand.

Saul felt Mikal's sharp nails dig into his palm, a warning not to humiliate her in front of everyone. Saul winced from the mild stab and tried to retrieve his hand, but Mikal kept a firm grip. He wisely took the hint and became more solicitous—more a father, not a king.

"Captain, my pledge to you, should you complete your deed of service, was the gift of my youngest daughter," Saul said. "A gift I would not offer to anyone because she and her older sister are worth more than any price for a bride."

Saul's words eased the intensity of his daughter's piercing nails.

"So, you could slay one thousand giants and an army of Philistines, and it would not be sufficient dowry for my daughter." Saul smiled as he bent over and kissed the top of Mikal's hand. He also used the distraction to take back his hand.

"My king, the gift of your daughter, and to be your son-in-law, is a great honor, but a greater honor still were she to accept before you and our companions."

At first, Mikal was lost for a reply. She had not expected to be called upon for a public declaration on marriage to David. She had certainly let it be known to her older siblings she considered such a union with the captain her greatest desire, but the captain now solicited her feelings, requesting she make them known before one and all. For Mikal, it proved her bright thoughts on their compatibility were justified.

She was surprised again when she opened her mouth to speak but could not. Tears burned in her throat, forcing her to swallow. Yet, these were tears of joy that this moment had arrived, and she had been asked by her future husband to express her heart.

"When you came to us in the Valley of Elah, I never imagined one day standing in the Hall of the Wolf King hearing these words regarding marriage," Mikal began. "You risked your life for the king and his people when you slew the giant. You chose to risk your life again on my behalf. Nothing would please me more than to be wed to you, Captain David."

Mikal's words and the purr of her blush landed on David's chest, dispelling his exhaustion and awakening flesh and bone. This must be the will of Yahweh.

Her public statement to be his wife could not be taken back. He had avoided entanglement in the royal family by refusing the king's first offer of his oldest daughter, but to reject this second offer would be impossible. It must be Yahweh's will to be so close to the royal family, though the closer he got, the more trepidation he felt. It seemed to risk more pain and suffering than any hoped-for joy, but to refuse the will of the king and the expressed desire of the princess would be folly.

There was no returning from this path.

"I gladly yield to the will of the king and to the princess." David returned once more to a bent knee. He reached inside his breastplate and removed a gift wrapped in fine linen. "I had this made for the princess in hopes that I would be able to present it as a pledge of my affection. What better time than now?"

David held up the gift to Mikal as an offering, and when she raised her hand to receive it, he noticed the dried blood on the fingers of her right hand.

"My lady, you have a wound," he said.

Mikal pulled back her hand. She did not want to stain David's gift.

"Captain, I too have a gift, though it is not finished. It is a banner with the insignia of the Lion of Judah, your tribal symbol." Mikal held up the bloody hand, the wound had had resumed its flow. "I pierced my flesh with the tip of the bone needle and broke it off. It remains it my fingertip."

"We have shed blood for each other." David folded back the layers of cloth wrapped around his gift.

"Your act required more courage and was the greater cost." Mikal fixed her eyes on the object in David's hand.

"And pain." For an instant, David remembered what transpired only days before.

"But for the superior reward, I hope." Mikal cupped her hand beneath his, which brought David back to the present moment.

"Yes, my lady, a superior reward." David peeled back the last layer of cloth to reveal a golden cuff bracelet with a lion's head at each end.

David could see in Mikal's face the thrill at the sight of the golden bracelet, but more of a thrill at his phrase of her being the superior reward. Blood had been shed in the forming of this union, and the reward would be a marriage between the Lion of Judah and the Wolf of Benjamin, a great and noble foundation from which to build.

David rose and took Mikal's hand, scraping away a streak of blood on the inside of her wrist before he placed the bracelet around it. Then he kissed her hand. When he drew back, he felt the red flecks on his lips.

Mikal reached up and brushed away the flakes of dried blood with her fingers. She whispered, "Your gift shall be ready by our wedding night."

"It is done then." Saul vigorously clapped his hands together. "Jarib, make the announcement that in three days both my daughters are to be wed."

"Yes, my lord." Jarib bowed his head. "We have much to get done."

"This great Hall of the Wolf King shall resound with feasting and celebration," Saul said, and in his exuberance, he leapt into the chariot and gripped the reins, pretending to drive a team of horses. "And I want my chariot, this gift from my future son-in-law, in front of the southern entrance to the Hall for all our guests to see as they enter."

At the king's exuberance, the sentries pounded the ends of their spears upon the stone floor. Others drew their swords and slapped them upon their shields. All began to chant: "For the love of Israel. For the glory of Yahweh. For the honor of the king."

David spoke the words but held his happiness in reserve. The complexity of this union kept him from fully embracing the joy echoing through the Hall. He did not want to trifle with anyone's affections, least of all, Mikal's, but marrying into a noble house on the death of two hundred men demanded by a king whose mind was fragmented, and at moments, bent on harming him, kept his heart on alert.

His future wife had lifted her eyes to the ceiling, chanting the praise. His future brother-in-law was clapping his hands, repeating the same phrase in honor of Israel, Yahweh, and the king. His future father-in-law was dancing now inside his chariot.

The Hall resounded in full exaltation, and yet his heart withered instead of bloomed, his mind filled with foreboding instead of elation. Was Yahweh doing this for him? If so, why? Was this bargain, this union, a boon or a trap?

He smiled at his future wife as she opened her eyes. He hoped she did not perceive his disquiet or that there lodged a needle of fear in a corner of his heart like the needle embedded in the fingertip of his bride-to-be.

Chapter 26

WHILE IN CAPTIVITY, SABA EMPLOYED HIS ARTISTIC SKILLS. Were it not for Jonathan, Saba would have been left destitute in the Valley of Elah, or worse, put to death. Prisoners were a luxury Abner could never justify. Strip the dead, finish off the wounded, and leave all carcasses to the vultures and vermin. Captives from battlefields required housing and victuals; enemy noncombatants could be used as slaves and servants but were never trusted.

In Saba's case, the prince prevailed. Saba was housed in a small quarter inside the military compound on Gibeah's northern city limits and put to work fashioning shields and designing personalized insignia on any shield at any soldier's request that represented his tribe or clan. Each day, Saba was escorted by two soldiers to an industrial unit on the compound equipped with forges, tools, and materials, which employed dozens of workers to repair weapons and fashion new ones. Shields were all Saba was allowed to decorate. He was never allowed to touch weapons of any kind.

After his capture, Saba never had access to the city even under guard. He was confined to his small cell on the military compound or to his workplace, but he was happy to be alive and pleased to be working even if it was for his enemy. Perhaps, if he were ever able to escape, what he learned about his captors might prove useful to the Five Lords of the Philistines in future conflicts. But this was not a primary concern. He had spied for the Five Lords in the past, but now his artistic life was his means of survival.

Saba did what was required of him: designing insignia and embossing reliefs on the shield-front of individual soldiers. Communication with the soldiers was usually by exaggerated gestures, belligerent shoves, or raised voices. Saba knew he had pleased a soldier when he was given a straight look into his eye and a nod of approval when presenting him with the finished product. The only way he was assured he would survive was the increased demand for his skills in designing a crest for a shield. No Hebrew artisan had so many requests for a personalized emblem.

Perhaps Dagon, his god, was looking out for him. Or perhaps the God of Israel had taken pity. He did not know.

The rare occasion he used his language was when the prince paid a visit and brought Jarib, the king's secretary. Jarib was able to translate. But the day Jonathan brought the giant-slayer to the workshop in the compound Saba's world took a brighter turn.

The giant-slayer wanted a bracelet fashioned in gold with the intricate detail of a lion's head on each end.

Saba took some coal from a pile near the forge and a blank parchment and quickly sketched a design for the bracelet. When he was finished, Saba watched as the eyes of the giant-slayer widened in amazement, his speed and dexterity to envision the bracelet as described held his viewers in awe.

Could he create it with haste? Yes. Did he have the required materials? Yes. Did he have the right tools to carve the faces of the lions? Yes, and from the pouch of his leather apron, Saba produced his small chisel retrieved from the battlefield of Elah.

Because of Mikal's reaction to the bracelet, because of the weddings of the king's two daughters, because of the appreciation the prince and now the giant-slayer had of his work, Saba was given a cart, a mule, and his freedom. He was deemed no threat to the kingdom of Israel, and though Abner grudgingly agreed to Saba's freedom, he thought there was no harm in letting an artist go back to his people. Perhaps this artist might harbor goodwill toward his enemy for the way he had been treated.

And so, on the morning of the weddings, Saba drove his cart out of the compound. He let it be known he would like to return to the Valley of Elah, and if the stone he had carved for the giant was still there, he would like to reclaim it. By the generosity of the prince, along with the cart and mule, Saba was given ropes, pulleys, and a wooden ramp to help in loading the stone. He was also given a box of carving and chiseling blades and different sized hammers to begin his work anew.

Before Saba departed, Jarib presented him with a new document of safe passage stating, "Saba, the Philistine artisan, is free to travel inside the borders of Israel. Any harm that comes upon him by a citizen of Israel shall answer to Prince Jonathan, son of King Saul." At the bottom of the document was the unmistakable waxed seal of the Wolf and the Crown.

In the early light of the rising sun, Saba drove his cart over the empty training ground in the middle of the compound. There was no training today, the marriage day of the king's daughters. When he reached the gates leading from the compound into the heart of the city of Gibeah, someone shouted his name. His heart froze. He was so close to leaving, and now he was being stopped for some unknown reason. Had the commander overruled the decision of the prince to release him?

He reached inside his leather pouch on the riding bench for the prince's letter of safe passage. When he saw the giant-slayer running toward him with a smile on his face, the pounding in his heart eased. It must be one last expression of thanks for his work.

David stopped on the opposite side of the cart and patted the passenger seat, indicating he would like a ride. Saba placed the leather pouch on the floorboard at his feet, and David climbed in next to Saba. David ordered the sentries to open the gates of the compound. Saba noticed David's white wedding garment tucked underneath the everyday robes he wore to protect it from smudges and stains, and his golden turban lay cradled inside his arms. As they passed through the gates, the cheerful sentries spoke to David which made the captain laugh. Saba concluded the words must have something to do with his marriage that morning to the princess.

Once they emerged from the compound gates, Saba expected David would want to be driven to the Hall of the Wolf King. He began to steer the mule toward the royal dwellings above the city. Even though the city was in a festive mood, Saba was fearful of the risk of hostile action against him once he delivered his passenger. Even a letter of safe passage from the prince might not provide enough protection from ruffians bent on tormenting him. So, he was surprised when David pointed for him to turn in the direction of the southern gates that would put him on the road toward the Valley of Elah instead of toward the king's palace.

His passenger sat somber and quiet as they rode through the streets toward the southern gates. David slipped the hood of his robe over his head. Saba assumed such an action was the captain's attempt to keep the townspeople and guests from around the country from recognizing him.

When Saba pulled the cart to a stop in front of the southern gates, he expected David to jump out, but he remained seated, scanning the open country, the plains to the south and the foothills to the north. Saba had a strange premonition that David was hesitating, that the giant-slayer might make a snap decision and order Saba to continue driving with him at his side.

David turned and raised his eyes in the direction of the royal dwellings on the hill overlooking the bustling city, then slowly turned back in his seat and resumed gazing at the vista of the open road. Saba knew there was no common language they could share that would express David's thoughts or any verbal response Saba could offer. Saba could only imagine what David was contemplating, but he could tell by the tenseness in the captain's jawline, the squint of his eyes, and the kneading of his fists into his knees that the man next to him was grappling within his soul.

The captain bowed his head and quietly moved his lips, but then he stopped and raised his head, his eyes appeared glassy.

Saba nodded for him to continue. David took a deep breath and reached inside a pocket of his robe and pulled out a fat, leather purse, rattling the contents. Saba was completely surprised when David dropped the pouch into Saba's hands. Then the captain laid his hand upon Saba's shoulder and spoke in a solemn tone.

Saba understood the reference to the Hebrew God when he heard the captain say "Yahweh," and he assumed David was praying over him, though Saba knew nothing of what was said. It did not matter. The words sounded kind and gracious to Saba's ears whatever they might mean.

Then David hopped out of the cart and marched through the city toward the dwellings of the king. Whatever the captain had been struggling with had been resolved.

Saba dropped the leather purse into his lap and snapped the reins on the mule's rump. The cart jolted forward, and once he was a good distance from the city, he pulled onto the side of the road. He unlaced the strands of the purse and poured out some of the gold coins; not Israelite coin, but Philistine coin, and in such great quantity. He had never received so generous a commission, not from Goliath or any of the Philistine patrons or the Five Lords.

He had to wipe his eyes to test the reality of his sight. He had to squeeze the coins to test the reality of what he felt.

Saba quickly realized he was the only one departing the city. Citizens of Israel unable to find lodging inside the city were stirring from their encampments along the highway and making their way into Gibeah. Saba returned the gold pieces to the purse and placed it inside the pouch with Prince Jonathan's letter of safe passage. He took the reins and guided his mule back onto the road, heading into the bright sun toward the Valley of Elah.

What kind of men would favor him in such a way? What kind of god?

David tramped through the city streets unmolested toward his favorite bakery. The early morning hour was to his advantage. The citizens of Gibeah were not yet out in full commercial force, and the shabby cloak covering his wedding clothes and the hood over his head concealed his easily recognizable face.

He had secretly rented a room on the top floor of the bakery with an outside entrance behind the building. No one knew of this with the exception of Benaiah who had rented the space on behalf of his captain, paying the proprietor a year's rent in advance.

With the bakery in sight, David ducked off the main road and into the back streets. When he arrived at the stairway, he looked up and down the street for any inquisitive eyes. Trust was hard-won. Few had it, and given the circumstances, David thought the less public attention drawn to him and his family, the better—for everyone's safety.

He had not played at the Wolf Den since the night Abner and Jarib approached him with the king's vile proposal to become his son-in-law. He had not felt like playing. Somehow, performing in front of adoring crowds had lost its appeal. He had not felt inspired to compose. His kinnor remained inside the lion pelt in a corner of the new rented room. David had deposited it there on his only visit to the room once Benaiah had secured the letting agreement. He chose to stay in the barracks until the day of the wedding and did not want the men to pester him to sing. The back street was empty, and he briskly climbed the outside stairs.

The door was cracked open, and he slipped inside.

Benaiah rose to greet him. "I installed hook braces on the door and the frame for extra security." Benaiah demonstrated by dropping a wooden beam inside the braces and sliding it across the doorframe. "No sentries will be necessary."

"Well done, Benaiah," David said.

"It is sparsely furnished, Captain." Benaiah extended his arm to the interior.

The lodging was empty when Benaiah showed him the room the first time. David requested just the basics; soft beds were a rarity, hard ground, the norm. He did not understand the charms of feminine décor. When David stepped from the entrance into the inner room, he saw a bed of skins and quilts in the center, a lampstand on either side, a table and two chairs beneath the one window looking onto a side alley, and his kinnor propped up in the corner. There were eating utensils on the table, a bowl of fresh fruit, a skin of wine, and selection of bread and cheeses courtesy of the bakery. Flowers in a pitcher in the windowsill were Benaiah's touch.

David eased around the room, patting the large pillows tossed onto the top quilt, smelling the flowers in the window, opening the top of the wine-skin and sniffing the contents, holding up an oil lamp to the sunlight to check the level of oil. It was full.

"Again, well done." David marveled at what this warrior had cobbled together. "The flowers are a pleasing addition."

"I hope the princess will find them a delight," Benaiah replied. "Though in time, she will want to add her own touch."

"I am sure of it," David said with a knowing smile. "I have said nothing about this to her. It will be a yielding from the luxuries of her royal room. I have not known how to tell her of my discomfort sleeping in the palace."

"May Yahweh bless your marriage bed," Benaiah said with a nod.

"Yes, though I doubt I will be giving Yahweh much thought tonight." David looked at the mound of quilts before falling eagle-spread over them. There was little spring, and he nuzzled his face into a pillow. "Benaiah, what do I do?"

"What do you do, Captain?"

David rolled onto his back; his arms wrapped around a pillow. "What do I do with the princess?" David said, his voice a parched whisper.

Both men were speechless: David thwarted by the prospect of marriage and the marriage bed and Benaiah by the fact that his captain had spoken to him with such intimate exposure of his soul.

David finally sat up but still clutched the pillow.

When Benaiah saw the tears in David's eyes, he looked away. David was thankful that his friend did not want to shame him by staring at something he never expected to see. David could not speak though Benaiah waited. David could only manage moist gulps of air.

Benaiah cleared his throat. "Captain, I have little knowledge of such things, except for the lewd talk among the men in the barracks. I know the way of war, not the way with a woman."

"I know nothing, Benaiah. I came out of the mountains having tended sheep. I slew a giant. I have trained for war and killed my share of men. I have been afraid before, but this is a fear I have never known, a fear that makes my heart freeze."

"I think there is little to fear, sir," Benaiah said in a reassuring voice to still the captain's soul.

"And you have never been with a woman in that way, I mean?"

"No, sir." Benaiah turned to look at David. This required an eye-to-eye, older comrade's wisdom and words to encourage, not dishearten. "Captain, my lord, my friend, this is not something you train for as in battle. You do not face the princess like an enemy to conquer. I do not think her affection is won so."

"Then what do I do? How do I reveal myself to her and not be a fool?"

"May I venture the notion that the princess is just as inexperienced as you," Benaiah said. "That she is just as anxious, fearful even, of this night. And then, may I suggest that you allow the impulse of nature to provide direction."

"It is very confusing to me, Benaiah." David sighed and clutched his head. "I just want it to be right."

"I suspect it does not have to be right the first time or the first one hundred times," Benaiah said. "It just needs to be full of passion expressed from the heart."

"The heart, you say." David swallowed hard. "Therein resides my deepest confusion. How did we come to this point, Benaiah? I may have been ready to abandon my life when I was tending sheep in the mountains, but at least it was simple. Now, it has become entwined with complications."

"I do not philosophize on life, Captain. I see the practicalities of each day, and I contrive my way through them. Now, stop fretting. You need to get to the palace."

Benaiah went to the door, opened it, and stuck his head outside. Satisfied, he looked back at David who had not moved from the edge of the bed.

"Such a healthy young man should not be so unnerved by the prospect of a wedding night," Benaiah observed. "How do you feel when you play your kinnor?"

"Joyful. Wild. Inspired. My heart abandoned to the motion of my hands and the sounds of my throat and the words from my lips." David spoke instantly without pausing.

Benaiah stepped away from the door for David to make his exit.

"Then let the princess be your kinnor and make her sing," Benaiah said as he opened the door.

Chapter 27

ABNER'S GAZE DARTED FROM ONE FACE TO ANOTHER AS HE moved between the thick walls and the massive columns inside the Hall of the Wolf King. The chieftains and their clans gathered around the column and carved insignia representing their respective tribe. The wedding guests had stepped toward the center of the Hall for a closer viewing of the high priest solemnizing the union of the king's daughters to their respective husbands.

One bridegroom Abner trusted. He would always be mistrustful of the other. Abner did not care if he was a valiant warrior, beloved by citizen and soldier and his besotted cousin, connected to the prince in covenant bond, or that he was an exquisite musician.

Abner glared at the singer's family clustered beneath the column and its insignia of a lion for the tribe of Judah. Abner made sure that David's brothers were searched before entering the Hall in spite of their bitter complaints that the family of the bridegroom should be so rudely treated. All of Israel may be obsessed by the singing giant-slayer, but Abner would not fall under his spell.

And what he hated most was the effect the captain had on his cousin. There was no controlling Saul's moods, and the presence of the captain and his men in court always seemed to provoke the king's heart to erratic behaviors and despondent tempers.

David rarely played for the king anymore. That was the only thing that seemed to calm his cousin but could no longer be counted upon to soothe Saul's spirit when the evil came upon him. Abner did not have the artful

tongue of a counselor to reason with his cousin when he was beside himself
with terror. There was no other word for it; the thought of David in such
close proximity to the throne brought terror to the king. In Abner's mind,
usurpation by force was always in the realm of possibilities regardless of cov-
enants, of marriages, victories in battles, or a pretty voice.

There had never been this large a crowd inside the Hall, and Abner did not
like it: too stifling, too noisome, too dangerous. Though he had ordered no
weapons to be carried by the guests, with this many people, some form of a
lethal weapon could be smuggled inside, concealed beneath a robe or a gown.

Abner slowed his pace as he approached the column of the tribe of Benjamin and caught the eye of Jeush, the loyal chieftain of the king's tribe. Abner
paused and motioned his head toward the column of Judah. Jeush cast his
eyes across the Hall, scrutinizing David's clan, then looked back at Abner and
nodded. Jeush was ever-faithful and ever-watchful, and his nod meant he saw
no suspicious activity on the part of David's brothers.

Before Abner continued his patrol, Rizpah appeared from behind the column and leaned her back against it. The torchlight above her head illuminated her smile, the long curls of her red hair encompassed her face and draped
over her shoulders like folded wings. The amethyst stone that hung around
her soft neck, the scarlet gown that clung tight to her body, and her slippered
feet that peeped out beneath the hem. When had he last seen her looking so
radiant?

Rizpah dislodged herself from the wooden column and moved quietly
past Abner. To him, she seemed to float, a scarlet ghost, only this ghost laid
her hand upon his half-bare arm and applied a gentle pressure. Then she was
gone, departing from his peripheral vision into the side entrance leading into
the royal chambers.

Was she a vision? The fragrance of her passing seemed to indicate not, the
hair on his arm resuming an upright stance from the rising chill where the
evaporating warmth of her touch had been. Abner rubbed the spot, reinvigo-
rating the temperature as his eyes scanned the Hall. No one had noticed the
moment. All eyes were upon his female cousins and their future husbands
kneeling before the high priest as he swiped his finger over their foreheads
with a daub of holy oil and offered Yahweh's blessing upon these unions. Even
the king seated upon his throne, with Jarib at one side and Ish-bosheth on the
other, had only his daughters in his sight.

Abner could not remember when he and Rizpah had last spoken. He had difficulty summoning the sound of her voice in his mind. Every exchange of late was nonverbal, so fleeting, so forced, so in the open and yet so subtle, the need to be concealed from the eyes of others. When had they last embraced?

He did not turn but took a step back and stopped. Might he risk it?

He took another step back, and then another.

The room paid him no mind. Dare he risk it?

He looked back at Jeush lost in the ceremony, and then the sons of Saul— three princes, arm-in-arm, surrounding their sisters. No one was looking in his direction. A few more steps and he stood at the entrance into the royal chambers. In a few steps more, he passed through the curtained portal. Before turning, he waited to see if anyone followed, but the curtains remained closed. The ceremony continued.

When Ahimelech spoke the final blessing, the celebrations would begin. He would not be missed.

After a few deep breaths, he turned around.

Rizpah waited at the far end of the hallway.

At first, his feet would not move, but once her arms opened to him, the restraint on his legs dissolved. He did not look back. Instead, he raced toward her, his own arms rising to meet her embrace.

Saul sat propped up in bed still clothed in his wedding robes. Ish-bosheth lay stretched out beside him sound asleep. Saul gently rubbed the boy's head and stared at the door into his chambers. Ish-bosheth had told his father that he did not want to go to bed until he saw his sisters ride away in the golden chariot after the celebrations, but the lad could not stay awake. The whole day had been filled with the bustle of a double wedding, and Ish-bosheth too often found himself in the way, ignored or pushed aside. Exhaustion and rejection finally took its toll.

After the extravagant feast, when the two couples were ready to depart for the night, the doors of the southern entrance into the Hall were opened and the golden chariot, captured by David from the Philistine general, now driven by two caparisoned, milk-white horses, entered the grand Hall. The wedding guests shouted, and the musicians blasted their shofars, plucked stringed instruments, pounded drums, and clashed cymbals. David and Mikal deferred to Merab and Adriel, allowing them the pleasure of a parade ride through the city in the golden chariot.

When Saul had searched for Ish-bosheth so he could see them being driven out of the Hall, he found the prince sound asleep on a windowsill. He plucked his son off the ledge and held him in his arms. He moved beside his throne and watched the chariot disappear out of the brightly lit Hall into the darkness of the night with the cheering crowd following.

Mikal and David remained in the Hall, the cast of desire covering their faces, oblivious to everyone, except Saul who glared at them from the platform of his throne. Mikal removed a piece of material from inside the sleeve of her wedding dress. She unfolded it, offering it to David who raised the fabric to the light. His face transformed into an expression of admiration and wonder at the exquisite design stitched upon the cloth. Then the captain lifted Mikal off her feet, causing a delightful squeal and carried her out of the Hall in his arms.

Saul listened to the echoes of Mikal's laughter reverberate in the Hall before he entered his private chambers behind the throne carrying his sleeping son.

Saul quietly rose from the bed and went to the trunk behind the stand bearing his armor. He had not worn this battle suit since the army returned from the Valley of Elah. He paused before it, running his hands over his belly and squeezing the fleshy roll of his stomach. Would this protective cladding still fit?

He exhaled in dismay and removed his crown, placing it on top of his helmet. He went around behind the stand and lifted the lid of the trunk, pushing aside quilts and garments until he found the wooden box he sought. He closed the trunk and returned to the edge of the bed.

Before opening the lid of the box, Saul glanced at Ish-bosheth who slept the deep sleep of a child. What did the future hold for his son?

His entrance into the world had been precarious. Were it not for his two sisters, who now were focused on starting families of their own, the boy would not have survived the rage of this father, a similar feeling that was taking up more space in Saul's heart. He hoped that in a fit of madness, he would not be so overcome that he would harm this boy. His growing fondness for the lad seemed genuine. He hoped this small budding of affection would provide a palliative. He hoped, but he could not be certain.

Saul removed the lid and carefully lifted the handkerchief Ahinoam made for him with the names of his children stitched along the border. The name of her last child—the child that killed her—was not sewn into the fabric. If his love for Ish-bosheth was sincere, then perhaps he would have Mikal stitch his name on this precious keepsake.

If only Ahinoam could have seen this day. If only she had lived, his mind could have remained clear, there might have been no confusion, no bad judgment, no madness and torment.

Saul set the handkerchief on the side of the bed and removed the torn sleeve off Samuel's robe from the box. In a fit of desperation to keep Samuel from leaving him, he had gripped the prophet's robe so firmly it had been torn from the rest of his garment.

The prophet turned the moment into an object lesson: "*Like this sleeve torn from my robe, Yahweh has torn the kingdom from your hands.*" Or something to that effect.

Saul just wanted to please. He desperately wanted to please, and nothing he did or could do appeared to make any difference. So, if this was what the prophet of Yahweh proclaimed, then so be it. If the prophet's opposition would never be withdrawn and there was no chance to be reinstated into the good grace of the prophet, then perhaps this linen remnant contained some mysterious protection against the worst impulses of his nature.

He laid the sleeve aside and pulled out the empty vial from which Samuel had anointed Saul when informing him he would be Israel's first king. He was the first. That was something, was it not, being the first?

No one could take that from him. Not the prophet or the people or historians. Not even Yahweh.

He held the bottle between his forefinger and thumb, raising it to the light. Such a small bottle. A portion of Yahweh was once inside this bottle. Would that its contents had never been poured upon him, that it had just been handed to him, the bottled symbol of Yahweh's favor, and that he could have returned it to the prophet unused and all would have been forgotten. So small a bottle. So stingy a portion of Yahweh's Spirit. So long ago.

"My lord, the guests have all departed and the servants are cleaning the Hall. Are you ready to retire? It has been a long day."

Saul had not heard anyone enter his chambers. He slipped the vial into his palm and made a fist around it. Then he looked at the intruder standing before him. It took a moment for Saul to place him.

"Did you see the way she looked at him, Jarib?" Saul spoke in a low growl.

"Who looked at whom, my lord?" Jarib asked, maintaining a smile.

"She did not look at me once the entire evening," Saul said. "Not once. She did not bother to kiss me good-bye or say good night on this last day of being my daughter."

"She will always be your daughter, my lord. Both of them," Jarib offered, though he suspected the king referred solely to Mikal. "And you can hardly blame your daughters for the distractions of the day, or for thinking of the pleasures that await them," Jarib added with an amused smile, trying to dismiss the perception of the slight as a minor offense.

"He shall be my enemy for the rest of my days," Saul said, his voice oddly composed for such a dire statement.

Jarib detected a threatening rattle in the king's voice. "Surely not, my lord," Jarib blurted, and then caught himself. The day had been long, and he did not want to get into a debate with the king or try to placate him. If this mood was brought on by exhaustion, then the quickest way to soothe it was to get the king into bed. "Come, my lord. Let me summon the servants to help you out of your wedding clothes."

Saul did not answer Jarib, but instead carefully placed the objects back inside the box before closing the lid. Then he returned the box to the trunk and covered it with the garments and quilts. He went back to the bed and looked down upon the sleeping Ish-bosheth.

"I will focus my wrath on David." Saul spoke as if formulating in his mind the possible consequences of this decision. "If I do so, perhaps the boy will be spared."

"My lord, I am not quite sure…"

"Oh, Jarib, I am very sure," Saul interrupted his secretary. "And if I am diligent in my purpose, perhaps I might even change Yahweh's mind about the giant-slayer. Yahweh certainly changed His mind about me. Diligence, Jarib, that is the secret."

Saul bent down and kissed the child on the cheek. "Sleep, my son," he whispered, stroking Ish-bosheth's hair. "As long as you have breath, there is a chance. If not your brothers, then perhaps you will wear the crown."

Jarib watched as the king reached down and pulled the fur quilt over his son's still body. What had the king meant by these words? What was he plotting?

Jarib knew in that moment that he too must be diligent, diligent to guard the king against his worst impulses. To keep the king from destroying himself and his kingdom.

Benaiah raced through Gibeah's streets, teeming with people celebrating the double wedding of the king's daughters. He assumed once Merab and Adriel returned to the Hall that David and Mikal would take their turn in the chariot, but they were nowhere to be found. He did not want to alarm Jozabad, Uriah, and Eleazar when they and all the other wedding guests returned to the Hall with Merab and Adriel after their tour of the city.

Benaiah had fully expected to escort the bride and bridegroom to their secret quarters, protecting them from unwanted exuberance from the crowd. The least David could have done was inform Benaiah of any alternate plans for how to get from the Hall to the secret rented room above the bakery, but the captain was always doing the unexpected. Benaiah just hoped he and the princess had made it without incident.

Benaiah pushed through the revelers until he arrived at the bakery. It was doing brisk business, the proprietor taking advantage of Gibeah's increased population from the four corners of Israel. Benaiah slipped around the side of the building into a passageway that barely afforded enough room for one man to walk between it and the adjacent building. He did not want to use the street on the opposite side of David's house for fear of bringing undue attention.

When the tight passage opened onto the back street alleyway behind the bakery, Benaiah found it deserted. All the citizens preferred the merriment on the heavily trafficked thoroughfare in the heart of the city. He looked back to see if he was followed then slipped to the stairs leading up to the rented room. The flame burning from a small container of oil attached to the wall at the foot of the steps provided Benaiah with enough light to see two garments cast aside like discarded skins of ghosts. The first he recognized as the cloak David had worn that morning to protect his wedding clothes. The second, smaller garment was not as plain, but not ornate enough to draw attention.

Benaiah raised his eyes to the door at the top of the steps. Could they not wait until inside the room to disrobe?

He threw the cloaks over his shoulder and went around to the other side of the building with more space between it and the next structure. Light from inside the room flickered from the window above, and two distinct shadows frolicked on the ceiling of the room like two fluttering birds hovering in flight, separating and coming together in passionate flow.

Benaiah lowered his head and smiled as he returned to the back staircase. He neatly folded the two cloaks and laid them one on top of the other on the bottom step.

"It seems the captain and the princess have begun their great discovery," Benaiah said to himself as he moved up the quiet avenue and headed back toward the barracks.

It took all day for Saba to drive to Socoh. With a few of the coins David gave him, he intended to hire some locals to help load the stone onto the cart. If he could locate the stone.

He arrived just before the gates in the walls were closing for the night. Socoh was the closest Philistine city that was partially fortified and nearest to the site of the humiliating military defeat. Though he was an indigenous Philistine, even heralded in the five capital cities as an artist of renown, he felt a tension in his heart at being back in his native land.

Saba secured his mule in the city stables, and to save money, he was able to camp in the commons beside the stables. He slept in the bed of his cart, and before drifting off, he gazed into the sky with its thin moonlight and thought about his captivity.

He was mystified by his survival. The approval of Prince Jonathan meant his treatment would be respectful. No captive of the Philistines would be so well treated, especially a Hebrew captive, and then to be set free with a purse full of Philistine coins to start a new life. This was absurd. There could be no other explanation for such observable facts but a divine source intervening. But what source? The Philistine gods were not known for benevolent dispositions for such personalized intervention.

At first light, local day-labor hires gathered in the city square. Saba needed stout men, not sluggards or those suffering the muddles of too much wine from the night before. He chose three who looked capable of hoisting a heavy object and intelligent enough to understand instruction. Saba told them he was looking for an artifact buried in the earth.

When he explained the location, the men hesitated. The land was cursed, they said. The Philistine army suffered a great defeat at the hands of her enemies. When Saba advanced them two coins each and promised an additional two coins apiece once the job was done, this seemed to appease their superstitions regarding any curse.

Saba did not tell the laborers the reason behind his interest in the stone. He knew the general location, and if he could not find it in a day that meant it had probably been looted by industrious treasure hunters. On the way out of town, Saba stopped at an outdoor market and purchased instruments for digging and supplied the four of them and the mule with a day's rations of food and water; a little extra for himself and the mule since he would not be returning to Socoh.

Saba entered the valley from the eastern outskirts. The countryside appeared to have changed, or was it that his memory had become hazy surrounding the details of the forty-day siege when every footstep of landscape seemed to be covered with tents and equipment, livestock and soldiers, and eventually corpses, thousands of corpses of his countrymen?

While in captivity, he learned not one Israelite died in that battle. Not one.

He stopped at the edge of the stream to allow the mule and the men to slake their thirst and stretch their legs. Saba stood in the driver's seat, shielded his eyes from the sun's bright glare, and tried to spot the area where he thought the monument might be located. The Philistine camp had been set up on the southern side of the stream running through the valley. He need not cross it. He remembered distinctly how Captain David charged over the stream toward Goliath. He told the laborers not to get back into the cart but to walk along the base of the hill and where the ground began to incline, keep their eyes peeled for a large, four-sided stone with carvings on its face, and perhaps pieces of iron scaffolding that had held it upright.

Saba remained standing in the cart as it rumbled behind the laborers walking through the former Philistine encampment. When they had reached the central part of the valley, one of the laborers shouted and started running in a circle, pointing downward. Saba leapt to the ground and grabbed an iron crookneck tool out of the cart and ran with the others to the spot.

The scaffolding was nowhere to be found. He got down on his knees and used his hands to clean off the layer of dirt and rock covering the large square impression sunk into the earth. The stone slab was the exact size Saba remembered, but completely smooth. He had expected to feel the bas-relief images he had carved. Perhaps, the stone had fallen forward.

After cutting a clean outline around the stone in the ground, Saba pulled the cart beside it. While the laborers dug a trench around the stone, Saba crawled over the square, meticulously brushing off its surface. He could not believe it remained intact. He could not find any cracks.

Once the laborers had burrowed a full span below the thickness of the stone, Saba tied three hooks to three ropes and secured them along one edge of the stone. Each laborer took the end of his rope and moved into position on the opposite side of the cart. If all went well, they should be able to flip the stone upon its side and then slide it onto the flatbed cart. On Saba's order, the laborers carefully pulled the stone onto its side. Once the stone was far enough off the ground, Saba was shocked by what appeared to be a dead body beneath the stone, but he did not bother to closely examine the remains until the stone was secured onto the cart.

While the laborers stood around the dead body, they jabbered away, speculating who it might be and how he had suffered this unfortunate accident. Saba examined the bas-relief images. The impressions he had designed for Goliath had suffered very little damage while buried, yet the story it told had a completely different outcome for his patron. At least, the giant had approved of the finished piece and enjoyed gazing upon it before his death.

"Hebrew! Hebrew!" shouted one of the laborers, and Saba looked at the excited man waving a scabbard and sword with Israelite markings. A second laborer held a worn, leather pouch and poured out Israelite coins.

Inside the deteriorated garments of the deceased were the smashed bones of what Saba assumed were an Israelite soldier facedown in the earth. The unsuspecting man apparently did not know what hit him. They had not found the iron scaffolding Saba had used to support the stone while he chiseled his creation. It appeared that once the victorious army had been paid and discharged, this soldier took it upon himself to plunder. The slab must have toppled when the soldier removed the iron supports and turned his back. So, an Israelite soldier had died after all, not by a Philistine sword, but by a work of art.

Saba gave the laborers their balance of payment once they rejoined him after bathing in the stream. They departed for Socoh still excited by the treasure they found and the coin they earned, yet indifferent to the stone slab they unearthed and loaded onto a cart for their eccentric employer.

After a final check of the tension on the ropes securing the stone, Saba climbed into the wagon and sat quietly in the driver's seat. In the absence of human voices, Saba could hear the sounds of the earth: the valley stream running between the hills, the wind blowing low over the ground at his back, carrion eaters swooping overhead eyeing Saba and his mule as a potential meal.

Then the moans and shrieks of the dead began to rise from the ground. This land was haunted, where war and death had prevailed against his kinsmen. This was where the mightiest among them had fallen at the hand of a stripling.

This was where he had carved his most beautiful creation. He turned in his seat and looked again upon the images. A little reconstruction and he could restore it to its original state.

He snapped the reins over the mule's rump and the cart rumbled forward. He headed west toward the city of Gath. He would make a new start in Gath, and he would place this stone at the entrance of his new studio. What better way to attract new patrons?

PART THREE

PART THREE

Chapter 28

GAD RUSHED OUT OF THE HALL OF THE WOLF KING THAT WAS filled with military officers and raced toward the royal stables. While the engineers were pointing out the design improvements of the new Israelite chariots, advance word arrived that David and his men had entered the gates of Gibeah and were parading through the main street to the frenzied welcome of the citizens, wagons overflowing with Philistine plunder. They were on their way to the palace, so Saul could review what the captain had pillaged from his latest campaign.

Everyone had greeted the news with enthusiasm, except the king.

"Is he invincible?" Saul erupted in fury. "Does every Philistine spear fracture when hurled at him? Every arrow splinter when shot at him?"

Ishvi and Malki ran for their father, wrapping their arms around him to comfort not constrain him, and Jonathan used the distraction to catch Gad's attention. "Warn him," mouthed Jonathan.

The prophet had slipped out of the Hall unnoticed. If Gad could reach the royal stables and prevent David from proceeding to the Hall with the wagons, then perhaps a humiliating disaster might be averted for Saul before his court.

Gad stumbled to the entrance of the stables, bent over and braced his arm against the rock wall to catch his breath. He heard the rumble of horses and wagons groaning under the weight of plunder and looked up to see David leading his column of militia flanked by his quartet of mighty men.

Gad stepped in front of them, waving his arms.

"Stand aside, Gad." David spoke with annoyance at Gad's obstruction.

"My lord, I implore you not to go to the Hall at this time." Gad kept his voice measured, so as not to reveal the king's current state of mind.

"Prophet, my men and I have been absent for weeks while on this recent operation against the Philistines. Yahweh has given us success. We desire to give the king his treasure and go to our homes."

David dug his heels into the flanks of his horse to go around Gad, but the prophet reached for the horse's bridle.

The horse snapped at Gad, as did David.

"Gad, you are either foolish or have newfound boldness." David pulled back on the reins. "Stand aside. I need to see the king, get a bath, and tend to my wife."

The men behind him chuckled at David's last stated goal.

"I understand, Captain." Gad massaged the slobbered spot where the horse nipped his wrist. "I beg you to dismount. Prince Jonathan sent me."

Invoking the name of the prince, meant David would pay attention. Once the captain dismounted and approached, Gad spoke under his breath only for David's hearing.

"We were reviewing the new chariots when word came of your arrival. Your unexpected return has infuriated the king. The prince thinks it unwise to present your treasure at this moment."

"Our arrival and our treasure should have brought joy to everyone," David responded.

Gad read the bewilderment in David's eyes at such a reception. "There was gladness expressed by everyone in the Hall apart from the king."

"I can do nothing to please the king."

Gad knew from David's grumbled reaction that he was weary of this burden.

"It is not that, Captain," Gad continued, glancing back at David's men. "The prince thinks it best if you delay your arrival until the king's spirit has been soothed."

"I must see Jonathan." David dropped the reins and darted around Gad.

"May I suggest that the wagons of plunder remain behind." Gad's short legs forced him to trot to keep up with David.

David spun to address the four horsemen of his elite forces, but he was unsure what to tell them. This was not the normal welcome for a victorious army. It was, in fact, shameful for the king not to receive the warriors he commissioned for battle upon their return, not to inspect their bounty, not to accept their offer of treasure. But if Jonathan had sent Gad, then something was amiss, and David did not want to subject his men to the unpredictable rage of the king, especially if he were the cause.

"Benaiah, dismiss the men," David ordered.

David had hoped his marriage to Mikal would calm the king's anger toward him. He had hoped that his friendship with Jonathan would ease the king's distrust. He had hoped leading successful campaigns against the Philistines would lessen the king's resentment, but none of this seemed to matter to the mad king. "We will present the king's treasure another time."

When David and Gad approached the Hall of the Wolf King, Abner's military officers, the engineers, and royal attendants were pouring out of the southern entrance. Few made eye contact with David. Those that did looked fiercely at him, their hand on the hilt of their sword in what David perceived as threatening. He was troubled and wanted desperately to understand why. Once inside, David barely noticed the three new chariots parked in the Hall. His eyes were riveted on Jonathan kneeling before an empty throne.

Gad grabbed David's arm, forcing him to pause in the middle of the Hall until the guards closed the doors at the southern entrance. The soldiers remained outside. No other sentries were positioned around the throne or posted at the king's chamber door.

David pulled his arm free from Gad's grip and moved toward the throne, an unsettled feeling in his heart.

Abner came through the door of Saul's private chambers, carrying the king's crown. He set it on the seat of the throne, and then looked at David. He said nothing until Jonathan rose.

"He tossed his crown on the floor." Abner pointed to the royal diadem, the wine-colored stones of the wolf's eyes sparkling in the torchlight. "Said it was the cause of his black headaches. He has crawled under the furs of his bed and buried his head beneath his pillows to block out the light. The twins are with him now, and Jarib has summoned Rizpah and your sisters to his chambers."

"Thank you," Jonathan said, his voice brittle and desolate.

"Thank me for what?" Abner grumbled. "I do not understand the cause of his lunacy, but it makes for a poor king. You should prepare to assume the throne."

"We will not make that decision yet." Jonathan shook his head.

"You are the natural heir, Jonathan. The kingdom is unsettled by his madness."

"Stop saying he is mad," Jonathan exclaimed. "Troubled and angry, yes. Frightened, yes, but not mad. I can calm him. I can bring him to reason."

David's pace was quiet and measured as he approached the throne.

"Even the great singer has lost his power to soothe the beast," Abner said, a sneer pinching his upper lip.

Jonathan stepped off the raised platform, and the two friends embraced.

"Will you tell him, or shall I?" Abner blurted, impatient to break off the embrace.

The month before, Jonathan and Adriel had come to David's encampment in the territory of the tribe of Dan. The Philistine armies from the city-state of Ashdod were raiding villages along the tribe's northern frontier, and Allon, the tribal chieftain, begged the king to send David and his men to secure the border and establish defensive positions.

The prince was anxious to get back to the battlefield, feeling his skills as a warrior were growing slack, but his father and uncle consented to this mission only if the prince did not engage in battle. He was ordered to gather information only. Jonathan could go if he remained in the camp with the cooks and the baggage and return in seven days' time with a report.

David did not expect the prince to obey the command, but he did expect Adriel, Jonathan's armor-bearer, to keep the prince safe. That proved difficult in the heat of hand-to-hand combat where the prince was required to take care of himself. After a week of heavy fighting, Jonathan and Adriel returned to Gibeah. David was grateful his friend had returned home in one piece with just a few scrapes and bruises that he could hide beneath his clothing.

"Tell me what?" David looked into Jonathan's face.

Jonathan was not immediately forthcoming. He gave a pensive look at the crown. "You heard the commander. He wants me to assume the throne," Jonathan began. "Gad, what do you think? Should I do as he asks?"

David felt a weakness in his legs. He glanced at Gad who would not return his look. David knew what lay ahead in the future kingdom of Israel. His dear friend would never be king, but he would do nothing to usurp the throne.

Jonathan did not wait for Gad to answer but took the crown from the throne and placed it on his head. Then he slumped into the throne. No one but his father had seated themselves on this royal chair. No one had worn the royal crown but Saul.

The reaction from David and the others at Jonathan's bold action was sufficient answer to the prince's question. He rose, reverently placing the crown back on the seat.

"By the expressions on each of your faces, I have my answer. If I took the crown, or it came by natural birthright, it would not be the will of Yahweh."

"What do I need to be told, Commander?" David shifted his focus toward Abner.

"My father believed that the love of his son would be stronger than his love for his friend," Jonathan said, raising his hand to Abner for him not to answer. "I do love my father, and that is why I will reason with him and talk him out of killing you."

David was painfully aware of the king's enmity, but to hear Jonathan, his trusted and covenant friend, utter such words of condemnation, brought cold dread to his heart.

"It is true," Abner said. "When the cheers went up in the Hall for your victorious return, the king became enraged and ordered your death."

"His inflamed eyes looked straight into mine, and he ordered me to kill you," Jonathan added, unable to speak the words above a whisper.

David glanced back at Gad with a knowing look, and the prophet received it as such. How could either of them ever forget the night the king had hurled his spear across the room while David was playing for him?

This was not just a momentary moral failure, but murderous intent flowing from a poisoned mind. Now, by kingly decree, the poison had been released to include anyone so inclined to carry out the order. The danger to David's life was a stark reality both on and off the battlefield.

"But do not fear." Jonathan gripped David's shoulders in his hands. "Go home to Mikal. Take pleasure in her company. Tomorrow, hide in the hills above the training field. We are testing the new chariots in the morning, are we not, Commander?"

"We are," Abner answered.

"I will see that my father will be there to observe. I will speak to him of you and tell you whatever he says, but I swear, as Yahweh lives, you will not die by my hand."

Once outside the Hall of the Wolf King, David devised a different plan.

"Home is too dangerous." David removed his breastplate, shin guards, and leather girdle and handed them to Gad. He kept his shoulder bag containing a waterskin, bread and dried fruit, cords of twine, bandages, a bottle of olive oil, his sling and several rocks, and a small knife. He tightened the strap for his sword around his middle. "Return to the stables and tell Benaiah what has happened, and that I will stay the night by the rock-face pool. He must tell Mikal. Now go, quickly."

David watched as Gad raced toward the stables. When he could no longer be seen, David jogged down the main road leading into the city. He then veered from the road and disappeared behind a row of houses. If Jonathan refused to kill him, plenty of people would, especially those of the tribe of Benjamin.

To avoid being followed by prospective assassins, David kept to the side streets and back alleys until he was sure no one was following. At last, he disappeared into the forest on the eastern side of the city. When the sun had set and the sky was a twilight blue, he slipped out of the forest and made his way to the rock-face pool.

David slipped below the surface of the deep, spring-fed pool, spinning his body in the clear waters and scrubbing with his fingernails the dirt and grime from his hair and flesh built up over weeks of fighting the Philistines. When he came up for air, he scanned the forest of trees and wild undergrowth that concealed the pool. Even with the sun overhead, the thick foliage fragmented the light, creating a patchwork of shadows. Satisfied that there was no danger, he took another deep breath and went under again to continue his scrubbing.

David had found this oasis while tracking a stag that was following a stream, leading to the pool tucked inside the dense woodland. The pool was fed by water gushing from two different crevices in a rock face and flowing out of the pool beneath the dense underbrush on the opposite end and forming a small stream that flowed into the open landscape. It flowed for only a short distance, splashing over the rock formations before disappearing into the earth.

He brought Mikal once to the edge of this remote forest before they were wed when they went riding one afternoon. They stopped to let the horses drink from the stream rippling out of the dense underbrush before vanishing into the earth.

When he surfaced again, the limbs hanging low over the stream swayed and bobbed. David could not tell if the movement was caused by human or animal. He slipped out of the pool, crawled onto the mossy bank and grabbed his sword lying next to his soiled and worn garments. David heard a horse neigh and a feminine voice softly calm it. He stepped forward as Mikal emerged from the thicket, her garments soaked to her knees from slogging through the stream. They stood still, each staring at the other in disbelief, inside the reverie of a dream.

"Were you followed?" David asked.

"I rode south out of the city, took the road east, and doubled back."

"Your clothes are soaked." David pointed with his sword.

"And you are without clothes." Mikal nodded her head.

"What's to be done?"

Mikal led her mare out of the stream onto the bank and wrapped the reins around the closest branch. Then she unlaced her top cloak and threw it over the back of the mare.

"I am starving," David said.

"So am I." Mikal pulled her arms through the sleeves of her undergarment, yanking it off her shoulders.

"There can be no fire tonight."

Mikal slipped off her sandals. "We will need no fire."

"The water is cool."

"The day is hot." Mikal untied the cord straps around her waist supporting her leggings. This layer of clothing was not thrown over the mare's back but was discarded on the ground.

"I have missed you, wife," David said, his face brightening, his flesh rippling at the sight of Mikal's pearl-white skin.

"I can tell, husband."

David dropped his sword onto the ground and leapt into the pool. He remained submerged as Mikal splashed right in front of him. They held their breath long enough beneath the surface of the water for the air bubbles to clear so they could gaze upon each other in the refracted light until the force of desire drove them together. Their muscles and flesh strengthened from mutual yearning. There was only one need to be satisfied. Their bodies swirled in a cauldron of froth, their feet gained purchase on the soft mud bottom, in this one-flesh passion their only uncertainty was how to keep from drowning.

Chapter 29

MIKAL'S TIME AT THE POOL WITH DAVID WAS NOT A ROMANTIC interlude. It was a stolen moment, a perilous reverie, for, if caught, it threatened not only their marriage but their very lives. She did not know how to exist under such duress. She did not know how to dream of a future. How to love a husband when her father wanted him dead, or when he was constantly at war or in hiding?

Would there ever be a time when they did not live in fear? Would it ever be possible for them to see a day of happiness that the king's unpredictable nature did not threaten to destroy?

Mikal clung to David's back as they rode her mare out of the hills toward the palace under the cover of darkness. When David was away at war, Mikal stayed in the palace and not in their room in the city.

Her sister had given birth to a boy and was expecting another child. It seemed that all Adriel and Merab had to do was look at each other and Merab was imbued with new life. Rizpah also expected another child, meanwhile keeping up with Armoni, a handful and not a particular favorite of the king. Ish-bosheth held that position except when her father was under the burden of his dark spirit. Mikal took it upon herself to protect her little brother from their father's rage.

Jonathan's wife, Levana, had given him a son, Merib-baal, the smasher of Baal. Not a name she would have chosen, but it suited his father and delighted his grandfather. Mikal was a dutiful aunt, daughter, and sister to a palace full of boys, none of them her own and only sporadic prospects for having one.

Merab had given Mikal the life-size teraphim to enhance her chances of success, but what good was a fertility idol if she only saw her husband on rare intervals? Mikal kept the teraphim in the rented room in town, not at the palace. She had no desire to be reminded of her childless state when she went to bed at night alone.

Mikal had to return to the palace before dawn. David guided the mare to the edge of an olive grove on a hillside on the outskirts of Gibeah. Soon, they should know if Jonathan was able to convince Saul to cease his hostilities toward her husband and rescind the directive to have him killed. Depending on the outcome, the couple would know their future.

David slipped off the mare and helped Mikal scoot forward on the leather padding before handing her the reins. He kissed her knee and laid his head on her thigh while she rubbed her fingers through his thick hair. They had spoken little. Too much time was taken with lovemaking, eating, lovemaking, sleeping, and waking to love again before departing from the pool while it was still night.

"I pray my brother convinces our father to come to his senses." Mikal kissed the top of his head.

"I wish for the same, my love," David said. "But I am fearful."

"If he does not succeed, what is to be done?" Mikal's voice caught at the possibility of this outcome.

"He must succeed." David raised his head from its resting place. "I do not wish to think of an alternate plan."

Mikal took David's face in her hands, kissing him hard on the mouth. If the hour was not so dire, she would have slipped off her horse and fallen upon her husband for one more amorous encounter.

"You must go. You must go," David said, breathless with desire. "You must."

David forced himself to break from his wife's clasp. He kissed her hands before helping her secure the reins between her fingers, and then took off running back into the hills.

David did not like keeping secrets from his wife. He had wanted to tell her about Samuel's visit to his home in Bethlehem, of the anointing, but she might consider this act treasonous, a betrayal of their marriage. He did not know how to confess to Mikal that Yahweh had chosen him over her father and brother. She had enough burdens to bear without this terrible knowledge, so he would hold on to this secret a little longer.

Jonathan stood beside his father on a wooden platform situated in the center of the field, watching each charioteer drive his chariot in a wide circle around the perimeter. The engineers had built prototypes of three different models, each a different size. The chariots had to be durable to withstand rough terrain, and the horses had to accept the harnesses as well as the training to pull the vehicle in tandem.

If the test of the new chariots went well, his father would be in a more favorable frame of mind. So, Jonathan waited and watched as each driver drove the chariots in endless circles around the field at speeds no faster than a trotting gait.

"How tedious," Saul grumbled. "They just keep driving in circles on a flat field."

"I know, Abba. The engineers are concerned—"

"We should be on the rough plains or in a valley," Saul interrupted. "They should be testing these contraptions by running them through streambeds and up rocky hills."

"You are correct, but before they do that, Abner wanted to test them on softer landscape."

"Do we request our enemies fight us on gentler landscapes?" Saul barked. "And we should be firing at the drivers with slings and arrows and spears—battlefield conditions, not parades and joyrides. The Philistines will not be throwing flowers at us. I do not want my men sent into battle driving a pretty piece of equipment only to have it fall apart when it runs over a rock...except for your friend. I should instruct Abner to send the captain into battle in one of these machines with a cracked axle or loose wheel."

This was not the improved mental condition Jonathan had hoped for.

He had anticipated the driving tests would go well and brighten his father's mood.

"Abner!" Saul yelled at the commander standing at the far end of the field with his military corps and engineers. "Tell them to stop driving like old men and go full bore."

"Why would you give the order to have David killed?" Jonathan interjected. If his father's frame of mind was not going to improve, then he must take advantage of this private moment and the fact that Saul had initiated the subject with his threat to send David into battle driving a faulty chariot. "This is an evil thing you have done against such a loyal servant who has done you no harm."

Saul waved to Jeush, who stood with the engineers huddled around Abner. He cupped his hands over his mouth and yelled. "Jeush, fetch me a bow, a quiver of arrows, and a rack of spears."

"What do you intend to do?" Jonathan was becoming more anxious at this request for armaments.

Saul ignored him.

Jeush immediately ordered soldiers to gather the weapons requested by the king and meet him at the platform in the field. Abner had a soldier raise the banner, signaling the charioteers to return to the starting point, so he could give them the king's new order.

Things were happening fast, and Jonathan did not want to lose this moment now that his father had spoken of David, even if in a threatening vein. All the more reason to argue for reconciliation. Soon, there would be too much action to distract his father and too many soldiers around the platform.

"The king has benefited by what David has done." Jonathan wanted to focus on advantages David provided king and country. He paused to see if his father would agree.

Saul stepped over to a table next to the stage with a pitcher and goblets. He poured some wine and guzzled it, spitting the last swallow onto the ground. He watched Jeush and the soldiers race toward the stage bearing the armaments.

Jonathan continued to make his case. "David risked his life to slay the giant. Yahweh gave Israel a great victory that day. You witnessed it and were glad. David is an innocent man, Abba. You have no cause to order his death. Why would you do such an evil thing?"

Jonathan could have pointed out multiple reasons for the king to rescind his order, but he chose instead to make the moral point of murdering an innocent man. Surely, his father could agree such evil action against a man so beloved would do irreparable harm.

"Where would you like the weapons, my lord?" Jeush asked breathlessly as he and the soldiers bearing the arms halted before the platform.

"On the stage would be fine, Jeush. Thank you." Saul turned the empty goblet upside down and set it upon the table.

Jonathan stepped off the platform to make way for the soldiers to lay out the weaponry to the king's satisfaction. He did not know how to interpret his father's silence, the lack of acknowledgment of the salient point that would appeal to any rationale mind. But then Jonathan knew in his heart that his father's mind was a fragile, volatile thing.

All three chariots had returned to the starting point, and Abner looked to the king to give the order.

Saul cupped his hands over his mouth and shouted to Abner. "Tell the charioteers to drive one behind the other full out," he commanded.

Dread filled Jonathan's heart as his father slipped the quiver of arrows over his shoulder and tested the tautness of the bowstring as he waited for the drivers to gain speed. By the time Saul notched an arrow, the lead chariot had reached the first turn in the track. Saul pulled back the bowstring and let the arrow fly.

The driver dropped to his knees to avoid being struck. The driver in the second chariot reined in his team and let the king's second arrow fly in front of him.

Saul shouted his praise for the driver's quick counter maneuver. However, this caused the third chariot to veer around the second stalled in the middle of the track, which proved a fatal mistake.

Jonathan watched in horror as Saul yanked a spear from the rack and leapt off stage, gaining momentum for his throw. The spear flew right between the spokes of the wheel, jamming the axle and causing the wheel to break away.

It required the full skill of the charioteer to bring his team to a halt as the chariot plowed through the field and track on one wheel.

Again, Saul extolled the driver for not letting himself be thrown from the crippled chariot or leaping out and abandoning it to a runaway team of horses. Saul spun, vibrant in the sensation of the moment. "Now that is a test!" he bellowed; his arms stretched out in triumph. "That is just a taste of what to expect on the battlefield. Chaos and death to those who do not know how to react and adjust. True, Jeush?"

"True, my sovereign, and were you not the king, I would demand you fight at my side." Jeush fell to his knees, a look of awe on his face.

The king bound onto the platform and dropped the empty quiver onto the wooden floor. The arrows had spilled onto the ground when Saul hurled his spear.

"If my spear can disable a chariot, then our engineers have designed death machines not war machines," he said. "Jeush, tell the commander to order the engineers to refit their chariots and make them sound."

"Yes, my lord," Jeush said, rising.

Saul watched as Jeush and the soldiers marched away, and then turned to look Jonathan squarely in the eye. "You were saying?"

Jonathan was so startled he momentarily forgot his advocacy of David. "You could have killed those men," Jonathan said, unable to comprehend his father's actions.

"Better to die by the hand of your king than an uncircumcised Philistine because you were ill-equipped." Saul hopped off the platform and headed toward the palace.

"Abba, I—"

Saul spun but continued to walk backward. "As surely as Yahweh lives, David will not be put to death."

Alone on the platform, Jonathan shuddered at what he had witnessed. In one moment, his father had caused turmoil on the training field, and the next, had calmly lifted the order to assassinate David. Jonathan could not possibly fathom what was going on inside the mind of his father.

He glanced toward the hill above the field. In the outcropping of boulders, David hid, awaiting word of his fate. He would go at once and tell his friend he had been restored to the king's favor, hoping this time it would last.

Chapter 30

DAVID DID NOT TRUST THE KING'S WORD YET DID NOT WANT to imperil Jonathan for taking such a risk in confronting his father on his behalf. So, when David was ordered to lead his men to the town of Zorah, in the province of Judah, and retake the city recently captured by the Philistines, he was relieved to be given a mission. Any mission had its dangers, but David would rather face the Philistines in combat than the unpredictable moods of the king.

On the battlefield it was fight or die, but with Saul he was in a weak position because of familial ties. He could be taken unaware, ambushed by loyalists wanting the king's favor, which meant David must always be looking over his shoulder. It was a precarious truce, for King Saul did not embrace David, made no personal acceptance he had wronged David—no attempt to explain himself and convince David of the sincerity of a changed attitude.

David and his men surrounded Zorah in the dead of night, scaling the walls and attacking with such brute force that those few who escaped did so only because of the chaos of battle and the cover of darkness. The grateful citizens of Zorah threw open their storehouses and prepared a great celebration for David's victory. The public heralded David, this son of the tribe of Judah, as the new "Samson," for the great judge had been a native of Zorah and had fiercely fought the Philistines all his life.

After making an obligatory appearance with the city elders, tribal chieftains, and Levitical priests—to accept a cart full of gifts that included beautiful robes and gowns, chests of silver shekels and wedges of gold along with jewelry and precious stones—David slipped out of Zorah unnoticed and returned to the camp nestled inside a grove of trees outside the city. He preferred to play his kinnor in quiet solitude.

Uriah first appeared out of the darkness, leaping upon the cart of gifts and offerings and pawing through the items. "Where is it? Where is it?"

"What are you shouting about, Uriah?" David set his kinnor on a table near the fire.

"The greatest weapon in the history of Israel," Uriah cried, stretching his body over a pile of quilts and blankets and opening a treasure chest.

"Get out of the cart, you fool!" Benaiah exclaimed, grabbing Uriah by the calf of his leg.

Jozabad and Eleazar stepped into the light of the fire, each carrying one end of a table laden with food and drink. They set it next to the fire and began to eat. Eleazar handed David a skin of wine, and he sipped from it.

"It has to be here," Uriah cried.

"What are you looking for?" Benaiah yanked on Uriah's leg.

"The jawbone of an ass." Uriah pulled back from Benaiah's grip.

"You are the ass," Benaiah said. "Now, get out of the cart."

Uriah sprang from the cart, grabbed David around the waist, hoisting him onto his shoulders and dancing around the fire, slinging David's legs and arms as if they were a weapon.

David dropped the wineskin and held on for dear life.

"And the mighty Samson slew a thousand Philistines in one day with the jawbone of an ass," Uriah cried. He plopped David in front of his cart and fell to his knees. "I bow before a new Samson with another victory to his credit and a cart of booty even if he did not use the jawbone of an ass to slay his enemies."

David grabbed Uriah's jaw, giving it a playful tug. "Next time, yours will do nicely." Then David pushed Uriah onto his back. "I could slay even more Philistines just by letting you talk them to death."

"How many Philistine ears between us this time?" Jozabad asked, tossing the wineskin back to David. "I collected four."

Benaiah opened his pouch and tallied the number. "Seven."

Eleazar licked the lamb grease from his fingers, and then gave his number, "Five and a half. I was set upon by a Philistine who did not appreciate me cutting off the ear of his comrade, so I only got half of one."

"And for you, Captain?" Benaiah asked.

David just shrugged. "No one died at my hand last night."

"And the winner is me." Uriah yanked his pouch from his belt and danced a little jig. "Eight Philistines sent to the afterlife deaf as a stone."

Uriah stuffed his pouch back into his belt and gave David an expectant look.

"Go ahead, Uriah, the first pick of the spoils is yours."

Uriah climbed back into the cart and resumed his treasure hunt.

David picked up his kinnor and began walking away. "I think I shall sleep alone tonight," he said casually over his shoulder.

When in the field, they slept together on the ground apart from the rest of the company of soldiers. They would converse on all subjects as they ate their rations and stared into the fire or up at the stars before drifting to sleep. On occasion when David felt inspired, he would give these loyal friends a private concert.

"Captain, are you troubled?" Benaiah asked.

David turned to face Benaiah and saw the look of regret for asking the question in front of the others. Benaiah should have waited until a private moment.

"I fear going home," David said. "I fear facing the king even though the prince assures me that the royal order to have me killed has been withdrawn. However, there are many loyalists within the king's tribe who would gladly plunge their sword into my back. And I doubt the king would punish any assassin who went against his order."

David had never spoken so openly, but to whom if not these men?

Jonathan would always hold a place in his heart that no man could supplant, but he was also the son of the king, and his loyalties would always be divided. Regardless of the covenant they shared, the father of his friend preferred him dead even if he had revoked the order.

"Captain, we will protect you," Benaiah said.

Jozabad and Eleazar rose. Uriah stopped pawing through treasure and climbed out of the cart empty-handed. All four faced David with a unified front.

"We stand with you." Benaiah raised his arms to include his comrades. "Go into any battlefield, endure any hardship, follow you to the ends of the earth. We swear."

David felt he had unwittingly manipulated the situation to elicit their fidelity, yet his heart swelled. The words of Benaiah and the four men facing him, cohesive, loyal, fearless, provided him a guarded strength.

"Your words are a balm to my heart but be careful what you swear to."

On the day David and his men returned from victory over the Philistines at Zorah, he had delivered his report, collected Mikal, and together they went immediately to their room in the city. Neither had returned to the palace but had enjoyed each other's company away from the pressures and demands made by family members and David's military duties.

His popularity among the people after liberating Zorah continued to grow. David had yet to suffer a defeat at the hands of the Philistines. Credited for slaying "his tens of thousands," this created a general rivalry and jealousy among many in the ranks of the king's standing army, but among the citizens, David was a hero with his golden arm and his golden voice.

In the days after his return from Zorah, the notoriety he and Mikal received as they moved about Gibeah required special guard details to protect them from being mauled by adoring citizens. The only time he could be in public and not be accosted was if he were singing. One night, he and Mikal went to the Wolf Den for supper, and in order to quell a potential riot, he agreed to sing. So, when a summons arrived for the captain and the princess to share an evening meal with the royal family, it did not surprise David that the invitation came with the directive from the king to bring his kinnor.

David and Mikal entered the brightly lit Hall and found it beautifully decorated with tables groaning under the weight of platters of venison, elk, and fowl; bowls of fresh vegetables roasted, stewed, and raw; washed leafy greens doused in oils and herbs; and mounds of cakes glazed with honey. Cushions and stools were set out in a wide circle for the family to relax upon while they feasted. On a low table in the center of the circle were pitchers of wine and baskets of breads and dried fruits all within easy reach.

David observed the room, the habit of a warrior to be alert for any possible danger.

The king was sprawled on top of a pile of cushions, his head tilted back, catching grapes in his mouth that Ish-bosheth tossed in the air. The twins were playing pitch and catch with ripe melons over the table of wine and bread.

No one seemed concerned that one bobbled catch could wreak destruction upon the neatly displayed table between them. Abner and Rizpah sat off to one side of the king. Rizpah cradling her newborn son, Memphi-baal, in her arms while Armoni crawled over Abner's broad shoulders and back like a little insect. Servants bustled about, tending to the needs of the royal family. The room was alive with frolicking, and the guards posted at each of the columns in the Hall were merely decorative, not looking for danger or threatening it.

Mikal broke away from David and moved toward her sister. She carried a small wooden chest filled with the jewelry brought home from her husband's latest conquest. Mikal had chosen something for herself—a crown with gold-beaded tassels hanging from its rim—before she made her selections for the women in the royal family to choose from the gemstone necklaces, bracelets, brooches, and pins.

Merab was ripe with the anticipated delivery of her second child. Her belly was so swollen she could not rise to greet her sister, so Mikal knelt and opened the lid for her to see the contents.

"A birth gift from us." Mikal held the chest before Merab. "May you have a girl this time. We are becoming outnumbered."

"Sister, if you want a girl, then begin making your own contribution to the family." Merab's harsh tone came as a complete surprise.

Mikal jolted back from her sister as if she had been scorched and the lid on the chest slammed shut. Mikal rose, her face flushed.

"Forgive me, Mikal. My belly is ready to pop, and I do not know what I am saying half the time. Adriel is always apologizing for me."

Merab's feeble attempt to apologize had no effect on soothing Mikal's wound. "You must be keeping him very busy then," Mikal blurted.

She did not wait for a response, nor would she stand there any longer and endure humiliation. Mikal spun and made her way to her husband who stood talking with Jonathan. David was just removing the skin pouch containing his kinnor from off his shoulder and setting it on the floor, so he could admire Jonathan's son, Merib-baal, perched on his shoulders. Mikal knelt in front of Levana and opened the lid of the chest. She would give her sister-in-law first choice from this jewelry. Mikal did not look back at Merab to see her reaction at the intended rebuff.

"The slayer of ten thousand and his princess have finally arrived." Saul's voice boomed above the royal family joviality filling the Hall. "And she bears gifts. What do you have for me?"

"Nothing, Abba," Mikal said sweetly just as Levana removed a necklace from the chest. "These are treasures only the ladies can appreciate, given to my husband from the city fathers of Zorah for vanquishing the Philistines."

"Another victory to your husband's credit." Saul grabbed Ish-bosheth and drew him into his chest. He pointed at David, and in a voice of fearful mockery said, "Beware, Ishie, my boy, soon the giant-slayer will run out of Philistines to kill and come after us."

"Abba, do not speak so about my husband." Mikal finished tying the necklace around Levana's neck and smiled at the pleasure it brought her sister-in-law. Then she scooted to her father and kissed his cheek. "Even in jest."

Saul ignored Mikal's chastisement and her affectionate kiss. "I hear you have been playing for the citizens of Gibeah since your return from Zorah. Now, it is time to play for your family."

"Yes, my lord." David removed the kinnor from the lion-skin pouch. He eyed Saul, trying to discern if his playful banter masked a sinister intention. David could never assume any unqualified acceptance by Saul after a successful campaign. But in this Hall filled with the king's family enjoying themselves, surely, any hostility Saul might hold against him, David could abate with a song.

"My lord, what is your pleasure?" David bent his ear to the strings while he tuned his kinnor.

"Since you asked." Saul stroked his beard, brooding over what to request. "You are fresh from yet another victory over our enemies, so why not a song celebrating the triumph?"

Saul wrapped his arms around Ish-bosheth and tightened his embrace. Father and son settled into the cushions to listen to David.

Jonathan sat next to Levana and plopped Merib-baal between his legs. He snapped his fingers for Ishvi and Malki to stop their play, and they dropped down at the table in the center of the circle and helped themselves to bread and wine.

"I have been pondering such a song, my lord." David bent on one knee and propped his kinnor on top of it. He cast his eyes about the Hall, not to see who might be paying attention, but to take the pulse of the room, to see if anyone might be anxious or sensing any danger. It was his shepherd instinct, finely tuned—like his kinnor—into a warrior's instinct to be alert to any peril. The family all seemed relaxed and ready to listen. The servants were still, and the soldiers stood at attention.

When Saul closed his eyes, David began.

> "Oh Yahweh, the Lord Almighty,
> The God of Israel;
> I will sing of your strength in the morning,
> I will sing of your love; for you are my fortress,
> My refuge in times of trouble.
> Oh my Strength, I sing praise to you;
> You, Oh Yahweh, are my fortress,
> My loving God."

Abruptly, Saul bolted out of his cushions as if they had turned to burning coals, causing Ish-bosheth to fall forward onto the floor.

"How did you come by your voice, Captain?" Saul blurted, unaware he had sent Ish-bosheth tumbling headfirst or that the entire family held their breath.

"My voice?" David replied, startled out of his melody.

"You were just a shepherd reeking of sheep dung when you came into my tent and charmed the hearts of my family with your voice. How could you come by a voice that charms every ear who listens? Is there no other voice in Israel who can sing with such enchantment? So yes, how did you come by your voice?"

David's throat constricted as if Saul's powerful hand and fingers wrapped around it, squeezing out the breath and blood flow.

"My lord, I believe my voice is a gift from Yahweh." David made no sudden move, but slowly set his kinnor on the floor and rose.

"Of course, Yahweh. Who else but Yahweh? Does Yahweh always dote on the singing shepherd?" Saul spoke with a mocking growl, and then he paced like a panther in front of the guards who stiffened their postures.

Without warning, a firm hand grabbed David's robe and yanked his body to the floor just as the wind of the hurled spear swiped his face making a terrible whir as it flew over his head. What followed was the deep, blunt thud of the spear's steel head penetrating the wooden wall behind him.

Jonathan gripped David by his shoulders, pulled him back upon his weak legs, and rattled him like a toy, trying to jolt him out of his astonishment. But David stared at Saul lying prone. The force with which he hurled the spear yanked from the soldier's grip had caused him to lose his balance and fall facedown into his cushions.

Malki and Ishvi rushed to their father, crying and screaming. Then the twins turned on David and cursed him until Abner pushed them aside and fell upon his cousin like a blanket of protection.

"Leave!" cried Jonathan, his voice breaking through the chorus of screaming in the Hall. "Take Mikal and go."

David's wife led him away. He was being dragged out of the chaos, out of the evil that had erupted and split apart the earth, and into the night whose primal darkness fell like a fierce assault to his eyes and flesh.

As they ran from the dining hall, he heard the wounded, self-loathing howl of the king like the cry of a tortured wolf.

David lifted his trembling hand and placed it upon the door. He cracked it open just enough to see the men moving about on the street at the base of the steps of his second-story loft.

In the torchlight, Jeush, the king's most loyal servant, spoke in a muffled voice to the others and pointed upward to the door. All were dressed in breastplate with leather bands wrapped around their arms and legs; their swords and helmets gleamed in the flickering light. At this late hour, these men should be in robes or tunic not military garb.

David knew they meant harm, knew they were there to carry out the king's order that meant either arrest or murder.

"Deliver me from my enemies, O Yahweh." David's lips moved at a rapid pace, his mind focused on the realization of imminent danger, his thoughts crackling in lyrical supplication. "Protect me from those who rise up against me. Deliver me from evildoers and save me from bloodthirsty men. See how they lie in wait for me. Fierce men conspire against me for no offense or sin of mine, O Yahweh. I have done no wrong, yet they are ready to attack me. Arise to help me; look on my plight."

"Come away from the door," Mikal whispered.

David did not move but remained fixated on the scene below. "They come at evening, snarling like dogs, and prowl about the city." He murmured his observations as if in prayer. "See what they spew from their mouths—they spew swords from their lips."

"What are you talking about?" Mikal's tone became more urgent. She removed David's hand from the door and closed it. "Please come away. They do not know we are here."

Mikal forced him to sit on the bed and knelt in front of him. Her hands touched his face. In the waning moonlight, he could see his wife's tear-stained face and the whiteness of purest fear in her eyes.

The words spilling from his lips made no sense to her. Yet, he could not stop them from pouring out of his heart. "In your might, O Yahweh, make them wander about and bring them down. For the sins of their mouths, for the words of their lips, let them be caught in their pride. For the curses and lies they utter, consume them in wrath, consume them till they are no more."

"You have got to listen to me." Mikal swiveled his head back and forth.

"I must remember this night. I must remember these words." David was not looking at Mikal, but through her, beyond her physical presence and into the dire consequences he imagined. No greater fear had gripped his heart. No greater threat to his life had ever occurred. No place was safe. No human was to be trusted, and only these lyrical words of hope that Yahweh might be aware of his plight brought him any sense of steadiness.

Without warning, his wife's hand struck him. "Stop this befuddled nonsense and look at me. You have got to listen."

David gave his wife his fullest attention. "Mikal, what have I done? What have I done to you?"

"I know I have lost you." She spoke in frightened gasps.

David knew that any fulfilling joy they might have had together was about to be wrenched from their hands.

"I do not know why this is happening. I have lost you. Why is this happening to us, to me? An eternity ago, the night before you slew the giant, your fingers plucked the strings of my heart the instant you began to sing. I was desperate for you, but now, more so, for I have had you in my arms and you are being taken from me. It is as though the spear of my father was plunged into my breast."

David pulled Mikal to his lips. Their kiss was severe as if invisible hands pressed against the back of their heads. Yet, when their lips parted, their panting breath had no sweetness, and the taste on their lips was bitter.

"What is to become of us?" All options brought sorrow.

"You must escape now," Mikal said.

"But how? They are gathered at our door."

"If they suspected we were here, they would have burst in by now," Mikal rose, dashed to the window, and peered out between the curtains. "The alleyway is clear. Quickly, we must gather your things."

David's warrior instinct took over. He pulled the satchel he carried with him whenever he was at war from beneath the bed with its supply of extra clothing, bandages, ointments, a long coil of rope, a small cutting knife, and his sling. He took the rope and wrapped it around the sturdy leg of the heavy dining table.

Mikal gathered dried fruit, a small block of cheese, and stale bread from the shelf and dropped them into a garment sack. Then she opened the wooden chest and poured in all the jewelry. Finally, she removed the golden headpiece she had worn that night and placed it inside before she tied the sack's neck with a strip of leather.

"Once I am on the ground, uncoil the rope from the table leg, and I will pull it to me." He tugged to test the reliability of the weight of the table. He drew back the curtains and looked out to see that the alley remained clear. David took the garment bag from Mikal, tied it with the other end of the rope, and lowered it to the ground. Then he slung the strap of his satchel over his shoulder and climbed onto the window ledge.

"When you have made your escape, I will distract the soldiers," Mikal said.

David gripped the rope in his hands before glancing below. Then he looked back at his wife.

"What of the king? What will he do to you?"

"What has he not already done?" Mikal answered.

David gave one final tug on the rope, and Mikal leaned against the table to add the support of her weight.

"I owe you my life, Mikal, but…" and here the words caught in his mouth, yet he must speak the thought. He must give her freedom. He must release her to an uncertain future, release her to the will of Yahweh. "Do not wait for me."

When David's feet hit the ground, Mikal uncoiled the rope from the table leg and let the end slither out the window. He had vanished. The window was vacant. She stood beside the table in a daze and faintly heard the escape—her husband's feet running away, running from her.

She moved cautiously toward the window, and bracing her hands against the ledge, eased her head out. The alley was empty.

He was gone, and the world suddenly tilted. The sky above was vacant and lonely and would never again hold its grandeur for her.

"Do not wait for me." Were those really his last words to her? Could she have misheard?

Mikal withdrew from the window and pulled the curtains together. The night air gave her a sudden chill, and she went to the fireplace and threw some straw and small sticks inside the center. A few strikes of the stone flints ignited the dry straw. When the room jumped with light, the image of a man stood in the corner.

She gasped and sprang to her feet. Had David returned? But how?

She was hallucinating. Yet, the male image did not move, only the shadows that bounced around it. The teraphim, the dumb idol she had brought from the palace.

Beating on the door brought Mikal to her senses.

"Princess Mikal."

She recognized the voice of Jeush as her door rattled from repeated pounding.

"Princess Mikal, the king demands to see Captain David at once."

She felt surprisingly calm, no panic or indecisiveness. "Tell the king, my lord is ill and in bed." She directed her voice toward the door. "He will come to the king when he has rested."

The rattling paused, and Mikal quietly approached the door and placed her ear against it. She heard muted voices from the other side devising a way to adjust to this unexpected wrinkle in their plan.

"Princess Mikal, if I am to report this to the king, I must see for myself." This time, Jeush spoke without rapping.

"Of course," Mikal said, clarity and inspiration coming at once. "One moment." She placed the teraphim on the bed and threw the blankets over the idol. A goat-hair coverlet lay at the foot, and she wrapped the head of the teraphim with it and placed a pillow on each side. She smiled at her ingenuity and crossed to the door.

Jeush entered, his sword drawn, leaving two robust soldiers, their own swords half-drawn from their sheaths, just outside the door. He peeked around the corner of the entry to view the life-size form beneath the covers.

He returned to the door satisfied. "Princess, forgive me, but I must send word to the king of the captain's ill health and your request to delay his audience. I will wait for the king's answer."

"I understand, Jeush." Mikal nodded. "But would you wait at the bottom of the stairs?"

"Yes, my lady." Jeush instructed the two soldiers to descend the stairs.

Jeush would return with the king's demand for David to be taken from his sickbed if need be, but David was not here. How far had he gotten by now?

The city gates would be closed, but he had his rope and could scale a wall. Her husband was resourceful. And so was she. Her trick had worked on Jeush, and in so doing, allowed David more time to escape. She lay in the bed next to the motionless form and ran her fingers through the goat-hair coverlet on its head.

"You were supposed to make me fertile. You had opportunities, fewer than I would have liked, but still, it only takes one. You withheld your power. Your magic worked for my sister, but not for me."

She rolled onto her back and watched the shadows on the ceiling. She folded her arms beneath her head and continued addressing the teraphim like a confidante.

"I will never see this room again. I will never return, nor will my husband. My father has driven him from me and with him all my happiness. 'Do not wait for me,' he said. 'Do not wait for me.' Why did he say such a thing? Why were his last words so bleak, so fruitless? Much like your power to make my womb productive…fruitless."

Mikal jammed her elbow into the side of the teraphim in disgust. "Why could my husband's last words to me not have been words of tenderness, of hope as, 'I will send word where to meet,' or 'Do not lose heart,' or 'I love you?' Why not a simple, 'I love you?' Something I could carry with me to face my father's wrath; something that might offer comfort. There was no comfort in his last words, in his last kiss, his last look before he vanished from the window. He just vanished, and at this moment, I feel the love I hold for him dripping from my heart. How could that be? How could that be?"

The pounding did not startle her. She expected it and invited Jeush to enter without rising. The door crashed against the wall.

Mikal watched with amusement as Jeush and the other soldiers, swords drawn, suddenly froze after rushing in and seeing her lying beside the form.

"Were you planning on killing us in our bed, Jeush?"

"Not you, my lady," Jeush answered.

"You are nothing if not honest." Mikal climbed out of bed.

Mikal reached over the cold, still form she had been addressing and ripped the goat-hair coverlet off its head and tossed it at Jeush's feet. Then she yanked the blankets down to reveal the clay image. She could not control her laughter at the shocked expressions on the faces of the soldiers. Mikal despised them for being susceptible to her deceit, for their slavish obedience to a mad king, for a lack of any compassion for her breaking heart.

She went to the window and pulled back the curtains, and then she leaned over the bed and gripped the clay idol. She had the might of a warrior and the detachment of a judge. Mikal lifted the teraphim off the bed and threw it out the window. When it crashed into pieces on the paving stones below, she felt liberated. Her future may be doused in bitterness, but she would meet it with strength.

"Come," Mikal said as she passed Jeush. "Let's not keep *the king* waiting."

Mikal's story was simple. Logical. And for it, her father struck her; he cursed her; imprisoned her in her palace bedroom, refusing to hear any viewpoint that did not support his malevolent obsession.

"Why did you lie and deceive me like this?" he had railed, rubbing his fingers after striking her across the face. "Why did you help my enemy escape?"

She wanted to say her husband was not his enemy, but the words stuck in her throat when she remembered her husband's last words: "Do not wait for me."

"David threatened me," she had told her father. "He said to me…" and here she paused. She did not want to speak those final words, those tragic words that left her heart bruised, a bruise that would soon be matched by the one rising on the side of her face. "He said, 'Help me escape, or I will kill you.'"

But he had killed her. Mikal had been slain twice in one night. Once by her father when he threw the spear at her husband, and the second time when her husband spoke his last words. It was a double death—a death of the heart, a death of the soul.

Now, all that remained was for her body to follow.

Chapter 31

JASHAR BURST FROM THE STABLES AND RACED TOWARD THE main house. The prophet and his wife would be eating their morning meal and would not wish to be disturbed. The prophet rarely emerged before midday, at which time he would visit the dwellings, the series of structures where student prophets lived and studied or stop by the archive building to check on the progress of those scribes copying the sacred texts.

What Jashar had to report would warrant interruption to a quiet morning.

Jashar did not pound on the door; such rapping would have matched the pounding of his heart. He stopped to catch his breath, then lightly knocked, paused, knocked again, and then stepped away.

When Shira appeared, her perturbed expression flustered the young man.

"Forgive the intrusion, my lady, but I just returned from my morning ride, and there was a dead body in one of the stalls."

"Beast or human?" Either way, Shira's morning routine was interrupted.

"Human, my lady," Jashar answered. "A man I did not recognize."

"You did not notice him before you left on your ride?"

"No. I went to gather straw to feed my horse after my ride when I discovered him. I thought the master should know."

Jashar was a rider like Shira which made him an unusual fit for the prophet's school and had endeared a special fondness from the wife of his master. Most of the students had little aptitude with horses, but Jashar came from farming country in the far north of the lower Galilee region and was accus-

tomed to dealing with livestock. Jashar's parents recognized his natural aptitude in language and decided the prophet's school might be the place for him.

Samuel was also fond of him but for different reasons. Jashar displayed
a grasp of historical narrative and lyrical wording and his lettering bordered
on artistic which was perfect for copying the ancient texts. For a young man
to be so well versed in the dual life of an agrarian and a scholar was a rarity.

"I could have used a beast's hide for writing material," Shira mused. "A
human will need burying."

Samuel appeared staff in his hand, still wearing his bedclothes, and scooted by his wife with such force she had to grasp the doorframe to keep from
tumbling.

"Take me to him," Samuel mumbled as he tramped down the walkway.

Jashar did not expect the prophet to move with such haste; the end of
his staff jammed into the ground with every step to maintain balance. Jashar
caught up and stayed beside his master as they made their way to the stables.

Shira raced ahead and disappeared into the barn before them.

"Any markings on his body?" Samuel asked. "Any signs of violence?"

"I did not look carefully. When I saw the body, I came at once."

When Samuel and Jashar entered the barn, they saw Shira kneeling on
the ground, observing a pair of legs protruding out of the stall. The body lay
facedown and leaned against the side of the barn. The head was covered with
a hood and rested upon a leather satchel. The leggings were torn and stained
with dried blood. The leather strings on the sandals were wrapped around the
ankles and triple knotted. The clothes were of fine quality but could be garb
worn by anyone of means.

"Could he be a citizen from Ramah, my lord?" Jashar asked.

Samuel ignored the question, inching forward, and raised his staff. He
roughly poked the body with the blunt end.

The body sprang to its feet, knife in hand, waving it at the trio frozen at
this abrupt resurrection.

Jashar yanked the staff from his master and put himself between the
prophet and his wife and the threatening knife of this stranger. At once, the
man dropped the knife, fell back into the hay, and was still.

All three stood transfixed, waiting to determine if the man would again
surprise them, but after a moment, they seemed assured he would remain
immobile.

"Carry him to the house, Jashar," Samuel instructed.

"Is that wise, my lord?" It was rare for Jashar to question the prophet's authority, but it was risky for this stranger to be taken inside the house of his master.

Shira seemed to agree. "He could be a vagrant, a thief, or worse. He could be anyone."

Samuel reached out and delicately brushed aside the loose cloth and curls of hair that concealed the stranger's grimy face.

"I suspect he is not just anyone," Samuel whispered.

Jashar had never been inside the house. It took a moment for his eyes to adjust to the darkness.

Shira picked up a lamp from the table as she passed through the common room. Samuel closed the front door, the satchel of the stranger slung over his shoulder.

Jashar followed Shira with the body to the last room at the end of the hall.

In the room, Samuel took the lamp from Shira so she could untie the straps that held the fold-down bed in place and lower it from the wall. Samuel pushed the table into the corner where he set the lamp. He laid the stranger's knife beside the lamp and removed the satchel from his shoulder. It bore weight, and the contents rattled inside when Samuel dropped it upon the table.

Once Shira pushed a clay jar stuffed with scrolls against the wall, Jashar entered and lay the body faceup on the bed.

The body groaned but did not move.

When Jashar moved back into the hall and made his way toward the front door, the prophet stopped him.

"We need more light, Jashar," Samuel whispered. "Collect a lamp from the shelf in the common area."

Jashar quickly fetched the lamp, and when he returned, Samuel ignited the wick with the flame from his lamp. The room bounced with shadows created by the illumination of the second lamp.

"Now, Jashar, hold your lamp over him and check the beat of his heart."

Jashar looked down at the body and waved the lamp above it. The hair was matted and dirty and the face was ruddy, yet its handsomeness undiminished by grime and blood. The soiled clothes were beyond cleaning or repair and would be discarded the moment they could be removed. Jashar knelt and laid his head upon the chest. He was surprised by what he heard.

"The beating is strong, my lord," Jashar said softly.

"And you thought he was dead," Samuel said reproachfully.

"Do not scold the boy, Samuel," Shira admonished.

Jashar rose. In the light of the lamps, his shadow danced on the walls. Jashar wore his riding clothes: russet tunic and girdle with a blue woven waist cord, leggings, and a leather headband. An insignia of a golden bowl with fruit, the sign of the Asher tribe, was embroidered on the front of his tunic in multicolored thread. He was proud to wear his tribal heritage. His youthful features both muscular and delicate, the combination of the early years of farm life and recent years spent in sedentary learning at the prophet's school. His long hair fell like brown curtains over the sides of his face.

"I am not scolding the boy." Samuel looked back and forth between his wife and pupil. "He did well. You did well, Jashar."

"Thank you, my lord," Jashar said.

"Look inside his satchel," Samuel said. "Its contents are weighty."

When Jashar removed the pieces of Philistine jewelry and set them upon the table, all three were amazed to see such splendor. Jashar stepped away, afraid that if this man was a thief, on the run, they could be in mortal danger.

"He does not bear the features of a Philistine." Jashar pointed to the stranger's face. "Or any other type of Canaanite. He looks like a citizen of Israel."

"Then he is a common thief," Shira declared. "We should report him."

"We could be harboring a criminal with stolen goods, my lord," Jashar added.

"He is not a thief or a Philistine or any type of criminal," Samuel said as he stepped toward the bed. "There is no need to report him."

Jashar stepped aside to make room for his master who knelt beside the bed. He grasped Jashar's arm and had him extend the light over the stranger's face.

Jashar watched his master quietly contemplate the stranger. Samuel cupped a hand upon the stranger's brow and pushed back the matted hair. He ran his fingers over the head and began to massage the scalp, whispering words Jashar could not believe he was hearing. When Samuel withdrew his hand, he held it to the light, fingers spread, showing his wife and young student.

"My hand has touched this head before. I was not sure until now." Samuel spoke in a tone of hushed awe as he looked back upon the stranger's grimy face. "This is a royal head, an anointed head. This is Yahweh's chosen. The next king of Israel."

He squatted on top of a boulder protruding from the mountainside. Far below the barren landscape stretched into a horizon that disappeared into darkness. He sensed movement around him, and to his horror saw wolves emerging from the crevices of the rocks. He froze. If he did not move, perhaps the wolves would not notice him.

They paced around him, sniffing the air, snarling, their claws clicking against the surface of the rock. Then all the wolves became motionless, no sound coming from them as their attention shifted to a presence behind him.

He felt the hot, moist breath. He felt the cold snout of a beast rove over his shoulders, behind his ears, and across his neck. Then drops of liquid began to fall on top of his head. He did not flinch, but let the fluid run down the side. The wolves around him were agitated but kept their focus on the creature behind him.

The liquid streamed upon his head and flowed down his shoulders. He shifted his focus and saw blood splashing upon his feet. The wolves cut their eyes from the creature behind him and locked onto him. Their hides bristled and rose; their chests expanded and contracted with heavy breathing. Fangs bared, and the drool flowing from their mouths was blood red.

With a burst of strength, he flung his body into the air just as the wolves sprang. In midair he spun around and saw the beast that had been dripping bloody saliva onto his head was a wolf twice the size of the others. The large brute reared onto his haunches and sprang after him. He flung his arms and kicked his legs just as the bloody mouth of the wolf was about to clamp its sharp teeth upon his throat.

David bolted upright in bed. He had no notion where he was or how he got there. He felt his hair, expecting it to be soaked and was relieved to find it dry and stiffened by dirt. He moved his feet and rubbed the calves of his legs. He was slow in coming to a sense of his present reality—a sense that whatever this room was and however he got there, he was definitely alive and grateful for it.

He braced his shoulder against the cool wall and ran his fingers over its cracked and peeling surface. In the dim light of the oil lamp, he spotted his satchel on the desk with his knife next to it along with a plate of food and a pitcher and mug. Clay jars lined the wall in an orderly fashion, containing

THE SINGER OF ISRAEL

numbered scrolls. Plastered on the front of each jar was a parchment label with writing David could not decipher.

Voices came from another room. His body tensed, his ear cocked, he quietly rose and eased to the desk. He picked up the knife and stepped to the door, cautiously drawing back the curtain just enough to see a woman moving about the common area and the back of a man hunched over the table. Though he could not make out their conversation, they appeared harmless, even disinterested in him.

David let the curtain fall back. He swapped the knife in his hand for the mug on the desk, which was filled with warm water. He took a bite of bread, vigorously chewed it, washed it down and bit off more. He stuffed into his mouth some grapes and a plug of dried beef, and while he took the time to chew, he poured more water into the mug. After gulping the water, he leaned against the desk, allowing the food and liquid to settle in his stomach.

His eyes were fully adjusted to the gloomy cast of the room, so he took a scroll from one of the jars. It was tied securely with two leather strands. He raised the tube to his eye and looked down the funnel but could not tell what was written. He replaced the scroll in its proper jar then opened his satchel. He held the lamp above it and saw all the jewelry Mikal had sent. This couple had taken nothing for themselves. He closed the flap of the satchel.

He pushed aside the curtain and quietly stepped into the common area. He could see openings to other rooms connected to the spacious area with thick curtains hung over each entrance. The door to the outside was closed with a rim of sunlight coming from the base where the door and floor did not quite meet. Several oil lamps burned brightly on the table, and along with these were lamps placed upon the shelving attached to the walls. The whole room glowed, and the air was pungent with the odors of burning oils, herbs, and whatever concoction was boiling in the pot on the cooking fire.

David took another small step into the room and saw the older couple examining with intense scrutiny a parchment spread on the table.

The woman stood beside the man, the fingers of her left hand running through the coils of the man's long, darkened hair as they read together: "May Yahweh make the woman who is coming into your home like Rachel and Leah, who together built up the house of Israel. May you have standing in Ephrathah and be famous in Bethlehem. Through the offspring Yahweh gives you by this young woman, may your family be like that of Perez, whom Tamar bore to Judah."

When they finished reading, the woman pressed her hands into her back to stretch the muscles. She turned and saw David standing at the hallway.

"My lord," the woman whispered and placed a hand on the table to give her balance as she bowed to David.

Samuel rose and performed the same respectful bow.

David had never received such deference or been referred to as "lord." It was a first, an act of reverence by the great prophet—the man who anointed him—and his wife.

"My wife, Shira, my lord," Samuel remained on bent knee.

"We are honored to have the king in our home," Shira said.

"Please, please." David waved for them to rise. "This is not necessary."

Samuel and Shira awkwardly rose.

David had given his first order as king, and after that he did not know what to say.

All three stood still in the uncomfortable silence, each struggling to speak. So much to say and yet how to begin. Finally, Samuel took the initiative.

"My lord, we were just going over the latest writings." Samuel gestured to the parchment spread on the table. "A history of begetting, I suppose."

"I beg to differ," Shira interjected. "It is more than that. It is the love story of Boaz and Ruth, your great grandparents, my lord."

"It is a love story, my lord," Samuel said.

The couple shared a sparkling glance.

"My wife corrects me often. The story includes your generational line going back nine fathers to Perez. Would you care to read it?" Samuel gestured for David to sit.

David tentatively took the chair. The leather seat still bore the heat of the prophet. He scanned the lettering and painted inscriptions across the wide page. His eyes darted from symbol to symbol, searching for any familiar sign. A word or lettering here or there bore some recognition: "Yahweh," "Israel," "Judah," his father's name, "Jesse," and finally his own, but taken as a whole, even written out in its neat and ordered hand, the page looked as if the chickens had been let loose upon calfskin.

"I am sorry, my lord," David said, his voice barely audible in an attempt to hide his unease. "I cannot convert what is written."

David was barely literate. He loved words and they tumbled out of him when he sang his heart to Yahweh, but he could with no confidence write the words he sang or spoke, nor could he recognize them even if the verses were written for him.

The people of Yahweh were people of the written word. If he were to be king of Yahweh's chosen, he could not just defend them in war or rule them in peace or bring them into prosperity or administer justice. If he would wear the crown, he must do more than sing words of praise to Yahweh, he must read them as well. He must know the words, speak them, use them with confidence and wisdom. He may have slain a giant, achieved the rank of captain in the army, and married a king's daughter, but he would be no genuine king if he could not read the written stories recounting Yahweh's covenant with creation, the words of Yahweh's covenant with the chosen. These letters and stories were etched onto the skins of beasts, but for these stories to become real and powerful in David's imagination, they must be written on his heart.

David offered up a helpless look to the prophet and was given a kind and tender expression in return.

"We shall remedy that, my lord." Samuel gently placed his hand upon the shoulder of the future king.

David did not venture beyond the house and courtyard. It took time for the nightmares to subside, for his aching muscles to heal from days on the run, to feel rested and safe, to develop enough trust in Samuel to confess all that Saul had done to him.

His only previous encounter with Samuel was the most astounding moment in his life, the mysterious seizing of Yahweh brought on by the prophet anointing him to be the future king of Israel. It felt as if the Almighty had whispered secrets of the universe into his heart. How would he converse with a man who could channel Yahweh in such a fashion?

Since the prophet's visit to Bethlehem, all David thought he knew or understood about himself and his future lay in fragments. Death was a menacing phantom constantly in pursuit.

Samuel and Shira did not seem to mind the minimal communication they had with their guest. David remained in his room or consumed his food in silence as the three of them ate meals together. Occasionally, Shira would hand him a scrap of parchment and point out a phrase she had written and repeat it for him.

David would whisper the phrase again and again while Samuel and Shira went about their business of writing and reading and mixing liquid potions to use for writing. The quiet company, the unhurried routine and dark confines of the house gave David a calm he had not known for some time.

The only visitor allowed in the house was Jashar who delivered blank parchments and took finished scrolls and pots of dyes and inks back to the dwellings for the scribes and students. When David asked if Jashar had seen any soldiers in the area, Jashar reported that none had been spotted.

David warned him to be on the lookout for strangers or unexpected travelers that could be spies.

One morning, Shira handed David a scroll completely filled with the nomenclature of his people.

"It contains inscriptions of our tongue," she said. "It will help you get started."

David unrolled the parchment and examined the individual letters along with corresponding phrases and simple sentences. To form these shapes and symbols into a comprehensive language would be the key to understanding the heart of Yahweh.

"We have twenty-two symbols," she said. "I have also inscribed words that feature the symbols and phrases to help you connect the letterings."

"My wife is the best copyist and writer among all my students," Samuel said, eliciting a humble smile from Shira.

"What is written on the scrolls in those jars where I sleep?" David asked.

Samuel set down his quill and blew his breath over what he had written, hardening the words onto the parchment. He picked up a damp cloth and wiped the dye from his fingers. He had been writing for so many years his skin was permanently stained.

"The first stories of our ancestors." Samuel leaned back into his chair. "Out of the world's beginnings came our beginning: the barrenness and begetting, the wandering and alienation, the treacheries and promiscuity, the myriad travails of those of our tribes all leading to Yahweh forging a nation into a chosen people. Stories of mystery, passion, and madness from ancient times. When you understand those symbols before you and can read the narratives written, you will be drawn into the blessed rhythm of Yahweh's heartbeat. The scrolls are the collections of our spoken stories and laws and traditions and have become a written gift to our people—the gift of the word of Yahweh."

David would fall asleep on his bed looking at the parchments in the clay jars. His imagination would soar with all the tales and sagas in them. He was drawn to words. His soul contained words. He had composed his songs from the spontaneity of his spirit and out of his mouth he had sung them to nurture his heart, to reassure his soul, to point others toward recognition of Yahweh. He was able to command the flow of the spoken word into melody but understanding the written word would begin a deeper movement inward toward Yahweh. The order of the heavenly spheres, the origins and wanderings of peoples of the earth, the actions of men and women exposed or held captive by their choices—all these wondrous stories were at the mercy of the written word, and Yahweh was at the center of it all.

Until now, the only world David had known was the one he walked over. It had proven all-consuming just to survive in such a treacherous and isolated place. When he became king, if he became king, he would devote himself to the language of Yahweh and commit to bridging the gap between the physical and spiritual worlds, the world of man and the world of Yahweh.

Chapter 32

SAMUEL CLIMBED THE STAIRS OUTSIDE THE HOUSE ONTO THE roof. Shira had insisted he carry fruit and wine with him, but he left the tray on the top step. This was not a time to eat and drink. David spent time on the roof at night when the students could not easily spy on him, and the dwellings and valley below were quiet and peaceful.

Samuel had chosen not to disturb him until this night. He carried a lamp and the two fur blankets Shira handed him as he went out the door. The air was cold, and neither the future king nor the prophet needed to come down with a chill, she told him.

When Samuel reached the top of the stairs with the blankets, he did not see David. The light from his small oil lamp did not extend over the whole roof.

"My lord?" Samuel called, squinting for signs of life.

David was nestled into one corner of the roof wall, scrunched into a ball to retain some body heat. When David rose to accept the fur blanket Samuel offered, the scroll Shira had given him of the Hebrew letters and phrases dropped to the floor.

"My head swims with the lettering," David said as he threw the fur blanket over his shoulders. He bent to retrieve the scroll, and then held it open and pointed to one phrase. "I do not understand what is written."

The moonlight was insufficient illumination for Samuel's eyes, so he held the lamp over the scroll. Samuel pointed his finger over the phrase as David held open the scroll.

"It reads, 'Yahweh says, "Abram, do not be afraid. I am your shield, your very great reward."' Now. say it with me, my lord."

They pronounced each word together. Then David repeated the phrase, pointing to each word as Samuel nodded. David repeated the phrase yet again. He stretched open his jaw, relaxing it before he began humming gradually, modulating his voice into a melody.

When David reframed the written words into vocal music it was as if Samuel heard the phrase for the first time. He stepped back, awed by the power of David's sound, by the deep understanding the melody provided these ancient words. His voice possessed a mournful quality, a hunger, a disconsolation, and as it trailed off into silence, Samuel was unprepared for the heaviness he felt. He lowered himself onto one knee.

"My king, I have never heard such art and beauty in melodic phrases," Samuel said, his voice quivering and breathless. "Would that my students and the young scribes and prophets could sing in such a fashion. But I doubt this can be taught. The way you sing is like pouring the words of Yahweh directly into my soul."

David did not respond to Samuel's praise, but stood still, gazing into the night sky, his ear pressed against the dark as if awaiting some heavenly response to his lament.

"What is done here, my lord? What is taught here?" David pointed toward the buildings scattered across the property.

"Much, my king. I call these young men who come from every tribe in Israel, 'sons of the prophets.' They are near to me as sons. We keep accounts of the stories of Yahweh. Copy them for priests and Levites to teach the chosen in their synagogues throughout Israel to observe the laws and decrees given us by Yahweh, so that we will be a great nation and become a wise and understanding people. To never forget what we have seen and learned in past generations so our children's children will love Yahweh with all their heart and soul."

"Would that I could live here and become one of your 'sons.'"

"You see the large meeting hall in the center of the surrounding buildings?" Samuel directed David's attention toward the complex. "That is our *nevayoth*. We have our assemblies in the *nevayoth*. There we worship, celebrate the Sabbath, and have our ceremonial initiations. Sometimes, the lively singing and dancing of inspired worship inside the *nevayoth* will spill into the assembly yard and ring out across the valley. I can see you leading us in such worship."

"I have only led men into battle or sheep into green pastures. Never have I imagined leading others in worship of Yahweh."

"Do not confine your future to your own imagination. The will of Yahweh is like a gust of wind. The pure breath of Yahweh is exhaled upon those whose heart is inclined toward the Almighty."

"My lord, this troubles me." David raised the scroll again for Samuel to see what was written. "These words Yahweh spoke to the ancient father gives me no comfort."

"Why is that?" Samuel asked.

"These words frightened me." David slumped upon the wall's edge. "I have no understanding why I am chosen. Yahweh is no shield. Yahweh has taken away my covering. I am alone and on the run. My song does not reach the ears of Yahweh."

Samuel sat next to David. He felt a pressure released into his heart by David's spontaneous lament and the wonder of Yahweh's attention upon him. Samuel understood the human response of reverence for Yahweh and then Yahweh turning from him. Samuel knew the turning of Yahweh's face, of Yahweh remaining silent, of being the recipient of bitter circumstances when there appeared to be no explanations for them.

"I know, my son." Samuel sighed, and the instant he uttered the words, "my son," he began to weep. The forlorn quality of David's refrain had plucked a cord in his soul that had remained silent a long time, and so the words gushed out, a force impossible to retain.

"I have lived too long and seen too much. There is a scar in my heart that has never healed. When I was a child, my parents left me at the Tabernacle in the care of an old high priest with two degenerate sons who despised me. I was fatherless. I believe it was the will of Yahweh, but it has been most bitter. In time, my own sons became wastrels, complete strangers to their mother and me, and I do not know how we lost them. I cannot explain why your melody brought back the feeling of failure…my failure as a father. I was angry with Yahweh's chosen for wanting a king. I took it upon myself to stand in the gap for Yahweh—to protect the honor of the Almighty—when in part, I was trying to deflect the attention away from my sons and blame Israel for my failure. Shira and I never speak of them.

"I cannot remember the last time my lips have uttered their names. Joel… Abijah; my sons. We cut them off like a worn patch of fabric from whole cloth. It is as if Yahweh did not withhold the knife in my hand as he did Father Abraham with Isaac on the mountain of sacrifice, that I killed my sons with my own hand."

Samuel paused to catch his breath. The visceral anguish ran deep. It had to be expelled. The hardened earth of his soul could no longer keep it buried beneath its crust.

David was no longer absorbed in his own distress. He felt humility at the grief and regret expressed by the prophet and understood that even Samuel at his ripening age carried an incomprehensible sorrow from the wounds of former years.

"Yahweh have mercy. Yahweh have mercy." Samuel rocked back and forth, the cries and bodily motion reflecting the anguish of his soul. "I have written it all. It is recorded. It must be read. It must be remembered."

David saw in the prophet's long duration of grief that life was more than personal survival: looking out for himself; fighting giants; dodging spears whether hurled by Philistines or a father-in-law; marrying a princess as a safety measure, in truth, not for love; of learning ways to kill to avoid being killed, of building up a blood-debt that could never be redeemed, this was all he knew. Samuel expressed his regret to the Almighty and accepted his loss for he had lost much, and within his own breast, David could feel compassion for Samuel for he too had lost much.

In David's eyes, Samuel purging his soul gave the prophet a dignity David had never considered possible. It was a dignity of confession, and that confession had the deep cut of a knife disemboweling his heart. Samuel had been given a fatherless life and he had passed that fatherlessness down to his sons. And while Samuel poured out his grief to Yahweh, he had done so without casting blame. It must be recorded. It must be read. It must be remembered.

"I have spent much time on this rooftop," Samuel spoke, the expulsion of grief finally subsiding. "Yahweh met me here. On this roof, I informed Saul he would be king. I have now confessed to the future king my despair.

The time spent on this rooftop has been costly. Perhaps, after tonight, I will descend the stairs and never scale them again."

David was startled when Samuel pushed off from the ledge of the wall and marched toward the stairs as though freed from a great burden.

"Bring the lamp, my lord," Samuel said over his shoulder. "There is something you must see before the sun rises and the young prophets assemble for sacred raptures."

Chapter 33

DAVID WAS SURPRISED BY THE PROPHET'S SPEEDY PACE AS THEY marched up the sloping hillside toward the dwellings and the *nevayoth*. Samuel did not even hold his staff. He had neglected to bring it to the roof and did not bother to collect it once they descended. David realized the prophet's mind was preoccupied with urgency and purpose.

David followed Samuel by the open area in front of the devotional center and straight up a flight of steps into the archival building. In the flickering light of the lamp, David saw a circle of benches in the center of the learning room. Within this circle, Samuel informed him that the students would read from the ancient books of the prophet Moses and listen to lectures and teachings from learned teachers and Levitical scholars on the history of Israel and her twelve tribes, from the collected writings of Joshua, the great military general who brought Israel into the land of Promise, and from the documented accounts of the exploits of Israel's judges. All around the walls were rows of desks placed in front of windows. This way the scribes could maximize the sunlight all year long as they labored to inscribe the words of Moses onto the scrolls.

Samuel paused to point out one desk in particular. "That is Jashar's desk, the young man who found you in the barn. He is currently writing the story of my visit to your home in Bethlehem."

"Is that wise?" David asked. "Having it written down puts our lives in danger."

"Following the will of Yahweh is always perilous," Samuel replied. "The truth is always more dangerous than a lie. But it must be written. It must be read."

"It must be remembered." David completed the words of Samuel. David must be gaining understanding for the prophet's face brightened after he spoke.

They came to a door at the far end. Samuel opened it and stood back for David to enter. The room had one table in the center covered with an orderly array of writing materials and lamps. A stool was tucked beneath the table with a large clay pot on either side, each filled with scrolls. A thick carpet of goat hide lay under the table legs.

"This is Nathan's room. He manages the institute, and this is where he proofs all the scrolls. Once he approves, the copies are stored below."

"Below?" David looked about the enclosed, windowless room but saw no access to any type of storage.

"Help me move the table," Samuel said.

David set the lamp on the table and the two of them rolled away the clay pots before moving the table off the covering. Samuel grabbed a corner of the goat hide and yanked it away. His face was beaded with sweat, and he was panting, but he was exhilarated. He took the lamp and held it over the exposed area and pointed to the floor.

In the dim light David could barely make out the edges of a trapdoor.

"We need another torch before we go down." Samuel pointed to a bucket full of wooden staves with the flammable ends sticking out. "Select one."

David took a torch, and Samuel lit it with his lamp. Once the end was in full flame, David could clearly see the outline at his feet.

Samuel bent and pulled opened the door, revealing pitch darkness beneath the floor.

"I will go first." Samuel gave David the lamp and took the torch. "Leave the door open behind you, so the flames can breathe."

David watched Samuel descend the steps until he had reached the bottom. All he could tell from his vantage point was that the prophet stood on solid ground.

"Come." Samuel waved for David to follow.

When David reached the last step, he stood on animal-hide carpeting that covered the whole ground, stretching from one jagged wall to the other.

"Before we began the prophet's school and built the dwellings, families who worked for my parents lived in the structures built along the hillside. Shira lived in one of those units with her mother after her father died. When we tore down the old housing, we discovered a cave and constructed the archival center into the hillside to conceal it."

Samuel pointed to a curtain hanging on a wall. He approached the curtain and placed the torch inside a bracket attached to the rock wall.

"My mother wanted a child so much that in her misery she vowed to Yahweh that were the Almighty to give her a male child, she would return him to Yahweh to serve the Creator all of his days. She kept her vow—the most courageous act a woman, a mother, could ever do. I had no part in this decision, no choice in the matter. She gave me the name of Samuel, which means 'the name of Yahweh, for Yahweh has heard.'

"The first time I heard Yahweh speak was in the Holy Place of the Tabernacle, and the first word the Almighty spoke to me was my name. I hear the voice now in the ear of my mind as clear as I heard it spoken long ago. In hearing my name spoken by the Presence, I began to understand my purpose in my mother's vow even though I have carried this feeling of abandonment all my life. When Yahweh spoke my name, I was given a resolve to carry forward my service to Yahweh, to honor the vow of my mother and the courage of my father who gave her the freedom to do what seemed best to her. That was my strange beginnings with the Almighty, and when my life and my heart has known turmoil, I listen and remember the sound of Yahweh speaking my name."

Samuel placed both hands on David's shoulders. "You feel abandoned and wonder why the Almighty chose you to be king. I cannot tell you. The ways of Yahweh are past finding out, but I hope what you are about to see becomes an altar in your heart, containing a fire that can never be extinguished."

Samuel released his grip. He leaned his back against the craggy wall, raised his leg, and began to unlace his footwear.

"Please remove your sandals," he said as he slipped a foot out of one sandal.

David removed his sandals.

The only sounds in the room were the snap of the torch flame and the breathing of two men, but David could distinctly hear the beating of his heart. He felt a weakening in his legs. He was not sure if this was some fanciful dream or if he was fully awake and engaged with reality. He placed the palm of his free hand above the lamp he held just high enough to feel the heat and slight burning of the flame. His flesh recoiled. He was in no dream but present in an underground room, beneath the academic center for the prophets of Israel, alone with the prophet whose name had been spoken by the Creator of heaven and earth.

In this mystifying moment, David felt he stood on the edge between sanity and delirium. Samuel pulled back the curtain and tied it off with a golden cord. What wonders were concealed in the thick darkness beyond the curtain? What phantoms? What secrets?

"May the king be inspired by what he is about to behold," Samuel whispered and stepped aside with a bow to allow David to enter before him.

The darkness was so profound that the simple flame in David's lamp barely provided enough light through the tight corridor. When the rocky walls on either side of the passageway disappeared, the room opened into an impenetrable blackness.

Samuel eased past David, taking the lamp from his hands and turned his back to him, obscuring the light.

David felt as if he were sealed up by the terrible darkness, absorbed into the deepest interior of the earth.

Then the light was almost blinding as it grew. David placed his hand over his eyes, shielding them from the brightness.

Samuel held a menorah of pure gold with three branches on either side of the center branch. At the tip of the seven branches was a blossoming almond flower that held the wick and oil. Samuel raised the seven burning flames above his head to reveal a room filled with wooden shelving containing jar after jar, all different sizes, of rolled volumes of animal skins.

"The words of Yahweh inscribed by the great prophet Moses," Samuel whispered, the awe in his voice retreating to moan before he was able to speak again. "I performed the rituals and duties in the Tabernacle. I studied the divine words. I copied them, and in the copying my heart was transformed by the sacred script. I was able to save these documents when Shiloh was destroyed. They are more than stories and histories and laws. This is the divine language of Yahweh, the manna of the wilderness become the divine Presence."

David could not speak, nor were there melodies he could summon to express what flooded through him. His heart was leaping at the sight of this library of Yahweh, a vision like no other. He would never leave. He would remain in this underground vault forever and devote himself to studying the ancient texts, consuming the words of Yahweh, absorbing the words of the Almighty indelibly onto his heart and soul.

Yahweh would never leave him, would never abandon him. David was hemmed in by the Presence. From all sides, above and below, the Presence engulfed him. David could never escape or flee from the Presence; to the four corners of heaven and earth, Yahweh would be there. Yahweh was there before him and would be there after him. David's eyes overflowed and the noisy exhaling heating up his mouth began to shape a repeated phrase: "Who is like Yahweh? Who is like Yahweh? Who is like Yahweh?"

Samuel placed his hand upon the small of David's back and gently moved him toward a four-horned stone altar in the center of the room. Upon the altar top where the sacrifices were offered laid a solid, wooden frame of smoothed and planed gall oak. The frame was lined on the inside with the finest goat hair.

"When I fled Shiloh and came home to Ramah, this was my first altar." Samuel carefully placed his fingers on the edge of the frame and opened it. Samuel gave David the seven-branched lamp and motioned for him to step to the side. He then lifted the top two layers of goat hide and put them on a shelf near the altar. Then he removed a thick parchment covering. Underneath the parchment was a layer of linen, and beneath it, a layer of pure lamb's wool. Before Samuel removed the final layer of protection, he looked at David.

"In the first forty days on the peaks of Sinai, Moses sat with the Almighty above the clouds. In the midst of billowing smoke like that of a furnace concealing the glory of Yahweh, Moses spoke with Yahweh as a man speaks with his friend. The great prophet neither ate nor drank. Yahweh was his food and drink, and out of the thunder and lightning, the finger of Yahweh inscribed on two stone tablets the Ten Sayings."

Samuel carefully lifted the two squares of lamb's wool and there on the gevil skin inscribed in hardened dyes were the Ten Words, five on each skin.

"From the holy and beautiful lips of the Almighty, the very words spoken to the great prophet," Samuel said in a hushed tone.

David was caught in the merciful grasp of the world in its fullness; in a world of perfection; in the world as the Creator meant for it to be where truth had no time or place, past or future, but forever present, opening hearts and eyes to what Father Jacob expressed when he awoke from his dream in Bethel and said, "Surely Yahweh is in this place; this is the gate of heaven."

"The Commandments springing from the imagination of the Almighty and expressed in words even the simpleminded can comprehend," Samuel said. "This is how the chosen are to live, entire with Yahweh and in loving community among the nations."

If David could whet the notes in his voice he would burst into song, but his body was consumed by weeping.

Samuel took the seven-branched light from David and continued.

"The first tablets of stone were destroyed by Moses when he descended from the mountain and saw the debauchery of the people worshiping a golden calf. In his rage, he smashed the stones against the base of the mountain. After melting down the golden calf, Moses ground it into powder, scattered it over the water, and made the people drink it. Then he returned to the mountaintop shrouded in thick clouds and had to chisel two new tablets and engrave the Ten Words upon them. Those tablets are sealed inside the Ark of the Covenant with Aaron's budding staff and a golden jar of manna."

David felt his spirit fly out of his skin and he fell upon his knees, his body trembling at the base of the altar. He had reverted to a nursling, lost and helpless. But his spirit floated above the altar, calm, his heart in complete possession of Yahweh, and he began to feel himself expanding outside the cave and into the dwellings, into the landscape, beyond to the whole earth, and into the heavens, the abode of the Almighty. It required that much expanse for his spirit to feel liberated.

"You felt the first rush of Yahweh into your heart when I anointed you in Bethlehem." Samuel rested his hand upon David's head. "When Yahweh gives you the throne you must be a king of the Ten Words, a king of the Covenant, a king of all the sacred testimonies written by the great prophet Moses. Make your place in the heart of Yahweh. Let these divine words consume your soul and pour forth from your tongue."

Samuel set the lamp upon the table and carefully enclosed the Ten Words back inside its protective coverings.

"I never want to leave this place, my lord," David gasped. His spirit was beginning to retake his body. "I want to remain in the Presence forever."

"In time, my king." Samuel knelt in honor of his weeping sovereign. "I believe I will never see you ascend the throne."

David lifted his head to protest but Samuel placed his hand upon the king's lips.

"You must rise, my king. You must rise and leave this place. It is not safe for you here. But do not despair. You are a shepherd of the Almighty, who will preserve you."

Samuel lifted David to his feet. The faint sound of singing accompanied by instruments began to drift into the cave. The barely audible music floating in from above set off an energetic droning inside the cave. The scrolls vibrated. The clay jars hummed. The light from the seven flames intensified and made the shadows dance upon the walls and ceiling. It was as if the written word and the spirit of the music were in a harmonious moment of divine intimacy.

Then a voice spoke from the outer room just beyond the interior room of wonders.

"My lord, are you in there? My lord, it is I, Nathan. You must come out and witness this miracle."

Once David and Samuel climbed the stairs out of the cave, David helped Nathan restore the rug and table over the trapdoor in Nathan's workplace. They moved briskly into the learning room. It should have bustled with young men, but it was empty. The open windows allowed the dawn light and the music to flow into the space. The bright sun and the loud music competed for David's attention. The sunlight came as a surprise to David. He had no awareness of night passing into day inside the sacred cave filled with the words of Yahweh.

David stood between Nathan and Samuel on the deck at the top of the stairs of the archival building, looking upon the open area in front of the devotional center. Musicians clumped together, vigorously playing their instruments. Trumpets, shofars, flutes, drums and cymbals, harps and lyres, and stringed instruments resounded with power. Before them was a sea of half-naked men, their clothes strewn about the ground, their bodies lost in ecstasies, leaping and jumping arm in arm in small groups or individually, but all with one mind, exalting the union with Yahweh. The clangor of music was not rude but offered the worshipers a perfect pitch and balance to singing their praises.

"Praise Yahweh you servants of the Lord.
Praise Yahweh you servants of the Lord.

Yahweh chose Jacob to be his own;
For Israel to be his treasure.
Yahweh is Creator of heaven and earth,
The seas and their deep places.
O house of Israel, praise Yahweh.
O house of Aaron, praise Yahweh.
O prophets of Moses, praise Yahweh.
Let all creation praise Yahweh."

David jerked his arms out of the sleeves and let his robe drop around his dancing feet.

Both Samuel and Nathan grabbed David to keep him from rushing down the stairs to join the celebration. Nathan pointed out that mixed in with the disrobed worshipers of prophets, students, and scribes were a number of soldiers.

David realized that much of the clothing tossed on the grounds and being trampled upon was military garb.

"The king has sent three contingents of soldiers to capture you!" Nathan shouted above the instrumental and vocal din. "They began arriving as we were starting our morning worship. We hear now that Saul left the great well outside the city and is coming to the dwellings. You must leave at once."

But David's path of escape was blocked by a wall of man: soldier and prophet dancing shoulder to shoulder in a divine hysteria.

"Look for Jashar." Samuel scanned the crowd.

A few musicians stopped playing, laid aside their instruments, and joined the other men in the center of the grounds, bouncing and springing until they all burst into a wild applause and began shouting praises to the Almighty.

Nathan found Jashar and signaled for him to join them on the decking.

David made a mad dash back inside the archival building as Jashar bounded up the stairs. David had moved so quickly he left his robe lying on the deck between Samuel and Nathan. Once Jashar was on the top step, the worshipers pressed together and formed a circle then widened out to the perimeters of the grounds, leaving an opening in the middle.

David thrust his head out an open window in the building and could not believe what he saw. King Saul had reached the top of the hill and entered the grounds of the dwellings, staggering as if ill or intoxicated. Saul's ungainly motions and lurching steps began to flow into the rhythms of singing and dancing. No one greeted Saul as the king should be greeted. No one bowed or halted their praise. No soldier attempted to assist or guide him in the pulse of worship. Everyone was caught up in the prophetic spell of adoring the Creator.

The king removed his protective headgear and let it fall to the ground. He danced in a circle, his lips moving in sync with the choruses of his soldiers and the prophets. He removed his sandals, and then his outer garments, his breastplate, the arm guards, the linen shirt, and leather skirt around his waist.

David was amazed at the king's outburst of piety.

Wrapped only in loin swaddling, Saul gradually slowed his movement until he became perfectly still. First his knees dropped to the ground, then his body spread prostrate over the worn earth, and finally he became still as though dead, deep in the entrancement of holy rapture before the Presence until the intensity of worship dissolved into sways and groans with a sporadic utterance from a prophet unable to return from the elation of worship.

"Wait here," Samuel whispered, and he began to descend the stairs. He looked back at Jashar. "Get his robe and be ready to take him to the stables upon my signal."

"Yes, my lord." Jashar stooped to grab the robe off the deck.

Samuel moved across the grounds toward the king lying facedown upon the earth. He was not sure if the king was asleep, entranced, or dead. Samuel had been in such a state many times after encounters with Yahweh.

Perhaps the Almighty had taken pity on the king lying bare before the Presence; a chance given to renew his heart and bring about a transformation. Nothing was impossible with Yahweh. The mercies of the Almighty endure for a thousand generations.

Samuel knelt beside Saul and gently laid his hand upon the king's head. He had loved this man once, counseled him, had done Yahweh's bidding and anointed him king, spoken truth to him, and had never ceased to pray for him. So much grief had flooded Samuel's heart for this man who lay prostrate on the ground beneath the weight of the Almighty.

How would the king rise up from here? What changes of the king's soul might have happened from this encounter with the Most High?

But the prophet would take no chances with the fate of the future king. Convinced Saul was incapacitated either by slumber or trance, he rose and waved for Jashar.

The near-violent state of divine worship had given way to a tranquil rapture, and David escaped through a gauntlet of prophets and soldiers overpowered by the Presence. David paused beside the king flat on the ground. He knew it was only a matter of time before Saul would have found him. Even in this miraculous escape, in time the king would again hunt him down.

No place was safe, not even with Samuel. He gazed into the old prophet's eyes sparkling in the light of the sun.

A smile formed on Samuel's lips, but he placed a finger over them. Then Samuel nodded to Jashar, and the young prophet led David out of the grounds.

While Jashar saddled a horse in the stables, David rushed into the house to gather his satchel. It was sitting on the table in the common area along with the scroll Shira had written for him and a shank of lamb wrapped in linen, dried fruit and flatbread, and a skin of water. He folded the scroll to fit inside the satchel and called to her, but she did not respond. She was likely making herself scarce, given that she and her husband were harboring a fugitive, and the king and his soldiers were on their property. He looked inside the satchel and saw the jewelry, and then he stuffed the food Shira had prepared inside and placed the scroll on top before closing the flap. He slung it and the waterskin over his shoulder and bolted out the door.

David's eyes enlarged as he raced up to Jashar waiting in the courtyard at the end of the garden path holding the bridle of the dark red horse he had saddled for David. He had never seen such a beautiful horse.

"Her name is Sela. It means 'like a rock.'" Jashar stroked Sela's long neck. The large muscles in Sela's legs trembled in anticipation of a new rider.

David hesitated to mount.

"She is anxious to be off, my lord. Unlike most mares, she has the grit and power of a stallion. Sela will live up to her name."

Jashar linked his fingers together forming a stirrup, and David planted his foot inside and slung himself across Sela's back. She did not buck or act skittish but pounded the ground, signaling she was ready for the rider's heels to give the command to depart.

"Send word to Prince Jonathan." David looked down on Jashar from his high perch. "Tell him I will meet him at the Stone of Ezel and to bring my kinnor."

"Yes, my lord." Jashar tossed David the reins and stepped away.

David tugged on the bridle and spun Sela in a complete circle. An instant bond between horse and rider was established. David felt confident this magnificent creature would take care of him.

"I could use someone like you, Jashar." David pulled back on the reins for one brief exchange. Sela's muscles tightened and clinched beneath his haunches.

"It would be a pleasure to serve the king," Jashar said with a bow.

"Do not be anxious for this job. It comes with danger," David warned. "You will be much safer here with the prophet."

"I trust the will of Yahweh, my lord."

"That is wise, but if you join me, you will never be far from death," David said, and then he dug his heels into Sela's flanks. David almost fell from his saddle at the explosive speed the horse exerted from her standing position.

Jashar watched David ride out of sight.

He had witnessed a resurrection. Jashar had discovered David's body, a body he thought lifeless, then carried it into the prophet's house and was told he had borne the body of the future king of Israel, his king.

Now, this king had requested he should enter his service. A service, should he accept, that would come with hardship, peril, and the constant threat of death. His heart beat fast. His body trembled at the prospect: the giant-slayer had requested his service, the slayer of ten thousand, the Lion of Judah.

He had carried the myth of this man in his imagination since he was a boy. He had carried his body in his arms. If it was Yahweh's will, he would serve this future king through every hardship and danger to the end of his days.

Chapter 34

GAD HAD HOPED THAT THE KING'S EXPERIENCE AT THE DWELL-
ings with Samuel would have produced a lasting effect. "Saul was among the
prophets," it was reported, and indeed, the king had returned a changed man.

When Saul initially received word that David had fled to Samuel in Ramah, he pursued him with murderous intent. But Nathan reported to Gad of
a miracle of Yahweh, that the king and all his men were overwhelmed by the
Spirit of the Almighty, falling into prophetic worship with the other prophets
on the grounds in front of the devotional center.

Gad witnessed this changed demeanor in Saul. To his surprise, the king
expressed enthusiasm about the upcoming New Moon Festival. He requested
Gad bring the scrolls and read to him details of the feast and the types of offerings and celebrations as set out by the prophet Moses. He was the old Saul,
the king in the early days when he would study with Gad. The king treated
the approaching celebration with special devotion even denying Rizpah access to his chambers until after the festival.

Gad was encouraged, all the royal court was encouraged, especially Jonathan. The prince had confided in Gad that, after his father's return from his
encounter with the Almighty, he hoped the darkness in his father's heart had
been burned away and that his dear friend and husband of his sister could
return to the court.

Princess Mikal was not as sanguine about her father's outward change,
and no amount of persuasion by her brother modified her mind. When Gad

brought word to the prince that David would meet him at the Stone of Ezel, they went to see the princess in her chamber where she remained in a self-imposed exile. She accused Jonathan of misplaced optimism and he was too quick to forgive their father for his irrational hatred of her husband.

The one thing the king had not done since his return from Ramah and his encounter with Yahweh was offer the princess his regret for treating her the way he had the night of David's escape. He had ordered the guard removed from her chamber doors and she was told she could move about freely, but he had not come himself. No amount of enthusiasm for a religious festival or expressed interest in the words of the prophet Moses would change her mind about what she believed: that their father's nature was beyond repair.

Gad was present when the king had accused her of betrayal. His heart flinched and he looked away when the king struck his daughter and watched when the guards dragged her away to her chambers. While Gad might be hopeful, he also knew the dark spirit could return to the king's heart, and who knew what havoc would be unleashed once the malevolence took possession.

The night before the festival, Jonathan and Gad had ridden secretly out of the city to the crossroads at the Stone of Ezel. Jonathan believed he would be able to sway David to return with them, but Gad had packed supplies for David along with his kinnor in case the prince was not persuasive.

Three roads converged at the Ezel marker, and just off these rarely traveled routes were ruins of a Canaanite village. Abner would use these ruins to stage combat exercises within city dwellings.

After the heartfelt greeting between the prince and the captain, Gad observed David's wariness when Jonathan told him about the king's change of heart. When David said he would rather the prince slay him where he stood if he thought him guilty of treason or any other crime than to be turned over to the king, Gad sensed more turmoil lay ahead for everyone.

David was to be the next king. Gad and Nathan knew it. The prophet Samuel knew it. David and his family knew it. And Saul believed it to the point of obsession.

Jonathan remained in denial, thinking there would be some reconciliation, some other path than the devastating one they were on, a time where the king would regain mental balance and peace would be restored in the household and the kingdom. But when?

David refused to return unless Jonathan guaranteed his safety, the prince devised a plan to test the mood of the king to see if he still bore hostility toward David. Once a plan was forged, the prince asked David to swear an oath between them that gave Gad an unsettled feeling.

"When Yahweh has cut off every one of your enemies from the face of the earth," the prince had stated. "Swear to me that you will not cut off your kindness to my family."

Gad presided over the covenant formed by these two men in the Valley of Elah. The bond between them was sealed by blood and held together by mutual love, but would this bond survive when faced by the severest of tests? Could the prince come to grips with the possibility that the relationship between David and the king might never be restored? By this oath, Gad knew the prince was protecting himself against the worst outcome.

That night, Jonathan had forced David to swear an oath to show mercy to him and his immediate family. Gad had expected Jonathan to admit that he knew he would never become king, that he knew David would assume the throne once the reign of his father had come to its natural end. But he did not. Perhaps, he could not for it would mean that this great man of honor would have betrayed his father.

Jonathan and Gad returned to the palace. In the wordless ride back to the city, all Gad could do was offer silent prayers to Yahweh for the agony he knew resided in the heart of the prince.

After the sounding of the trumpets over the burnt offerings for a memorial to Yahweh on that first day of the festival, the royal family sat down to eat together. The king had asked Gad to read from the Sacred Scrolls of the prophet Moses relating to the New Moon Festival.

Gad had written out a special copy of the passage, and after the meal, he stood before the royal family and read of the cloud of Yahweh that hovered over the Tent of Testimony, in the days of the wanderings after the flight from Egypt.

That first evening, Gad did his best to ignore the vacant seat. No one, not even the king, referenced the empty place next to Mikal reserved for her husband. And Mikal never looked at anyone, just stared down at her plate, nibbling at her food in silence.

Not even Merab attempted to cajole her from beneath the weight of her sorrow. As far as Gad was aware, the two sisters had barely spent any time together since David's escape and Mikal's internment in her room. Gad had tried to encourage Merab to visit her sister, but she had refused. It looked to Gad as if both sisters had accepted a permanent strain in their relationship.

When Gad had finished the reading, the king thanked him and requested that he return for the second night of the festival and read another passage from the Sacred Scrolls at the evening meal. So, on that second night, Gad took his position behind the pedestal and opened the scroll. He looked to the king to indicate that Saul was ready for Gad to begin, but the king signaled for the prophet to wait.

Saul sat in his usual place by the wall with Jonathan and Abner on either side. David should be seated between Jonathan and Mikal, but again his place was vacant.

"Why has the son of Jesse not graced us with his presence for two days now?" At first, the king directed the question to no one in particular, but when no answer was forthcoming, he looked at Jonathan. "Yesterday, I thought he must be ceremonially unclean. But that was not true. Look at this wife. How unhappy she is."

Saul chuckled, amused by his mocking wit at Mikal's expense.

No one joined in the laughter. Indeed, everyone averted their eyes both from the king and Mikal.

"So, my son, why would the son of Jesse not join us for the meal, either yesterday or today?" Saul asked again, his humor replaced with a growl and a wild, erratic look.

Gad had never known the prince to express a falsehood to anyone. It was just not within his character. But when Gad saw Jonathan head bend forward, his eyes downcast, and his face become loose and expressionless, he knew Jonathan was about to do something he had never done…lie to his father.

"David asked my permission to go to Bethlehem," Jonathan replied, his voice almost imperceptibly soft, forcing the room to become still, mothers to silence their children, and the prophet to lean over his pedestal to listen.

"Bethlehem?" Saul raised his arms in a gesture of curiosity.

"Yes, Abba, his family was to observe a special sacrifice, and David said his eldest brother had insisted, commanded even, that David attend."

Jonathan took a deep breath and raised his head to look at the king. He had said just enough to bolster his courage and finish his story with another layer of deception by looking squarely into his father's face.

"He begged me, saying, 'If I have found favor in your eyes, let me get away to see my brothers,'" Jonathan continued, his body becoming limber as if in anticipation of the need for a quick reaction. "That is why he has not come to the king's table."

Once before, Jonathan had tried to convince his father not to harm David. He used his power of rational argument to show David's benefit to the king and kingdom. Now, the prince resorted to blatant lying to save his dear friend.

Jonathan observed the king looking at Mikal as if she would verify her brother's story, but what could she add? Jonathan would have known if David had gotten a message to her, but she had heard nothing since his escape.

"Mikal knows nothing, Abba."

Jonathan knew Mikal may not be allowed to speak to her husband for the rest of her life, that it was best if she not be dragged any deeper into this infection of hatred the king had for her husband. She was wise to remain silent, sip from her goblet, and nod as if to confirm her brother's tale.

Saul's face went blank as if absorbing the veracity of his son's story and his daughter's silence. He could have asked the prince to clarify. He could have solicited the princess. He could have questioned the commander sitting on his right if he had received any word of the captain's whereabouts. Instead, Saul sprang to his feet with such violence it caused everyone to recoil as if assaulted by an invisible force.

"You wretch. You are a perverse, rebellious wretch," Saul roared. "Your mother's death came too early in my life, but this is the first time I am glad she is dead, because her firstborn has shamed her nakedness by siding with the son of Jesse, by lying for him, by defending him when you know that as long as he walks the earth, your kingdom will never be established. Now, bring him to me, for he must die."

Jonathan leapt to his feet. "What has he done? Why should he die?"

"You think I am mad. You think I am the one who has lost his mind. I am the only one who sees clearly; the only one who recognizes this usurper in our midst."

Saul began pacing the room, his hands clawing at his face, his mind grappling in the onslaught of dark images.

No family member rose to calm him. They all remained still like animals hoping the predator would not spot them.

"Your mother must have played the harlot with me," Saul railed. "You shame her. You shame me. You are an utter fool to befriend a rival. What will the tribal chieftains think letting a son-in-law replace me? You have no right to the throne. You are not fit to reign. You are not my son, and you will not bring down my kingdom."

Gad dropped behind the pedestal.

The family burrowed into the cushions or hid underneath the coverings. Even Abner cringed in fear, his body draped over Rizpah and her sons, attempting to shield them.

When Gad lifted his eyes, Saul held a spear. Surely, the king was not so out of control that he would hurl a spear at his own son. But the black waters of madness had drowned the king, and he threw the spear with such force that when it struck the massive support beam directly behind the prince—the beam dedicated to the tribe of Reuben—the vibrating shaft echoed in the hall until the screams of children and mothers overwhelmed the sound.

When Jonathan crumpled to his knees, Gad thought the spear had gone through him. The king had murdered his firstborn son in front of the entire family. The king was so possessed by an evil presence he had slain his beloved son.

Gad rushed to Jonathan, fully expecting to see blood and entrails, but the prince's body was intact. Trembling violently with anger and shame, but still in one piece.

Gad lifted the prince onto wobbly legs and rushed him from the hall. He must save the prince. The rest of the family could fend for themselves. They could deal with the king, howling on the floor in his madness. Gad's only concern was to remove the prince from the threat of death.

Once Gad brought Jonathan to his chambers, the prince realized his wife and son were left behind and sent Gad to fetch them.

"Bring Ishie as well," Jonathan said, his raspy voice trembling at what had just transpired. "He must not spend the night with my father."

When Gad returned with wife and young son and Ish-bosheth, they were hysterical. Levana collapsed into her husband's arms. Merib-baal held onto his father's leg, confused and panicked beyond comforting. And Ish-bosheth stood to the side, his young face stricken with horror.

Before Gad departed for the night, Jonathan asked the prophet to join him at the royal stables before sunrise.

Most of the ride to the Stone of Ezel was in silence. They left at dawn after a sleepless night for both the prophet and the prince. Ish-bosheth rode between them. The young boy fretfully looked back and forth at the weary faces of Gad and his older brother.

Sensing the boy's fearful heart, Gad periodically patted Ish-bosheth on the shoulder and head and presented an encouraging smile but offered no words in an attempt to calm him. Gad was at a loss for words. It was impossible to explain what he and the others had witnessed the night before.

As they neared the Stone of Ezel, Jonathan finally broke the silence. "I promised Ishie that I would teach him to shoot his new bow this morning," Jonathan said, his voice hoarse from lack of sleep and the strain of misery.

"Yes, my lord." Gad was relieved Jonathan had spoken at last and on a subject other than the king's near-fatal impaling of the prince. "Excellent plan."

But the promise of target practice with his elder brother did not distract Ish-bosheth from what was foremost on his mind, and he barraged Jonathan with questions regarding their father's state of mind and what had possessed their father to do such a thing. When Jonathan did not—or would not, or perhaps could not—answer his little brother's frantic queries, it only increased the anxiety in the young lad.

Gad laid a hand upon the young boy's back to calm his fear. He squeezed the boy's shoulders and directed his attention toward the rising sun on the eastern horizon—a good sign that the beauty of this dawn should begin to replace the horror of the previous night.

Jonathan led them off the road and to a wide, bald mound of earth a good distance from the Stone of Ezel. Jonathan jumped from his horse, letting the reins slip from his hand. Imitating his brother, Ish-bosheth swung his leg off the side of his horse but misjudged the height and tumbled forward, driving his face into the hard earth.

His brother helped him to his feet and brushed the dirt from his robe. Any other time, they might have all laughed at the incident, but there was no place for laughter in their hearts.

"We are going for distance today, not accuracy." Jonathan pretended not to notice his little brother's clumsy dismount or his red face. "Let's string your bow."

Jonathan was patient with Ish-bosheth, giving detailed instruction on tying off the string at each tip of the bow and the tautness of the string itself, how to notch the end of the arrow into the string, where to place his hand in the middle of the bow, how to sight and aim, how to test the string with the arrow notched without releasing it.

The distraction of details provided a calming effect on the hearts of all three of them.

When it came to firing at the Stone of Ezel, Ish-bosheth's arrows fell short of the marker. But Jonathan never criticized or made his brother feel he was displeased. Jonathan complimented his little brother for his steady hand and good concentration. He saw potential in him becoming a fine archer someday, and he would give him exercises to strengthen the muscles in his arms, so he could pull back the bowstring to its full extent.

Ish-bosheth beamed at the encouragement he received, and when Jonathan displayed his prowess with a bow firing two arrows far beyond the stone marker and into the outside wall of an abandoned wooden hut inside the ruins, the boy was awestruck at the distance the arrows had flown.

"Now, Ishie, I will fire a third arrow, and it will strike the wall right between the other two."

Jonathan could tell that Ish-bosheth did not doubt his big brother's confidence to do exactly as he stated. He marveled at such self-assurance and looked at Gad to see if he believed as he did, which Gad immediately confirmed with a nod and a smile.

"When I fly my arrow, run as fast as you are able and fetch all three arrows."

Ish-bosheth took a runner's stance and expanded his lungs with several deep breaths, waiting for Jonathan to give the signal. Jonathan pulled back the bowstring and held it.

"Run," he shouted, and the boy sprang from this starting position.

Jonathan let fly his arrow and it sailed over his little brother's head as he raced past the Stone of Ezel and into the ruins of the village.

Gad took the waterskins from his saddle blanket and gave one to Jonathan. "He knows nothing of what we are doing here, does he, my lord?"

"He does not," Jonathan said, opening the spout of his waterskin. "Nor should he. He should know nothing of this. He should never have known any of this."

They both looked toward the ruins when they heard Ish-bosheth squeal with delight and saw him pointing to the arrows lodged side by side into the wall.

"Hurry and bring them back!" Jonathan shouted.

The boy immediately worked to remove the arrows out of the wall.

Jonathan took a long drink from the waterskin then handed it back to Gad. He took a few steps toward the Stone of Ezel, shielded his eyes from the sun with his hand, and scanned the ruins for any signs of life.

"By now he has seen the will of Yahweh in the flight of my arrows," Jonathan said. "But he will not show himself until you and the boy are gone."

"What will he do?" Gad asked. "Where will he go?"

"I do not know." Jonathan was on the verge of weeping. "Far from here."

Ish-bosheth skipped with delight as he approached the Stone of Ezel, arrows in hand. He paused before the towering monolith and rubbed his hand over the surface of the boulder smoothed from years of exposure.

"Master Ishie, the ancient stories tell of giants who placed those very rocks," Gad called out. "You are standing where giants once walked."

"Giants!" Ish-bosheth exclaimed, and he rushed back toward Gad and Jonathan. He held up the three arrows as he approached as if they were prizes of honor. There were splinters in his fingers and streaks of blood from digging the arrows out of the hut wall.

"You are bleeding." Jonathan took the arrows from the boy.

"I feel nothing," Ish-bosheth replied, and he wiped his hands on the sides of his tunic. Splinters and blood would be pleasant reminders of one of the most joyous days in his young life.

"You and Gad must be getting back now. Your sisters will start to worry."

Jonathan made a stirrup with his hands and boosted Ish-bosheth into his saddle.

"You are not coming with us?" He reached for the reins.

"I shall follow shortly." Jonathan handed the reins to his little brother.

"Jonathan," Ish-bosheth said, his voice quivering. He took in a deep gulp of air to speak the most courageous words he had ever consciously uttered. "I know you are friends with the giant-slayer, and I think you would make a great king."

Jonathan's face crumbled, and he lowered his head to gain his composure.

"And you, little brother, would be the greatest prince ever to rise from the tribe of Benjamin and from the house of…of…our fathers."

Jonathan had to walk away, leading his horse toward the Great Stone of Ezel.

"Come, Master Ishie," Gad tried to distract the boy from watching his brother. "I do not know about you, but my stomach is growling fiercely. Your brother forced me out of bed this morning without my breakfast."

Gad tapped the sides of his horse with his heels and started for the road that led back to Gibeah. Ish-bosheth's mount followed automatically. Once they both were on the road, Gad reached into his pouch for a bag of dates as Ish-bosheth pulled beside him. Gad kept their pace at a slow gait so as not to raise suspicions in the young prince. He handed the boy the dates. "These must suffice till we get back to the palace."

While the young prince was focused on stuffing dates into his mouth, Gad causally turned and looked behind them. He saw David stumble from hiding inside the ruins and fall to his knees in front of Jonathan and repeatedly bow his head to the ground. When Jonathan lifted David to his feet, they fell into each other's arms, kissing each other on the cheeks. Whatever would transpire in these last moments between them, Gad knew Jonathan would share with him later.

"Gad, look!" Ish-bosheth shouted.

Gad spun in his saddle, trying to think of a quick explanation as to why his brother was embracing the giant-slayer.

But Ish-bosheth was pointing to the sky and a flock of ravens circling overhead.

"Quick, my young master, we must hurry back to palace before those scavengers attack us for our dates." Gad took the bag from the boy's hand and stuffed it into his pouch. "Now, the great question is, who will win the race back to the palace?"

Ish-bosheth dug his heels into the horse's flanks. The young prince laughed with delight as he bounced on top of his horse as it raced down the road.

Gad waited until Ish-bosheth disappeared around a bend in the road before he followed. He spun his horse for one last look and saw the prince and captain embracing. They were both weeping, though the captain wept the loudest.

"May Yahweh bless you," Gad began the great prayer of the first high priest of Israel. "May Yahweh bless you and keep you. May Yahweh make His face to shine upon you and be gracious to you. May Yahweh turn His face toward you and give you peace."

Epilogue

THE ANIMAL HIDES COVERING THE TABERNACLE FLAPPED AND shook from the battering of strong winds whipping through the hilltop village of Nob as Ahimelech finished his evening prayers. The high priest had eaten the week-old bread of the Presence with his fellow priests in the Holy Place earlier than usual and sent them home to wait out the windstorm with their families. The unusual circumstances of the relentless gales meant Ahimelech had to wait alone for the arrival of the fresh loaves to replace the ones eaten by the priests. But it gave him the chance to be alone in the Tabernacle, an opportunity he relished.

After removing his priestly garments and mounting them carefully on the stand in a corner of the Tabernacle, he knelt in the center of the Holy Place and offered his prayers. Dressed only in the fine linen robe he wore beneath the Ephod with its breastplate of twelve precious stones and the Urim and Thummim hidden behind it, Ahimelech enjoyed these quiet moments with Yahweh. Though, on this night, it was not so quiet. The winds were so fierce even the thick insulation of the Tabernacle's coverings could not keep out the noise of the violent air currents. The twelve fresh loaves of bread should have arrived by now, but Ahimelech surmised that the windstorm howling through the village had delayed the courier.

When Ahimelech felt a blast of wind come through the entrance of the Tabernacle, he rose. The gust blew around the Holy Place, extinguishing all but three of the seven flames on the lampstand before the flow of air was absorbed into the thick curtains. The high priest turned, expecting to see Doeg entering the Tabernacle carrying a basket filled with the fresh loaves, but in the decreased light, Ahimelech could not distinguish the obscure figure.

"Doeg, just place the basket beneath the table, and I will set out the loaves." Ahimelech waved for the shadowy form to approach the table of Presence with him.

"My lord, I need your help," the form spoke.

Ahimelech knew instantly this was not Doeg. Ahimelech stepped closer, squinting to bring the image into sharper focus. When the form dropped his arm from concealing his face, Ahimelech began to tremble.

"Why are you alone? Why is no one with you?" Ahimelech did not mean to be so blunt, but he was caught off guard, unable to believe who stood before him. He knew of this fugitive's recent narrow escape from the king's spear and of his flight to Samuel's home. He knew of the king's pursuit of the fugitive, but that Yahweh had descended upon the king and his men in a miracle of ecstasy, allowing the fugitive to escape.

Now, the man the king had gone to great lengths to murder was in the Holy Place asking for his aid. The arrival of the king's son-in-law in his ragged, travel-stained condition and without an escort struck fear in the heart of Ahimelech.

Nothing good could come of this.

David did not want to lie, certainly not to the high priest of Yahweh, certainly not in the Holy Place of the Tabernacle. But what could he do?

Lives were in the balance, especially his own. He looked around the interior of the Tabernacle and saw that no one else was present. His story should be safe, but would the story be believed?

"My lord, I am on a secret mission for the king," David said, moving away from the entrance toward Ahimelech. "Under orders of the king, no one is to know about this. And I am not alone. My men are instructed to meet me at an undisclosed location."

Ahimelech took a step back and raised his hand to stop David's approach. He wanted to believe the captain's story. He wanted to believe that the king had a change of heart toward his son-in-law after the encounter with Yahweh at the dwellings of Samuel. Yet, how to explain David's choice to come to Nob seeking him and asking for assistance. It just did not seem plausible.

"And how can I assist you on your secret mission?" Ahimelech asked.

"I need five loaves of bread or whatever you have on hand," David blurted.

Ahimelech almost laughed at such an absurd request. How was it a man of his rank and station could possibly need bread? Had he no coin? Had he not carried supplies?

"Captain, I do not have any ordinary bread, but—"

Doeg, carrying his basket of fresh bread, stumbled inside the Tabernacle with a burst of wind and pressed his back against the heavy door to secure it. Even the double-thick curtains hung in front of the door could not hold back the powerful sustained winds.

"My lord, I could not get here before now," Doeg panted, his shortness of breath due to fighting through the gales. "Please forgive me."

David locked eyes with Doeg, then he slowly turned back to face Ahimelech.

"Leave the basket, Doeg." Ahimelech sensed David's discomfort with Doeg's surprise entrance. He sensed that David did not wish to be recognized by anyone but him. "I will place the loaves on the table. Do as I say. Go now."

"As you wish, my lord." Doeg set the basket of bread on the floor. He raised the sleeve of his robe to cover his face before braving the storm.

Ahimelech slipped around David and opened the heavy door, hastening Doeg's exit with a shove through the double-thick curtains. After closing the door, Ahimelech moved to a small acacia wood table overlaid with gold, carrying the basket of bread.

"Why is the king's chief herdsman among the priests of Nob?" David asked.

"Doeg had a falling out with the king over some trespass," Ahimelech offered. "Something to do with his ill-treatment of those under him."

"I know how he treats his shepherds."

"He came to us to do penance by serving in the Tabernacle." Ahimelech removed a stack of six loaves of bread from the basket and placed them on the table.

"He will serve no better in the Tabernacle than he did as the king's chief herdsman," David said. "Beware of him."

"Rather harsh judgment, Captain," Ahimelech said with a slight scolding tone.

David shrugged but offered no retraction of his appraisal of Doeg's character. David moved beside Ahimelech, eyeing the fresh-baked bread as the high priest placed the second stack of six loaves beside the first.

"You really should not be in the Holy Place." Ahimelech brushed breadcrumbs off his hands and robe. "You should not travel on the Sabbath to come to Nob. And you should not be eating any of the bread of the Presence. It is for priests alone."

"As I said, I…we…my men and I are on this mission, and we left in such haste there was little time to prepare."

"You are fumbling for words," Ahimelech said, but when David remained silent, he continued. "And these men of yours, are they pure?"

"My lord?" David said, unsure of the high priest's meaning.

"Have they had sex with their wives, or whomever?" Ahimelech asked candidly.

David could not control his laughter, but when Ahimelech did not retract his question or alter his humorless expression, David looked around the Tabernacle sheepishly, trying to regain his composure. Time to formulate another lie.

"No, my lord. I have not been with my wife for many days," David said, which was true. "And my men are pure. We just left home. Their clothes and travel bags, all pure," which might be true, but he had no way of knowing, and if he had to guess, remaining pure for a loaf of bread would not be worth the trade-off. The real truth was that he had not set eyes on his closest companions since fleeing Gibeah, and he did not ask Jonathan to get word to them to meet in a secret location. He was too grief-stricken at their parting. Even if he had the presence of mind to make that request, it would have placed the prince in deeper jeopardy with the king were it to be discovered.

Ahimelech looked deep into the eyes of David, but David did not allow the high priest's gaze to linger inside his soul. He must change the subject from purity to arms.

"My lord, would you have a sword or spear?" David asked. "I did not bring my sword with me or any weapon." When Ahimelech did not answer immediately, David added, "The king's business was urgent and I left in such haste, you understand."

"You know, Captain, we are in the Holy Place, standing before the bread of the Presence." Ahimelech held up his hand to prevent David from uttering any more lies in such a sanctified place. He understood David's need for self-protection. Perhaps the captain was even acting out of concern to protect him from harm, but Ahimelech could no longer tolerate the charade.

"This is Yahweh's table. These twelve loaves stand for the twelve tribes of Yahweh's chosen people. The meaning of this table, this bread, is that Yahweh is breaking bread with His people, communing with His creation, an extension of Yahweh's love. You may take this bread of the Presence, and you may have the sword of Goliath, the giant slain by you in the Valley of Elah. But you must leave here and not return. You put all the priests of Nob and their families in danger."

"Yes, my lord." David bowed his head before the high priest.

Ahimelech lifted one stack of six loaves off the table and nodded for David to pick up the basket at his feet. Ahimelech dropped the loaves into the basket and then added the second stack of six.

"Eating this bread of the Presence is an act of fellowship with Yahweh," Ahimelech said reverentially. "Never forget that."

"Yes, my lord." David held the basket close to his chest.

Then Ahimelech went behind the Ephod displayed on its stand and opened the lid of a long wooden case. He lifted the sword from the receptacle and handed it to David. It was wrapped in Goliath's military cape. While David's eyes brightened at regaining possession of the weapon used by the first man he had ever killed, Ahimelech sighed in relief at this opportunity to be rid of something that had no place in the Tabernacle.

"There is none like it." David held the blade up to the weak light provided by the seven-branched lampstand. He returned the blade to its sheath and laid it across his shoulders. He tied the basket of bread on one end and started for the door.

"Yahweh be with you, Captain." Ahimelech bowed to David.

"Yahweh be with you as well," David said, and he pushed through the doorway.

The captain had come to the city of priests not to see him, not for prayer or protection or to seek guidance from Yahweh by oracle either through consulting the Ephod or by casting the Urim and Thummim. The captain had come to the Tabernacle to plunder.

The violent wind blew open the door and powered its way into the Tabernacle with a force so great that it extinguished all the light inside, plunging Ahimelech into pitch darkness.

READING GROUP GUIDE

Discussion Questions for
The Singer of Israel

1. At the beginning of the book the army of Israel is camped on a hill above the Valley of Elah. On the hill across the valley the Philistines army is encamped. There has been a forty-day siege with the Philistine champion, Goliath, daily taunting the army of Israel to fight, but fear has griped King Saul and his army. Inaction has depleted the spirit and courage of the army of Israel. Have you ever experienced a similar situation where you have not known what to do and felt paralyzed by fear? When has it been difficult for you to make a decision to move out in faith?

2. David was sent by his father to the Valley of Elah to take supplies to his three older brothers who were conscripts in King Saul's army. When he left his hometown of Bethlehem, David had no intention of meeting the royal family or facing-off with Goliath. Recount a time in your life where you have been surprised by dramatic circumstances that you never expected. What was your emotional response? What course of action did you take to navigate the situation?

3. Eliab was David's oldest brother. He and all David's brothers witnessed Samuel anointing David to be the next king. Yet Eliab did not have one good thing to say to David when he came to deliver the supplies to his brothers. Have you ever expected or hoped to be encouraged by someone and instead been ridiculed by that person?

4. Friendship is a key component of this story. In our modern world it can be difficult to establish close relationships with people. After David defeats Goliath in battle, he and Jonathan, King Saul's firstborn son, enter into a covenant bond of friendship. There is even a ceremony that marks this lifetime bond. What does a bond of friendship mean to you today? What form does the commitment take? How has life shaped this bond of friendship?

5. Back in the time of this story, marriages were normally arranged between families. The modern experience of "falling in love" was just not the norm. But it is clearly stated that Mikal, King Saul's second daughter, was "in love" with David. However, it was not a smooth path to the altar. There were many obstacles along the way. While the historical context of the circumstances for David and Mikal to be married were unique to them, what obstacles have you observed in other people's romantic relationship or personally experienced that might be similar?

6. Jealousy is a most destructive emotion. Shakespeare refers to it as the "green-eyed monster" in his play *Othello*. When King Saul sees that the people of Israel have turned David into a national hero his heart becomes consumed by jealousy. Can you describe the circumstances around someone you know who has experienced the effects of jealousy? Such a shared story is in itself a cautionary tale.

7. The character of Shira, Samuel's wife, is created out of whole cloth. We know Samuel must have been married because we have record of him having two reprobate sons. But the "wife" of Samuel is never mentioned. Even though Shira is a woman set in biblical times, is there anything about the character of Shira that strikes you as unusual, even modern? And how does she humanize the character of Samuel?

8. David was certainly a complex human being. He could play his kinnor in such a way that it brought comfort to King Saul's troubled mind. He could also face a giant in battle. This is a beautiful combination of tenderness and courage. He certainly displayed many other traits that modern society would consider admirable or shocking depending on the context. What does it mean for a man to possess both tenderness and courage? How do we encourage these and other qualities in a man?

9. There are instances in the story where many of the characters are given an opportunity to acknowledge God as one who is the "living" God, one who is an active participant in a person's life and then move out in faith based on who God is. Can you identify those moments in the story? Can you cite examples in your life when you were met with similar challenges? How did you respond?

10. Who was your favorite character? Who was your least favorite? Why?

11. In every story there is the protagonist and antagonist. Sometimes there is more than one. What character did you identify with the most and why? Were you able to empathize with all the characters, even the ones who might be considered an antagonist?

12. What were some of your favorite themes in the story? Identify some ways these themes resonated with you.

ACKNOWLEDGMENTS

Gratitude begins with my parents, Henry and Bernie, and ends with my wife Kay and daughters, Kristin and Lauren.

Michael Blanton, Steve Brallier, Michael W. Smith, Jim Davis, and John Brewer. These men of God gave of themselves to me for decades. They sacrificed their time and treasure on my behalf just because they loved me and believed in me even when I didn't believe in myself.

Brian Mitchell, President of Working Title Agency/Media and Dave Schroeder, Director of Publishing at WTA/Media. These two eternal optimists never took a "no" as a final answer. They have brought the multi-volume *The Song of Prophets and Kings* historical fiction series across the finish line.

The father/son team of Ben and Derek Pearson for their work on the promotional videos, and to Jillian LaFave/Robotic Fox for her fabulous web design work.

Jim Reyland, and the studio team at Audio Productions, Inc./Nashville for making my audio book sound terrific.

All my theatre artist collaborators and friends who inspired me to be a better storyteller.

David and Roseanna White of WhiteFire Publishing for taking the risk on an unknown. And for the editorial team of Roseanna White, Janelle Leonard, Wendy Chorot, and Kim Peterson for their insightful and "gloves-off" editorial guidance. This series has achieved a higher level of literary craft because of them.

And finally, to God...I have been carried between His shoulders all my life.

HENRY O. ARNOLD

Henry O. Arnold has co-authored a work of fiction, *Hometown Favorite*, with Bill Barton, and nonfiction, *KABUL24*, with Ben Pearson. He also co-wrote and produced with Steve Taylor (director) and Ben Pearson the film *The Second Chance* starring Michael W. Smith, the screenplay for the authorized film documentary on evangelist Billy Graham, *God's Ambassador*, and the documentary film *KABUL24*, based on the book which is the story of western and Afghani hostages held captive by the Taliban for 105 days. He lives on a farm in Tennessee with his lovely wife Kay. They have two beautiful daughters married to two handsome men with three above-average grandchildren. For more information please visit: www.henryoarnold.com

ALSO BY HENRY O. ARNOLD

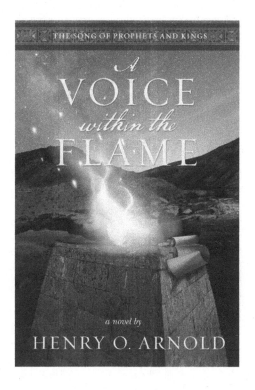

A Voice within the Flame
The Song of Prophets and Kings, Book One

A son of the vow. A voice for a nation.
When Israel's enemies threaten to destroy his world, it appears as though
everything Samuel ever held dear may come tumbling down around him.

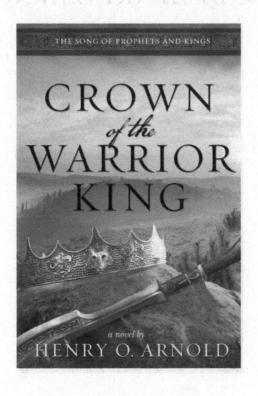

Crown of the Warrior King
The Song of Prophets and Kings, Book Two

The desire of Israel…
the first to wear the crown is the warrior king

Under the banner of the wolf, the symbol of his tribe, Saul rises to prominence, winning the hearts and minds of the people of Israel with his success on the battlefield and benevolent leadership.

CPSIA information can be obtained
at www.ICGtesting.com
Printed in the USA
LVHW091209101122
732777LV00006B/8

9 781946 531292